AMERICAN WILD

A Story of Resilience and
Redemption After
The American Revolution

MARISSA HALE

ISBN: 979-8-9895149-0-8

Produced by Publish Pros | publishpros.com

DEDICATION

To the overlooked and the unsung.

*To the generations following me: that you might understand the hearts
and sacrifices of those who lived—and how they died—before you.*

*And to Robert Hale, who told me in the beginning all I needed was time
on our couch with a pencil and some paper.
This book is dedicated to you, Love.*

She watches his last breath evaporate. For her it is the breaking of promises, the splintering of dreams, and the end of everything she understands.

French-born of pedigree and class, she shivers beside her husband's dead body high on a rocky hillside in the uncharted wilds of America's first colonies. With no one else awaiting her, nor anyone expecting her return, a dark sky overhead and shadows below converge with a vengeance, stabbing into her mind how small one soul really is in this world.

The plan to continue ten miles further to the homestead she has yet to see disappears with the warmth of his body. That place was home in hope and down payments alone, its geography unknown and unmapped for her. Looking again into the night, she marks a pattern in the stars and their alignment with the treeline points her onward.

But somewhere else in the darkness, a war party composed of vagabond thieves lingers in the shadows. They tighten their grip on the reins of three new horses loaded down with Spanish-milled coins, French francs, rifles, building and garden tools, and an intricate gold crucifix. Also buried in the trappings are legal documents—an honorable discharge, a marriage certificate, and two deeds for acreage along the Green River, past the Appalachian Mountains.

One woman is worth something. You just need to know who
to sell her to.

1

1781 - Nantes Cathedral. Nantes, France

She pounded on the ornately carved door, desperate to be heard. Her small fist barely made a sound above the storm, so she hit it harder.

Disguised in a hood and cloak, Vittorie pressed her body closer and cupped her fingers around her mouth. "Père Benét!" she shouted into the old wood.

A swirling wind sucked up her words and howled her plea into the spindly trees. It whistled up the hollow passageway of road behind her and threatened to subvert the very sanctuary she sought. The church of rock and mortar stood unmoved as the rain drenched her. She searched for any movement beside the storm. Seeing none, she knocked again, standing on the doorstep of the cathedral as a fugitive might, pausing, afraid of who might be watching. As she sidled the thin form of her body further into the shadowed curve of the pointed doorframe, the decision to leave her petticoat home and wear a simple *robe a l'anglaise* proved wise.

Metal twisted and the ancient door opened. An old priest peered out. The rain pelted his pinched cheekbones and pale forehead. He held a lantern just inside. Recognizing the woman as she pushed back her hood, his expression changed.

"Victoire!" he said, looking past her at the violent night once more. "*Qu'est-ce que c'est, mon enfant?*"

She slipped inside and together they shoved the thick door shut.

"Lock the door, *rapidement!*" she said.

He twisted the key in its hole, still unsure of her reason for appearing, cloaked, soaked, and informal. The bulky key ring disappeared beneath the folds of his cloak.

She undid the clasps on her gray coat, soaked black by the storm. "I'm sorry, Father," she said, puddles forming on the massive stones of the vestibule floor.

"*Qu'est ce que tu fais ici?*" he asked, motioning her away from the door toward his chambers. "Why are you out in this storm?" The look on his face did not bring comfort.

2

1781 – Nelson House. Yorktown, Virginia

"Confound Clinton!" British General Charles Cornwallis smashed the thin paper in his hand and ground his fist into the desk, his lips puckered in rage. "We have no time for this pettiness! Yorktown shall be lost over his idiocy!" His eye twitched repeatedly, an old wound that flared with his temper.

Cannons had been firing for so long, the silences in between seemed unnatural. Allied forces of American and French troops continued to bombard the British-occupied port city of Yorktown. The frequent shellings broke through fortifications, decimated buildings, and shattered the confidence of the Red Coats, as intended. The town, and morale, crumbled.

In what was originally the drawing room of the house, Cornwallis' highest officers crowded around him. All of them were in want of a shave. Decisions were overdue; supplies were gone. The blockade of colonial and French forces continued. A large map lay open on a beautiful cherry desk. Major Alexander Ross pointed to a narrow strip of blue in the middle. Lieutenant Colonel Charles O'Hara stood beside him and examined the waterways.

"If the Royal Navy had arrived weeks ago, even one week ago, our situation would be greatly altered," O'Hara said, dark eyebrows shading his hazel eyes. "Now, the French have taken the harbor. And the force we face on land is three times our size." He tapped the map with dry knuckles for emphasis. "At the least."

Lieutenant Colonel Thomas Dundas spoke next, his Scottish lilt apparent. "We must find help, sir, if we are to maintain our position here." His r's rolled just so as they passed across his tongue. "We've no defense left against the rebel blockade."

Dundas' words spurred a murmur of agreement. These were facts in the crisis they faced. Resources were exhausted. All aid cut off. The senior officers looked to their general.

"Entreat God! For we are alone." Cornwallis squeezed his oversized belly up from between the armrests of his chair. "Five days until reinforcements *may* arrive, Clinton says." His fair English skin flushed red to purple. "He's a failure to the Crown! I've no respect for him."

An officer appeared in the doorway. He snapped a salute and crossed the floor.

"Make your report," Cornwallis said. "Out with it! Speak, man!"

The young officer's eyes were bloodshot. "Major Campbell says we've pulled back from the outer redoubts, General, but munitions are insufficient for the force besieging us." His pant legs quivered. "Also, those disabled by smallpox number in the thousands, sir. Our numbers of able bodies are minimal at best." He swallowed hard and stepped back, the message delivered.

Cornwallis glanced at O'Hara. "How long can we last...?"

An explosion cut his sentence short. The entire house shook. The ground to the South had been struck by a cannonball and sent the shock of it through the rafters. Pieces of plaster dislodged from the ceiling and crashed to the floorboards.

"Blast!" said Cornwallis. "How many rounds can those Continentals have? What are our…"

"We are depleted, General, sir," O'Hara said. He steadied himself with a tight hold on the thin-legged table. Another nearby explosion shook the room. The golden candelabra swung perilously and scalding wax dripped onto the map below.

Cornwallis paced the room. The report confirmed what he already knew. "And Clinton doesn't feel bothered enough to help us, does he? Stay with his forces in the North, eh? Well, Clinton," he said, shouting to the air, "you are a *coward*!" He stormed to the window, yelling epithets. "Among cur dogs you haven't an equal!" He yanked back the brocade curtain. Its light blue pattern complimented the walls impeccably in this makeshift headquarters.

As if in direct defiance to the tranquil paint of the room, outside the transomed windows the mood was austere, smeared dark and red. Dark were the sky and the smoke billowing; red were the fiery bursts and the flaming embers. Red also were the thin waterways trickling through the streets, mirroring the sky. Or maybe they weren't mirroring anything; perhaps that was blood. The world had punctured an artery.

"He's here," Cornwallis muttered. His thoughts rambled through the impossibilities facing him on behalf of his king and country, of England and her revolting colonies. "Not in the North, but here, at my window. Washington's come 'round and forced the war where I am, while Clinton plans theaters for no audience in New York!" The implausibility of the situation stunned him; the inevitability overwhelmed him and he laughed. Only once.

Cornwallis faced away from his men, away from the stain of defeat that would certainly taint his military record. "Parliament *will* hear them now…pompous idiots wouldn't listen when I spoke…" He peered through the bubbled glass at the bludgeoning atmosphere of the day. "The colonists mean to be heard, by God." The eye twitch intensified. "They *are* Englishmen."

He let the curtain fall back, blocking out the bleak scene. "Get the sick and dead away from those who are able enough to stand." He buttoned the collar of his shirt and walked back to his men around the table. "I will not lose Yorktown for Clinton's error." He looked at none of them, his full attention on the map. "Give every slave their freedom if they'll fight. Arm them."

Another violent explosion pounded the house. The windows shattered, scattering glass shards across the narrow plank floor.

The lieutenant steadied himself under the doorframe. "Sir, I have nothing with which to arm new men. May I suggest…"

Cornwallis yelled orders. "I want no horse left for enemies on either side after we are gone! Take them to the river. Kill them all."

Reverberations from the barrage of twenty-four-pound cannons came now with barely a pause in between. Smoke seeped through the walls, choking them.

"I will not dishonor the Crown! The city may be lost, but…" Cornwallis spat on the ground. "Go!"

O'Hara saluted and left. The rest followed, leaving the General alone.

Cornwallis faltered, grabbed at the desk, and sank to his knees.

3

Father Benét's study was sparse, adorned only by the curiosities a man dedicated to his life's work might attach himself to. His garden tools hung by the door. In the center of it all, his writing desk. Glowing torches hung from several wall sconces, giving the space a cathedral feeling, though the curved ceiling was actually quite low. A wide fire crackled away in the open hearth.

He moved a three-legged stool closer to the fire and spread Vittorie's wet cloak over it. "*Asseyez-vous,*" he said, pointing to half a hewn log that doubled as a bench. His desk chair creaked as he eased himself into it. The papers on his desk were arranged in one stack to the left. His quill rested next to the inkwell, and his blotter had a thick, tortoise-shell handle. In the corner of the room, an armoire, painted in parts with gold leaf, glowed when the fire flickered, and a large tapestry with the picture of an urn and pheasant in a garden hung on one wall.

"*Pardonnez moi,*" Vittorie said, "but I must show you something." She tried a smile but it didn't work. Lying didn't fit her. "I don't know who else to tell."

He nodded at her, but the creases deepened around his mouth and eyes. Priests come to know many things.

"*Il est temps que j'en parler*," Vittorie said, moving to show rather than tell him. Loosening the string at the neckline of her *chemisier*, she blushed, and turned her body and face away. The pale pink linen dropped over her shoulders and caught around the curve of her hips. Her fingers trembled as she snatched the front up to cover herself there.

"*Mon Dieu!*" he said.

Deep burgundy welts covered her back, the haphazard lines of a blunt whipping. From her neck to her tailbone, a dozen clusters ranged on both sides of her spine. The bruises were grotesque, purpled and swollen. He reached to touch the wounds, but stopped short. His hands hovered over them instead, praying silently. He limped to the armoire and returned as fast as his aged body allowed, placing a silver bowl on the desktop. With fresh linens over one arm, he plucked herbs from several different bundles drying above the mantel. These he crushed in a practiced roll of his fingertips against the pulp of his palm and sprinkled them into a cloth.

"Tell me," he said, twisting the cloth into a poultice. He reached for the kettle. Water poured from the spout painted with *Chinoiserie*. The steam rose in lackluster puffs until he plunged the herbal remedy into its warmth.

"It's difficult…to say, Father."

"The best way to begin is to not begin. So, first," he said, extending the bowl beneath her nose, "we review. What do you smell?"

She closed her eyes and inhaled. "Cassia. Cinnamon."

"*Quoi d'autre?*" He nodded, pleased with her knowledge. "What else?"

"…lemon. Cloves…" Her shoulders relaxed and her breathing became normal.

"Good." He wrung the excess water out but paused before placing the poultice on her skin.

"…Rosemary."

"Very good," he said, rinsing out her wounds, applying as little pressure as possible. "This may be painful."

She nodded once. "It already is."

"Who would do this to you?" He moved the bowl to the floor and wrung the poultice out again. "You are not unprotected. Your father will…"

The color drained from her face. "Please, don't tell him!" she said, her head of brown curls shaking.

"*Pourquoi?*"

"*Peut-etre* it's me who is too…" she said, pulling her shirt up to cover her back. "I wouldn't give him what he wanted."

"Please," he said, raising his hands but quieting his voice. "Please, you came to me for a reason. Let me help you, *mon enfant.*"

She took a leather pouch from between the folds of her skirt, untied the knot, and removed a small package. It was just larger than the surface of her palm, its velvet fabric tied with a pale green ribbon.

He wiped his hands on his robe, twisting the fabric this way and that to be sure they were thoroughly dry. He pulled the ribbon loose. From inside, he unwrapped a worn, wrinkled parchment.

"Gilbert's letter?" he asked, recognizing the paper. The beads of his rosary swung back and forth. He unfolded the parchment and smoothed it out over the worn planks of the small table beside them. "Why anyone would fight you at all, let alone over this?" He glanced over the familiar words, folded the letter, and handed it back to her. "You could have let it go and lost nothing *de grande valeur*, child."

"How can you say that? You know Gilbert and my love story better than anyone. I pray for his safe return with every breath." The pain of his response hurt so profoundly it forced tears to her green eyes. "But this man," she looked at the paper in his hand, "isn't worth the…he wanted me to…but I didn't! I would never! I told him I was Gilbert's alone. I held the paper out for him to see, to show him Gilbert will return for me…and that's when… he wound my bed sheet around a candlestick from my side table and…"

Father Benét looked from her back to the old love note. "You can't read! What difference does the paper make?" His lips trembled with emotion as he moved to look into her eyes. "You aren't married and your father is away at court…How was this man in your parents' house past dinner?" He paused and made the sign of the cross over her. "You've been my Vittorie since your christening *et je me sens…* I feel…responsible."

"Because I showed you?"

"Because I read you Gilbert's letters. I may have given you false hope."

The logs hissed in the fire. He knelt in front of her, choosing his words carefully. "Someone close to your father did this?" He peered into her down-turned face, forcing her eyes to answer his question.

Her nonresponse confirmed his suspicion and he whispered something unintelligible. Kissing two fingers in blessing, he laid his hand on her head. The brown curls were still wet. Among all his parishioners, she, with her passion, piety, and intellect, was most precious to him.

"Whoever hurt you is a fool. Fools hold power over others any way they can, but freedom comes with truth, Victoire," he said, calling her by her given name. "I know the courage it took to speak to me. This last letter is three years old. We've prayed for God to protect Gilbert, but…to be a soldier means to understand the danger and walk forward anyway." He folded the paper and gave it back. "Can loving a soldier mean any less? We don't know his path before God, Vittorie."

"Hope deferred makes the heart sick. Hope extinguished snuffs out the soul." Vittorie cried quietly, the tears descending in succession over the mound of her cheek. "What is my path, *avant Dieu*, without him?"

He took one of her hands and held it. The rain resumed its beat on the roof. "You know every word on this worn-out scrap by heart." He bent her fingers around the envelope. "You should have let it go."

She breathed in sharply but stopped her objection before she got it out. "I did run."

"*Ne pense pas que je ne sais pas!* I've watched you." His eyes moistened, reflecting the light of the fire within them.

"Why does He not save me?" she said.

"Gilbert?"

"God."

"Victoire! God gave you a good mind and an able tongue, but you have only just begun to use it! And," he said, softening, "about the other, perhaps you should have let him go when he sailed away. Married another as other of your friends have."

"Like my sister."

So. She had told him. Her sister's husband. Father Benét made the sign of the cross.

"Gilbert *est en vie!*" she cried. She did not mean to fight with her priest, but he was wrong. "He is alive! And he will return to me. That's the reason I can hold on here, alone. I am no one's but his." She looked in the direction of the door. "That's how I stood up to…him. I won't be…"

A sudden banging on the door startled them. He put his finger to his lips.

"Father Benét!" A man's voice called out.

Vittorie's reaction confirmed what Father Benét already knew. He tossed her cloak to her, and pulled aside the tapestry, revealing a small door. One swift key-turn later, it opened to a long, dark hallway.

"I may be unprotected," Vittorie said, easing the cloak over her bandaged back, "and insignificant in the eyes of some…" she added, glancing toward the angry voice. "But I won't be snuffed out altogether!"

He handed her a burning torch as she fled into the darkness. "Run!"

4

October 16, 1781 - Yorktown, Virginia

The quiet company of soldiers advanced through the darkness, not with rifles, but with shovels. Each man cut the ground in front of him, the thrust of his body forcing the Virginia hillside apart. The battle trenches were nearly complete. To the east of them, a battery of slaughtered horse carcasses ebbed against the sandy shoreline. The wind, invisible, hovered over the water, compounding the stench. The rain continued its drizzle.

As the men sliced into the ground beyond the marsh, the air shifted in their direction. The river beat against wooden hulls cloaked in the darkness of the surf. The sound licked the diggers' ears, carrying with it hope for reinforcements. This caused an uptick in the tempo of their maneuvers.

Fifteen hundred yards away, the rest of the Allied army increased firing. The volleys came on the minute, their timing part of a choreographed charade. The diggers staggered onward, carrying out their secret, definite plan. The syncopated sounds of their trench-makings were concealed from the British by the resonating cannon-fire of their fellow colonials to the northwest.

Falling cinders from the constant explosions burnt the exposed forearms of any soldier who rolled up his sleeves.

Three distinct taps on the arm and the Frenchman stopped mid-stroke. He spat the gritty paste of earth through his teeth and straightened up a bit, the muscles in his back wrenched in pain. His right hand rubbed the soreness as his left fist punched into the darkness. There it found the arm of the next soldier, passing on the signal to stop digging. Gilbert LeClerc, French born and serving under General Rochambeau, tipped up the front corner of his hat to see how close they were to the enemy stronghold.

Logs with pointed ends protruded out of the ground just ahead. Hessian Jagers hired to guard the British-occupied fort at Yorktown were very close. So close, he could see the spring fern color of their tall hats. Continuous pre-dawn explosions flashed, but the Jagers' steady gait proved they hadn't seen the Continental Army crouched in the covert trenches below.

It had been six years, three months and seventeen days since Gilbert had gone to fight in the Americas. The King of France had responded to the American colonies' call for aid in their fight to overthrow Britain's rule. Gilbert had answered his King's request to fight overseas. Though he may have been only one soldier of many from the Crown's point of view, he was the only one who mattered in the heart of a certain green-eyed woman. And his duty had kept him long overdue.

Leaning hard on the handle of his shovel, he all but collapsed to a sitting position. The mucking of feet muffled and all movement hushed. Of the two hundred men hiding with him in the night, Gilbert could see only a handful in the trench beside him. He surveyed the others folded into smaller versions of themselves, grabbing at sleep.

Like the ragged, drawn lip of a wanderer's sack cinched together, his mouth sucked in air through a crack in the center. His right hand clenched into a fist and then released again. He wiped his palm down his chest trying to relieve some tension. It didn't help.

The rawness of wet uniform on sweaty skin itched less as the mud seeped through his clothes, chilling him. Grabbing the front of his coat with a calloused fist, he tucked his nose and chin inside the collar. The heat of his breath warmed the first few inches of his neck and chest, then vanished. Nothing stopped the cold night air from infiltrating his thin coat.

It took three swipes before his fingers locked onto the hole in the elbow of his left sleeve. Poking inside, they retrieved a bit of cloth. A cannonball exploded nearby, breaking soil loose from the embankment above his head and spraying dirt everywhere. Snatching the fabric as if from a fire, he brought it tenderly to his face. He puckered, attempting to blow the object clean. Satisfied at last with its preservation, he unfolded it delicately.

It had no military insignia or wording. There was no map. The fraying around one edge threatened to unravel it completely. His eyes drank in the image stitched for him alone. Fashioned in knots from multicolored threads and filling the square, a large tree grew resembling a wild apple or cork oak. The trunk swept over from the side and twisted as it rose into a cascade of foliage. Sweat and time had marked it so that the profusion of the original details colored only his memory, no longer the piece itself. He held the fingers of his other hand just above its surface, allowing himself only the faintest touch.

As he held it, his breathing eased. The muscles of his face relaxed.

A flash of white lit up the clouds, shrouding the British bulwark before them.

Unfastening a button on his chest, his hand disappeared inside the jacket. His wrist swept up and down, side to side in the symbol of the cross. Looking up for a marker, he squinted, brushing his three-cornered hat further back off his forehead. Orion should have been high by then, but he couldn't find him.

"Watch her for me tonight, *un Vieil Ami*," Gilbert said under his breath.

Someone kicked his boot in the dark.

"Shhh, *vas-y*" the voice of his commander whispered. "Let's go."

A volley from the cannons shook the ground, rousing the sleepers. Rifles passed hand to hand. Gilbert brushed the cloth across his lips and replaced it deep in his sleeve. Clenching a rifle, he rose to take his place in the file of men.

5

Candles flickered around the small room with Vittorie's mother's abrupt entry. "We start for the country as soon as your father arrives in the morning." She spoke the directives from just inside the door. "I need your help, Victoire. What are you fooling with at this time of night?"

Hearing her proper given name, Vittorie dropped her hands and the luxe material she was sewing into her lap. "But I'm expecting more trim on Tuesday by post." She pulled the needle taut from the satin, finishing a knot in an exquisite series of details, hating that her voice trembled as she spoke.

"The light, Vittorie. Nearer. Your eyes are not good as it is." Her mother's eyelids fluttered as she shook her head. "Go and help Cook first thing in the morning. Last time she neglected to pack Père Benét's cheese. I forced her entrées down for a month."

"I thought Father was at court for another week," Vittorie said.

"No," said her mother, waving off further conversation with a flick of her over-jeweled wrist. "Vittorie, *vous savez que nous vous aimons.* As your mother I am asking you to consider the convent. You would be well suited and there is no shame in it. You seem

17

happy whenever you return from visiting the nuns." She delivered the words without hesitation, as if hastening their pace cushioned the blow. "Are you listening?"

Vittorie nodded, green eyes locked on her mother's, giving attention, not agreement. "I am happy with them as I wait for Gilbert."

The skin over her mother's cheekbones looked especially translucent, sharpening the contrast between their height and the hollow underneath. "Things are happening that affect more than just you." The cupping of skin underneath her eyes had darkened since last night. "The country will be better for your sister. She is not well."

"I know."

Vittorie's mother, Marie Monet, led the household and the family estate in all matters. "You should sleep now." The candles in her hand never dimmed. "The sheep need milking. In the mornings Paul is so slow. See if you might put a hand in there."

Vittorie poked the needle through the lavender fabric. "I'd like to talk to you, *Maman*, about..."

"Not again. Not now. He's your sister's husband and family. *Alors…*" The velvet hem of her mother's skirt swirled as she turned to leave. "Gilbert may be a dream, Vittorie. Perhaps a ghost. Your life is ahead of you, Gilbert or no Gilbert. Choices need to be made and there is no shame in choosing a life of service to God in the Church."

"I know," Vittorie said, her voice a whisper. It was the truth.

Marie moved her own candelabra back into the hallway. "There is hope and there is folly, *cherie*." The wax light lengthened her dark shadow into the room. "Don't be the fool."

The drop of the door latch clinked.

Vittorie snipped the string and pierced the needle through the fabric, settling it half in, half out for safekeeping. Decisions were not her strength. Cradling her project like a precious newborn, she walked over to the window. There, she arranged the embellished bodice inside a trunk on the floor and closed the heavy lid.

6

Yorktown, Virginia

Washington's aide-de-camp, Colonel Tench Tilghman, threw the reins of his dappled mare at the tent peg. He'd barely dismounted before announcing the report of the battle.

"Hamilton's and Deux-Ponts' battalions victorious, sir!" he said, saluting. "The Reds laid down arms! We barely fired a shot, just leaped over the abatis and they practically laid down their arms. A great victory, sir!"

"Casualties and wounded?" Washington asked, his forehead stern. He stood up from the small writing table, melting a blue wax stick in the flame of the candle. His other hand pinned the fold of a letter closed.

"Count's still coming in. What message for de Grasse?"

Moored just offshore in the York River, commander of the French Navy, the Comte de Grasse, and his fleet had blocked British supplies and escape by water. Recently arrived from the West Indies, de Grasse buoyed more than hope in his hulls; he brought enough ships for a sturdy naval blockade plus 500,000 silver pesos from the citizens of Cuba as payment for the Continental Army.

Washington stamped the parchment with his seal. Wax sizzled under the press of his large hand. Giving the roll to Tilghman, he said, "Tell him he has the gratitude of a new nation, and my deepest thanks. This letter," he said, "goes immediately to Martha at Vernon."

"Yes, sir."

"Jacky's fever has worsened." The jaw muscles in the General's cheek tensed as he grit his teeth.

Tench held his head high, color filling his cheeks as though life was never more full nor more satisfying for him than this moment. His hair had grown long in the front. "Martha has a way of bringing thing's aright. Hasn't she, sir?"

George looked past him through the triangled tent opening to the battle victory on one front, the potential death of his wife's son on the other. "Yes." He nodded. "She has."

Humidity was rising, and the cicada's hum increased with the higher temperatures. The tide of the Revolution had now turned in the colonies' favor. Yorktown had fallen.

"I'll see Martha returns to camp immediately, sir."

"Thank you, Tench."

Tilghman tucked the orders under his arm, mounted, and kicked his horse in the ribs.

✵ ✵ ✵

General George Washington granted General Cornwallis a two-hour cease fire. Consecutive negotiations were enacted later at the Moore family farm, outside the line of fire. The little white house was one of precious few still standing. It was after midnight when the two British representatives, Lieutenant Colonel Thomas Dundas and Major Alexander Ross met with the allied officers, Lieutenant Colonel John Laurens, representing the Americans, and Second Colonel Viscount de Noailles—the Marquis de

Lafayette's brother-in-law—representing the French. The parties agreed to terms.

The British conceded the battle. The Americans were victorious.

✳ ✳ ✳

Disregarding the solar eclipse mid-morning when everything momentarily grayed, the day's colors were in stark contrast to those of weeks prior. The skies blued to a royal shade, as though the heavens smiled on the colonists' victory, pleased to have them placed equal in rank to any other country.

Not to be outshone despite their defeat, every British soldier wore a brand-new uniform. Their parade snaked its conciliatory way before the Continental Army, gold braid gleaming on stooped shoulders. They marched behind their leader, but not their commander. General Cornwallis was too sick to attend and had sent O'Hara instead.

Astride one of the only remaining horses, Lieutenant Colonel O'Hara rode forward, paced by the beat of a solitary drum. His uniform at the forefront of the formal ceremony of surrender further illustrated the absence of his superior officer. He sat straight up in his saddle, but his face slouched as he rode to meet the rebel leaders.

A clean white flag flapped forlornly around the sentry's pole. O'Hara dismounted, handing the reins to the crimson-coated soldier beside him. He stepped up to a handsome man with striking features in a ruffled waistcoat, complete with sash and saber.

The French General, Jean Baptiste Donatien de Vimeur, comte de Rochambeau, whose invaluable assistance helped the fledgling colonies of Britain in turning against her, pointed Cornwallis' second toward the American general. "There is the commander of this army."

O'Hara stepped sideways, this time to stand in front of a man who towered above him. He took a long breath, but before he could speak, Washington turned his head away and extended his arm.

"May I present my second, Major General Benjamin Lincoln."

Mr. O'Hara looked as though he was working to prevent a difficult sneeze. He swallowed his curse and stepped to the side yet again, this time arriving in front of the Major. Bursting into speech a bit too loudly and decidedly too soon, O'Hara said, "We request terms of surrender as set forth by…"

Here, Washington interrupted. The rebuff of General Cornwallis feigning illness and not attending the ceremony himself had not yet had its final acknowledgement. Turning to Mr. Lincoln, Washington said, "Major Lincoln, you had the misfortune in this war to be overtaken by British troops at Charleston and forced to surrender, did you not?"

Lincoln held his head high. "I did, sir."

"Good," Washington said. "I call upon your excellent understanding of British diplomacy at such a time to extend to Mr. O'Hara that same courtesy now. Set forth our terms. The power of the Continental Army and that of all the American Colonies stands behind you."

Lincoln took a moment, setting his shoulders. Staring squarely into the face of the red-coated man before him, he said, "You will not be granted any traditional honors of war. Your battalions will leave in disgrace—your flags tightly wrapped, your muskets shouldered upside-down—marching to a tune honoring American bravery. I have in my memory a city in ashes behind the defeated but since this is *our* city wherein you have trespassed, we shall take it back and restore it and this nation to its rightful institution, free from British colors, British taxes, British law, and British leadership."

Stiff, but accomplishing the task he must, O'Hara held out the sword of his absent superior officer, thus surrendering the battle, the city, and his pride with an acknowledging nod.

Lincoln gripped the handle of the sword, lifting its weight before him. "I accept your unconditional surrender." With a decided swivel of his heel, he marched to General Washington, lowered his eyes, bent at the waist, and gifted the ceremonial defeat of the British—and with it the crippling blow to tyrannical rule—to his commanding officer.

Washington raised the sword high in the air. That simple act caused an eruption of sound from the hillsides. Tens of thousands of men saw their general stand, verifying the victory of their long battle at last. They huzzahed the issue of their souls and the cause of their spilled blood in one unanimous cry of victory, a glorious, symphonic shout of freedom.

7

Monet Family Home. Nantes, France

Wiping sleep-dust from the corner of her eye, she waited and clutched her bedcover to her chin. *What was that noise?* She fluffed her pillow. It was a short, quick motion, but done quietly, just in case. She stuck it back under her head.

Pierre, the rooster, crowed.

It couldn't be morning yet, could it? The warmth of her dream clung to her. Gilbert was there, handsome as always. He laughed and smiled, sobering just long enough to gaze into her eyes. There was a boat. A ship. *Was he leaving?* She was waving on the pier. *Even Father Benét said let Gilbert go...*

There was Pierre again, alarming the estate. She was fully awake now. Her decision for the convent struck. She would never marry. Vittorie threw off the blanket and twisted carefully through her clothing. Her body would heal, in time, but her soul felt feverish. She would get to mass early today. She didn't want to be caught...

There was a knock. Before she could answer, her sister opened the door with a quiet, *"C'est moi."* She entered, pregnant belly first, and the rest waddled in after.

"What are you doing out of bed?" Vittorie asked, rushing to her sister. "Did Netta take the bell with your tray again?"

Annabelle was three years younger than Vittorie, but she was five centimeters taller. Her yellow hair was wavy and thick, pretty even in her nightcap. She raised her thin, slender fingers in protest, but Vittorie escorted her into the bed anyway.

"I'm feeling better. I am. *Vraiment.*"

"You shouldn't be up yet," said Vittorie. "Come. *Ici.*" She waited as Annabelle sidled herself into the embroidered sheets.

"Vittorie," Annabelle said, taking Vittorie's hands, "*Je sais que...* I know that…I know…you…" What she had to say was nearly impossible to do. She let go of her sister, covered her face, and burst into tears. Every sob shook her belly.

"Oh! Don't cry!" Vittorie moved a pillow behind her sister. She pulled Annabelle's feet up onto the bed and coaxed her sister to lay back. "*S'il te plaît*, shh... Please, I'm fine. The important thing is for you to keep well and healthy." She removed damp hair from her sister's wet cheek.

Annabelle's bottom lip sucked in each time she gasped, but her breathing slowed. "Mama and Papa praised him…but we know. Don't we?" She stared at Vittorie, eyes wide, her full lips whispering terrible words.

Vittorie sank down on the bed beside Annabelle. They found each other's hands and held tight. Pierre repeated his song just outside the window this time.

"He has never betrayed his vows to you…with me," Vittorie said.

A tear streamed down Annabelle's face. "*Je sais*," she said. "I know you could never."

Vittorie kissed Annabelle's cheek and pressed her own to her sister's. "You will be brave."

"*Non.*"

"*Oui.*"

"I am the fool."

Vittorie sat up and wiped Annabelle's cheeks dry with the back of her fingers. "You'll teach your children differently than we were taught."

Annabelle nodded. "You, too."

"*Moi!*" Vittorie snorted. What her sister lamented, she'd dreamed in vain. "I don't see any children in my future."

The noise of the wooden cellar door scraping open in the kitchen beneath interrupted them. A flurry of chickens cackled, and a woman's voice clucked soothingly to them. The sisters sat holding hands in quiet until their breathing synchronized.

"*Arrivé*," Vittorie said. "Cook will have breakfast for us soon. That will do you good."

8

Western Virginia, unmapped wilderness west of the Appalachian Mountains

Wrinkles in the honey-brown skin of the longhunter's forehead softened. With aqua-blue eyes he watched the gray morning fog thin over the barrens, and though it was cold, he didn't feel it. His attention was elsewhere.

Unaware of the interloper, the doe's head remained down. Her graceful neck pulled at the sweet greens near her feet. Then, her left ear cocked and she was on alert. Jerking her head up, without hesitation she leapt over mature goldenrod fronds and lean, willowy grasses. Her young muscles worked effortlessly, springing the smoothness of her body out of the meadow and into the woods. Instinct darted her past a dozen maple trees. She changed direction between trunks as wide as her outstretched form, endeavoring to outpace and lose her attacker.

But all his instincts were in play as well. His pursuit never lagged. He scrambled over massive, gnarled tree roots and ducked sapling branches in full flower to keep up. Worn creases framed his eyes. Like arrows, they compelled this man of the woods forward. His ears, trained to the sounds of the trail, heard not just her footfalls but calculated her intentions. He was gaining ground.

The doe led down deeper into the cool cover of the wooded hollow, where the early dawn barely pierced the canopy of the treetops high overhead. The pair separated, but then she reappeared, now just a few paces away. He followed, keeping her at a constant pace above her average escape speed. And he never let her rest, predicting the outcome of the run. Their two heartbeats and panting breaths echoed through the dew-dropped forest—the doe and the man.

All morning, prey and pursuer matched stamina over rocky ledges and brambles taller than the average Scotsman. Her pointed hooves dashed through soggy stream-beds. His moccasins left human footprints with no sound in the soft dirt. Her eyes wild, her breathing labored, she couldn't keep up that pace. She was overheated; her systems peaked. She faltered. Her knees buckled. She went down, struggling and frantic, no longer able to outrun him.

With eyes never leaving her and lips parted in muttered homage, he watched her ribs pulse until at last, the doe released her final breath through wide, rounded nostrils. Her body shuddered, then was still. She was dead, the race over.

He unslung a strap from his shoulder and pulled a string from around the thigh of his pantleg, releasing a leather satchel secured there during his run. It fell into a bed of leaves by his feet. Barely winded, he squatted beside it, unlatched the toggle on the satchel, withdrew his knife, and went to work.

9

1783 - Hotel d'York. Paris, France

The commission of delegates from the Continental Congress were being led down an ornately gilded hall. John Adams and John Jay followed closest to the French guards escorting them. Thomas Jefferson held a large assortment of papers in one arm, which he flipped through as he walked.

"It must say 'free,'" Thomas said, unsettled. He glanced at Benjamin Franklin beside him.

Ben readjusted the wire of his glasses over his ears. "Fine, Thomas."

"We've settled it already," said Adams, his pace quickening to keep up with Jay's. "'Sovereign' suffices. When dealing with a king, speak like one." His forehead, now reddish to the top of his head, exploded into bushy tufts of hair the color of wheat ale with shocking white patches overtaking his ears. "His Majesty must acknowledge the United States of America to be sovereign, no less than he is, or we risk succumbing again to tyranny by lack of proper rhetoric," he said, tucking his round chin further into his neck, emphasizing all the hard consonants of the last word.

"Precisely why I tender the word 'independent' for final consideration," said Ben. His pudgy nose bounced above his lips as he spoke. "There's no confusion about what 'independence' means when speaking to a sovereign, in my opinion." The natural wisps of his uncurled hair flounced around his high collar. "Besides, Laurens already agreed and signed it as 'independent'."

John Jay stopped walking and brought the argument to a halt in front of two tall doors. "Gentlemen, it is *our* document." Dark eyebrows hung dangerously over his deep-set eyes. "We may define our terms as best suits the needs of the American people, thereby establishing our free, sovereign, independence from Great Britain and honoring those signers, like Henry Laurens, who have approved what Thomas already had." His fair hair covered the tops of his ears. "Adding words for completion here isn't heresy." His curved lips returned to the straight line befitting a man in the legal profession. "This isn't the Bible."

"Amen," said Benjamin. The humor of his own wit wasn't lost on himself, and he diverted a short laugh in the direction of his shoe buckles. "Thank you, Jay," he said, straightening his spine and pouching out his belly. "The lawyer among us."

A middle-aged Frenchman joined the guards at the head of the procession. His was a compassionate face inside a wig that curled just over his shoulders. His eyebrows arched steeply above large gray eyes, and three folds of skin bagged beneath them, giving the impression of tireless dedication. He now waited on the commissioners, speaking English with French tones. "Gentlemen, welcome," he said, twisting two adjacent door handles to the floor and opening two opposing doors. "*Messieurs* Hartley and Oswald await you."

"No King George?" muttered Benjamin.

"We're just farmers, Ben," said Adams. "We'd have to be at least a duke. Maybe an earl." Then, bowing to the Frenchman, he added, "*Merci, Monsieur…*"

"*Monsieur* Monet," said the gray-eyed Frenchman. "Auguste Monet. I am here to help, *Messieurs,* in any way I may be of service."

The Americans each dipped their heads in thanks.

10

Chateau de Monet. Bretagne, France, near the Bay of Biscay

Built in the fifteenth century, the country house impressed without being overdone—ivory stone construction with twin round towers capped by quintessential French blue turrets. Its windows on the first and second floors boasted newly painted shutters. The third-floor windows were smaller, shutterless, and appointed the seven gables on the southwest side. Everything about the home evoked history and class, including a dozen brick chimneys festooning the top. Overlooking meadows and vineyards, the views lacked nothing.

Annabelle's seven-year-old son jumped down from the carriage and ran all the way up the stone steps to the chateau. "The ships are back!"

Vittorie caught the boy on the steps in a hug.

"*Alors!* François, wait!" Annabelle ushered the other children out ahead of her, then accepted the footman's hand. Getting out of the jostling carriage herself was not easy in her maternal state. Once safely on the ground, she snatched the littlest two children by the hands.

"It's true," Annabelle said, confirming the boy's announcement. The driver snapped the reins and the empty carriage lurched toward the stables.

"He's home," Vittorie said, kissing her sister on both cheeks. "I'm sure one of these ships is carrying him to me!" Overjoyed, she stretched her arms above her head and spun around. She swept one arm across her body, then down to meet the outstretched point of her toe peeking out beneath the embroidered hem of her silk skirt.

"Stop dancing a *courante*!" Annabelle said. "What would Mama say?"

Vittorie ended with an exaggerated curtsy, and the children squealed in delight for their aunt's performance.

"Yes, *bravo*, but no more!" Annabelle warned with a look in the direction of the house. Her smile returned as she saw what her sister was wearing. "When did you finish that?"

"Yesterday," Vittorie said, beaming. The gown complemented her eyes, green silk damask with cream, peach, and raspberry embroidery for trim. The waist was small, and the hem higher in the new fashion. "There was a rider earlier with a message for the de la Motte Rouges," Vittorie continued. "Arles sent word as soon as he heard." She scooped up her youngest niece and cuddled the child against her cheek.

"*Non!* Put her down," said Annabelle, alarmed. "She's jostled around in the carriage and you can't risk getting dirty. Let me have her." Vittorie kissed the girl's cheek as Annabelle took the baby from her.

A ship's bells sounded over the hills. Vittorie stretched onto her toes as if she might see a mast just past the stone wall of the courtyard. The pull of Gilbert's anticipated arrival was strong, and she broke into a run.

She got halfway under the arched gate before Annabelle shrieked, "Victoire Alexandra Claire Monet! You cannot run across the fields!"

"Annabelle," Vittorie called back breathlessly, "come with me!"

"With the children? No!" Annabelle held the little heirs closer to her. "I can't…we can't…go running anywhere. It's not ladylike, it's beneath our station, and besides…I don't want to."

"I'm glad you're standing up for yourself!" Vittorie called over her shoulder, feet still striding over the pebbled area. She whirled around like a spindle stuck in place, head high and arms free. "Now is the perfect moment to run! He's right down there! *Je pense qu'il est!*" She raced to where the wall was broken down and stepped up on the rocks, stretching her neck to see. "He's home. He's come back to me!" She straightened her powdered wig. "I can't see the banners, but I'm sure it's Gilbert's ship! Come with me, Annabelle! Come with me!"

Her hope had endured. Her love was as close as the masts bobbing in the surf. She was giddy with anticipation.

Annabelle gave in. "It will take Phillippe time to change horses…"

Vittorie ran through the iron gate and past the perennial gardens. She wasn't listening in the slightest. "Find me when you get to the docks!" She raced over the sloping hillsides, every step crushing blossoms beneath her feet. It filled the air with the smell of lavender, apple mint, and moss.

Her heart beat ferociously. She laughed out loud as she ran, uncorking the happiness inside her. The dreadful years were behind her. Gilbert was so close. She didn't want to spend one more moment without him.

11

Bay of Biscay

The docks were full of people. It wasn't every day a ship returned from fighting King Louis' wars to anchor in their port. All Vittorie could really see were masts and flags, ears and armpits. People with no business there nor family returning stared up at the wooden hulls and bobbing decks high above their heads. So many bodies loused up the order of things. It was madness.

Vittorie charged into the noisy crowd, elbowing her way closer to the enormous battleship. A few people crushed themselves over a bit to allow her a small passway; most ignored her.

"*Pardonnez moi,*" she said.

A little man with bad breath faced her. He took one look at her—the smooth skin of her face, her ridiculous white wig and dress—and his face scrunched in disgust. "*Attendez!*" he said, grabbing at her neck. "One less little noble." His top lip curled with hatred showing black caverns where God intended teeth.

His rage shocked Vittorie, and she pulled away. Afraid, she pushed against the movement of the people, away from this stranger with the dark mouth and anger and…whatever it was he was after. She ducked under an elbow, which jostled her wig askew. She got it straightened just as the man beside her found who he was looking for.

"*Alors,* Gilbert!"

He thrust his arm through the mass of bobbing heads to wave it above them and collided with Vittorie's wig. The pins tore her hair from her scalp, and the wig fell to the ground. *Could he know my Gilbert and be calling him?* She wasn't tall enough to see who he was trying to summon. From her space next to his shoulder, she saw tears pool in the man's eyes.

"Gilbert!" he yelled again. "*Alors, ici!*" He whisked the cap from his head, making the sign of the cross between his forehead and shoulders.

Gilbert! She turned to snatch her wig up from the ground, but it was gone. It must have been trampled underfoot, kicked aside, lost in the tumultuous sea of soiled aprons and patched trousers. Someone pushed her from behind and she stumbled forward. The man who had called out for Gilbert grabbed her arm, preventing her from hitting the ground and being trampled herself. He pulled her back to her feet, avoiding lengthy eye contact.

"Stop!" he said, rebuking two young boys pushing through. "There's a lady here!"

The boys ignored him and grabbed hold of a man wearing a white soldier's jacket. "Papa! Papa!" they chorused. The returning soldier caught both children around the shoulders and fell to hugging them, kissing the tops of their heads.

Vittorie's indignance at being pushed changed to forgiveness in watching their reunion, awaiting her own. She clutched onto the stranger who'd helped her up. Embarrassed for such a familiar hold, she blushed. "*Pardonne-moi,*" she said. "I'm sorry…"

His hands released her, waving off her apology. "No problem." His teary eyes and kind smile reassured her.

"Gilbert!" she yelled, standing on her own again. She glanced at the man beside her, returning the smile.

Surprised to hear her call for Gilbert as well, the tall man resumed his own shout. "Gilbert!" He patted Vittorie on the shoulder. "He's heard us! He's coming!"

Wagon wheels came to a stop behind her and horses whinnied. "*Mademoiselle Monet?*" said a male voice behind her.

Vittorie flinched and spun around on the defensive. Annabelle's husband, the Count de Lousan, emerged from between the shrouded curtains of the family carriage. His appearance stiffened her and she turned from him.

The gold buckles across his shoes glinted in the midday sun as he approached. "My dear, are you alright?" His eyebrows arched high in concern he did not mean.

The crowd surrounding Vittorie scurried away as he approached. Their presence—moments ago so stifling to her—evaporated.

"Gilbert," she said, looking around, "is here."

"Is he?" His eyes narrowed but he never turned his head. Instead, they swept over the scene with a casual disinterest. "Well," he said, taking her hand, "if he is, we can greet him together."

She pulled away but he'd taken hold. She felt the knuckle of her middle finger dislocate. Pain shot up her arm and the suddenness of it unnerved her. Her knees went weak.

He coiled an arm around her waist and spat into her ear. "He is not on this ship. You need to come home with me."

As he released her hand, her knuckle corrected itself and the searing pain eased. He stood so close it was uncomfortable to look up at him. She stepped away and looked him in the eyes. To her, they were chamber pots ready to be thrown out on the street.

"You are a liar and a thief." Now that Gilbert was home everything would change.

He laughed. "I am your future. Embrace me."

"Gilbert!" the tall man shouted again nearby.

Vittorie spun around, anticipating the dark-haired image of her dreams. Instead, she saw the teary-eyed man clasping forearms with a long-faced soldier in a white jacket. His Gilbert had reddish hair. The men spoke to each other, but the voice was certainly not the voice of her Gilbert.

"Gilbert!" she cried, her voice shrill, panic-stricken. She searched the dock for him, running, hand shielding her eyes.

Parents embraced sons. Wives nestled into the arms of returned husbands. Fathers tussled children's hair and flung them above their heads to carry them on their shoulders. The contented laughter and soft sobs of reunions echoed from every direction. Every white jacket raised her hope. Every soldier not him erased it. She stood still, panting, chest pain intensifying.

"You see?" said the count, sauntering up behind her. "He is dead."

"No." She walked, slowly at first, around each family group. She must have missed him. He had to be here. Had to be. The possibility that Gilbert wouldn't return hadn't been allowed in her conscious thoughts. Now, framed against the scarring reality of the count's bouncy carriage and her own empty arms, she shrank away from him.

Her feet never ran so fast.

12

Vittorie collapsed high up on the hillside, far above the docks and the carriage roads, where only gulls and the wind spoke. She laced her fingers through the grasses until her fists grabbed handfuls of the green reeds. She held on tight, as though without their tethering her fears might shake her off the face of the earth.

He was too conceited to chase her up the mountainside. Looking down, she saw his carriage take the southern road. She might make it home before him if she ran, if she took the path through the vineyards. It would be too rocky for his fine wheels. She leaped up and beat the dirt off her dress. These vines were her second sanctuary. She knew them by heart.

The deep call of the tower bell on their small stone chapel sounded. She had raced its tones her whole life. Still, one peal having sounded already, she had only four more to reach the family vineyards.

The weight of the count's words settled once again, binding her spirit and buckling her legs. She fell down on all fours and swayed back and forth.

"Lord,..." she prayed, but added no more.

"Victoire!"

Father Benét's voice carried from a hill below. Looking around, she waited to see from which way he appeared. The sun was relatively high, not having speared itself for the night on the row of spindly cypress trees Turgot's engineers had planted. The workers leaving the fields for the day plodded over the gravel road until, individually, they peeled off, ducking through a hedge or under a trellis with a shout toward home.

She could see the town, shops closing, merriment stirring as more small groups welcomed men. An unfamiliar bay horse stood at the fountain. Its head ducked low into the basin for a drink. The saddle was empty. She coughed out some spit. Something must be wrong. It wasn't five o'clock. It was too early for the bell.

"Vittorie!" Father Benét called. He was limping up the hill to find her. "At 78, and the fourth oldest man in our village, I can still best this hill!"

Seeing him amble up the hillside sent Vittorie into motion. "*Alors!*" she said. "I'm here!" She slipped between the strings training the grapes.

"I can outrun you still, you know. I just don't want to," he panted as she reached him. "Your mother's been searching for you for longer than she's pleased with." Leaning into his staff for support, he waved her past him. "Run home! *Vitement!*"

Moistness in Father Benét's eyes, plus his permission to run, said enough. Gathering her dirty skirts, she darted through the breaks of warm, baked earth in the long rows of the future vintage. With each step, she prayed for the courage to confront whatever evil the count had conjured up for her when she arrived.

$$13$$

She raced through thin streets to the square, propriety thrown to the ground. Whatever happened, she would face it. Her whole body worked to power her legs under the awkward, cumbersome dress. She tucked the billowy fabrics into the crook of her elbows to get some of it out of the way. Her legs free, her fists pumped forward and back propelling her home.

As Gilbert had taught her, she focused on her upper body in the run. Her neck lengthened. She relaxed her shoulders. Her gaze settled on a spot about a meter ahead of her stretching toes, and her breathing eased as she found her stride. Turning the corner onto *Rue de la Paix*, Vittorie caught sight of her mother waving a piece of lace frantically. Cook and Netta were squeezed in beside her in the annex kitchen doorway. Cook's face, always red, looked plum. The auburn ringlets escaping Netta's cap were sweaty too, a sure sign of duress.

Vittorie's cheek muscles tensed. Whatever news she was about to hear apparently affected every level of the household, for they were all here. Her heart pumped violently in her throat even after her feet stopped at the threshold.

Mama pulled her inside and shut the door. She spat directives and undressed Vittorie all at once. *"Pour l'amour du ciel,* you look worse than a peasant. Turn around." The skin between her eyebrows pinched tightly. "Peasant" was Mama's favorite unfavorite word. "We've been searching for you for hours." She hated waiting. "Didn't you see the messenger in the square?" she asked, as though her daughter loitered there regularly.

"No," Vittorie replied, watching her mother. "Just tell me, *Mama.* If your eyelashes don't stop fluttering so violently, you'll have bruises under your eyes for a week."

"Victoire Alexandra!" Marie said. "I don't appreciate your humor." Her voice held a check, the studied tone of the offender offended. "And where is your hair?"

"I am sorry about that." Vittorie offered no explanation. Turning to run upstairs, she asked, "Is Papa home?"

Perfumed with the morning's preparations, Cook pulled the corner of her wide apron up and wiped her eyes. She smelled of the underground kitchen, with its stone walls and floor, and the stirrings of home. She hugged Vittorie, bosomy and comforting and warm. The scents surrounded them both: nutmeg, currants and mutton, butter browning, yeast, cream, and mushrooms.

Netta covered her mouth but nodded. Her cotton cap bobbed above her eyes.

Vittorie stopped. "What has happened?"

Instead of answering, they grabbed her arms and waist and ushered her through the kitchen and up the stairs. Together, they prodded, held onto, unbuttoned, and untied her. Bustling as one multi-tentacled human through the narrow back hall, they talked among themselves, ignoring her.

"...*un spectacle!* What do you think I thought seeing you *running* down the road...have you no upbringing?"

"...you must be thirsty, dear..."

"...Oh *non!* Your dress is ripped! It's with the grain so I'm sure you could stitch it, *Ma'am'selle...*"

The moment they entered Vittorie's room, she felt the dress slip down to her ankles. Mama took her hands to help her step out of it.

"Netta's got your taffeta ready," Mama said. She continued, but not to Vittorie. "Wash her neck, too, Netta."

The girl nodded, setting the cap to bobbing again. She propped Vittorie's hands over a basin and took the pitcher from Cook's outstretched ones.

"*Merci,* Suzanne." Only Mama called Cook by her first name.

Warm water poured out. Netta scrubbed Vittorie's arms with a soap ball. The scent of lavender was refreshing.

"Whatever for?" Vittorie asked, her pitch rising. "*Qu'elle est la problème?* Is Papa alright?"

"No, he's not alright anymore," Marie said. The matriarch looked at her daughter and threw up both hands multiple times, as if that explained everything. "*Ils ont commencé...* They've started in to...politics."

"Mama, stop!" Vittorie shouted, bringing the activities in the room to a halt. "What's going on?"

A woman of pedigree with taste and a talent for knowing what to do, Marie Monet held out her hands. All motion ceased. She looked at her daughter. "Gilbert is here. He's in the garden with your father."

Vittorie didn't move. She looked from one to the other, wanting to believe. Netta smiled. She grabbed Vittorie and spun her around with a delighted shriek. Marie came over and touched her arm.

"*Vous voyez,*" she said softly, "perhaps your faith was not misplaced."

Vittorie threw her arms around her mother and squeezed. "Oh, Mama," was all she could get out between giggles and a fresh outburst of tears.

"*Déjà assez,* he's waiting!" Mama said. She was twirling her wrists around again, lace waving emphatically.

"He's waiting," Vittorie repeated, dreamlike. Her trembling hand went to her mouth. Resting a finger above her top lip, her mother's words were still sinking in. "He's waiting!" she said again, nodding this time at each of them.

Their smiles confirmed that it was true. Cook wiped her eyes on her apron again.

"Netta," Vittorie said, running over to the window to see for herself, "*où est ma robe?*"

"Vittorie! Come away from the window and get dressed!" said Mama.

Netta rushed to grab the garment laid out on the chaise. Cook and Mama held Vittorie's elbows. She stepped through the back, deep into the petticoat skirting. Cook fluffed the hem at the bottom while Netta buttoned the *comperes*.

"How many more can there be, Netta?" Vittorie asked, the pitch of her voice unable to hide a moan.

"*Maintenis en place,*" said Mama. She took Vittorie's shoulders and squared them in front of her. "He's asked your father for your hand, but he's got some ideas Papa isn't happy with."

"Like what?"

Netta finished and stepped back to admire her mistress. Mama spun her middle finger around delicately, indicating for Vittorie to turn around. Cook and Netta gushed approval.

"*Les plus belles broderies que vous avez fait,*" said Netta.

"*Perfect,*" said Cook.

Vittorie had created the dress herself. It had all the accoutrements of her station, yet lacked any hint of being overdone. The moss green color of the linen chintz was accented by the even pleating of the matching petticoats in a wide border above the hemline. The evergreen color of the plant motif cascaded down from a small bouquet of appliqued flowers surrounding an emerald stone above the *comperes*. Floral silhouettes, embroidered in three shades of the berry family, bloomed out in clusters dotted across the bodice, while stems and leaves in an ethereal green vined their way in lavish abundance between them.

Vittorie gathered her skirts to run.

"Victoire Alexandra Claire!" her mother cried. *"Pour une fois,* act your station, please!"

Vittorie let down her skirts. Straightening up, she pushed her shoulders down and back and dropped her chin lower. A demure smile creased her lips. Catching her own reflection in the gilded mirror, she smiled with a heartfelt exuberance. This was her moment, and she gazed with complete joy at the face Gilbert would see. She lingered, pleased with her own smooth brow and tiny etched mouth. If she were honest, she knew she was marked with beauty, and she was grateful. Her eyes sparkled, fresh from crying but greener because of it.

"Will you be enough for him, now that he's come home?" she silently asked her reflection.

"Let him do the looking," Mama said, cutting short her doubts. "Go on already!"

With a low curtsy for her mother, and a nod toward Netta and Cook, she snatched a fan from the settee. Embracing the accomplished air of a noblewoman, Vittorie exited with a genteel, *"Merci, Mesdames."*

✵ ✵ ✵

When Vittorie entered the sunlight of the courtyard, Gilbert looked as though heaven had opened to him in the form of one woman. In an instant, the two were joined into one—their eyes reflecting each other's image, their hearts humming the same tune, their souls intertwining with their bodies soon to follow. Gilbert had returned, finally, across the sea and over the hills to close the distance separating them. What were a few more lengths of open ground? But these were the most precious. In these steps, he saw with his own eyes the outline of her shape, the light in her hair, the softness of her dress, and the way her lips were parting into a smile only for him. Oh, to be the air slipping in past those teeth…

"Victoire," said her father. Auguste Monet wore his informal family wig, a good sign for Gilbert. But his shoulders were pinched up and he wasn't seated.

Vittorie curtsied to her father, holding the low position extra long in an effort to remind him of his love for his good daughter. But her eyes couldn't keep from searching for Gilbert.

And there he was. With several intentional strides, his feet erased the world between them, and the embodiment of her love stood in front of her. He came so close she felt the warmth of his breath as he spoke.

"*Bonjour.*"

He stepped back to complete an acceptable bow. His white jacket was decorated with tassels twisted at his shoulders. The collar, stiff and short, stopped just under a scar on his neck that hadn't been there before. He was shaved clean and his brown hair was tucked under a freshly curled white wig. He looked into her eyes, searching for the answer to his long-held question.

"Yes," she smiled.

Auguste Monet cleared his throat. "You'll stay for dinner, Captain." It wasn't a question that needed an answer. Auguste couldn't keep a smile from his lips when he retired into the house.

"Victoire," Gilbert began, but that was as far as he got. He stepped closer and took her hand. His fingers touched hers as though his eyes were unnecessary and he could memorize her intent by feeling.

"Here I am," she said. "Gilbert…"

He kissed her lips lightly, requesting a permission she granted with another smile. He pulled her to him, arms and lips and hips fitting precisely into a kiss that could have been painted into a golden frame.

He knelt in front of her and ran his hands over the chintz until they grabbed hold, then pressed his cheek against her bodice. She had waited for him. He had proven himself in battle; let anyone say he was weak and they would be shown differently. But here, with her, it didn't matter. The burden of worry and war lifted and dropped the hero to his knees. His arms clutched her tightly and he held the little waist of the woman who had prayed so long for him.

His appreciation for this one good thing leaked out his eyes. To have expressed it any other way would have been false.

14

The count smiled at Gilbert across the dinner table. It was not a friendly smile. It was the practiced sneer of a man so absolute in his position he'd forgotten what fear was. "What are your plans now that you've returned to society?" He slopped a large morsel of beef through the *au jus* in his plate, stabbed at it with the two tines of his fork, and bit the meat off. The sharp edge of his pale jawbone circled as he chewed.

The family paused. All eyes looked at the returned hero. Gilbert rubbed the fabric of the tablecloth between his fingers. He hadn't touched his food.

"Sweetheart..." Vittorie whispered.

Seeing her face, his smile appeared and he reached to take her hand. He looked from her to Auguste.

Auguste's long eyelids lengthened under a raised eyebrow. He laid his napkin in his lap and said calmly, "The idea Gilbert has is to marry Vittorie."

Most of the small party erupted in cheers. The count stabbed into a morel.

"Oh, Blessed..." Marie clasped her hands together and kissed the rings on her own fingers. She looked heavenward and wiped tears away.

Annabelle, seated across from Vittorie, reached past the count to touch Vittorie's arm. "*Merveilleux!* Wonderful news!"

Gilbert stood to shake hands with Auguste and kiss Marie on both cheeks, the traditional *bisous.* Vittorie hugged everyone, avoiding the count.

Once the well-wishes and tears abated, Auguste pulled three times at his nose. He did this whenever he wasn't certain on a matter yet. "And…for them to make a life together in the New World."

All merriment hushed. Auguste took his fork back in his hand, staring at his plate.

No one had been surprised when Marie was courted by and wed Auguste Monet, ten years her senior. His family was a favorite of the king and he was a mild man. Having four daughters, each a vision in their own right and three married well, reflected on her. But having her fourth daughter journeying to the New World? She hadn't accounted for that.

"Surely, not," Marie said. "I hear it's only savages and Englishmen there."

"Is there a difference?" asked the count, laughing at his own joke. "*Vraiment*, Gilbert, if you're unsure of your place I can inquire for you at court. Louis and I have grown…what would you say, Papa? Quite close?"

Auguste wiped his mouth. "The king has favored you, Simon, but history shows that to be a precarious position. I think it wisest to refer to him with reverence at all times."

The count lifted his wine glass in apology and downed the ruby liquid. "No harm intended."

Marie waved her lacy wrist for the dinner dishes to be cleared. "Tell Suzanne we'll take dessert on the patio tonight. I long for some air."

Netta removed the plates, ducking her head meekly at each person's chair while she reached in. "*Oui, Madame.*"

"France will change now that this war is over," Gilbert said. "Too many of us didn't return from fighting for freedoms France doesn't even offer her people, yet. But I believe the time is right for France to grow in this way...." He looked at Auguste and continued, "...as the colonists have in the Americas. I've seen what rights free-thinking men afford each other, and what costs they'll pay to retain them."

Vittorie caught the grief with which he spoke the last words. She took his hand.

"You're drunk with ideals!" the count replied. He rolled the stem of his wine glass between three fingers. "Treasonous thoughts and poisonous words fresh from the American colonies, I'd say. Probably something you heard some Brit spout off."

The count's spite soured the conversation. Marie wished to change the mood. "Auguste, will you have dessert *à l'extérieur?*" She waited for him to pull out her chair, but he didn't.

Gilbert folded his napkin and pressed it neatly to the dark wood of the table. "As a man of education, I'm enamored with the beauty of America's vast, unexplored countryside. As the son of nobility and a sincere Frenchman, I find the possibility of men under God governing themselves intoxicating. As a soldier I've closed the eyes of too many men...friends...whose last catches of breath were sucked in under banners of kings and nobles they'll never meet, nor be appreciated by. And as a Catholic, I fought for people who believe in ideals meant for *all*. I fought with General Washington, bled with my men, and many foreigners, united in one cause. A cause initiated by our noble King Louis when he sent us as aid. While you, pert and wriggling under your tiny, powdered fop, would reduce France to a piece of beef raised and fattened to extend your own belly. *Et pour le pire.*" Gilbert pushed his chair back and stood up. "Forgive me, Madame Monet. I know better than to speak harshly at your table."

Marie blinked ferociously again, her face flushed. "Of course, you're forgiven, Gilbert. War is unspeakable and you haven't been in society…" Her voice trailed off as Auguste cleared his throat.

"Have they made Washington king, then, in the American colonies?" Annabelle asked. "Or will King Louis rule from afar?"

"*Non*," Auguste said. "There will be no king."

"How can there be order with no ruler?" Marie said. "They will become savages!"

"They've formed a government similar to ancient Rome, under Caesar. Washington refused the crown. I spoke with the American delegates during their time at court. Very interesting. Instead, he wants a tri-part government, written by and subject to the people."

"He'll be sorry for that," said the count. "What a fool to be so close and not attain the prize. I don't think he can be quite as great as you believe, Gilbert. But then, you've been living in nothing more than a hut for too long yourself."

It was Gilbert's turn to smile. "Yes, in a tent like the Hebrews, from whom comes our Christ." He crossed himself. "I think my horizons were broadened greatly by the experience." With that, he took Vittorie's hand and raised her up from her seat. "May I have the honor of escorting your daughter through the gardens *ce soir*, Viscount Monet?"

Auguste's jowls jiggled as he nodded approval. He motioned for them to proceed outside first then pulled the chair out for his wife to accompany him.

Marie removed her fingers from Auguste's hand. "Please stay, Simon. I've had Cook fix something magnificent in your honor."

"Of course," said the count with practiced formality. Hatred burned in his eyes.

15

Vittorie stared out the window into the morning sky. Aquamarine with pintucked clouds bathed in pink that dripped, still wet, with what looked like golden chiffon. Today, she would be married, caught up, and swept away. It was already written for her in the sky and she leaned out into it, soaking in every color and tone.

"The ceilings of the palace at Versailles captured a moment no less heavenly, but of lesser effect in my esteem," Vittorie said. "I'll stitch this," she added dreamily, "when we're settled in New France."

"You didn't wait all this time for a curse, did you?" Annabelle said, slipping her arm around her sister's elbow. "Come in! Gilbert may see you."

"No!" Vittorie said, laughing at her sister's superstition. "Look out there, Annabelle!"

The sisters paused, arm to arm, gleaning warmth from each other in the early chill of the day. It was the last time they would be together like this.

Annabelle broke the moment and threw a swathe of linen toweling at Vittorie. "Come away from here and take your bath!"

"*C'est tellement beau,*" Vittorie said. "Today is my gift from God and I'm soaking it in."

Netta poured the last hot drops from two white pitchers into the tub. Steam curled up luxuriously. Camellia blooms floated in the waiting water. She set her pitchers down and took fresh lavender sprigs from the fold of her apron, crushed them in her palm, and sprinkled them over the calming waves. Their heady scent filled the *salle de bain*.

Annabelle smoothed Vittorie's long hair and twisted it up, fastening it with a pin. "Well, soak it in while you bathe. Come." She nodded to Netta, who exited, daring a quick smile and a nod to Vittorie.

Vittorie disrobed. Tiny purple buds bobbed inside the round tub as she tried out the water with her toes. Satisfied, she tucked her bare bottom beneath the bride's traditional bathwater, its heat eradicating every imperfect occasion from her mind.

Annabelle stared out the window. "I see what you mean, in one way," she said.

"*Qu'est-ce que c'est?*"

"This." She looked over the garden wall, past the vineyards, to the small stone chapel they'd grown up with. The church was set into the rise of a hill, flanked by a grove of wild apple trees. Its tower point glinted as the sun appeared over the eastern mountains. "Father Benét worked so hard to keep the chapel grounds looking well for you today," she said, changing the subject.

"I asked Pére Benét for some clippings of the old apple trees to take with us," Vittorie said. She scooped several large blossoms into her arms. Melon-colored and sweet, the petals brushed her skin above the water.

"*Pourquoi?*" asked Annabelle.

Vittorie sank lower. Warm water covered her shoulders and wet the curls at the nape of her neck. "Because I will need something…it will be good for me to have something from home that I can take with me."

"I wish you weren't going."

"I wish you were coming with us."

"You know I can't. Simon is too important."

"He wasn't invited," Vittorie said, serious. "And you know I'd take you with us."

Mourning doves cooed. Essie bellowed from her stall in the barn, waiting to be milked.

"*J'ai juste…*" Vittorie said, "I hope you'll be alright…by yourself."

Annabelle snorted. "*De quoi tu parles?* It's *you* we're all worried about."

"*Moi?* Why me?"

"You're going across the ocean." Annabelle flicked the bathwater carelessly. "Not to mention you're marrying…a soldier."

"*Ce qui?* What does that mean?"

"Did you see how fast he was to contradict Simon at dinner his *first* night with the family?" Annabelle stroked her own hair, avoiding eye contact with Vittorie. "Mama was in shock. I'm sure you noticed."

"I'm sure she got over any shock she may have felt within seconds."

"*Ne parlez pas ainsi.* It's unholy."

"Unusual, but not unholy. Are you so…."

"*Quoi?*"

"Simon is not without his own faults." Vittorie selected her words carefully and sat up a bit, eager for the breeze to cool the sweat on her temples.

"Just because I've married above you, and first, is no reason for you be hateful." Annabelle tipped a pitcher sideways in the tub, refilling its mouth with water. "Is this how you intend to leave me? With rude remarks of what's been bothering you all this time?"

"*Quoi? Non*, Annabelle. *Ce n'est pas mon intention.* It's just that you don't see him the way I see him." Vittorie leaned forward, exposing her back.

"No. Nor do you see a soldier the way I see them." Annabelle poured the hot water out over her sister's shoulders, oblivious to the bruises healing beneath her sister's skin.

"And that's the way it's supposed to be, I guess," Vittorie said, picking lavender seeds from her freckled arms, "or *tout le monde* would want the same few men. And what would become of the rest of them?" She squinched up her nose to lighten the mood and forced a smile for the love of her sister. "Or the rest of us!"

"We would not be saved through childbirth." Annabelle turned pious. Her manner stiffened as she smoothed the *chemisier* over her swollen belly. "You have a chance now, sister."

The statement hung awkwardly between them.

"For what?" Vittorie asked.

"Salvation. Through childbirth."

"*Je ne pense pas…*" Vittorie said. "I don't think that's how it…"

Annabelle wasn't listening. She sat by the window and rubbed her belly.

Vittorie let her be.

16

In thirty minutes, Vittorie Monet would stand before God, family, neighbors, and friends, and receive a new name. She would be a LeClerc before sundown.

"*Penser*," Vittorie said aloud, gliding over the stone floor in her lavender wedding gown. "It takes years to build a city and nine months to incubate a human, but two lives may be combined into one in the space between breakfast and lunch. *Extraordinaire*."

Whispers and giggles filled the air beneath the arched ceiling. Marie, Annabelle, and the other Monet women busied themselves in the fun and frolic of marrying off their spinster sister. The hallowed occasion kept the merriment reverent.

"*Regardez celui-ci!*" said Annabelle, brandishing a sumptuously petalled camellia flower in front of Vittorie and Marie. "This coral color is a perfect foil for your gown."

"Yes, you are right," Marie said, making the decision. She tried the flower against the bodice but changed her mind, pinning the tender blossom below her daughter's ear amongst the cascades of her almond-colored hair.

Gentle light shone through the estate's windows. Fine fabrics danced as the ladies bustled throughout the chamber. Vittorie bit into a wild plum, sending juice down her chin.

"No eating *dans votre robe*." Marie thrust a loose glove under Vittorie's chin to catch the drip.

"But it just ripened this morning," Vittorie said, reluctantly depositing the rest of her treasure into Annabelle's outstretched palm. "I've been watching it all week."

Marie cinched the lavender silk and taffeta wedding skirt Vittorie had painstakingly created up over the *panier*. "Hold still," she said. "After six years of watching you sew this thing, I'd like to see it on."

Designer and seamstress, Vittorie twisted around to see how the final form fit. The stitches were even. The floral pattern unique. It was not gaudy in its lace nor its ribboning, its billows nor its pleating. Its perfection lay in the details and, as a whole, it was sublime.

"Such an even hand, Vi," Aunt Eloise commented as they finished getting Vittorie dressed. "The colors complement each other exceptionally. *Parfaitement adapté à votre coloration et de la personnalité*, Victoire. I could tell you crafted it without anyone telling me. In the three years since I've seen you, you've grown so much. Elegant. Mature. Whimsical and feminine."

Her approval warmed Vittorie. "Thank you, Aunt Eloise."

Aunt Eloise kissed her fingers and brushed them against her niece's cheek. "You would rival any queen and outdo anyone less."

"I didn't make the fabric, Auntie. I merely stitched it together."

"Hardly!" Marie added. "It took seven months to get the silks once they were ordered from the Orient by the best *atelier* in Paris."

Annabelle sniffed. "If she'd had it made by a seamstress as I did it would have taken only a year, with fittings." She fanned herself quickly. "But she vowed she would sew the dress herself."

Marie continued the story. "The shop promised her they could finish the dress for her if she came into any trouble with the fine points or details. 'Oriental fabrics are a breed of their own,' they said." The lace around Marie's wrists twirled as she held the *chemisier* for her daughter. "But you've done well, Vittorie."

Vittorie slipped her arms into the sleeves. "Thank you, Mama. I prefer to work with my own hands."

"It's old fashioned," said Annabelle, still fanning. "It's 1782! Paris is only a three-day journey now over the new roads." She glanced at her mother for boldness. "But she *had* to do it herself."

Aunt Eloise let out a little sigh. "You had a gorgeous ensemble for your marriage, Annabelle. Let Vittorie marry how she chooses." She fastened several embroidered buttons, stunning accents to the fabric's pale hue.

"It's backward." Annabelle spoke with the same pious tone as earlier. She flipped a ribbon correct side out and it cascaded below a gather of fabric and flowers.

Vittorie's youngest sisters, Noelle and Marie-Claire, chirped in through the doorway. "Father Benét asked how much longer." Noelle had married a duke last year, and her growing belly showed.

"Tell him we need a few minutes more. Then Gilbert can come for her," Marie said with another wrist wave. Turning her attention back to Vittorie she asked, "Where is great-grandmother's cross?"

"*Oh, ici,*" said Marie-Claire, handing it to her mother. Reserved and elegant, Marie-Claire was two years younger than Vittorie and taller by eleven centimeters. She'd married a viscount five years earlier. They had twin boys, Luc and Pierre.

Vittorie put on the stiffer coat made of the same lavender silk with pretty, curling details covering the corset vest. Tiny matching wristlets were added.

Aunt Eloise snapped a needle and thread from a cluster of pearls on the dress. She handed them to Marie-Claire who walked over to Vittorie's carved *trousse* trunk and tucked them inside a drawstring pouch on the left side.

Marie took Vittorie by both shoulders and turned her. The light streaming in the latticed window shone on her fashionable hair, face, and *décolleté*. "Let Papa pin this on you," she said, handing Vittorie the family cross. Its fine wrought gold shimmered with jewels—a diamond, a sapphire, an emerald, and a pearl. Etched vines flowed in four directions, and a red ruby graced the heart of it.

"I'm going to hold it, Mama," Vittorie said.

"Nonsense, you need your hands free to hold his. Papa will pin it on."

"Everyone is gathered outside!" Noelle said, interrupting the moment with her happiness. She waddled over in a rush and helped to button up the bride.

"Did you pack my thread?" Vittorie asked her mother.

"*Dans votre coffre, Cherie.* Everything is in your trunk. You won't need it anyway till you're on the ship." With that, Marie went silent altogether, but Vittorie saw her mother's thoughts puddle in her eyes.

"I love you, Mama," Vittorie said.

Her mother nodded but didn't speak. Instead, Marie kissed her on each cheek, then once more on the temple. Vittorie watched her mother's blinks with new understanding. This time, no antagonistic comment spilled from her mouth. She could see her mother's struggle and her own heart softened.

In an uncharacteristic gesture, Marie took Vittorie's hands in her own. "You are already a woman. But now you will be a woman with a man, which can be very different." Her voice was hushed in the stone chamber.

"*Oui*," Annabelle said, her eyes downcast.

Marie-Claire closed the lid on the trunk and buckled the leather straps. She blew Vi a kiss and opened the double doors. Joyful noises from the families gathered in the courtyard crescendoed, quieting again as she closed the artfully painted doors behind her.

The women bestowed their final wishes. Noelle took Vittorie's hands and kissed them. Aunt Eloise kissed Vittorie's palms. Annabelle kissed her forehead. Vittorie kissed each on both cheeks and all five held hands in a circle. Then, her aunt and sisters left the bride and her mother alone.

"It is easy for a woman to get lost in love," Marie's eyes were intent on her unmarried child. "A man is a king. Every man. Even a poor man if he has a good woman." She blinked. Emotion was difficult for her. "But it is not so easy for us." Her cheekbones softened and she smiled a moment. "Gilbert is a good man, I think. You will be a good wife. May love lead you safely. And always remember who you are."

There was a soft knock at the door.

"Are you sure of your decision?" Marie asked, sincerity flushing her face. Her green eyes flashed a warmth Vittorie had forgotten.

"Yes, Mama."

"Open the door," Marie said, signaling the men.

Auguste entered, captured as only a father can be seeing his daughter standing there, beautiful and resolute. He motioned for her to turn. "So I may see the entire vision," he said as she spun in place. By the end of her turning around he was so near that she reached out to brush the wetness off his cheek.

"*La plus belle*," he said, his voice barely above a whisper. "The most beautiful."

Marie held out the cross. "When you have a need, listen for God's voice." She gave her husband the cross to pin on their daughter as she continued. "He will speak in your heart and tell you what to do."

Auguste winked. "The voice of God may sound a bit like your mother's voice inside your head, for a time." Knowing his daughter's preference to hold the cross, he placed it in Vittorie's hands.

"But it will grow to sound like your own voice. You are well loved, my brave girl." He hugged her tight and kissed her hairline.

"*Je connais*, Papa," Vittorie whispered.

Auguste took her arm, but as they stepped toward the archway Vittorie stopped. "What if I can't get them to agree? The voices in my head and my heart?"

"*Ensuite*, you do the best with what you have and pray," Auguste replied. "God will sort out the difference."

All three looked at themselves in the same long mirror. Vittorie smiled at her wedding dress, finally complete. Her father, gaunt and grayed, held her left arm in his. Her mother, eyelashes beating, stood on her right, resplendent in her own gown of cream and raspberry.

"You are your mother's daughter," her father said at last. "*Belle. Forte. Et bonne.*"

With that, they all kissed each other one last time. Auguste pushed the tall doors apart, and they walked as one through the doorway.

✣ ✣ ✣

Gilbert waited alone in the *salon*. As soon as he heard footsteps in the hall, he sighed in relief. He was at the doors as they opened, and at Vittorie's side once she stepped under the doorframe. He kissed Marie's hand, and both her cheeks. When he shook Auguste's hand, he did so with a firm grasp, communicating to his future father-in-law how grateful he was. How deeply he understood his responsibilities as a husband. Auguste kissed Gilbert on both cheeks, then put his daughter's delicate hand into Gilbert's, keeping his own around theirs for a moment. It was hard to let go.

Gilbert tucked Vittorie's wrist around his arm and pulled her closer beside him. "*Tu m'etonne,*" he said softly into her ear. "Will you walk with me?" he asked, leading her toward the waiting crowd.

She blushed. "I'd race you, but I don't want to cause you any embarrassment. Not today anyway."

Nearby wedding guests startled at hearing Gilbert's eruption into genuine laughter. It was loud and boyish and heartfelt. He kissed Vittorie's fingertips.

"Come with us!" Gilbert shouted. "Today, I wed my true love!"

What joy on the lover's faces! What happiness for both sets of parents to see their sweet children walking to the chapel to be forever wed. At last, the hope in the hearts of these two faithful lovers would be fulfilled. The whole village rejoiced. The procession to the church steps was triumphant and endearing. The distance between the Monet estate and the chapel was not far, but every home they passed had doorways and windows filled with relatives and friends waving and blowing kisses. Children ran ahead of the couple, pudgy fingers holding crisp, white ribbons that streamed out behind them. With giggles and shouts, they carried out the tradition of unrolling fresh ribbons across the new couple's path.

"Oh," Vittorie said, glancing up at Gilbert and leaning into his side. From her silk pouch, she pulled a delicate pair of embroidery scissors. "How many obstacles we have overcome," she sighed. With several snips, she cut through a wide piece of the plain linen weave blocking them, symbolic of obstacles faced and conquered to reach the wedding day. It fluttered to the ground. As she stepped over it, a profound sense of goodwill filled her. She laughed, tossing away the years of worry and grief.

"*Regardez,* every face holds joy for you today," Gilbert said.

The wedding procession grew as it passed through the town. Neighbors joined in behind Father Benét, Gilbert and Vittorie, the Monets and the LeClercs.

Wreathed in festivity, the stone chapel hung with grapevines, lavender sprays, and stunning camellias in blushed hues. Plucked fresh from the king's botanical gardens outside of town, they gift-ed the air with divine sweetness. The old bell sang in the belfry with boys dangling from its ancient ropes, urging all to enter.

At the steps of the chapel, Father Benét stopped before the great wooden door and turned to face Vittorie and Gilbert. The ceremony was simple. His tenor voice filled the air as he administered communion to them.

Gilbert took a gold ring off his finger, similar to the one Vittorie had worn all the years of promise. As he slipped it on her finger, the rings interlaced into one. She noticed how strong his hands felt.

They each lifted a chalice with wine from their family vineyards and poured it into a third, two-handled goblet, signifying the creation of a new wine, a new vintage, the joining of their individual lives. From this goblet they both drank. It was finished.

Wedding guests thronged the steps. Flower petals rained on the laughing newlyweds as *Monsieur* and *Madame* LeClerc turned to face the crowd.

 Poor beggars reached their palms out from beyond the steps. Gilbert did his best to fill each dirty hand with a few coins.

Netta and Cook each kissed Vittorie on both cheeks and led the couple to tables laid end to end. Cook had outdone herself. She spent the rest of the morning serving enough pastries and tarts to feed all of France.

17

Later that day, everything that could be was crushed under the lids of three large wooden boxes. Locks were closed and the boxes were hauled outside. Their metal framings clanked against the stone of the street.

Vittorie was packed. But she wasn't ready to go.

It took three men to heave and hoist each trunk up over the carriage wheels. After that, Papa and Noelle's husband, Albert, slipped leather strappings through metal braces and pulled them tight. The cinching was simple and quick. The black mares pointed their noses in the air and shook their manes, anxious for the use of their legs.

Vittorie wished everyone would slow down. The wind smacked her face and she looked in the direction of the sea where it came from.

"Papa," Marie said, "remember the time!"

She'd harped about the straps, the time, and how the ship wouldn't wait for the newlyweds. Her mothering the morning of the great departure could be boiled down in one of Cook's copper kettles to "efficient officiant." Today, everyone forgave her.

Vittorie gazed at the cluster of family before her. She would have waited longer to fix the image, but her two oldest nephews rushed at her and clung tightly with their pudgy fists. She scooped them up together.

"Don't go 'way, Auntie," one of the boys said.

"I love you very much." Vittorie dried a loose tear of her own on the children's silky hair. After some tight hugs the boys were deposited again with their mother. The frothy curls on Marie-Claire's neck were pale as cream, like her sons'. Vittorie touched her sister's round belly, letting her hand rest on the future child. Her sister's hand laid lightly over Vittorie's. They stared at each other as in a mirror, reflecting thoughts as sisters can, *sans* distracting words. Wrapping Vittorie into a hug, Marie-Claire squeezed her hard, twice, without letting go in between. Her husband, Francois, had business in Montpelier, so his goodbyes had been said weeks earlier.

Everyone smiled through tears and took their place for hugs and kisses. There were no easy words, though the time had come to send them off. Gilbert and Vittorie caressed family and friends in tearful goodbyes. Each loved one offered a gift—a book, a doll, a rock from a nephew, a flower from a niece, a kiss from the mothers, money from their fathers.

Gilbert kept his arm around his bride the whole time, then helped Vittorie into the carriage loaded with their trunks. Taking his hand, she was up into the seat and he sat down beside her. The carriage door was shut and secured. They felt the movement of the driver as he arranged himself in front. A snap of leather and they were leaving her family behind.

Dreaming of adventure was not the same as actually beginning one. Vittorie willed herself to fix these images in her mind: the way Papa's chin sank into his neck while he forced a smile; how her parents held each other when her carriage jolted forward; how her sisters held their arms in lace sleeves high in the air until her neck pinched from straining backward to see them.

"Now that we're really leaving, I don't want it to be over," Vittorie whispered into Gilbert's shirt collar.

"Beginnings and endings are always difficult," Gilbert said. "*Toujours.*"

"I hope the middle is spectacular."

Gilbert chuckled and rubbed a tear from the apple of her cheek. "Me too."

As the carriage was passing by the steps of the chapel, Father Benét hailed the newlyweds. The staccato of hooves slowed to a stop before the great wooden door of the church.

The priest's smile creased several times through each wrinkled cheek. "I've been watching for you since the ceremony." He stuck a slip of well-folded paper through the window flap.

"*Oh, Père!*" Vittorie said. "Thank you for all you have done for me."

Gilbert took the paper and shook the priest's hand. "For us."

Father Benét's eyes twinkled. "God bless you, my children, as you go. May God go before you and behind you and flank you on both sides. And," he added, pointing to the paper in Gilbert's hands, "I have written some notes for the young bride on her journey."

"*Dieu vous benissez, mon Pére,*" said Vittorie. "*Merci, toujours.*"

"God bless you both." He kissed two fingers and pressed them to the ledge of the open window. Signaling the driver, he backed away from the high wheels.

Vittorie watched him as he made the sign of the cross over them. She kissed her own fingers and held her hand up in acknowledgement of his blessing. He was the last thing she saw of the home, the hills, and the people that had cradled her into a woman.

The wheels jostled and turned beneath them. With the trunks and all their possessions fastened securely upon it, the carriage took them away. Hooves of the four horses pulled their weight, found a rhythm, and trotted steadily. The priceless scenes of her existence thus far rushed past outside the heavy velvet curtain.

"*Il est très difficile…*it's very hard to leave what you love." Gilbert gave her the priest's note. "And those who love you."

She nodded. He was right. "*Presque impossible.*" She stroked the paper like the nose of a colt, then tucked it into a small pocket on the inside of her vest.

"Almost impossible," he said, pulling her closer. "But I have hope."

She stuck her head out the window, willing her eyes to take in each neighbor's house and bend of the road before it was gone, washed away by tears and ocean. She tried to memorize each tree and fencerow, how the hilltops gilded before the sun set. "Dear God, I shall miss home."

The vineyards waved goodbye in the wind. The scent of lavender and camellia blossoms came to her once more. The white pebbled ground stretched out before and behind them, as though this path had been laid out intentionally.

"Can I read his letter for you?" Gilbert asked.

"*Non, merci.* It's too much, looking behind. My heart is breaking." The cross was still in her hand. "Would you pin this on me?" She held it out to Gilbert. "I don't want to lose it."

He kissed her lips and did as she asked.

18

Gilbert woke with one ferocious jolt of the carriage, took a second to remember his surroundings, and burst into a smile. Kissing his new wife tenderly, he pulled the window covering aside. The deep angle of the sunlight over the passing landscape told him it was late in the day. His arm settled around her again.

"I'm hungry. And you ate less than I did." He patted his stomach. "Are you hungry?"

"Yes, *mon mari*," she said, taking this first of many moments to call him her husband.

Gilbert's smile widened, his face radiant as he looked at her. "*Encore, ma femme*," he whispered. "Say it again."

Her eyebrows gathered together in a small furrow as she repeated, "My husband?"

"Yes, my wife. All is as it should be with you here. In my arms." She snuggled in deeper as the coach sped on with its cargo over the endless ground.

"Did you know this is my favorite time of day?" she asked, yawning.

"I do now. We will arrive at the inn within the hour. Dinner there, and rest."

"Look!" she said, turning his chin from her to the gilded hills and cypress trees beyond. "The shadows are longest now. Everything is dipped in radiance for about thirty glorious minutes."

"Mm-hm." Gilbert looked out the window. "Tide's up."

She sat up. "Those last precious moments when the sun hovers just above the edge of the earth, stretching goodness and warmth as far as it can."

"It'll circle around and come up on the other side, sure as morning."

"Circle around!" Her eyes narrowed a bit and she let out a deep breath. "I learned all about *Monsieur* Newton and his new philosophy. The world as a circle. Never mind about that. Can't I just want everything to be still for a few moments?"

"Our life is ahead of us!" He turned her chin from the window toward him. "Be excited about that. And besides," the tone of his deep voice sobered, "mornings and moments happen whether we like them or not. Let's be grateful we get them at all."

She moved a piece of his hair off his forehead. "Aren't you sad about leaving everyone behind?"

Her touch softened his response. "The one I care about is right here in this carriage with me. I've let go of what's behind me."

"I know, but…"

"Victoire…"

"I am happy." The tears splashed out of her eyes and ran over her cheeks. "And sad. I don't know which to feel first. Nor how to express them. Neither of them. It's too much. Leaving and marriage…." She looked at him, crying. "…and America, too."

"Think about your sunlight then." He kissed her wet cheek. "Unless it's too late to stretch any more goodness from it today, as you say." He handed her a crisp, white pocket handkerchief.

She stared at her old embroidery. "I rushed this one. You can tell," she said, touching a knot.

"I didn't give it to you for critique. I'm in love with the woman who stitched it. Blow your nose and give it back, quick. I feel its absence acutely."

She obeyed with three exaggerated blows into the linen before handing it back. "When do we board your ship?" she asked, her face and eyes pinker.

"Tomorrow, according to Admiral Lagasse's letter. And it's the king's ship, not mine. We sail under command. But nothing is certain about the sea except the stars, if you can find them."

"I've heard that. Do you remember our stars?"

He nodded, tucking the wet handkerchief inside his blue jacket. "They are the same where we are going."

Vittorie brightened at that. "Truly?"

"*Oui,* truly." He shifted in his seat. "Where we're going is a wonderful place. You are going to love our home in the colonies." His face turned serious as he took her hands in his. "But it is not France."

Vittorie laughed out loud. "I know!"

She was so beautiful when she smiled, but he knew she didn't understand. "America has no king," he said, deciding how to teach her. "When I was fighting there, I fought beside some colonists. They fight for something they believe God gave every man. Something we, in France, do not even have."

"What is it?"

"Freedom."

"What do you mean?"

"Well, freedom from well-intentioned kings who don't understand their people. From taxes with no voice in leadership. And more than that, too. They've created a new kingdom…well, not a kingdom…it's called a 'government.' It's by the people and for the people. They will not have a king." He scratched under his jawbone. "Nor aristocracy."

Vittorie's face lost its humor. "Shhhhh." She pointed ahead to the driver and pulled Gilbert's ear down to her mouth. "Papa told me about this. He said a country with no king will destroy itself. How do people with no leader know who they are?"

The carriage slowed to a stop and disrupted their conversation. Gilbert helped her step out onto the street and spoke to the driver about the trunks. The sound of the sea lapping at the wharf posts held her attention until he wrapped her arm around his elbow.

"The Americans have skilled leaders. Most of the colonists are there by choice," he said, walking them up to a sign hanging above their heads. "Here we are. Our trunks will be brought up shortly." He opened the door and ushered her in. "They will live by laws, just like we do in France, but the people choose the laws. And the leaders, too. Something called 'election.' Every few years the people choose if they want new leaders, so no one person grows too powerful."

A thin man with an ill-fitting wig welcomed them to the inn, speaking pleasantly to both of them. They followed him up a stairway, barely wide enough, with a landing after three steps where it turned sharply to the right and continued upward. The lapping sound grew louder. He retrieved a key from his waistcoat pocket, handed it to Gilbert, bowed, and left them at their chamber.

"We can eat first, then unpack," Gilbert suggested, twisting the key in the lock.

The room looked as expected, small and comfortable, decorated in blues and greens with sparse accommodations. It boasted one window with a pattern of panes emanating out from a center circle. A yellow cord, snagged by a bent spike in the wall, pulled a heavy woolen drape to the left. The view over the street beckoned past the docks and beyond to the frothing ocean. In front of the window sat a three-legged table, set with a small repast of bread, *fromage*, grapes, and a tiny ramekin of paté. Gilbert pulled one chair out for Vittorie to sit. She arranged her skirts while he sat opposite and leaned over the table. They folded their hands to pray and smiled at each other. Vittorie blushed and looked away.

"*Notre Pére*," he began. "Our Father," he repeated, unable to put more into words.

"Thank you, Father…" Vittorie took up the prayer, but sat quiet herself.

They stayed like that in silence until he cleared his throat and made the sign of the cross from his forehead to his chest and shoulder to shoulder. "Amen."

She finished her own cross. "Amen."

Vittorie tore a piece off the baguette and smeared paté on it, scraping the knife clean on the hard crust. "Where will we live in America? In town or in the country?" She handed the first piece on a delicate plate to him.

"The country. America is so big. Every man may have a small kingdom." He bit, chewed, and swallowed, then bit and chewed again. "It is immense," he said after a second swallow. "Grander than any construction of man just in its landscape. The coast stretches as far as the eye can see in either direction." He eyed her second smeared piece of baguette and she handed it to him, open palm. "It's enough to restore man's faith in God." Bite. Swallow. "Only His hands could have designed and crafted so magnificent a spectacle."

It was unlike Gilbert to be so taken with something. He was a man of letters and learning, of order and soldiering. It was as if he had fallen in love. This talk of land was new, not as a nobleman's son speaks of entitlements and dowries and of being his, but as if the land existed outside of him and instead, he wished to be a part of it.

"Is it like Asia?" she asked, spreading paté on a third piece of bread for him. "Like when you went with your father for those two years? You were how old?"

"Fifteen. On errand for the king." He plucked three grapes and set them on her plate. "No." he stuck his knife in the wine cork and pulled. The resounding pop echoed against the plaster. "That was completely different. All the structures there tipped up at the corners. China is centuries older than France. America is a nation waiting for its umbilical cord to be cut."

"I remember you saying everything in China was red when you came home," she said with another smile. "'Red, the color most used in pageantry and in court.' But their art was black and white, with pale watercolors added to punctuate." She put a grape into her mouth,

"Very good." He swirled the wine in his glass and breathed in the scent, tasting in its juices the lavender and mint of nearby fields. His eyes never looked anywhere but her.

Vittorie scooped at the brie and added its soft white texture to the bread crust. "Impressed?" she asked, teasing.

His eyes sparkled as he handed her another glass. "Yes." Their fingers touched.

"I remember you saying how the Chinese women's hair was mostly long and black and every eye was brown." She held the bread with cheese out to him.

"It was quite an adventure." He took the food and put it down on his plate. He was intoxicated with the curve of her mouth, the way her chin moved when she spoke, the rise and fall of her chest as she breathed.

"You were certainly the talk of all of us children when you returned to the village that summer." She avoided his gaze with the practiced art of a gracious hostess and plucked another grape from its stem.

He put his hand over hers to stop her movements. She swallowed once and looked up at him. His blue eyes drank her in. The grape she held fell from her fingers. It made a "thap" sound on the edge of the table and rolled to the floor. She laughed. He moved and grabbed her up into a kiss that was warm and wet and wonderful. It tasted of earth and sky and salt and brie.

Two sharp raps on the wood door interrupted. "Your trunks, *Monsieur.*"

Their faces separated enough for him to say, "Leave them. *Merci.*" His arms held her close to him, and he kissed her again, quietly.

They waited to hear footsteps, hearts pounding. The floor creaked with the pile of their luggage and the porter's weight shifted. They were alone. Gilbert yanked the yellow cord and the drape came loose from its stalwart position. The trunks would wait.

19

After weeks on the open water, it was the second time Vittorie had thrown up that morning. The thought of being pregnant did cross her mind, but the lurching waves clamored for the credit. They thrust the ship hard to starboard. It was awful. The raucous sea and rank aromas from the lower decks overwhelmed her. She lay still on her bed, fearful of retching up more of whatever was disagreeable inside her at the moment.

Above deck, crates, barrels, ropes and seaman's tools left little room for extra bodies. Most of the time, the passengers stayed below. The noises from the lower decks of the vessel could be heard clearly throughout the wooden hull: children chattering, mothers soothing, old men letting out air and apologizing. Almost always someone groaning and someone crying. Only above deck did the wind and sea drown out all else.

The door latch sounded and Gilbert's face peeked in. "You're awake!" he said, hiding something behind his back. He crossed the space between them in one step. "Guess how many souls are aboard?"

Their quarters were generous for a voyage like this, yet barely fit the two of them. To say the space was small would be saying too much. It was miniscule. One felt like a giant opening the door; to duck inside was to wish to be out again. It offered no luxuries, no frills. Fashioned as an extra berth for dignitaries, or anyone who could pay for their travel expenses, it was what it was: solitary passage from one shore to another.

"Two hundred and eighty-seven souls," he said, answering his own question.

The room's one comfort was a bunk fastened to the interior hull, with a mattress made of clean straw stuffed between two linen sacks sewn longways. It boxed out into the space and stretched a meter and a half along the wall opposite the door. To call it the far wall would be a misrepresentation. Nothing in the whole cabin was untouchable from a full step inside.

Gilbert tossed himself into the bunk next to her. "I'm used to shifts. This two-to-a-bunk thing will take some getting used to." He pulled a piece of salt pork from behind him. "Look!"

"Oh, take it away! The smell…" Vittorie said. Color drained from her face.

Gilbert anticipated the worst and picked up the dirty chamber pot from the floor. He held it out to her, ready.

She closed her eyes and pinched her nose. "The smell is awful."

"I agree," he said, replacing the chamber pot on the floor, "but I'd rather not have to launder the linens in the rain if you throw up in the bed." He bit a hunk off the pork and chewed. "Wind's picking up."

Vittorie opened her eyes but kept her nose pinched. "Whad uz dat mean?"

"Storm, probably. Seas'll be grievous for a time. But we'll be fine, you'll see." He ran his thumb along the rough-hewn pine where an ax had cut cross-hatch lines. "That's where a branch needed hacking off."

"How do you know?"

"I've prayed for the Father to watch over us across *l'Atlantique*."

"Oh…no…I mean about the wood markings." Vittorie said, unpinching her nose. "A thousand new and interesting things surround me and I should be taken ill!"

"Did some work with an ax for his majesty during the war. Not everything happens with a rifle."

"Tell me about being a soldier." Her tone was gentle as she watched him.

"*Un soldat*…no. Not today." He stuck the pork under her nose. "Want some?"

"Oh, me!" She waved it away. "I'm strong. I can run. I just, *apparemment*, can't sail."

"You will." Gilbert patted her hand. "I was the same on my first crossing. I had it so bad," he said between swallows, "it felt like my knees came up through my gullet. But once it was over, it was over. I never got sick like that again."

"'You could have warned me," she said. "This is awful."

"You look awful." Gilbert felt her forehead, but she wasn't feverish. "I mean…hm."

"That's not funny. I do feel awful. I want to go above deck with you, but if I lay very still here in the bed, I feel the best. If I don't think about moving and just lay very still."

"You can't go with me anyway, and it's a bunk."

"I don't think that's important right now. Oh, my stomach!"

Gilbert put a hand out for the chamber pot, but she quieted so he left it alone. "I have only the three and a half months in this ship to teach you what English I know."

"You've been at it for six weeks already. How much English do I need? Everyone knows French."

"No. There are French in America, but many languages are spoken. English mostly."

"They should speak French, like the rest of us."

"I'll tell them." He cleared his throat and raised a thin eyebrow at her. "I don't want you to be ignorant of what others might be saying."

Vittorie's lips pulled together. "Please leave. I don't feel well. You're trying to be funny but not succeeding. I'll speak French. It's been good enough until now and it will be good enough where we're going. So long as my maid and cook understand French, what should I care?"

"What if your maid and cook plot to cheat you right in front of your face because you can't understand them?"

"Why would they do that? Why are you planning for the worst right now?"

"I'm not." Gilbert got off the bed. Their trunks piled floor to ceiling took up the rest of the available breathing room. "It's true, Vi. You've got to learn more than just the little world we come from."

"I'm trying. I know 'please' and 'why' and 'yes' and I'm vomiting across the Atlantic Ocean. I thought you were going to be happy with me."

The boat shifted portside, swinging the candle above Gilbert's head and spotting wax on his shirt. "I am happy with you," he said, taking his knife from its sheath and scraping the wax off. "But I know what I'm talking about."

"*Mon Dieu*, protect us." She gasped at another lurch of the ship. "Gilbert, I know you paid handsomely for us to have our own small cabin. I am grateful for how you're trying to care for me."

"I knew it would be hard for you. It is for every person, not just a woman. I wanted to offer what comforts I could. We have become pilgrims, venturing to become pioneers in the foreign land of America."

She reached out for his hand and he clasped it. Chorused shouts echoed from above them. Gilbert's eyes scanned the four corners where the ceiling met the walls. He leaned in to kiss her forehead, pointed deeper into the bed, said "stay there," and left.

20

August 1787 - Carolina Foothills of the Appalachian Mountains

The man didn't duck low enough as he stepped outside into the warm night. The roof thatch brushed his dark hair. He blinked up at the stars, blurry through tears, and released a long, guttural moan. Nearby, grasshoppers quieted. His horse stood, ears forward, alert.

Inside the hut, his mother began the song. Her voice rang out clear, the call to loved ones in the village to gather. The time was ended.

They filed past him into the house—his sister, female cousins, his wife's friends. In their arms they carried cloths to wrap her body, beaded necklaces, corn husks, and other items for his wife to have in the spirit world. His brothers carried large strips of cypress bark inside to line her circular grave. The digging of her burial pit continued, silencing the tree frogs.

He stood, unable to move forward, fingers clenched around his dagger. Hatred swelled inside him, revenge the only sound he heard.

"*Cap po ce.*" The old warrior's voice spoke soft, like the fur of a young rabbit. "My son," his father repeated, this time placing a hand on his son's shoulder. "Each of us must carry the cypress for one he loves. Now is your time."

"Why does she go to the Master of Breath when the *ika hal h* grow white? Why is she the one who sits in the earth?"

The old warrior moved to face his son and wrapped his gnarled knuckles around the grown man's muscled arms. "It was her time. Bury your dead. Mourn her. That is our way."

The cries intensified, overpowering the late summer night. The digging ceased. The mourners swayed, their beads jingling.

"She grew pale after the French came to our village. Her skin burned like fire from inside her." He shook his father off, eyes smoldering. "I will take their scalps, the hair of the French and the men of…."

"*Cap po ce, isti atcagagi*, you speak in hurt. Now is the time to mourn. Let the wisdom of our people be heard in your ears. Ahanu, the Creek way is peace."

Instead, Ahanu sliced the dagger across his own bicep to scar the memory. Blood ran down his arm. "Call me Ahanu no more. Your ways are no longer my ways."

21

September 1787

"Mermaids off the starboard bow!" rang the call from the crow's nest. Sleek and glistening in the dappled sunlight, the dolphins splashed out of the water just as near as the rosemary bush from the kitchen door back home.

The walkers all moved to one side of the rail. Each strained to see, afraid of falling overboard, yet eager to catch a glimpse of the shining forms. Choruses of *'Alors!'* echoed stern to aft.

"My, you are a sight at sea!" Gilbert said, looking at Vittorie.

Wanting to keep that vision ever before him, her nimble fingers tucked rebellious curls back under her *chapeau*. Fresh sea air smacked against her cheeks and pulled her hair loose again.

Fellow passengers walked a path between barrels and crates. Their schedule of times above deck worked in shifts like the sailors, allowing only a certain number topside at once.

Caught up in the excitement, Vittorie took the man's hand to her left, only to have Gilbert put his arm around her from her right. Startled, she released the hand to her left.

The sailor grinned as wide as his puffy cheeks allowed, his gray eyes settling on the woman who'd taken his hand. Several wisps of long, red hair hung down in scattered spots from beneath a worn turban.

"Excuse me," he said, taking off his hat. *"Pardonné moi.* An honor to be noticed by a lady like yourself." He held the salty rag before him as though it were a fine bouquet. His head resembled the large rock she used to jump off as a child. His nose was red. He grew no beard. His forehead, wrinkled and brown, stuck out in stark contrast to the pasty color of his scalp.

While Vittorie stood aghast, her attention focused on the adoring man before her, a large gust of wind whisked her hat far out into the waves. The hairs she had so painstakingly made obey the rules for a woman in her station came flying free.

Her shock at holding hands with a sailor, the immensity of the voyage they undertook, plus the grieving of all they'd left behind caught up with her in this instant. The stupidity of the whole thing made her burst out laughing. She snorted and doubled over.

"Qu'est ce c'est?" Gilbert asked, surprised by her sudden outburst. "What is it?"

Hysterical giggles continued as she tried to catch her breath. She put out a hand but laughed harder, eyes stuck shut. Tears streamed down her cheeks.

Gilbert took her hand and wrapped it around his arm, taking charge. Retrieving his handkerchief from inside his waistcoat pocket, he stuck it in Vi's other hand.

She dabbed at her eyes and sighed. "I'm alright."

"Amour," Gilbert said, low enough for her ears alone.

"I know!" Vittorie said, but gulped and giggled again.

He nodded *adieu* to the sailor, cleared his throat, and spun his bride toward the lower levels. "What would your mother think?"

"Suis désolé!" she said, unable to control herself.

"Alors," he said, opening the hatch to the lower decks.

Someone shouted clear and unmistakable: "Land!" All heads turned to see.

Gilbert dropped the hatch. Vittorie sobered. After months of endless rolling waves, seeing that shape on the edge of the horizon took their breath away. The sailor in the crow's nest shouted it again and all the crew on deck cheered.

"Gilbert pointed off the port bow. "There is our America!" He tightened his arm around her waist and asked a sailor passing by, "How's the tide?"

"We're on a flood tide," the sailor replied, understanding Gilbert's intent. "Supposing we don't need to give way, I'd say we'll be docking by dinner."

"*Merci.*" Gilbert took Vittorie's arm and marched toward the hatch. "Let's be ready before the tide turns."

"What?"

"…before everyone else!"

She turned her glinting eyes up toward him to rejoice and found her mouth stopped with a kiss right there in front of captain and crew. She laughed it off, but her cheeks reddened.

"We made it!" he cried and kissed her again.

She wiped at her eyes in mock seriousness for Gilbert's sake and to hide the blushing for her own. Gilbert kissed her hand and she leaned hard against him as the ship cut through the last of their waves at sea.

22

Held fast by a series of ropes attended by sailors below, the white-washed dory bobbed in the waves, a mere thimble beside the large ship. Squawking seagulls floated above, their cries heralding arrival and the promise of land.

"I'll go first," Gilbert said. "Don't come over until I call for you."

"Why?" Vittorie asked. The wind wrapped her skirts tighter to her knees as they waited for the boatswain's whistle. They'd be the last to board the first tender. As she peeked over the side of *L'Aventure* to the little boat, the distance looked daunting.

"So the men look away."

"Ah."

"Wrap both arms fully around the ladder rungs before you move one foot." He made two fists and cocked one leg around an imaginary ladder side rail. "Three hold tight, one moves."

She nodded one short nod.

"And don't look down. You'll know when you're there." With that, he was over the side and out of sight.

Gilbert scrambled down the narrow rope ladder, stepped off at the end, and spoke to the boatswain. Both men looked up. The boatswain looked away, and Gilbert shouted up with a wave.

Vittorie climbed down, three appendages locked on the ladder while the fourth found its next hold. Her heart beat so hard she could feel it in her ears. Even without much wind the ladder swung her into the side of the ship several times. The pain of each crash reminded her to be careful, to think about what she was doing. Falling would be worse.

Gilbert grasped her hand at the bottom while the dory rocked. She let go of the ladder and felt the boat balance out again as he ushered her to an empty seat.

"Focus on the horizon," he said, "not on the waves. You're doing fine."

The small boat pitched violently until the oarsmen found their rhythm. She tightened her stomach and thighs, forcing her weight down on the flat board under her bottom.

"I'd rather lay down in the bottom of the boat," she said.

"If there were any room…" he replied, holding her tighter. "We'll be ashore soon. I've missed your humor."

"I meant it when I said I was feeling better. *Was.*"

"Horizon," he ordered, his tone returning to that of a soldier.

"I'm teasing," she said and felt him relax.

The bow of the boat cut through the waves, the horizon leveled out, and the deep azure blue of the water changed to a paler green as they neared shore. The white of the wave caps curled higher and crashed heavier, an exhilarating sound.

The boatswain's whistle blew a piercing call. Every oar raised straight overhead, save two. Those made rounded movements through the waves. The oarsmen twisted the shaft of the wide blade down and away to skim the whitecaps, plunged the end under enough to catch the water, and pulled hard against the current. Their skill apparent, the tiny craft wedged neatly into place. With a dainty wallop, it tapped the edge of Charleston's dock.

Two sailors, one fore and one aft, each stretched a blue-panted leg to the high side of the boat and stepped onto the pier. Long ropes were thrown to them. These they tied like an "X" around an anvil-shaped piece of metal affixed to the dock with immense bolts. The men's arms moved with familiar speed, creating multiple knots. Secure, they reached to help the others.

Once on the dock, Gilbert shook hands all around then turned to face Vittorie. "What do you think of *Monsieur* Franklin's America?"

Vittorie looked to her right. The low, red-brick seawall stretched along the coast as far as she could see. To her left, the land curved back and out of sight, giving way again to the Atlantic.

"It's beautiful," she said, taking Gilbert's hand. Two steeples punctuated the horizon—a white one that ended in a point to her left and another built of red brick to their right. "What is this place?"

"Charleston, the city is called. In the colony of South Carolina. It's the wealthiest colony of all thirteen. Do you like it?"

"I don't know yet." She lifted her hem to walk up the several steps to street level. The smell of mud at low tide returned as they walked over puddles. "Oh, the ground! The feel of solid earth beneath my feet!"

"Ha!" Gilbert laughed at her enthusiasm, but enjoyed her response. "To sense that the world is not always shifting and pitching, but that it does somewhere anchor down below."

She smiled and clutched Gilbert's arm as they walked into the crowd. "I think you're laughing at me and not with me."

A couple in clean aprons sold tiny lumps from trays strapped around their necks. *Bread!* Her mouth salivated for it, even if it was dark brown and only one shape. It smelled like heaven.

"Stay close to me," Gilbert said.

"I am."

"I'll do the talking."

"That's fine," Vittorie said. "You're the one who's been here before."

"No, I haven't. Not here. I was in Virginia."

"Where's that?" Vittorie's back muscles tensed. "I thought we were going where you were before."

"Captain decided Charleston was best. I had nothing to do with it."

"How will we know where to go?" she asked.

"I can find our way from here as from anywhere. Charleston is called 'the holy city' as its open to more than just one faith. That's a good starting point for two Catholics, I think."

An old tree bent upward. Its glorious green leaves dripped with long, silver tassels swaying in the warm breeze.

"That's a wonderful tree." The steady wind blew her skirts against her body and pushed her forward. "And that's a pretty house."

Gilbert chuckled. "That's a government building, *Cherie*. Not a house."

The grandest building in view jutted out toward the water from the rest. Its symmetrical construction pleased the eye with false columns, a gabled roof, and a flock of sculpted birds perched evenly across the parapet. An arrow weathervane swung Northwest above a tall, white cupola. Its small, rounded roof softened the rectangular shape of the building as a whole. Seven recessed, arched windows accented the second story, its fanciest level, presented as three across the middle with two more on each side. Above that, the third story windows matched the number of those on the second, but remained flush with the stucco wall. Instead of the stone headers which decorated the second level, triangular canopies topped the third level sashes.

"Well, it's still *joli*," Vittorie said.

The same kind of barrels she'd dodged on the ship filled the docks, and she followed Gilbert through a myriad of them. "What's in all these?"

"Some export the colonies produced awaiting shipment, *apparemment*." He called above the wind to a man rolling a barrel: "What's in these?"

The man stopped rolling the barrel and straightened, his stance powerful despite horrific rips in his clothes. His dark forehead beaded with sweat. The salt colored his skin pale where it dried. "*Indigofera Carolinians.*" He spoke with a voice that carried deep currents. Scars striped his chest, readily visible due to his absent shirt collar.

Gilbert glanced around. Being more alone than not, he leaned closer and asked, "Is it the best? For export?"

The man returned to pushing at the barrel, head bent low near his elbows. "*Indigofera Anil* suits better, from the French Indies, *Monsieur.*"

"*Merci*, friend," Gilbert watched the man go back to work, running a hand over the gold buttons on his own coat.

"I didn't think…slaves would be here," Vittorie said.

"Come, we've got to register with Customs. Here," he nodded at the three-story building before them. "Exchange and Customs House."

Double stairwells led them from the street up to the main level. Its ascending design offered visitors an opportunity to bypass the lowest level. Except for large wooden doors below the stairwell, and some other crude features, it seemed as though the structure had been raised up to escape the bottom floor altogether.

"Have they decided the government already?" Vittorie asked.

"Yes, Vi. After Yorktown, the British surrendered claim to these colonies. That's what the whole war was about. Self-government of the people." He stopped to look in her green eyes. When he bent nearer to her, his brown hair brushed across his forehead. "That's what I fell in love with. That men could be free, with a moral compass inside each soul to guide them, and make decisions for themselves, as a whole, and as individual parts."

"But how does that work?" she asked, looking across the barrels for the tattered man.

"We shall see."

A rough cart pulled by a mule ambled across the rounded stones of the street. It stopped just near the stairs, its bed filled with bulbous, orange things. Most had a short, broken-off stem. Some retained a remnant of curling vine, light green in color.

"What are these?" she asked, reaching to touch them. "Feels like leather."

"*Je ne sais pas*," Gilbert said, feeling the orange gourd himself. "I don't know."

Another wagon heading the same direction overflowed with crimson apples. It passed a flat cart stacked high with countless layers of animal pelts. Boys ran by, beating round hoops with a stick. They rolled the circle in front of them, careful to avoid running into any adults. A burly man in a ruddy-colored apron shouted something she didn't understand. He waggled a silver fish in each hand. Behind him, three barrels brimmed with more.

"What's he saying?" she asked Gilbert.

"*Poisson.*"

"Oh. No fish. No. Thank you."

"Had your fill of the sea?" He winked at her. "Never mind. Our path lies inland."

"Not too far from the water, I hope. Not forever. Just for a little while, maybe."

"We'll find good land, Vi, with water on it for crops and livestock. There's more space here than you realize. Not like home, not like France."

"They've used our colors!" Vittorie exclaimed, abruptly changing the subject.

Gilbert glanced up. A flag waved with the same colors as France, though with thinner stripes and the addition of several stars. "*Oui.*"

Every import had to be registered whether passengers, crates, barrels, or produce. An endless queue funneled toward the Exchange and Custom House. The crowd narrowed at one door on the bottom floor. Gilbert stepped on a crate to see over the mayhem. His face clouded over, not seeing a better option than waiting in line.

Vittorie drank in her surroundings, eager to understand them. "The world here is so different from home! *En France,* the style is wigs, outlandish ones at that. Most of the men on this shore show their natural hair." she said, opening her fan.

Gilbert grabbed her arm and scurried to the outside edge of the crowd. "*Viens, ici,*" he said.

"Where are we going?"

"There," he said, pulling her along. "You see? The stairs lead up but everyone just goes below. Come."

A colonial man with a narrow face and full bottom lip hurried around the south side of the building. He arrived at the stairway just before Gilbert and Vittorie.

"Good evening," he said, nodding at them both.

"*Bon…*Good evening, *Monsieur…*sir." Gilbert ran a hand over his mouth. Americans spoke English. "*Comment…*Must us register before…sleeping?"

The American shifted a leather satchel from his right arm to his left. "Go downstairs." He pointed below them.

Gilbert followed the American up the stone steps two at a time. "I fought in the war at Yorktown *avec* General Washington. We are now arrive." His voice shook with passion.

Vittorie leaned over the stone railing to see the door with a rounded top closing behind several wagons of sheep. A seagull dropping landed on the railing beside her. She gathered her skirts and rushed to keep up with the men.

Gilbert put out his hand as was the American custom. "LeClerc. Gilbert." He nodded back over his shoulder. "My wife, Victoire."

Without much attention to the woman besides a curt nod, the man continued. "French?"

"Yes, *Monsieur,* sir."

The man spun around and leaned very close to Gilbert. "Yorktown, you say?" Even in the shadows of evening, the man's eyes seemed to come alive with an inner light. "Did you?" He held the question between them on the steps.

Gilbert sensed the challenge but couldn't explain in English. "*Parlez-vous Français?*"

The man nodded. "Some."

"*Avec de Vimeur, comte de Rochambeau. Un Chausseur de… Expedition Particulaire…de Deux-Ponts. Et le 64th Royal de l'Artillerie.*"

The man wore his hair tied back in a short black ribbon. He shook his head. "Can you speak Latin?"

Gilbert shook his head. Something about this man emboldened Gilbert. "I dig the road. Secret road. At Yorktown redoubt."

The man's facial muscles relaxed. "You dug the trenches." He readjusted his shoulders and put his hand out. "Heyward," he said, with a solid grip. "Thomas Heyward Junior. I signed the Declaration of Independence for South Carolina and spent eleven months in prison for it. *Bienvenue.* Welcome."

Gilbert clasped the man's outstretched arm and their thumbs interlocked.

"I've got a meeting above stairs tonight. Legislature. But I'll get your names first, then you can rest." He took a step up and cocked his head for Gilbert to follow. "Come for religious freedom?"

Gilbert's eyes widened at the word. "Freedom, yes. Every kind America has."

Captain Lagasse, freshly shaved and in a clean shirt, interrupted them on the steps. "LeClerc! Heyward!" He nodded at Gilbert but bowed to the American, coattails flapping in the wind. With a quieted voice, he asked, "How goes it with you, Thomas?"

"Good." His answer broadened the word. "And good to see you, Captain. I've just met Mister LeClerc." He nodded in Gilbert's direction but continued to speak to the captain. "You'll join us tonight above stairs? 'Twill be fine to hear all the news you can share."

"Yes. Very much so," the captain said, bowing to Gilbert and to Vittorie, the braiding on his jacket swinging as he did.

"Captain," she said, switching to French once she had his attention. "*Merci*. I want to thank you again for your special care of my husband and me. I know you took great pains…"

"*Pas de tous*. The sea shall be what the sea shall be and every sailor must make sail. I'd be honored to passenger you again. The truth is," he added, his eyes catching the lamplight, "I'd rather hear you sing than any man aboard." Offering immediate escape from the compliment, in a demure tone he added, "Madame, you do your country proud."

Vittorie ducked behind her fan. "*Merci*," she said with a curtsy, "but your praise is too high. I carry France in my heart, but I think I must make room for a new love now. America is her name."

"*Bien sûr*! You must ask Monsieur Heyward to sing you *his* song!" the captain said.

"Here, here!" At that, Heyward chuckled. "Though I would prefer the lady."

The captain continued with a playful smile at Vittorie. "And don't let him fool you, this soldier of yours," he said, stepping closer to her. "God doesn't make finer mud than this man here." He put a hand on the shoulder of Gilbert's military coat, relishing the obvious unease at which the young captain now stood. He bowed himself nearer the newlyweds. In a whisper loud enough for all to hear he said, "He spouted tales of you the entire passage home to France."

"Captain!" Gilbert said, waving him away.

"Newlyweds!" Captain Lagasse explained to Heyward.

"'*Suis désolé*!" Vittorie said laughing, embracing the lightness of the moment.

The full moon topped the live oak trees, its reflection lighting a choppy path across the waves. A warm wind played with the tendrils of gray moss hanging from its branches.

"I am," Heyward said, brightening a bit, "newly remarried myself." Contentment washed over his face. "Elizabeth," he added, saying the name with care.

The captain straightened up and with a mighty jerk threw his fist high into the air. "*Bravo, Liberté! Bravo, Amour!*"

Hearing something worth shouting about, two men tugging carts through the yard cheered, "Huzzah!" The bleating of sheep echoed from somewhere below.

"Are you coming up?" Heyward asked Gilbert, extending an invitation to the events on the second floor. "'Tis where all the goings' on are learnt at evenings here above stairs." Flames from the dancing lamps reflected in his hazel eyes.

"*Je pense que…*" Aware of himself, Gilbert stuttered into English again. "Tonight, I retire. À *demain*, adventure begins."

Captain Lagasse ended his laughter in a sigh. He looked at Gilbert, then Vittorie. "Fair winds and Godspeed." His smile lingered long before he turned away.

Gilbert spoke for them. "*Vous, aussi*, Captain."

Vittorie clasped to the last familiarity she knew and waved, even though the captain had already departed.

"Come," Heyward said. "I'll see you're registered and let you to your freedom." He hummed a cheery tune and marched upward, leading his new friends up the steps.

23

Gilbert looked out the window during the following Thursday's *le déjuener*, munching a hunk of brown bread. The second story room at the inn gave them a view of the street named King's Highway. His other arm, lifted above his head, leaned onto the low rafters of their present accommodations. "We're to have a third member join our party," he said. Reaching across several peaches on the table, he selected the bananas and ripped one from the bunch.

Vittorie held her spoon in mid-air, paused between the pewter plate and her small lips. "What?" she asked, deliberately swallowing the knot in her throat.

"Who, you mean." He peeled down two strips of the thick-skinned fruit. "The man I spoke with after mass yesterday. Smuthers is his name." He replied, pronouncing it with a hard 't'. Taking a large bite he returned to watching the scene in the street. "This island fruit is wonderful, firm without too much sweetness. The blessings of dining in Charleston. Let's remember that."

"How is it he's joining us on our wedding tour?" Some rice pudding dripped on the table linen. "*Oh, put-tut.*" She scooped it up and licked it off her finger.

Gilbert's eyebrows clenched. "What? This isn't a wedding tour, Vi. I'm trying to give you a new life. A better one."

Vittorie set the spoon down inside the dark gray bowl. "*Oui.* I know. But we're supposed to start it together." She watched the lumpy white liquid engulf the utensil's end. It disappeared.

"We are together," he said, lifting his thin eyebrows. "We've been together every minute since we left Father Benét's steps." He tapped a knuckle on the window pane. "There he is." He grabbed his hat and pecked her a kiss on the cheek. "Hurry down, quick as you can. I want to make a proper introduction."

A lift of the latch, a flutter of coattails, and clink went the door jamb. Gilbert had escaped the four walls. Vittorie's stomach turned. She put her hand to her lips. Smuthers was not the third party she hoped for.

✲ ✲ ✲

Once across the street, Gilbert talked to a man taller and broader than him. Vittorie followed several paces behind. The morning crowd filled the path between her and the men, and she spent a long minute gauging how to wend her way across. Suddenly the wind blew Vittorie's skirt out ahead of her, pushing her toward them as she rushed through the passing carts and vendors. Her arrival surprised them.

"Bon-jer." Smuthers' introduction to Vittorie held all the French he could say. The large, reddish man held out a dirty hand to shake hers, noticed the fault, and wiped his big palm down the leg of his soiled breeches. Then offered it again.

"I'm sorry, ma'am." He tipped his hat and laughed a genuine, embarrassed chuckle that quickly ended. "It's been a while since I've needed to clean up for a lady." He smelled like a stable.

Vittorie didn't answer. He irritated her. His horse, however, whinnied and cocked both ears forward. He lowered his head and bobbed his dewy nose in her direction. She rubbed down the gelding's forelock.

Gilbert cleared his throat. "Smuthers' family are good Catholics. *Les grandparents* came over from England. He himself was born in Maryland." Gilbert smiled, eager to bond the trio. "He fought at Yorktown with the Maryland regiments..." He waited until Vittorie looked at him. "...where I did."

"Do you know each other..." she asked, hesitating. She didn't want to be rude speaking French in front of this stranger, even if he was English. "...from fighting?"

"He was *at* Yorktown," Gilbert repeated. "I was *at* Yorktown." His mouth twitched a bit.

"So, you don't know each other."

"Excuse me," Gilbert said to Smuthers. He removed Vittorie by the arm, walking her behind a standing cart. "We shouldn't travel alone. When I met Smuthers at St. Michael's I thought he may be the answer to my prayers. To have someone else with us. Someone American."

"He's English," she said, correcting him. "And what's Maryland?"

"Another colony, and *everyone* here is from another country." His eyebrows raised. "He's a good man. I trust him. I want him to join us."

"What does that mean? Who will pay for him? And I don't trust him."

"He has his own pension from the war, like I do. He won't be any trouble."

"You discussed this with him before you consulted me?" Anger caused the green in her eyes to intensify. "I don't like him."

"He's good with horses and a good Catholic. A good soldier too. We need him." His sentences came bursting out one on top of another. "I want another man around to protect you."

"Me?"

Gilbert nodded. "How many women have you seen since we landed?" Concern colored his words.

"'*Sais pas.*" She shrugged. One well-dressed woman passed by in the throng of foreigners.

"Mostly men make this voyage. Soldiers stayed after the wars. Women are..." Gilbert took her hands in his, "precious."

"What do you mean? Am I not safe here?"

Gilbert blew a puff of air from between his lips and closed his eyes, frustrated. But when his eyes opened and saw how she looked at him, he hung his head. "I don't know."

A string of half-naked, dark-skinned people shuffled past them tied together by ropes looped around their necks—men, children, and women. They walked barefoot, linked together like chattel, inhuman.

Vittorie couldn't look anywhere else. The procession arrested her attention. The children's eye sockets, dark and sunken, hinted at the survival necessitated at their tender ages. They tugged at the ropes, unable to break away, inconsolable. Most sobbed, desperate for comfort, but found none. Women marched at the end of the line. Mothers with swollen stomachs drug onward by their hands and necks. They cooed and spoke to the children roped ahead of them in feeble tones, drenched in sweat, worn out.

Tears sparked Vittorie's eyes, hot and fast. The noise of these captives arrested her speech.

Gilbert caught her as she slumped, weak-kneed. "*Amour.*" He stood her back on her feet, and kept one arm around her as he dug out the handkerchief.

"I'm alright," she said, but leaned her cheek into his coat and spoke again with a whisper. "If I had the chance to start a new world, I would begin it differently."

"I know," he said, changing his tone.

She looked across the street. The overhead sign in front of the inn swung a gilded pineapple on a pale blue background back and forth. People in clothes with little lace and no ruffle went about their business in a quick and solitary way, hurrying past, winding through the maze of elbows, wheels, and puddles as fast as they could, as if on their way to something important.

"The faces on the people here don't look the way they're supposed to," she said. "I don't understand this country." She wiped under her eyes and blew her nose. "But I thought you did."

"I don't know everything," he said, "but I know enough. The people here are not all French, that's all. There are more kinds of faces than you're used to, but you'll adjust. *Alors*." He stepped in front of her. "*S'il vous plaît...*" His eyebrows drooped.

"I will try to do what you think is best for us."

He ran his hand over his mouth. "There is a place called New France. Many French journey there. I think that may be best."

A bell rang at the Exchange a few blocks away. It tolled eight times. The market opened. Shouts and noises erupted, carried on the wind. The bartering began.

Vittorie looked in the direction they'd left Smuthers, reconsidering. "He's not French."

"But he will come. He'll be what we need."

"How do you know he..."

"His wife died with child last year." He spoke the words in a rush, like he hadn't wanted to say them at all. "He needs a new start."

24

She stood just outside the oversized door of the stable on the edge of town. Several stalls faced each other down the length of the building. The men stood inside in a cluster, discussing things. Three horses, tied out in the middle area, pulled at their bits. One horse dwarfed the others in size.

Gilbert and Smuthers conversed. They talked in foreign words, and shut her out with common experiences and an education she lacked. The stench of urine stung her nostrils. Manure piles needed attention. She lifted her skirt hem to look down at her boot. Horse clods stuck to it. She stepped toward the doorframe, put a hand on the rotting wood, and scraped the dirty sole off against the stones on the street.

Another clanging bell rang out from deep within Charleston's bustling seaport. Its echoes ran light-footed atop the retreating waves nearby. Every time a new tone danced out of hiding, the song grew, crescendoed higher and lifted her up with it like a bird. Its similar sound to home in France spoke to her. She stood still, listening. The bell stopped; the final chords played themselves out on the waves around her. The gulls soared inland.

A man with very black hair and pale skin took off his hat. He bowed as he passed her. "¡Hola, Senorita!" he said, before crossing the street. His stockings stretched past his knees, half-way up his thigh. There they met short, blousy *pantalons,* more suited to the puff on a French sleeve.

Startled, she darted back into the stable, this time more careful where she placed her feet.

Gilbert ran his hand down the foreleg of a chestnut horse with white speckles on her rump. As mares go, she stood with beautiful lines, muscular and lean. "What do you think?" he asked Smuthers.

Smuthers said something in English. He looked at the large horse's teeth. Gilbert nodded. Vittorie ran every syllable around in her head, checking each sound against the teensy repertoire of English she'd retained. *Nothing matched. Wait.*

They kept repeating two words. "Sixteen…hands." She remembered! "Sixteen hands good Smuthers!" she said, triumphant.

Gilbert spun around at her voice. "What was that?"

"Sixteen hands," she said again, "good Smuthers." She untied the big horse from the wall and handed the line to Smuthers.

Smuthers mashed his hat forward on his head. He looked from the Frenchman to his wife, and back again, confused.

Gilbert bit his tongue not to laugh. He took a handful of coins out of his pouch and tossed one to Smuthers. "You heard the Frenchwoman," he said, provoking Smuthers. "You purchase 'Sixteen Hands.' I'll take the chestnut mare and the bay." He handed the money pouch to the stable manager.

"If you'll just sign for them here," the man said, wiping the sweat from the back of his neck on a handkerchief and holding out some parchment.

"Victoire, *Amour,* what will you name your new addition?" Gilbert asked, rubbing the mare's mane and shoulder with a firm hand.

She felt the velvety nose. "*Vignoble.*"

"I like it!" he said, then interpreting for Smuthers, added, "It means 'vineyard.' Mine shall be called, 'America.' What about you, *Macaron?*"

"No," Smuthers said, shaking his head, "It's Macaron-*ee...* Macaroni. That's what we Marylanders are called. Distinguishes us," he said, flicking the brim of his hat, "in the crowd." He sucked his tongue from between his side teeth and his horse stepped forward.

"Alright, *Macaron*-ee," Gilbert acquiesced, emphasizing the last sound. "What will you call your *grand cheval?*"

"Not that." Smuthers winced at the French word. "How about Ol' Mac? You looks like an old Macaroni to me, huh, boy." He puffed some air between his lips at the horse. "What did you name yours again?"

"America," said Gilbert.

"*Bien sûr,*" Vittorie said.

Smuthers chuckled. "You're one focused Frenchman."

"Are we ready?" Gilbert asked Vittorie. He led the hooved procession out into the sunlight. Vittorie walked beside him as Smuthers and horse followed. The ocean breeze whipped the horses' manes and blew their tails a northwesterly direction.

"My trunks are packed and latched, if that's what you mean," she said, turning to look at him. "I don't know how we'll be received where we're going. When I heard the bells...I was saying *au revoir.*"

"Good. We'll rise early and load the wagon, then start before dawn. I want to get as far as we can every day. New France is a far journey."

25

His boot never found the ground. The force of Gilbert's body projected him downward. Something shot through him. The earth opened up. A cavern gaped beneath him. Falling took as long as the realization that he was, followed by incredible, wrenching pain through his left shoulder and ribs. He couldn't breathe. His chest burned. His mouth opened wider in search of air. No oxygen came. Panic.

A sudden rush of air sucked in his cheeks. He flung back his head and lifted his chest nearer the life-giving force. The action caused more pain. His mind blacked for an instant in an effort to lose consciousness. Every breath felt like a thousand knives tearing into his lungs, neck, shoulders. He needed to get his bearings…couldn't…

"*A j'ai tirer dessu, trop?*" he shouted out loud.

Someone touched him. *Who?*

The charge of the rest of the battalion flooded past him. He lay shocked, alone, overlooked in the bottom of a shell hole. The battle continued above him. He heard the swish of legs running by without him.

The momentary lapse of control over such a necessary function as breathing startled him. The probability that he had been shot, and lay dying, made him angry. The impossibility of moving to fight or protect himself now brought a third emotion—terror.

A hand hung in front of him, about the size of a good shovel. It reached out of the darkness attached to a large, barrel-chested hulk of a man. The man's mouth moved, Gilbert grasped at its meaning. *"Foreigner."* Understanding crystallized. Another shovel hand waved something gold and familiar. Long black waves stretched across Gilbert's field of vision. He strained to see the man.

As the stranger leaned over him, Gilbert checked for insignia or distinguishing colors on the other's clothes. He found none.

"Amour?" Vittorie's clear voice pierced through the darkness. She pulled away from him.

Gilbert woke up disoriented. The unfamiliar setting spun around until he felt Vittorie beside him. *"Bien sûr,"* he said. "What?"

He lay on his left side under the wagon. A dark sky with no moon had replaced last night's constellations. He reached out to touch the dew on the grass, then back under the makeshift shelter to feel their covering. It was dry. They'd slept like this for over a fortnight. This wasn't the first of his night memories.

"You asked if you'd been shot," she whispered in the dark, "in your dream."

He found her hand under the blankets and moved it to his chest. Resting his own hand on top of hers, he patted her hand twice. "I'm fine."

"What do you dream?"

America and Vignoble snorted, tied to the wagon. They bent their heads near Gilbert's left shoulder. Sounds of ripping grass and fleshy horse lips smacking told Gilbert all was well.

"From the war. Don't worry," he said, "I'm awake now. Sorry I woke you. You need your sleep."

"As do you." She snuggled closer to him, aligning the curves of her body to match his. "If you don't tell me, I can't help." She traced small circles on the back of his hand. Her delicate fingers warmed him despite the brisk morning air.

"Dreams don't matter," he said.

Her movements ceased. The sound of grazing horses continued.

"If you don't want me to know, fine. Shut me out of something else."

This was heading in the wrong direction. Gilbert sat up fast, knocking his head on the wagon's wooden underbelly. "*Sacre...*"

Her feminine giggle spooked the horses and made them shake their heads, rattling the ropes securing them and clinking iron against iron on the rings fastened to the wagon. Those simple noises sounded grandiose in the still morning.

He didn't want to draw attention out here in the woods. They needed another fortnight still to pass until they reached the Wilderness Trail. "Shhh...." He spoke peace to the animals and they quieted. They had a long way to go. Crossing himself, he rose and stretched in the usual way—arms high above his head, left shoulder rounding, flexing and releasing. Last, he brushed his hands up and down his arms intending to get the chill out.

"Where's the flint?" Vittorie asked. Her nearness calmed him.

"I thought we'd break camp early instead. Don't we have *vitailles* left?" He heard her collar rustling as she nodded. "That'll do."

Smuthers snorted, pounded the ground, and spit. "Mornin'." The bulk of him roused from the earth. He belched and groaned and beat the dirt from his pant legs.

"Good morning," Gilbert replied.

"Welp, guess I'll go soften up some leather."

Gilbert smiled at his friend. "Find a wide tree."

Above the treetops, the new day brightened. Bruised purples from the shadowed night disappeared as a rush of pinks and saffron yellows smeared the aqua atmosphere.

Vittorie handed him some salted pork strips and dried beans in a cup. "If he didn't drink as much, he'd sleep lighter," she whispered, her disdain apparent.

"Gentle, Love," Gilbert replied. "He's lost enough things to drink over, even by God's estimation."

"Give them to God, I say, and let them go."

"Victoire!"

"He's coarse!" she said and ducked around the other side of the wagon.

"Yes, he is," Gilbert growled. "He's not fancy and he certainly wouldn't pass your mother's inspection!" He spun her around by the shoulders so she'd look at him.

Tears streaked her cheeks and her eyes burst with new tears. She flung the stew pot and ladle down, spewing a week's eating across a meter distance.

"What's the matter with you?" he cried.

"Me?" Vittorie glared at him a moment, then turned and ran into the woods.

"Vittorie!" Gilbert sprinted after. "Stop! *Arrête!*" He dodged several large tree trunks, keeping her in view.

"*Laisse-moi!*" She yelled at him but stopped running.

Gilbert caught up. "*Sil vous plaît…*never leave me like that."

They stood together both breathing hard. Sunbeams reached through the forest canopy.

"There, you see," Gilbert said, "the sun forgives me. Why don't you?" He raised his hand to shield her eyes from the sun.

"It's so hard here. I'm not good at anything. I don't understand. You talk to Smuthers and I try but it doesn't make sense to me…"

He folded her in his arms and kissed her hair. She smelled of pork and earth with a hint of lavender, and she felt good to hold. "I know," he said, kissing her again. "It will come."

She exhaled, long and breathy, with a sniffle on the end. Her nose rubbed against his jacket for lack of a handkerchief.

"I promise." He added those words looking deep into her almond-shaped eyes.

They walked, arms around each other, back to camp, between thick tree trunks and over ferns waist-high. Everything was new. But they were together, as it was meant to be.

26

Dense forest gave way as the trio emerged into a clearing. The ground, black and smoldering, stretched across several kilometers of open field.

"What happened here?" Gilbert asked. He leaned forward in his saddle, causing his horse to snort.

"Natives burn it off like that," Smuthers said. "New grasses draw game and buffalo. 'Ere's a fort yonder, I see."

"What's a buffalo?" Gilbert asked.

Smuthers laughed and lowered his voice. "That's French! Buff-uh-low. Boof-a-loo. I don't know. You say it."

"Ah! *Boeuf a l'eau! Oui.* Yes. Water…ox…cow." The corners of Gilbert's mouth turned down in thought. "Big. And horns." He grunted more than once as he pondered the animal.

Looking over Gilbert's shoulder to see how far behind them Vittorie was, Smuthers added, "The largest herd of horses that mated with seed oxes you ever saw."

"*Vraiment?* Is that true?" Gilbert whispered.

Vittorie's seat atop the wagon with the trunks lurched to a stop. The horses swished insects off their rumps with their tails.

"Naw. But that's about how to describe 'em. They're huge beasts that roam wild this side o' the Appalachians. Stand taller than a horse at the shoulder, built like a gentleman cow with horns, an' have a dark, wooly mane." He removed the stick of sassafras he'd been gnawing on from his mouth. "Hair like a lion…," he continued, "… 'cept theirs covers the whole head to their navel." He waved the chewed branch around his head in a circle and ended by poking it in his belly. Nodding once for emphasis, he replaced the stick between his teeth.

Smuthers dismounted. "That oughtta be Fort Caswell."

"*Forte?* It doesn't look all that strong. It's only wooden poles," Vittorie said, quieting her French for Gilbert to interpret.

"Not *forte*," Gilbert said. "Fort in English means…." He looked at the irregular shape of the fort. It consisted of a series of rooftops viewed above rough spikes chopped into the ends of logs pointing skyward. "It means…." War stockade. Revolution. Smoke. Fire. Pain.

"*J'entends une rivière!*" said Vittorie.

Her voice broke his memory and Gilbert ran a hand over his face, proof of the present. Dismounting, he threw the reins over America's ears. "What river is near?" he asked, interpreting for her. He grabbed the reins off the ground and led the horses toward the sound of rushing water.

Lifting her face, Vittorie breathed in smells of pine, dried leaves, and woodsmoke. The sound of water rushing over shoals caught her ear. Giddiness of arrival encircled her and she smiled with her eyes closed, savoring the scents of autumn in civilization again.

"Watauga River, I think. We'll have to ask the locals," Smuthers said, retrieving his hat from his satchel. He ran the long feather on the top between his thumb and two fingers to refine it. Satisfied, he stuck it on his head, perched over an eyebrow.

"Who live here?" Vittorie asked, practicing her English for Smuthers' sake.

He acknowledged her question without turning around. "Don't know. Gonna find out."

27

*N 36.83853, W -84.33849. Cumberland River. Virginia west of
the Appalachian Mountains*

The longhunter scraped the edge of his knife over the grayed
stubble of his cheek. He held a second dagger before his face, its
smooth shaft sufficient for a mirror. His breath fogged the reflection and he wiped the condensate off on the thigh of his britches.

The canvas of the Cumberland River's banks lay strewn with
immense boulders above and below the falls, their origins in the
horizontal strata of sandstone layers most apparent on the western bank. Deciduous leaves lacking chlorophyll overhung the top-
most levels of ancient sediment; yellow xanthophyll and orange
carotenoid pigments trumpeting their annual glory. Autumn
victorious.

He sat on a flat stone downstream from the great falls. One
leg hung over the side of a boulder with his foot braced on another rock below.

In the early morning light, two nuthatches landed beside him.
The monogamous pair took turns, one drinking the cool water,
the other keeping watch. In a repetitive, medium tone the male
sang, "Wa-wa-wa-wa-wa-wa-wa."

"Quench your thirst but get back to hiding your seeds, friends," he said. "Winter comes early this year."

When the pair fluttered up then descended again not far from him, he puckered his lips and repeated the nuthatch's call. "Wa-wa-wa-wa-wa-wa-wa-wa."

The birds turned their heads at his mimicry. They poked their pointed beaks skyward, looking for others with similar feathers.

He smiled at them, then sobered. "You can trust the word of Henry Skeggs."

Drawing the blade down from his high cheekbone again, shaving close, he stopped short and dropped his arms. He heard something. The pale aqua of his eyes scanned the far side of the riverbank. The cry came again but the waterfall overpowered its clarity. Bobcats sound very much like a woman shrieking. On instinct, he sheathed both knives and matched his shadow to the rock nearest him. He waited, able to remain still for days if need be, and watched.

The shriek echoed again. But this time he saw. On the eastern bank opposite his hiding place, four figures emerged from the tree line. All looked native-born and, except for the woman, indistinguishable as to tribe. Two men carried a canoe. The third male seemed to be the leader. He wore the winter pants of a Creek, but his chest was bare. He dragged the woman by her hair. She stumbled and fell to her knees at the river's edge. The canoe-carriers hoisted the hollowed cedar up the rocks beside the waterfall. The leader gripped the woman's face in one hand and yanked her to her feet. A long, white scar striped his bicep. He stepped close and licked the woman's face. She clawed at him. He spun her around, pushed her down, kicked her.

Unseen, Skeggs left his rifle behind and slipped under the water. Frigid torrents engulfed him. He swam, bracing himself on the upstream side of every submerged boulder, resisting the river's pull. Sometimes he could gauge well, other times the swells took him further downstream.

Skeggs surfaced, stayed low, and dragged his belly against the rocks. Crawling like a salamander, knees wide and low, he maneuvered along the shadowy side of their crevices. On the eastern side of the river lay another rocky outcropping. He slithered, movements muted by the 58 feet of falling currents, until he could stand up under the stone ledge where the men and woman now stood. Listening, he heard two of them on his right unshoulder the canoe. It rattled against the stone. Based on other noises, the scarred one tortured the woman near the precipice to his left.

Finding a solid fingerhold to climb the rocks on the side of the waterfall, Skeggs took three short breaths for focus and hauled his lean frame up and over the edge. *Attack.*

A slice to the achilles' tendon of the closest native, he then turned the blade up the bone, filleting the calf muscle to the posterior cruciate ligament. *One downed.* He raced forward.

At the edge of the rock, with the falls clamoring beneath, knelt the woman. Her dark hair blew upwards in the mist. Blood dripped from her nose.

The knife in Skeggs' left hand punctured the thigh of the second native at the pectineus muscle, just below the pubic area. He pulled down and away on the handle to cut across the sartorius and rectus femoris. *Second one slowed.*

The native with the thigh wound regained his wits and threw a club. Skeggs dove into the canoe, rolled it over on top of himself, and peered out from under its smooth edge. The club soared over the canoe and landed at the scarred one's feet. Skeggs jumped out, surprise no longer an ally.

From the opposite direction, the scarred native threw his tomahawk. Its feathers and shaft spun end over end. Skeggs dropped, gut flat on the sandstone ledge behind the cedar canoe frame. The weapon's blade stuck in the boat's bottom. He lifted the canoe and dragged it before him as a shield. Three satchels and a silver ladle spilled out.

The scarred one picked up the thrown club with his left hand and shifted his weight. His shoulders relaxed and he stood prepared to kill. Skeggs tossed the canoe at him, but the native pivoted and ducked. The canoe rocked to a stop above the falls. Skeggs unsheathed one knife and readied himself. Now they matched.

$$28$$

Fort Watauga. Sycamore Shoals

The structures at Sycamore Shoals boasted escape from the elements, safety from whatever couldn't scale the perimeter, and the hope of civilized humans.

Smuthers hallooed, rifle in hand. An Englishman's voice answered. Several calls and responses and a pause followed before the sound of wood scraped iron, then more silence. The wall lifted from the bottom rather than being hinged from the side. It created a doorway of sorts, a passageway in.

"Look at those spikes. This is frightful," said Vittorie.

"Shhh." Gilbert replied, focused on the conversation between Smuthers and the voices from the fort.

Smuthers led his party under the yawning beams. While the gate stood open, two men and a woman kept a rifle to their shoulder with an eye trained on the woods beyond the newcomers.

"We've got word of hostiles about these parts." The man who spoke rolled his r's. His coarse gray beard frizzled into black at the ends; his close-set eyes cloistered under bushy brows. "Water's short till we trust heading out again. We've water enough for your animals; beer and vittles for your'n. My name's Detweiler." His bottom row of teeth protruded in front of the top. "You kin get your'n animals water and kin shelter here awhile. Lord knows, two more men on our side's a help."

"*Bedankt*," Smuthers said in Dutch.

Hearing his mother tongue spoken by a foreigner, Detweiler's face brightened. "*Bedankt?*" He called something out which brought surprised looks to the other colonists' faces.

The people here looked haggard and spent, dark under every eye, dirt on most everything. They had none of the ease of Charleston. Men's jackets sported coattails, but they stopped at least ten centimeters higher. The women proved some familiarity; while not the large dresses of Versailles, and lacking detailing or lace, their wide skirts flounced with layers of petticoats. This didn't put Vittorie at ease. She clung very near Gilbert who had stayed with the horses and wagon.

Smuthers' first forays at diplomacy a success, he continued to make friends over a basic need. "D'ya have any waffles?" he joked.

The man with the underbite laughed. "*Wafels?*" He slapped Smuthers on the back and walked him toward a humble structure. "You'll stay with us! *Wafels!* Ha! I should ask you what you've brought us from Charleston!"

"Again, *bedankt*. Thank you," Smuthers said. Raising his voice a bit louder for more to hear he added, "And to our new Dutch friends we bring cookies."

At that last word, a collective sigh went up from several colonists. A child with bright blue eyes, hidden before, peeked out from the open doorframe.

Gilbert walked the horses to the trough. "Go with Smuthers to the house," he told Vittorie. His French stuck out within this barricade like a broken limb. "*Vas-y.*"

"I'm staying with you!" she said. "What language are they speaking?"

"*Neerlandais.*"

Vittorie put her hand to her lips and walked in between America and Vignoble. That way she couldn't be seen.

Despite the sucking of water by three horses, Gilbert still heard her sniffling. "*Qu'est-ce que c'est?*"

She shrugged and turned away from him. He handed her his handkerchief.

"I'm no good here," she said, blowing her nose. "I can't communicate, I'm scared, I don't know how to shoot a gun… What can I offer these people? A song? A handkerchief?" She waved the embroidered silk cloth around in a *laissez-faire* way. "In France, I was a nobleman's daughter. I understood things. I could speak. I laughed. Do you know the last time I laughed here?"

Gilbert lifted her chin with his knuckle and gazed at her. His intention to cheer her evaporated as her question remained unanswered between them.

Her eyes still flashed bright green, but worry-red threads coursed through the white of the sclera. "Here," she paused, "in your wild America…I'm good for nothing." She blinked a new flush of liquid over her cheeks. "And all I see is fear! Did you see their faces? The children?"

She let the handkerchief go and it fluttered to the ground, startling Vignoble. He jerked his head up, knocking her into Gilbert. "Ooof!" she said. "*Alors!*"

"Shhh…," Gilbert soothed, holding her close. He stroked her undone hair, long and flowing over her shoulders. "I understand you. You're good for me. And we're closer now to our new life than ever before."

Vignoble settled into drinking some more. The water had a green tinge inside the trough and Gilbert mumbled a short prayer to St. Francis to keep the horses healthy.

Though still early in the day, the sun set behind the tall tree tops, causing a noticeable drop in temperature. Between the heat of the gulping horses' bulging bellies, husband and wife huddled closer to each other. Vittorie sobbed hot tears into his collar. He looked at the handkerchief now under Vignoble's foot. His shoulder would suffice.

29

Cumberland Falls

The native looked at the ragged man before him. His brown skin meant nothing. Many non-natives burnt in the sun. His eyes didn't hint at any particular lineage either, though the lines of his face told of many winters. His body moved like a bobcat. Ahanu glanced at his two companions, downed, bloodied. The knife of this new warrior pierced like a bear claw.

"Where do you come from?" asked the man.

Ahanu did not show his surprise when the enemy spoke his tongue. "From far away, sitting down. Where do you come from?"

"Before the fog."

No clan came before the fog. Ahanu waited. This enemy intrigued him. "How are you called?"

"Henry Skeggs," said the fog man in deerskin pants. "And you?"

"My name is No More. Why do you quarrel with me?"

He looked past him to the captive. "Woman is equal. Mother of us all."

The dark-haired woman started to sing, low and mournful. Her voice came to his ears, echoing another song from his past.

Ahanu listened only a moment. "Go away now," he said to the interloper. "Walk on your legs and I will not send you to the Master of Breath."

"The One Who Is Sitting Above Us knows where I am."

Ahanu saw the ragged man's eyes glance at the scar on Ahanu's arm. Then he looked to the woman. *Why does this man watch her sway on the precipice?*

Skeggs looked again into Ahanu's eyes. "Where does this daughter of Corn Mother belong?"

Ahanu no longer desired this man's words. The club, held high since picking it up, grew heavy in his hand. No more Ahanu. No longer Creek. The One Who Is Sitting Above Us does not see. His wife sits in the ground because of those who had no fire, those who came in boats with white faces, those who did not bathe, those who gave the sickness. The Creek people came out of the fog. This enemy spoke in circles. He would come under Ahanu's club.

Ahanu looked at the two others who writhed in agony. They would go to the ground, but no one would seat them. *Perhaps the woman sang the song for all of them.* The woman's pitiful tune in his ears stung his heart. He shifted to look at her. *She will bring a good price.* The waterfall thundered. From her kneeling spot at the edge of the falls, her song ended. She looked past him.

Ahanu heard the stone speak under Skeggs' foot. Ahanu spun around, caught the enemy's wrist, and steered the bloody knife away. His other hand, holding the red club, struck out but got caught in the enemy's free hand. Their arms latched and swayed like tree branches, sinewy strength against lean muscle.

The canoe shook. Too late he realized her intent. One moccasin stayed behind as canoe and woman fell over the limestone edge into the rushing waters.

Ahanu swept a leg out and knocked the ragged man off his feet. He would pay. Skeggs twisted and pulled Ahanu down with him. Both men landed hard, shoulders and thighs against the sloping rock. Skill against skill, soul against soul, they grappled for mastery over each other, tumbling head over shoulder over knee, nearer the swallowing currents.

Ahanu felt the scratch of Skeggs' unfinished shaving. He used his broad forehead as a weapon and busted Skeggs' nose. Skeggs pulled back and responded in kind. He caught Ahanu's chin. Ahanu bent his wrist, still caught in Skeggs' hand, and clubbed him hard in the back of the skull.

"Ugh!" Skeggs cried, limp from the blow to the head.

Ahanu felt the weakness and pulled his arm free, still wielding the red club. A victory cry filled his lungs and shrieked from his mouth. "Ah-wahhhh!" He reared up, red club and eagle feather aimed for descent into his enemy's face.

Left hand and knife still pinned by Ahanu's right hand, Skeggs saw the impending club. He cringed and rolled toward his pinned hand. Ahanu's club collided with rock and shattered where Skeggs' head used to be. Only the club's shaft remained clenched in his fingers. Seeing its jagged edge, he flipped it in the air. It spun halfway round. He caught it again, point down.

Seizing the moment, Skeggs' punched at Ahanu. His fist caught him in the throat. Ahanu fell backward, mouth gaped open. Lack of air stabbed at his chest and paralyzed his response. Skeggs leaped up and pounced. His left knee landed in Ahanu's groin. His right heel connected with a shin.

Ahanu heard the crack of bone. Pain sliced through his leg. Air sucked in his throat and he yelled out the injustice with a guttural, "Ahhhhhhhhhh!" His arms instinctively reacted. Grabbing Skeggs at the shoulders and throwing him off to the side, Ahanu lay still, broken. If he wasn't in so much pain he would have looked sooner. He heard the scrape of a knife on the rock and saw his severed finger roll to a stop, disconnected forever from his hand.

30

Fort Watauga

It took a moment for Vittorie's eyes to adjust inside the log hut. She smelled men's bodies, dog, smoke, and…*something to eat?*

Gilbert moved away, beckoned by their host, and sat at the tables with the men. A dog brushed past her skirts, shooed out the open doorframe by a thin woman with full, round cheeks who clapped her hands at the canine.

The woman smiled at Vittorie, revealing tiny indentations in each rosy cheek. "No dogs allowed when we eat! Right? I'm Ina." She took Vittorie's hand and shook it with a nod, considered it insufficient, and pulled Vittorie closer, planting a kiss on each cheek three times. More satisfied with the fullness of her greeting she added, "Would you help me serve?"

Except for the warm acceptance and that the woman's health must be good by the redness in her cheeks, Vittorie understood none of what the Dutch woman said. She followed the foreign woman between two long benches of males seated at narrow tables to a kettle supported by a three-legged stand.

Once there, Ina scooped a ladle of stew into a shallow bowl and handed it to Vittorie. She waved her hand and held out her arm toward the men.

Vittorie nodded but didn't move. Her face flushed hot with embarrassment and she stared into the food floating in her hands.

"That's good stew, there," Ina said with a boast. "Lentils, cabbage, some root vegetables, venison John got, and a bit of quail," she nodded to a young lad at the table, "from my boy." She stopped filling bowls and hung her ladle on the lip of the iron pot. With playful directness, she took Vittorie by the waist and pushed her to the nearest seated male.

Taking the bowl from Vittorie's hand, she placed it in front of a lad about twelve years old. She removed the handkerchief from off his head and stuffed it into his shirt pocket, and kissed the top of his straight yellow hair. He muttered something. She pointed at his pocket and removed the spoon from his dirty fingers to replace it on the table.

Detweiler clunked the butt of his spoon on the table. "*Waar is het eten?*" he shouted. His loud laugh ignited the table in cheers and more spoon clunking from the others. "Where's the food!" he interpreted with a laugh in Smuthers' direction.

"You'll wait your turn!" Ina called out. "And ye've not given thanks!" She delivered the words with her hands on her hips and a thrust of her bottom lip. Her glare served its purpose. A hush fell over them all and two more souls removed hats from their heads under her roof.

She nodded at John, folded her own hands before her apron, and shut her eyes. John looked around the table, breathed in deep, leaned a forearm over one knee and in such a bent position, shut his eyes. The rest of the men in the room did as much. Every eye closed and all foreheads fell a bit lower. They stayed quiet like that for a minute or more. Then, almost in unison, Ina and John's heads perked up, as did the others, and the rustle of clothing at the wooden table echoed end to end.

The hearty scent of venison and root vegetables wafted around the room. Vittorie's stomach grumbled aloud.

Small as she was, a passion worked through Ina Detweiler's viens. She filled four bowls and handed two to Vittorie. "I'll not have our guests thinkin' we've no manners. Mind yourself, John Detweiler," she said, walking the length of the dirt floor and placing a bowl before him.

"Aye, wife, I'll mind!" With a twinkle in his eye and a wink at Smuthers, he landed a gentle wallop to the backside of her skirt with the broad side of his spoon.

"Ohpf!" Ina said, turning to wag a finger at him.

"We're all of us family here, Ina," he said, chuckling between slurps of his soup.

"Manners, John. For the little ones."

"Aye, that." He elbowed the man beside him and winked at the boy with straight yellow hair. "Alright men, Ina says we must abide the rules of society still."

"You first, John!" shouted a man with his hat still on.

"Don't look to me," he answered with a stein raised to drink. "I'd lead you all astray. Ina knows," he said, winking at her.

Ina turned from him to face the stewpot. But Vittorie saw a smile cross her lips.

John Detweiler gulped down the beer and rattled his empty stein against his bowl. "John Carter's the gentleman o' these parts. God bless his hospitality." A chorus of agreement sounded from several lips.

Once the men had eaten, Ina and Vittorie sat too. They ate at a separate small table of rough-hewn sycamore.

"I've made a treat for after dinner. Did you ever eat a waffle?" Ina asked.

Vittorie didn't understand. She shook her head.

Kindness washed over the Dutch woman's face. "*Beste me*, I just go on and on." She patted Vittorie's hand, her touch smooth and warm. "It's so good to have another female around."

A shout came from outdoors. Merriment turned to sobriety and the men made hand signals as they moved. They jumped up from the benches, grabbed their rifles, and raced through the doorframe one after another. Even Ina armed herself, gathered her skirts, and ran outside.

Through the open doorway, Vittorie saw them running, ducking low, assembling at strategic spots inside the spiked fort walls. Smuthers plucked his rifle as the others and walked out last into the dimming sunlight.

Gilbert stayed, rifle in hand. He waved Vittorie back from the door, but she didn't move far from his side.

"*Qu'est-ce que c'est?*" Vittorie whispered.

"I think it's a who," Gilbert answered as they peered out. "Wait. We'll see."

More calls and shouts. Several men exchanged places along the wall. They ran bent over with sloped shoulders. John Detweiler stood up full height and called an order. Three men pulled a rope, and the great door lifted. No-one moved as the passageway yawned open. Everyone waited. Only the sound of the Watauga River could be heard.

A small group of travelers made an appearance, dressed unlike anything Vittorie had ever seen. They wore pale colors of smooth fabrics that clung close to their bodies. Not silk nor chintz, yet something sparkled from it. Their hair hung loose, long and straight. Feathers twisted in the breeze. The women carried large woven baskets without handles full of produce. Several men pulled a hollow log full of large, round vegetables.

Vittorie realized she'd been holding her breath and inhaled to correct it. "Look!" she whispered. "*Magnifique.*"

"Yes. Magnificent, aren't they?" Gilbert replied. "Their skin is naturally darker than even the Spaniards. Those are the tribe of natives here called Indians," Gilbert continued, "but they aren't from India at all. They are the natives of America itself."

"*Les auchtones?* I thought you said everyone in America was from another country!" Vittorie said, still in a whisper. "They have such long, dark hair, I thought they might be Chinese."

Gilbert couldn't stifle a short laugh through his nose. "No," he said, struggling to regain his composure. He ran a hand through his straight brown hair. "If they are, we've sailed entirely in the wrong direction. It looks like they've brought gifts of…is that a vegetable? It must be a vegetable." He leaned further out into the evening air. "See, John is clasping the arm of the one with all the feathers on his head."

Vittorie remained captivated by the small group. "What are their clothes of?"

"Leather," Gilbert said. "Shells for decoration. Painted clay for beads."

"Leather?" Vittorie's mind worked to imagine clothes made from such materials. "From Italy?"

He burst into another laugh. "No, America."

The nearest people turned to look at them. Vittorie's cheeks flushed and she looked away from the objects of her interest. "You don't have to be so loud." Being laughed at in public did not sit well with her and her hands went to her hips. "I know bunches of things you don't."

"I'm sure you do."

"I hope you don't laugh at everything I don't know, or you'll be in stitches the whole trip and I'll hate you by the time we get to wherever it is we're going."

"No, no. Now that's not what I want at all," he said. Taking her hands in his, he added, "I'm sorry, though that was funny, from my point of view."

"Where *are* we going after this?"

"Lexington Town."

"Well, I hope they speak French there."

31

Cumberland Falls

The fight had lasted too long. Skeggs half slid, half scrambled down the rock face trying to buy back time. Seconds counted. He dropped the last twenty feet of the climb and bent his knees as he landed to cushion the impact. The pad of his right foot hit first. Pain shot up his leg to his lower back. He chose to ignore it.

Looking once over his shoulder up to the ledge he'd just descended, he paused, waiting. No one followed. The blood in his nose clotted. He breathed only through his mouth, awkward as it was. Like a squirrel, he raced over the surfaces of the rocks, tracing the river's edge downstream. *If she relaxed, surrendered to the falls, perhaps the water would have let her go. The river takes those who defy it. She was humble…let her have been humble…*

The midday sun crested the red cedars. The flow of the Cumberland River raced. As he distanced himself about 200 feet, the sound of the falls quieted. Instead, the rhythm of his own movements over the landscape could be heard like the soft soles of his feet squishing against green moss, his gaping exhales and tensile inhales. *Did the river suck her down?*

Where the Cumberland widened downstream, the river slowed. On its western bank in the shallows, strewn limp across the embankment, he saw her body. Splashing through water across the sandy bottom, Skeggs hesitated just a moment before touching her. She lay face up, mouth open, wrapped in the drenched tentacles of her long, dark hair. The cold pool puddled around her, playing with the fringed edging of her knee-length skirt, as though its offering may be rescinded at any moment.

Skeggs scooped her tiny form up in his arms and carried her to a wide rock outside the river's flow. Laying her on the warm limestone, he placed two fingers on her neck just below the jawbone. He forced his breathing to slow down to stop his own heart pounding in his ears—long breath in, deep exhale out. He couldn't feel a pulse. He moved his hand in front of her nose.

The wind blew. It rustled the hemlock leaves causing a crimson cascade to flutter downward.

"Almighty, please…." His hand moved her head to the left and he pulled her shoulder to turn her on her side. "We are only dust."

Water trickled from between her plum-colored lips, splattering the rock.

He raised her lifeless torso up and let her flop forward over the rounded edge of the boulder. "Let me not have run in vain," he prayed.

Her back arched and she vomited river water. Life surged through her as she convulsed several times. He put his hand between her torso and the rock, letting his arm be crushed by her convulsions. He caught her forehead to protect it and when she stopped, he helped her sit up.

"What's your name?" Skeggs asked in the Muscogee tongue.

She blinked watery, brown eyes at him. Gratitude flowed without words. With great effort, she lifted a wrist and dropped her hand on his shoulder. Her eyes fluttered shut.

"Come, little bird," he said, lifting her like a lamb over his shoulders. "Let's get you home. I believe your mother's people are still camped by Eagle Falls."

His feet found their way out of the sand. Once at the treeline, he stepped through a grove of red cedars and broke into a run.

32

Lexington, Virginia, west of the Appalachian Mountains

It was none too soon when Vittorie stepped down from the wagon onto Lexington's main street. Weeks on the trail had worn her through. She hungered for warmth, comfort, linen, and the security of indoors.

Gilbert held her hand extra-long as he helped her from the buckboard to the ground. "This is Lexington," he said. "We're still in the statehood of Virginia but over the mountains here things are…"

A group of three men passed by. Each wore high boots from the hair of some animal, pale colored clothes and rope belts. From the belts hung multiple pouches and between the three of them there were powder horns, rifles, and a musket. They hauled a makeshift contraption behind them made of skinny poles and twine. On this they'd piled the exploits of a bountiful hunting expedition.

Smuthers called out to them. "Looks like the varmints just raised their hands and threw off their skins from the height of that pile. What's the secret?"

Unlike the camaraderie Smuthers found at Watauga after his jovial greeting there, these men glanced his way without breaking stride. "No secret," said the nearest man, "unless you've no skill with a rifle." They walked past, said no more, leaving two ruts in the dirt behind them.

Vittorie, Gilbert, and Smuthers watched the men get farther away. The shuffle of their haired boots, the scrape of the travois laden with furs in gray, red, and brown, and the dispassionate way they cared not for the newcomers had a depressing effect.

"*Alors*," Gilbert said to no one in particular. He unfastened America's bridle, worked it over her soft ears and slipped it down her nose, removing the bit. The thankful mare rolled her jaw once and lowered her lips into the water trough. Gilbert brushed his hand down the strong muscles of her neck, each stroke a reward for her faithful burden-bearing. His focus on the animal broke with a last glance in the direction of the hunters.

Vittorie looked from Gilbert to Smuthers. Both men tended the horses but when she followed their gaze, found it elsewhere. "Have you been here before?" Vittorie asked.

Smuthers looked at her, then to Gilbert for the interpretation. He dug three fingers into the ruddy scruff of his beard and itched with vengeance. "Eh?" He hadn't understood. After a low belch, he bent Macaroni's foreleg up. Picking earth from the frog of the gelding's hoof, he split his interests between farrying and watching the Frenchman ignore everyone. He licked his lips and made a bird sound.

Gilbert looked up at him. "What?"

Smuthers nodded in Vittorie's direction. "What's she saying?"

"I don't know," Gilbert shrugged. Turning, Vittorie's arched eyebrow met his gaze. "…*qu'est-ce que tu dire?*"

A red-breasted nuthatch landed near a puddle not far from the wagon's front wheel. It hopped once and twisted its head, listening.

"Avez-vous été ici avant?" She stomped the cold from her feet and leaned into Vignoble for warmth. The wind picked up and whipped Vignoble's mane. "Is this where you've been before?"

"No," Gilbert said, "but land prices are better here for us." He slung the bridle off his shoulder and looped it over his saddle. "New France is just West."

"I wish it was New Paris. Everything here is wood. I miss...."

"Don't say it. Just makes it harder. We'll be home soon."

"Home?" She spun around, looking up Lexington's main street, then around again to see the other direction. "Where? All I see is forest, dirty men, and...."

"Victoire!" Gilbert's anger came quick.

She took a deep breath but bit her tongue. *"Suis désolé."*

The horse exhaled, sweaty belly shrinking in girth. Vittorie dropped her forehead against the animal's strong shoulder. Vignoble's familiar smell of leather and hide and heat calmed her some.

It wasn't much compared to Paris *but how could it be?* Instead of carved stone edifices, the architecture of nobility from centuries prior displayed for Parisians and the world's travelers to experience, this America of Gilbert's was a newborn babe still struggling with its bindings.

A gusty wind blew a chill down her neck. She shook it off and clutched her collar closed. Her stomach rumbled.

Gilbert came to her side of the horse. He stood close, breathing apologetic gusts into the December air between them. He offered his arm and she took it. He lifted her delicate fingers and kissed them inside her rose glove. When she nodded her own apology and leaned her head on his shoulder, he kissed her hair, too. They stepped up together onto a wooden walkway. Smuthers waited there for them under a large sign with gilded lettering.

"What is this place?" she asked, unable to read the sign.

"Indoor sleeping."

Her whole demeanor brightened and she squeezed his arm. *"Merci."*

She couldn't resist the temptation to touch the intricate carving on the large wooden door. It was the most elegant thing she'd seen in weeks, God's handiwork notwithstanding. But finery like this, expensive and detailed, had become out of her reach and was likely to remain so for some time.

Inside wrapped the newcomers in another world. Candlelight gleamed from wrought-iron sconces. Several chairs and one settee by the front window displayed curved legs and brocade coverings. Three tables covered in clean linens with place settings caused Vittorie's heart to leap. The fireplace beckoned with warm bubblings and a ready ladle.

"Madame Brown," Gilbert addressed the middle-aged woman crossing the plank floor to greet them.

"Mr. LeClerc," she began, with the French prefix pronounced with a long e sound. "Oh, you dear things, come in, come in! Your letter said you'd be here last week and I worried what may have happened to you." She ushered them in like long-lost children, shut the door, and stood back to look. With a hefty sigh, she paused and stared at Vittorie. "Dear me, all that harsh road and you so teensy. And all the way from Charleston."

Vittorie smiled at the woman while she babbled on. She seemed a pleasant woman, in her late fifties and rounded in all the places women that age are prone to be—plus a few more rounds. Her dark hair had grayed everywhere except for just behind her ears and down the nape of her neck, still visible under her cap.

Gilbert and Smuthers exited again and Mrs. Brown took Vittorie's hand. The woman's grey-blue eyes sparkled when she talked. Based on rapidity of movement, she'd earned every line detailing her wide mouth. Vittorie found herself focused on how the woman's bottom lip came up crookedly whenever she closed her mouth, so her pucker pulled to the right in a scowl that contradicted her demeanor. Vittorie startled when the door blew open and Gilbert and Smuthers entered, toting the largest trunk.

"My wife is learning English, still, Madame Brown," Gilbert said. "Which room is ours?"

"Oooh, par-lee voo Fran-see?" Mrs. Brown's eyes sparkled as she turned her whole person to face Vittorie.

Vittorie looked from Gilbert to Mrs. Brown and back again. She couldn't understand more than Gilbert's head nodding up and down indicating an affirmative and so she meekly added her own "yes."

After only a few more language barrier embarrassments and a personal vow to master it sooner than later, Vittorie and Gilbert were unpacking in their own room on the third floor. Smuthers had taken a room on the second floor and they had promised Mrs. Brown to take her up on her offer of dinner at half past six.

"What should I wear to dinner?" Vittorie asked Gilbert as he unlocked her trunk.

"You look beautiful now," he said without looking up. He focused on unfolding papers from inside his own trunk.

"Thank you, *Cheri*, but...." She waited, but he'd obviously missed her intent with the first question. "What will the other women be wearing?"

"It doesn't matter." His forefinger traced a line across a rolled piece of paper. "Things are different where we are, Vi."

She looked out the window at the setting sun. "*Est-ce que le soleil se dissipeuilse encore dans l'ouest ici?*"

"*Oui.*" He looked up at her, eyebrows scrunched close over his nose. "Of course the sun still sets in the west here."

"Oh." She lingered at the window, feeling the weave of the curtains between her fingers, and letting the majesty of the sky speak to her. Glorious orange streaked an aqua horizon under a falling canopy of plum. The Creator was showing off.

If the heavens could change gowns nightly then so could she. Vittorie took out a new dress and pressed it with her hands. "My mother and I chose this fabric in Lyon."

Letting out a long breath, Gilbert moved to her and took both her hands in his. "Why do you love me?"

"I don't know," she teased. "But I always have."

"You are so good." Here he paused and began again with no humor. "This is too hard. You could have married any man you wanted. Why did you wait for me?"

Taken aback by his new insecurity, she put her head on his chest and stayed there a minute, then threw her arms full around him. "I find myself in you." She shrugged, still connected. "I admire you. And I trust you." She picked her head up as if a new thought struck her and moved apart enough to look him full in the face. "You have proven faithful to me all these years, together or apart. You have an uncommon strength of soul."

He kissed her and she felt his wet cheeks against her own. "I love you," she added.

"I will always love you," he replied, folding her deeper into his chest and letting the moment linger between them. "And you make anything look beautiful when you wear it."

"I'll just be a minute," she said.

He sat on the bed and watched, contentment on his face, the papers forgotten.

33

A fire burned hot in the narrow hearth. Conversations sparked among growing acquaintances seated all around. The inn's few guests made interested listeners.

"I wanted to purchase land and plant crops before winter," Gilbert said. He leaned on the mahogany mantel over the fireplace and spoke to an older gentleman from Scotland. "I correspond with three land proprietors before return to America and now, to review the lands."

"Yes, you'll want to scout before you buy," said the Scot. He listened with his bottom lip pooched out. "Too many disputes nowadays."

"But winter weather has already come." Gilbert looked over his shoulder to the curtained window behind him. Dried leaves bounced against the outside panes. "I think we're too late."

Crouched in the place he felt most comfortable, Smuthers had taken responsibility of feeding wood to the fire. "It's no problem a' t'all, Mrs. Brown." He pushed a long wedge of hickory deeper onto the firedogs. Red ashes spewed outward as dry wood enflamed. "I'm very much at rest keeping this fire, I assure you."

"Really, Mr. Smuthers, I normally don't expect guests to do the work, but my leg has been acting up again." She leaned forward in her chair, located midway around the circle of furniture so as to enter any interesting conversation she pleased, and rubbed her left knee. "Must be a weather change coming through."

Gilbert continued his concerns. "I searched out land north and south of Lexington on maps. I'm most anxious to spy it out with my own feet." He tapped the ground twice with the toe of his boot and leaned again on the mantel, unaware of his wording error.

"Yes." The old Scotsman spoke slow and deliberate. "You'll want to survey and purchase land and be moved well before the autumn. Any later and it won't be ideal for crops, hewing lumber for a home…"

"*Exactement.*" Gilbert nodded and finished his sentence "…building shelter, gathering wood before the winter month. Do you have much…*eu*…how to say…." His dangling fingers waved around as he thought. "Smuthers! How to say…*eu*…white…winter falling?" He straightened up and moved both hands in one motion from above his head downward.

Smuthers glanced at him, but kept his attention on the task at hand. "Snow and ice."

"Ah! *Merci. Oui.*" He turned back to the Scotsman. "Snow and eyes."

"I-ce." Smuthers said, emphasizing the soft 'c' sound meaning cold precipitation. "Not eye-z." He pointed to the feature under his bushy eyebrows and chuckled at his friend's mistake.

Gilbert laughed, too. "I-ce. *Oui. Merci.*" He made the snow motion again and turned to Mrs. Brown. "Do you have much snow and i-ce?"

Mrs. Brown spread her hand out flat a little ways above her lap. "Some years as much as this high. But that's unusual, really." She nodded at her own information and dropped the height of her hand some. "Last year was as expected, only about this much."

Gilbert's eyeballs bulged and he sucked in his bottom lip a bit. "That's much."

The Scotsman smiled. "Aye, people hunker down about this time, like a bear." The wrinkles around his eyes deepened. "Don't poke their noses out again until about the third winter." He jabbed the blunt end of his walking stick into the air between himself, Gilbert and Smuthers.

"Third winter?" asked Smuthers, finally distracted from the fire. "What's that?"

"Oh, we have what we call the seven winters here," Mrs. Brown said, rejoining the men's talk, "though I can ne'er recall them all. Do you know them, Mr. Thompson?"

The Scotsman scrunched up his wrinkles and looked at a ceiling beam. "Redbud winter, dogwood winter, locust winter…."

Smuthers laughed. "Seven winters is about six too many for me! What're yew two talkin'?"

"Oh, I remember," said Mrs. Brown. "Blackberry winter, britches winter—maybe there are only five. It warms up some but then another winter follows. It ain't really Spring till all the winter's pass." She put her needlework down in her lap. "How many are there, Mr. Thompson? Five or seven?"

Mr. Thompson shrugged. "Folks around say 'em but I don't keep track. Just know 'em when they come."

Mrs. Brown nodded and resumed her handwork. She drew a long blue thread up with her needle and yanked it tight. "Me too." She sighed and sat still a moment. "Things change so much here."

The Scot leaned into his cane and rose from his chair. "Good talking with you." He bowed to Mrs. Brown and nodded at the others in turn. "I'll see everyone on the morrow."

A soft chorus of '*bonsoir*' and 'goodnight' followed. The wind howled louder.

"Another log, Mrs. Brown?" Smuthers asked.

The hostess perked up again, found a smile, but shook her head. "I'd best take my leave. Eggs don't gather themselves in the mornin' and it's been a good, long day." She smiled her wide smile until the pucker pulled her mouth crooked. "G'night and God sleep, all."

"The delays could not be helped," said Gilbert, speaking out loud to the licking flames. *"Je ne sais pas qua d'autre..."* He circled a hand through his dark hair twice and threw up his hands. "I don't know what else we could have done. Winter or snow…we must see the land right away. I have to foot it myself."

Smuthers leaned the poker against the warm bricks and stood up. "Walk it." He put a hand on Gilbert's shoulder and with the other, pointed to his foot. "This is a foot. The foot walks. You have to 'walk it' yourself."

"Oui," said Gilbert, but his cheeks flushed. "Many mistakes."

"That's how we learn," Smuthers said. "We'll meet Mr. Vaughn in the morning." He yawned wide and patted the buttons over his stomach. "Not to worry, Frenchman. There'll be scouting parties headin' out, blueberry winter or not. I'm sure."

Gilbert nodded and looked over at Vittorie. She slept, tucked into a soft-back chair and wrapped in one of Mrs. Brown's quilts. "She's not going."

Smuthers shook his head. "That's the most peaceful she's looked since I've known her." He looked back at Gilbert. "Mrs. Brown will watch out for her."

Gilbert shook his head. "I don't like to leave her."

"She won't like it either, at first. But it's the best choice now."

34

"Can't we wait here till spring?" Vittorie asked, buttoning her skirts. They hadn't lit the candle yet. When Gilbert didn't answer she changed topics. "Listen to the sound of our feet on the floor." She walked over near him. "Who would have thought I'd be thankful for a floor?"

Night lifted outside. The darkness in their room heathered into shadows.

"We'll be behind on vegetables and the garden for next year," Gilbert responded.

"'Let us eat cake, then," she said, spinning again and listening to her toes on the floor, "as the queen would have us!"

"*Ne parlez pas de la France!*"

Vittorie stopped. "Why can't I talk about France?"

"I'm sorry." Like a child, he knelt to put his head against her belly and wrapped his arms around her.

"What *would* you like to talk about, my love?" She placed one cool palm on his forehead. It felt sweaty. "What's wrong?"

His shoulders slumped but he squeezed her tighter. "I wanted better for you than this."

"Than what? Life with you?" She knelt beside him. "What's the matter?" Her eyes adjusted to the ambient light as she searched his face. "What is it?"

He traced her forehead, nose, and cheeks with his fingertips. Then they found her lips. He kissed her once, twice, and again, drinking her in. "I am a soldier of France," he said. "I fought every day for my king, for my country, for my fellow Frenchmen. I was so proud of my station, my class—more during that time than ever in my life." Tears pooled in the corner of his eyes. "I amounted to something. I knew who I was and what I was about, whose orders to follow, what orders to hand down and see that they were obeyed." He pinched off the tears. "Men saluted me when I walked past, as I did them. Life had an order and I fit into it."

Vittorie kissed him. "*Qua d'autre?*"

"We missed our time. Now the weather's changed. I want you to stay with Mrs. Brown while Smuthers and I…."

Vittorie held his gaze. "No. I won't think like that! I don't want you to speak it out." She took his face in her hands and smoothed his rough cheeks. "I want to stay with you. Look what we've accomplished already!" Her whisper got louder. "You survived the war, but I know the fear is still with you." She exhaled. "Every warrior's wife must know that." She kissed his rough palms. "We've had a wedding, a sea voyage, we crossed the mountains…. I'm learning a whole new land and coming to love it, as you do."

"Smuthers and I will go spy out the land, then return for you." He bent his forehead down until it touched hers. "Please."

She looked through the panes to the wilderness beyond. "Like Joshua and Caleb. What am I supposed to do here without you?"

Gilbert put his cheek against hers. "You've had a wedding, a sea voyage, and crossed the mountains. Now out of the wind and rain and not camping in a new place every night, perhaps you might get some sewing in." His breathing calmed.

The morning outside cast off its nightshirt, revealing the day's ensemble in brilliant ribbons of magenta. Blue satin crested the distant treetops at the horizon, dotted with tufted white clouds and gilded in gold.

"Come back for me." She put four fingers over his lips before he could answer. She could see the moisture of his eyes in the morning light. "I'll wait. And pray."

He ran a hand through his straight brown hair. "We'll need it."

"You *will* find a place. And we'll build a home there."

Gilbert laughed. "What will Madame Brown think when we are so late to breakfast, eh?"

"She will think, 'the French are great lovers,' *oui*?"

His fingertips brushed across her cheek. *"Oui."* He tucked his favorite curl behind her ear and leaned forward so their foreheads touched again. *"Merci,"* he whispered.

"For what?"

He kissed her nose. "Marrying me."

She kissed his lips. "You're welcome."

35

Gilbert stood with his hand on the doorknob and repeated his question. "You're sure his office opens at half past nine?"

"Yes, Mr. LeClerc." Mrs. Brown picked up a dirty breakfast plate and added it to the pile on her little tray. "Unless he's gone to see his sister in Boonesborough or is traveling with a scouting party. Then he mightn't open till ten or half past that, or sometimes not till noon." She turned back to clearing the china from the table, her shawl swinging behind her. "But if ye'll wait on him, he'll be there, by the by."

Gilbert walked out on the porch and held the door open behind him for Vittorie. He offered his arm and she linked elbows. "Unless he has business…his business is to be at business!" Gilbert bristled. "Don't pat my arm, Vi. I didn't travel all this way to do business with men who aren't about their business. Let's go. Walking will warm us up."

Smuthers followed and shut the door behind him. "Righty-ho! Which way?"

Three steps and they were off the porch and onto the frozen, cracked road. Vittorie stamped her feet the next several steps to beat the cold off her boots.

The inn stood in the center of the main street, with a courtyard to one side and a large grove of trees to the other. Past the

161

trees was the livery for the coaches and horses bringing travelers, and next to it was the smith.

"Smith must keep a decent business between the farmers and the passengers," said Smuthers.

Gilbert glanced but said nothing.

"'Round behind the livery is said to have the best drink in town." Smuthers licked his lips.

"How do you know?" Gilbert asked.

Smuthers cleared his throat as they came to the rough-hewn siding of the livery. The waft of manure and fresh hay met him as he breathed. "Man keeps his ear to the ground, don't he?" His long legs carried him past the stable and carriages in a couple of strides. "Think I'll check in on the horses after we see Vaughn."

"I'm anxious to hear what he has to say." Gilbert focused on the shops as they passed. "Might get that harness looked at when we're done."

"Ay-yep. Thought the same."

"*Regardez!*" Vittorie pointed with her glove at a grove of trees that towered above them. "Look how beautiful!"

"Those trunks must be eight feet 'round!" Smuthers said. "Bark looks like some kind of an oak."

"There! Gilbert said, spying a blue sign across the street. "R. Vaughn, Land Proprietor." Its gold letters glinted in the morning sunlight. His walking speed doubled in its direction.

It wasn't a morning Mr. Vaughn had business out of town, as Mrs. Brown warned. Through a small window they could see a figure moving about inside. Gilbert knocked and turned the handle. An overhead bell jingled as the door scraped an arc across the plank floor. The trio entered.

The office had one desk, three chairs, stackable bookcases, one tiny window which looked out onto the main street, and served just one man, Robert Vaughn. The single interesting thing in the room was a cabinet which had some inlay and paint on it.

The fact that it was held up by three legs and a small boulder added to its curiousness. Little by way of decoration complimented the space except several hand-drawn maps. These hung on two walls, tacked up with horseshoe nails at the corners and a few other nails pinned along waterways.

Mr. Vaughn, hearing the jingle, spun around from the bookcase. His eyebrows lifted as though surprised by the event. "Good morning," he said, more of a question than a statement.

"*Oui, Monsieur Vaughn.*" Gilbert stepped around the side of the man's desk, took him by the shoulders, and kissed him on both cheeks. "Gilbert LeClerc!" Gilbert stepped back, elated. "*Finalement!* We meet!"

Mr. Vaughn's expression flipped from stupor to surprise as he retrieved a handkerchief from his pocket. "Yes, I'm Robert Vaughn. And you are…?" He rubbed both cheeks with the hankie, caught sight of something on a map, and turned back to the bookshelf.

Gilbert looked at Vittorie and Smuthers. Vittorie sat down in the chair nearest the window and took her embroidery out of her pouch. Smuthers shrugged. Gilbert waited a moment, then cleared his throat.

Mr. Vaughn muttered something indistinguishable, turned a page in the book he held, and ran a finger down the line of type.

Gilbert looked at Vittorie and Smuthers again. Smuthers walked to the door, opened it, and shut it again.

When the bell jingled, Mr. Vaughn slammed the book shut and spun around. He moved to shake Gilbert's hand, stopped, and immediately busied himself about his desk. Then, turning to see the three people in the room, an odd expression came over him. "What was the property in question?" he asked, as if he hadn't forgotten they were there. He opened a cabinet door and stuck his head inside.

Gilbert looked at Smuthers again. Catching Gilbert's unease, Smuthers moved closer to Vittorie.

Robert Vaughn could only remember his business at every third movement. In constant motion, he entered into and out of his own carousel of action and conversation. Turning away from his patrons—for reasons known only to him—he came back to the table startled to find anyone waiting for him. To his credit, Mr. Vaughn appeared as frustrated by this queer happenstance as the rest of them. As many gentlemen who have fallen on hard times, he bore the demeaning cycle with charisma and ballast. It isn't respectable to forget what one is at so often and need to be reminded by outside prodding—a childlike state in a very grown man.

Vaughn's distraction carried on too long for Gilbert's patience. "Mr. Vaughn, do you or do you not remember my letter of April this year to which you responded you would see me once I arrived in Lexington? Be so good to show me the holdings you wrote about."

Mr. Vaughn's back was turned from them. Hearing the tone in Gilbert's voice, he emerged from behind the cabinet door and closed it securely behind him. There followed a loud clinking of bottles and a long gastrointestinal sound, after which no one spoke for five full seconds, despite the fact Vaughn had turned to face Gilbert. He maintained an expression during the prolonged silence of such a mix that Gilbert worked hard to tell if it were indigestion or embarrassment. Standing up rather tall but not at all straight, he then looked at Smuthers, assuming him to be the speaker, and said, "Mr. LeClerc, I will see you now." He flipped his coattails, sat down with a flourish, and folded his hands across the papers on his desk.

Gilbert sat across from him. "Thank you. Mr. Vaughn, I should like to see the land you wrote about near Big Buffalo Crossing.

Two hundred acres with water dissecting it the full length. And another two hundred acres beside it for Mr. Smuthers, here."

Smuthers came over to stand by the desk. His frame towered over it.

Vittorie understood little of the conversation between the men. She watched and listened and poked her needle up and down through the fabric in her hand.

Robert Vaughn raised his head to take in Smuthers' full height. He tapped his quill pen in the inkpot twice.

"Yes, yes. I remember. Make your marks here." He lay the quill down for their use.

"We're gentlemen. We'll sign our names." Smuthers plucked up the pen, scrawled a fine signature, and passed the feather to Gilbert. "I can pay you one-third once the papers are drawn and one-third each year for the next two years, as can he," Smuthers said. "But we'll need to see it before we pay. How soon could you get a scouting party together?"

"Longhunters run the scouting parties here. Know the woods better'n any. But by the chill in the air, you must know you're late in the season for such things?" said Vaughn. "Take about three weeks to find a guide. Skeggs ought to be back through about then. He'll deliver you."

✻ ✻ ✻

Smuthers walked as far as the livery and went to check the horses. Gilbert and Vittorie stopped at the grove of huge trees before the inn. The sun hadn't warmed the December day much.

"Vaughn said the next scouting party might not be through for another three weeks yet," Gilbert said. "Which is much later than we planned for planting. We'll be away for maybe…up to two weeks."

"What will I do without you?"

165

"Aren't you the woman who waited six years for me?"

"Yes. Six years, three months and seventeen days. But that was in France among everything and everyone I loved, and we are not in France, as you have been so fond of reminding me."

"But you are the same, Vittorie. The same woman who knows her mind and who knows me, and who crossed the sea and who sat in the back of a wagon for weeks at a time."

"I don't wish to remember that, thank you. Next time we travel the countryside I would like my own horse, please."

"On her own horse next time, for weeks at a time. You have the spirit of a thousand horses and the courage of a lioness," Gilbert continued, interpreting the weight of his words by the touch of her hands, "and who I know is tender as a new spring vine, but who the world sees as…"

She shook her head. "The world doesn't see me at all. Only you do. To everyone else I am a single blade of grass, blending in with all the others. A woman. And of no consequence."

"I think you are a queen."

"A queen? I thought we have no king or queen to rule us in this New World?" She'd caught him in his own words.

He loved her, and her cleverness encouraged his enamoring of her. "True," he acknowledged. "So, I will choose you then as the one above all others in my soul; my gift from Holy God Himself."

"So, I am your gift?"

"If it suits you. What gift can I give you?"

"Please plant the apples and grapes when you go. Give them as much time to germinate as possible."

"If I can, I will."

36

The small scouting party stood among thousands of trees on the crest of a giant hill. Thanks to winter's stark view, Skeggs, Gilbert, and Smuthers surveyed the rolling landscape in every direction. The eastern sunrise warmed the men's shoulders and caused every ice-laden limb in the forest to glisten.

"The Green River is 320 chains south from this ridge." Skeggs leaned on the trunk of a large black walnut tree, rifle secure over his left shoulder. "There's a spring ahead. We'll drink there." He reached into the sack strapped to his side, pulled out a long strip of salted meat, and bit off a decent bite.

The quiet beauty of the clearing before him took Gilbert's breath away. A thin rush of fogged breath threaded from between his lips. "*C'etait incroyable.*" He wiped thawed wetness off his mustache down the sides of his mouth and blinked moisture to his eyes. "Vittorie will fall in love, I think."

"I hope my land looks just like this," Smuthers said. He squatted down against a larger walnut tree. "Look how tall these trees are! Bet they grow nuts big as my fist."

"*Qu'est-ce que c'est?*" Gilbert asked.

Skeggs dug deeper into his pouch and pulled out three black balls. Their striated casings had exterior ribs running from top to bottom all over. "Black walnuts." He tossed one Gilbert's direction and another to Smuthers. "Crack 'em hard." He lay the nut on a flat piece of sandstone, walked a pace, dislodged a small boulder and smashed the nut between them. The outer shell split. Picking it up, he pulled the largest crack apart and nudged the meat inside loose with the tip of his bare thumb. He held the exhibit out in the palm of his hand for closer inspection from the others.

Smuthers placed his nut down about where Skeggs had his. Gilbert did the same. Smuthers smashed and Gilbert smashed. The noises reverberated in the stillness, and several squirrels chattered their complaints as they careened further away in the sinewy treetops.

"That'll do!" Smuthers said, munching the knobby meat from his shell. "Mmmm. Yep! Let's get going. I'm ready to gather walnuts on my own land."

Skeggs led the way downward, nimbly picking the quietest route. He moved like a bobcat, silent and quick.

Gilbert's feet shuffled through brown leaves. He bent over and picked a few up. "What trees are this?"

Smuthers looked. "Uh…ask him."

Gilbert ran to catch up with Skeggs. "*Qu'est-ce que*…I mean, what tree are this?"

"*Nous peut parlons Français, s'il vous voulon.*"

Gilbert straightened. "*Vous parlez Français? Mon Dieu!*" Amazed at his fortune, he crossed himself and turned back to Smuthers. "He speaks French!"

"Ay-yep. Guess you can't tell who'll meet in these woods." He urged his large frame to catch up. "Are your people from France then also?"

"No," Skeggs said. "My father was Ulster Protestant, but, I believe men are free to seek God as they will. Anglican, Puritan, Quaker, Roman Catholic, and the native tribes here."

Gilbert nodded but hung closer to Smuthers as they approached a level basin with low hills bordering each side. The gully, insignificant except for the explorers' inquisitive eyes, welcomed the scouting party as a child takes a bird in its cupped palm.

"My mother was born in Virginia, Fincastle County. But they settled an' raised my brothers an' me in Maryland," Skeggs continued. "He was a fur trader and taught us boys." His head tipped toward his left ear. "But it was the land I ended up loving. Not the skins."

"But not a tobacco farmer, eh?" asked Smuthers. "Whereabouts in Maryland?"

The wind calmed, causing the canopy of narrowed branches to cease moving above their heads. Peace, the kind found only in the depths of a forest where life teems yet rests, enveloped them.

"No. Not a farmer at all, as you see." He waited for them near the ring of poplars. "My mother died young. Grief expands a person." His conversation shifted. "Either of you know Latin?"

Gilbert nodded once. Smuthers nodded with a slow toggle of his head.

"It'll help you out here, knowing Latin. Might'n't think it, but it's true. Learn the laws. Know your rights, and others' rights, to keep safe."

Skeggs trudged up a hill heading east. Gray clouds covered the sun as they do on December days. Reflected light washed the woods, casting no shadows. Midway up another steep incline, just below a huge felled oak, Skeggs pointed to the ground. "Here's the next spring. You'll tell it by the oak for now till you memorize the topography. That oak fell two winters ago…no, three…winter of 1784, in a storm. It's the last water till the river. Source comes from deep underground so you know it's pure." He bent his face under the trickle and lapped it with his tongue.

Gilbert and Smuthers looked around, uneasy. Smuthers motioned and Gilbert drank next.

"You're right to be aware," Skeggs said, wiping his wet beard on the sleeve of his brown skin coat. "Most tribes camp farther south this time of year. But can't never tell who's in these woods."

"You seem to know 'em," Smuthers said.

"I do," said Skeggs. "I say you can't never tell who's around, but you'll learn. This is nearly your backyard here. Your land's just south."

Cold spring water pinged into the bottom of Smuthers' little iron cup. He drank his fill, stuffed it snug inside his sack, and knotted the drawstring.

"That's as fast a knot as any I've seen," Skeggs said.

Smuthers smiled. "Kept the *Alosa aestavalis* on the line back home." He hauled the bag over his shoulder and interpreted for Gilbert. "Blueback herring…little shiny fish. Tastes delicious smoked, fried, in a stew." He licked his chapped bottom lip.

Gilbert's expression changed as he interpreted the word for stew. "*Bouillaboisse.* Fish soup." His stomach growled.

"Yes, but Bouillaboisse has mussels or shellfish and vegetables, too. In St. Mary's we'd have mussels or oysters a-plenty, right Skeggs?"

Skeggs laughed a deep belly laugh. "It's good to see two, so very different men traveling as friends. I think I understand your common interest—food!"

"I am French," Gilbert said, with sincerity. "Do you think I could settle so near a man who doesn't appreciate good food?" A twinkle lit his eye.

Smuthers laughed. He moved side to side, following Skeggs around three trees. Running his hand over the dark brown bark, he analyzed the vertical grooves. "Sugar maples!" Still excited about the sugar maples, he added, "Sap boils down so sweet." A dozen yellow and black birds flitted above them. "He lets me tag along because he thinks I'm gonna haul his timber when it comes housebuilding time."

"You'll each have your pick of timber. What do you think?"

The merry party halted. With their happy banter they hadn't noticed before, but now, in the quiet, the unmistakable sound of slow-moving water could be heard.

Through a final ridgeline of trees, with a gray winter sky beyond, ran the Green River. It yawned from bank to bank with a generous gape and lazy flow. A small, steep decline held its edge below ground-level. It seemed quite content within its borders. Matching, large swathes of trodden dirt could be seen on either bank.

"That's where the buffalo cross." Smuthers took off his hat and clutched it to his chest. "Prettiest place I e'er laid eyes on." His jaw hung loose and he gazed up the waterway and down as far as he could see. Putting his wrist to his eyebrows and twisting to look skyward he said, "Can't make out no sun."

"The far side's the one Vaughn's held for you," said Skeggs. "This side of the river is *Monsieur* LeClerc's."

Gilbert hadn't heard a word. He knelt, kissing a handkerchief. After crossing forehead to belly and shoulder to shoulder, he pulled his knife from his right boot. He held it in both hands above his head, paused, then jabbed it into the ground to bore a hole. Into that hole he deposited three seeds. Before he covered them up again, he leaned over them, whispered, and spit. Sighting the tallest pine on his right, he lunged one large stride toward it and plunged the dagger into the earth again, beginning the orchard for his love.

37

A flurry of snow crossed the plating of Mrs. Brown's hotel doorway as Gilbert and Smuthers stepped in. Two weeks living outdoors was evident on them, from their thick beards to the compacted dirt on their clothing.

As soon as both of Gilbert's snow-covered boots were inside, Vittorie jumped from the settee and flung herself on him, her needlework landing on the plank floor.

Smuthers sniffed. His eyes lit up like fire in full blaze "Mrs. Brown!" his voice roared through the tiny space. "It smells like ye've been cookin' an entire feast jes' fer me!" His beard got twice as wide as he grinned.

"Now, Mr. Smuthers," said Mrs. Brown, "you just wash and change and we'll have dinner here for you as early as you like." She pulled the kettle off the iron balance beam and spoke over her shoulder. "I'll have water brought for you both. Constance!"

The younger woman pulled a brass pan from the flames and set it on a stand in the center of the table. Her long forehead, bereft of eyebrows, made her eyes appear tiny. Wiping her hands on a worn apron, Constance threw a shawl over her head, picked up two buckets stacked by the back door, and headed out into the weather.

"A bath can wait, but," Smuthers said, "a body could use some vittles."

"Alright then," Mrs. Brown said, replacing the kettle and swinging the iron arm back over the fire. "You can wash hands and eat first. Mr. Lee-clerk, you're hungry, too, I'm sure."

"*Oui, Madame*," Gilbert said, Vittorie still attached. He unwrapped his arms from around her, but she kept her hold, face buried in the collar of his coat. Holding his hands out wide, he shifted to show Smuthers the wife clasped around his neck.

Smuthers' belly heaved a laugh. "Don't make me wait on you for dinner. I'll eat your share."

Vittorie relaxed her grip. "How is the land?" she asked. "What does it look like? Is the river far?" Her eyelashes fluttered and she looked up at him. "Did you plant the seeds?"

"I missed you, too," Gilbert said. "Fruitful. Old forests with rolling landscapes. *Non.* And yes."

"Dinner!" Mrs. Brown sang out. "Table's set. Constance brought fresh washing waters there in the basin." She pointed to a pitcher set on a three-legged table in the corner. "Sit as you like and we'll begin."

Dinner was a veritable feast. Boiled root vegetables salted and swimming in butter, summer pickles, pasties filled with various meat and tubers, brown bread sliced thick with gooseberry chutney, and all the beer they could drink.

The men wasted no effort on ceremony. As soon as their plates emptied, Constance or Mrs. Brown passed another dish. They traded excerpts of the trip between swallows.

"We got stuck coming over one ridge to wait out some snow, but traveled along well after that," Smuthers said. "The way between Lexington and the land was mostly foothills." He guzzled more beer. "The highest hills lay just before the site."

"It's bordered on one long side by the river." Gilbert spooned more chutney on his second slice of bread. "Wide enough to travel by, wash by…we'll build a waterwheel…and swift enough to keep vermin that cultivate in putrid areas of still water away." He nodded at Constance with the pickle plate. "*Merci.* The land has a low plain area at the river that slopes steeply uphill, then levels out again for several hundred feet and then…."

Vittorie sat, utensils in hand, breathless. She leaned close to the table and looked between each man as they spoke. Every detail ignited images in her mind. Transfixed, she relived the journey with them.

"…it just rolls away into hills and forests, far as the eye can see. The view from our house," Gilbert leaned closer to Vittorie, "will take your breath away." He pulled another pasty apart while he chewed. "Smuthers' land, west of ours, is just as delightful. In no way faulty or lacking."

Grabbing a pause while both men chewed, Vittorie asked, "How about the orchard?"

Smuthers swallowed. "We come upon the area just before noon. There's a ridge at the river but a long, wide plateau on the bluff. Perfect timber. Nut trees.

"Walnuts." said Gilbert.

Vittorie stabbed a dice of turnip with her fork and wiped it across her napkin to get the butter off. "Can it really be so perfect?"

Gilbert smiled. "God has opened his hand and blessed us, *Amour.*"

Mrs. Brown refilled Gilbert's beer. "Good you're back safe, Mr. Lee-clerk. I can't say I was as successful in getting your bride to eat."

"Really?" He looked from one woman to the other.

Vittorie slid the buttered napkin under the table, away from view. "*C'est pas?*"

Gilbert's thin eyebrows lifted. "Thank you, Mrs. Brown." He downed half his beer but watched Vittorie over the rim.

Mrs. Brown groaned. "She barely took her eyes off that window. Save for sewing."

"And teaching us how to make this!" Constance brought an earth-colored pie dish with blue stripes to the table and served a large spoonful to everyone. "Apple cinnamon compote, for dessert." A teensy smile spread her mouth.

Smuthers kept his plate up after being served. "More please."

Constance blushed. She dug the spoon into the gooey sweetness again, tapped it twice, and released the dollop onto the edge of his china plate.

"When do you think we can go?" Vittorie asked, raising her eyebrows at Gilbert.

Gilbert pushed the last of the pasty into his mouth, chewed twice, spread more chutney on his bread and added it to the mouthful. "Loths of thime layer to thalk aboud thad."

38

"But it's much colder than you're used to," Gilbert said. He leaned against the wall.

"I've been inside for over a month and won't stay in another minute!" Vittorie insisted.

Gilbert's jaw twitched in annoyance, but he put on his long coat. "Well, you're not going by yourself," he said, holding up her coat.

She put her left arm through the sleeve. "*Merci.*"

"I know," he added. "I hate it more than you do."

They marched downstairs toward the front door. "I doubt that."

Mrs. Brown looked up from her knitting. "Smuthers has gone out, too." She pulled her shawl around her and crossed her ankles. "But it's not the finest of evenings to be going out in."

Gilbert reached for the large brass door handle. "A little walking will do us both good this evening."

Once outside, January's frozen breath filled Vittorie's mouth. They hadn't walked long before she could feel the ice crystals inside her nostrils. She pulled on her nose to dislodge them.

"Now," Gilbert said, taking her hand, "tell me about you."

"I've ached for a walk, but didn't feel comfortable here without you."

"And, what else?"

One blue ring haloed the round moon. It threw unusual light on the little town, almost daylight radiance on the empty street.

"What's the matter?" Gilbert asked.

"Nothing." With her arm linked in Gilbert's, Vittorie looked up at the orb. "I couldn't wait for your return. Now that you're back, I don't really want to leave."

"Are you cold already? Because I'm fine, we can go back. I don't need to walk tonight."

"I do."

A month ago, the livery smelled robust and warm with hay, manure, leather and horse all mixed up in it. The new year's temperatures had removed those smells. She peered inside as they passed the barn's door. About half a dozen horses—mostly bay or chestnut, with one paint—whinnied low. The nearest horses lifted their heads, hearing syncopated footsteps against the silent evening and the wooden sidewalk planks. Vittorie smiled at the creatures as she passed.

"Since when have you come to love horses so much?" Gilbert asked.

"I guess since leaving France, really." She tucked a curl back under her hat. "I've always liked horses, but now they're something familiar to me…in a world of not familiar things."

"I thought it might have been the carriage ride from the sea that enamored you of them so much." He squeezed her hand.

"Ha ha! That, too." She leaned into him a little more, his arms strong and warm next to hers. "No, I've missed my own two feet under me. The freedom of knowing where you are." She stopped to face him and he wrapped his arms around her. "Does it sound silly to say I miss running? At home I ran wherever I wanted. I knew everyone and…."

"Everyone knew you and forgave your indiscretion if they saw it."

She chuckled and nodded. "But here, who knows what Americans think of a grown woman who runs around the streets. It can't be decent, I know that. And it makes me sad." Hot tears ran down her cheeks. She let them continue, expunged into the wool of Gilbert's white soldier's coat.

"Is that all that makes you sad?" He pulled the worn handkerchief from his breast pocket and offered it to her.

As soon as she touched it, she stopped crying. "My handkerchief!"

He smoothed tears and new-fallen snowflakes off her cheeks with his glove. "No, *my* handkerchief."

She smiled, though the liquid still spilled from the ledges of her eyelids. "I remember." She sneezed into it. "Surely you don't want it now?"

"More than ever." He retrieved it from her and tucked it into his bosom again. "Come on, Mrs. LeClerc."

The lovers stepped off the sidewalk at the end of town and stopped, arm in arm. Gray breaths curled out between them in the frigid night air. Moonlight glazed the pebbles of open ground a bit further. Then thick, wild forest took over. With Lexington behind them, away from the kindness of strangers and not knowing what lay before them, they gazed into the frosted darkness engulfing the horizon. The snow fell heavier.

Gilbert cleared his throat. "I wish our families could see this." He removed his glove this time and smoothed her wet cheek again.

Vittorie nodded her head and cried harder. She kissed his palm as it moved past her lips. "You are a good man, Gilbert."

"And you are the best woman in the world. We'll be fine, you'll see."

"How do you know?"

He lifted his face skyward and let frozen crystals land on his skin. "I have faith."

"What if I cannot make this my home?"

"You haven't come this far to turn back," he said. "You are the perfect woman and I am not afraid."

She laughed out loud at his boldness. "I don't mean to be afraid, but I am."

He stopped looking at the sky and kissed her. "Come," he said, unbuttoning his coat.

She glanced around, shocked. "What are you doing?"

"We're almost home. Why shouldn't you run?"

"What?"

"We're going to race." He reached for her coat buttons. "Coat on or off for you?"

"I'm leaving my coat on, thank you. It's freezing!"

"Fine, but no excuses when I beat you to that hemlock tree over there because you chose to leave yours on. *Allons-y!*"

Vittorie looked around her in all directions. Spectacular snowflakes fell everywhere. She stuck out her tongue to catch some, but he still had his coat off when she faced him again. "You're serious!"

"I spoke French…you understand me! We're going to have a race for those little running legs of yours."

Looking back down the street she could barely make out the fronts of the buildings. Only yellow light from inside select ones shone out, illuminating winter's falling curtain. "Well, if I can barely see the door frames and sidewalks, perhaps no one could see us this far away if we are to have an indecent race to the tree." Her eyes gleamed. "Go!" she yelled and took off with a belly laugh.

Gilbert slipped on his first step over the slushy ground but scrambled to his feet.

The hemlock grew less than thirty paces ahead. Its perfect cone shape rose taller into the milky sky with every touch of her flying feet to the covered ground.

Looking once over her shoulder at him in full pursuit, she doubled her efforts. Her legs stretched out, each stride kicking her coat before her. She ran, fists clenched. Her arms pumped front to back like she'd done a million times before.

The exhilaration coursed through her body—warm blood, cold air. Winter wind punched at her lungs. She forced her lips closed to keep from chilling her teeth. Her hair tingled. Her thoughts were so clear. She loved this moment more than any that had come before it. From joy deep and excitement overflowing sprang satisfaction. As her body raced the gap between behind and before, she was herself, relying on no one, accomplishing what was hers alone to accomplish with no aid nor reprimand.

The hemlock loomed. She stretched out her right hand to take hold of the lowest evergreen branch almost within reach. With a swirl and a whoosh, she felt her body captured and caught, wrapped and tumbled with Gilbert's to the cold cushion below the tree.

"You cheated!" she cried, her heart pounding in her chest.

He laughed out loud. "I won!"

"Ha! You call this winning? You still haven't touched the tree." Her sides ached. She couldn't control her laughter, but she stretched to finish what she started. Her hand brushed against the trunk first.

His arm pillowed her head and his breath warmed her face. He panted above her as he caught his breath. "I wasn't after the tree."

They kissed, wet and deep, and pure as the snow. Nothing else mattered. They held each other beneath the hemlock branches on the outskirts of the village.

After a time, Gilbert looked out into the weather. "Come, Mrs. LeClerc. I do not think your mother would approve of you kissing outdoors." When he looked back at her, he puckered and kissed her once more. "Not with an inn so nearby."

Snow blanketed their world with peace. They said little the whole walk back to town.

39

"My! Isn't it just bucketing down?" Mrs. Brown said for the fourth time that day. "I don't remember when we've had such a rainy spri…."

Lightning flashed with ferocious intensity. Sheets of rain swept across the windows.

Vittorie looked up but continued stitching the hole in Gilbert's knee-breeches. She pulled the needle up but it caught. The thread got knotted on the underside. Frustrated, she sucked the inside of her teeth and frowned.

"You're so dedicated to your work," said Mrs. Brown. She left the fireplace and came to stand beside Vittorie. The skin around her gray-blue eyes bunched into pleasant wrinkles. "You really do have the finest handwork I've ever seen." She leaned over the deep-yellow velvet pants and nodded. "Mm-hm. I've never seen a rip so evenly restitched. And the linens you were attending to yesterday…."

Vittorie paused to acknowledge the older woman's conversation. She smiled and turned the floral and cartouches fabric inside out.

Moving back to the fireplace, Mrs. Brown took hold of the mitt and removed the kettle. "That pattern has such curves and details." With a grunt, she leaned over the table and set the kettle on an intricate brass trivet. "I would offer to buy some from you if I didn't know you were setting up house."

"*Je voulais*...I want sew...." Her English vocabulary faltered. She pinched at the knot with her fingernails. "*Je voulais les réparer pour qu'il puisse s'habiller pour les dîners... après la construction de la maison*...build house."

"Well then," said Mrs. Brown, nodding without understanding. She took cups and saucers from the dresser and ambled around the table to place them just so.

Vittorie took a deep breath and set down her work. Rising, she smoothed the cotton fichu around her neck, checked the buttons down the front of her dress, and went out the front door.

Growing rivers raced in haphazard rivulets down the street. Smuthers stood with his shoulders leaned against the outside front wall of the inn, arms crossed, mouth turned down.

With long strides, facing away from the door, Gilbert walked the length of the porch. "What do they pay in New France to be a courthouse? English pay 13 pounds here!"

"They're not all English. And they're paying that to the custodian, per annum. Courthouse is the building." Smuthers ran his hand over his nose and wiped it down his beard. "I know. What do you think about joining the militia? Wear the red feather in our hats, summer here until the fall so we can get the planting...."

"No!" Gilbert spun on his heel. "*Mon Dieu*, will this month ever dry out?"

"*Gilbert*..." Vittorie said, "...*du the*."

Pounding raindrops drowned out her words. Gilbert bent his neck toward her and cupped his hand around one ear.

"*Du the*." Rain splattered the colorful drawn work of her petticoat. She stepped back, nearer the doorway, away from the bouncing puddles at the edge of the porch. "Tea," she said to Smuthers.

Smuthers stood up and stretched. "Mare-sea, Vittorie."

Gilbert stuck his palm out into the deluge. Water drenched his sleeve.

40

The wet spring continued into April. The sun had yet to break the horizon. Moisture hung in the air, hot and thick.

Gilbert whipped America's cinch through the buckle and yanked the billet too tight around the horse's girth. Startled, America yanked at his tether and stamped the puddle under his hooves. "*Arrête!*" He shouted at the docile bay.

Smuthers stopped combing Macaroni and stepped in front of Gilbert. "They've a long way to go, Gil. No sense riling 'em up at the beginning."

The deep furrow between Gilbert's eyebrows relaxed. He hurried on, checking the saddle straps with snug pulls followed by a quick rub and two pats on the animal's rump.

Mrs. Brown was in tears. "I can't help it." She blubbered into a hankie. "You've stayed so long and been so kind, I hate to see you go!"

"Too long," Gilbert said, bending over Vignoble's hoof.

Smuthers stretched up to his full height and answered for the group. "Thank you, Mrs. Brown. We'll likely be back through for supplies come summer."

"Good," Mrs. Brown said. "Vittorie'll need some woman's company, too, mind you. Don't keep her out there lonesome. Change comes best with friends." Mrs. Brown dabbed at her eyes again and moved around the hitching post. She put a pudgy arm around Vittorie.

Her gentle touch made tears sprout in Vittorie's eyes, but she didn't cry. Instead, she forced as amiable a smile as possible.

For the first time in five months Mrs. Brown said nothing. She took Vittorie in her arms and squeezed her tight to her chest. Vittorie put her arms around the woman, squeezed her back, and released her. The best way to keep emotions in check was brevity.

But Mrs. Brown did not let go. "Lord, bless her as she goes. Keep her path straight. Guide and protect her. In Your name, I pray, Amen." She stroked Vittorie's back several times and patted her head like a good child.

The warmth of this woman's touch, her blessing, and approval caused Vittorie to cry. She could not stop the tears falling over her cheeks or running over her lips any more than she could hold back the sunrise. The uncertainty of her faith, the gravity of her past decisions, the ever-present dangers, and the horrifying doubts kept at bay in France by tradition, familiarity, and ignorance had been stripped away. She laid the weight of her head on the older woman's shoulder and bawled.

Gilbert came to take Vittorie from Mrs. Brown, but the matron rebuked him with a look. He stepped back and checked the ropes which tied Vignoble's load. The knots held. Vittorie's tears stopped and her steady breathing returned. She raised her head off Mrs. Brown's shoulder and wiped sweat and tears off her face. Mrs. Brown removed her hand from Vittorie's head and released her. She removed a satchel from her own shoulder and placed it over Vittorie's capped head. It was heavy around Vittorie's neck. Inside, there was a bottle. Removing the lid, she saw a dark substance, neither liquid nor solid.

Mrs. Brown dipped a plump finger into the sticky substance and stuck her finger into her mouth.

Vittorie did the same with her own finger. The taste was sweet, strong, and good. *"C'est bon!"*

"Sorghum," Mrs. Brown said.

"Merci." Vittorie's eyes had hope in them. *"Tu es celui que ma mère aurait espéré que je rencontre ici."*

Mrs. Brown looked to Gilbert once Vittorie was silent. Her handkerchief shielded her eyes from the early morning sun.

"You are what her mother would have hoped for," he translated.

With a happy clap of her hands and a look that said it all, Mrs. Brown hugged the girl again. Turning with a swish of her skirt, she returned to her porch.

Smuthers tipped his hat and bowed low toward Mrs. Brown. "Thank you, Ma'am. You've been very kind." He and Macaroni led the way onward.

Gilbert unwrapped Vignoble and America from the post and walked them away. *"Merci.* Thank you for taking care of everything."

Vittorie looked behind her several times as they continued out of town. Mrs. Brown stood with her hand raised beside the front porch railing for as long as Vittorie could still make her out, etching the woman in her mind. How her russet brown skirt hid the lavender petticoat she denied owning. Her simple grey boots with eight buttons. Her pretty, blue-trimmed blouse and periwinkle shawl secured in front by the pin her late husband had bought on their trip from the coast. Her hair, as always, fastened back with three pins underneath a piece of crocheted handiwork she used for a cap as long as Vittorie had shared a roof with her.

Heading into the wilderness, letting go of the last familiarities they'd come to know, Vittorie, Gilbert, and Smuthers were quiet. No one would be there to greet them when they arrived. No candles would be lit. No fire going. No camaraderie nor meals to be shared, except what they brought with them or gathered on their own before making camp.

Vittorie shot her arm high into the air and waved back, long and slow. *"Au revoir, mon amie."*

Gilbert trudged beside her. He clutched a horse rein in each hand. "You'll see her again."

41

"What?" Gilbert asked.

"Can I lead Vignoble?" Vittorie hurried to keep in step with him.

Four days without shaving grew on his jawbone and upper lip. He ran a hand over his beard. "The ground here is uneven. I'd rather keep a hold."

The horses carried everything they could under the wrapping Gilbert had attached to them. Covered in canvas, linen, and strong rope, it seemed paltry.

"Let's play a game," she said as Vignoble lumbered beside her.

Gilbert didn't respond, so she ran ahead to Smuthers. Holding his rifle under his armpit, Smuthers led Macaroni around a massive tree trunk by a rope.

"Game?" she asked.

Smuthers nodded, glanced back at Gilbert, and said, "Aye. You start."

"Name the cover!" She skipped a few steps to keep up with Smuthers' and Macaroni's pace. "Remember who is pack! *Alors!*"

"Remember *what* is packed," Smuthers corrected. He looked up to find the sun but only leaves glinted above them. "In English!"

Walking backward a few steps beneath a towering maple tree, Vittorie put a finger to her chin and then pretended to stir a spoon inside the curved shape of her other arm. "Bowl for mix."

Smuthers pulled a twenty-centimeter blade from a sheath strapped to his left thigh. "Knife."

The horses maneuvered around wide tree trunks. High above their heads, new green leaves shimmered and spun. Growing unhindered for so many years, the tall, thick trunks supported great foliage. Thin petioles quivered as the west wind intensified.

Vittorie tested a rock with her foot. It didn't wiggle so she put her full weight on it. "Pee-share."

Smuthers shook his head. "Nope."

"Pee-share?" She placed her hands on two oak trunks and stepped over a large root growing between them. "Pee-chair?"

Macaroni shook his head. His strong shoulder muscles flexed.

"She's trying, Mac. Be nice." Smuthers spoke to his horse and led him around the far side of the surfaced root system. "Pitcher," he said to Vittorie. "You mean pitch-r. To pour out." He made the motion with his free hand.

Vittorie's expression changed. "Ah. Pour out. Pitch-air. Yes. I mean this. *Come ça.*" Avoiding one mossy rock, she stepped up and to the right on another. "I am hunger."

Yellow finches flirted above their heads, singing. Their ascent through the leafy canopy disturbed a collection of raindrops which sprinkled down around the travelers.

Smuthers looked up through the swaying green leaves to the darkening sky. He scanned the path ahead. "Let's camp under that ridge tonight. The rock hollows into a bit of a cave. Keep you out of the wind."

"T-ank ee-you."

Smuthers couldn't help but smile. "I meant Ol' Mac here. But you're welcome." He turned Mac's bridle in the direction of the ridge. "Horse."

Vittorie smiled. "Sor-gum."

Smuthers sighed. "Mrs. Brown's biscuits and bread. I wish we still had those." He led Macaroni around an outcropping of boulders and up the western side of a small hill. "Gilbert!" He shouted behind him. "It's your turn. What do you remember that's packed under these heaps?"

Gilbert watched three black birds fly up into a redbud tree. Their dark forms contrasted with the bright purple buds. "Two axes, a pick, extra leather and iron, plus tools to work them should there not be a smith nearby, a lathe, her pans." He took a deep breath before he continued. "Silver candlesticks—wedding present from Father Benét—her sewing, my father's pocket watch, lead…"

Vignoble raised his tail and kept walking. The smell of hot manure mixed with honeysuckle and pine.

"…candles, wax, wicks. Too much. More than I want to think about!"

"Seeeeds!" Vittorie said. "*Et mon mariage ensemble.*"

Smuthers let Macaroni's rope hang free while he touched the moss at the base of the rocks. "Not too wet." He waved Gilbert up, but addressed Vittorie. "English, please."

"Her wedding vest and clothes," Gilbert answered. "*Vittorie, tu veux bien l'apporter un morceau de bois.*"

"Een-glish, please." Her eyebrow and forefinger raised and she laughed at her own joke. "Yes, wood to fire. I go."

42

Smoke columned to the sky from an odd structure in the center of a long field. The building, made of sideways logs stacked atop the other and filled in between, had a roof that began a little lower than it ought to. Vertical wood pieces bound together served as a door, plus there were two tiny windows and the chimney. The prettiest thing about it was the short porch extending along the entire front. Skinny sticks held up the porch roof. When Smuthers stepped out from the woods into the sunshine of the field, he bent his chin lower and squinted. "There's Highbaugh's Mill again."

The light shone sideways through majestic maples and pines. Long shadows pointed eastward.

"Good," said Gilbert. He nodded for Vittorie.

"You know this place?" she asked, taking the reins from him.

He brushed his hands on the thighs of his pants. "*Oui*. We stopped here with the longhunter *en Decembre*."

The field they walked through boasted a creek. Its clear water meandered along one side of the woods for an even pace and then veered off to the left, past the cabin and out of sight. Vittorie led the horses to it. They tested the soft river mud with their hooves and lowered their long noses for a drink.

"Ah!" she said, dipping her arms into the water. It cooled her wrists. Cupping her hands together, she scooped up a good drink and slurped it from her palms.

"Now that makes me proud!" Gilbert said. "Cupping her hands like a true pioneer in the wilderness!" His cheekbones raised as he laughed and his beard wiggled.

"*Bien sûr, Monsieur LeClerc,*" came Vittorie's response from the creek bed, "and I'll have you know I've peed out of doors more than once, too. But I'll not admit it again. All these weeks walking this trail and being outside all the time make me grateful for a roof, and a bed, and a chamber pot."

She sat back in the tall grass by the stream and leaned onto her elbows. "The blue of that sky is just like the delphiniums in the Southern garden back home," she said. "Or…in France."

Gilbert tipped his hat in her direction. "We're so close, Vi." He jerked his head to the right. "It's just over a few more hills. This mill is what we've been aiming for. We've finally met up with the trail Smuthers and I took in December."

"Why did we take the long way?"

"As narrow as it may seem to you, the trail we took you and the wagons down is much better defined, and without as many perils as the one we took with the longhunter. Stay here. We'll be back."

Just above the tops of the swaying grasses hummed a swarm of flying gnats. Over the treetops she saw light gray clouds. Gilbert and Smuthers ascended two steps to the porch and conversed with three men and a woman who met them. The woman looked about 30. Her shirt and skirt were both the humblest cotton and not very far off from the meanest shade of brown. Fair colored curls framed her face under a blue scarf.

Whatever passed between the parties on the porch left the horses uneasy. The tones of the talk that she could see on the faces and hear when the wind blew in her direction was civil, peaceful, and friendly. But then the stranger's faces gathered a look of concern. Their eyebrows gave a disapproving shade to their faces. They shook their heads. The baby in the woman's arms began to wail. With a parting glance in Vittorie's direction, she removed herself and the child back inside the cabin.

"What is it?" Vittorie asked Gilbert when he returned. "Can we not stay the night?"

"I don't want to."

"Are they not good people?"

He stepped around her to fetch Vignoble's reins from the water. "It's not for me to judge if someone is good or not." He handed the leather straps to Vittorie.

She pursed her lips at his deliberate avoidance of her questions. "*Gilbert.*"

"We're less than a few hours from our land, Vi." He knelt and splashed water over his face and hair. "We're almost home." He glanced at her as he brushed fresh water over America's salty neck.

Smuthers stepped closer to his friend. "We could take their offer and stay the night. We'd all be fresh in the morning."

Gilbert checked the ropes over America's load, and with a hand over the gelding's rump, rounded the back side to check on Vignoble. "We're already late for spring planting," Gilbert said.

America's tail swished the gnats from his legs. Smuthers patted the horses and spoke to them in a low voice. Gilbert took hold of a bridle and turned the horse back toward the woods. Vittorie's hand slipped into his open palm. She stood firm. He turned to face her. Her other hand reached to soothe his tense jaw. His face, and then his shoulders, relaxed at her touch. His blue eyes looked into hers.

She spoke, just above a whisper. "I know you want to be there already," she cooed at him. "I know you wanted to be there all winter long. But look at you. Look at me." She threw her arms wide open. "We *are* here. We have each other." Sincerity washed over her demeanor and she looked around a little. "We are home."

She was beautiful. He looked at her now and his eyes drank her in. She was shaped the way a woman should be. Her hips, waist, and breasts curved in perfect pairings. Her skin, soft to his touch, was smooth and fresh despite the weeks of outdoor weather. Her eyes, green and bright, had an intelligence behind them that no amount of schooling can produce. They shone in laughter and in sadness and met him at every level.

"I love you," he said. "And I want to provide for you with everything in me. But I need to do it with my own two hands. I'm tired of waiting. Tired of relying on strangers or weather or time! I want to move on to the next part of what I know is ahead of us. What I promised you and our families back in France."

"*Je connais…*"

"…And that starts with getting to the land, building a house…." He waved his hand around in the air while the words came to him. "…planting, and we will grow into a home." He kissed her mouth. "That's your job. Mine is to get us there first."

He turned her little hands over in his own. Dirty and calloused from the unusual tasks of the last many days, he kissed her palms. Here she stood, loving him still. Holding nothing but him and dirt, and standing lovelier than ever, stronger, patient, and wise. "Let me show you," was all he managed before he grabbed her, kissed her. When they finally broke apart, they turned to see Smuthers watching them.

Gilbert ran a hand through his straight brown hair and reset the hat on his head. "Are we ready?"

"I've been ready," Smuthers said. "Waitin' on you." He winked at his friends and clicked his tongue at the horses. With a snort and a stomp, they were off.

43

37° 21' 17" N; 85° 52' 25" W. April 1788. American wilderness

Smuthers struck out in front, gun in his left hand, reins of the big bay horse in the other. Tethered by an extra length of rope, Vignoble followed wherever America led. Gilbert shouldered his rifle and held Vittorie's hand. She walked beside him through the dense underbrush. Thorns caught at Gilbert's shirt. When he yanked his arm away, they ripped a long gash.

Vittorie sighed.

"What's the matter?" Gilbert asked.

She poked a finger through the newest hole in his dingy linen sleeve. "Just thinking about how much needs to be done once we get there."

"Here," he said, lifting a loose fold from the mound atop America. He pulled his military coat out, shrugged into it, and fastened the buttons as they walked. "I'll put my coat on so you don't have to look at it. Besides, it's gotten colder." He retrieved hers also and held it up by the shoulders.

She pushed her arms through the sleeves. "Yes, I agree," she said, buttoning buttons. "When the sun drops behind the trees the warmth vanishes with it." She pulled the collar erect.

Dusk settled in and the shadows grew. The horse's feet dropped heavily along the feeble trail through the old forest. They followed Smuthers through thick brambles with dense leaves and around tree trunks rooted there since the foundation of the world. A waxing crescent moon glinted.

Ol' Mac's ears went back and he stopped. Smuthers cocked his gun and turned around with the steady motion of a man comfortable with a firearm. He pointed its barrel in a wide circumference, waiting.

In quick, quiet motions, Gilbert moved Vittorie behind him. His eyes scanned the horizon. His fingers found their familiar places on his rifle. Vittorie held on to him from behind. She felt the hilt of the dagger on his belt.

No one moved, not the people nor the horses. An owl's hoot resounded into the falling night.

Gilbert unknotted Vignoble's tether and brought the horse shoulder to shoulder with America. He put a finger to his lips, moved Vittorie between the two horse's bodies, then ducked under the lead line and retied the animals together near their bridles.

Vittorie put a palm on each of the horse's sides. Her heart raced. Their steady breathing calmed her. She inhaled long and held her breath, then let it out without a sound. Seeing the excess rope hanging before her, she reached out and took hold of it.

Gilbert walked to the back and whistled a bird sound. Hearing the signal, Smuthers urged Ol' Mac forward.

A bird rustled up on Gilbert's left, darting into the air.

Vignoble whinnied. America startled. The two horses crushed Vittorie between them.

In the confusion, Vittorie lost her balance. Her shoulder plunged into cold mud.

Gunshots exploded. Orange sparks spewed around her.

Smuthers fell like a wet shirt to the ground.

Ol' Mac reared up. He landed backwards. The ropes broke. The load burst open. Pans and fabric spilled out. Mac's legs kicked in erratic movements.

From the bushes on her left, human eyes glared at Vittorie, red-rimmed, full of hate. The black and white striped face disappeared into the dark.

Vittorie shrank back between the horses. *"Gilbert!"*

Shouts erupted. Bodies jumped from the woods. Gilbert shot one square in the chest. Vittorie gagged. More thieves joined the attack. Two grabbed Vignoble's and America's reins. The horses spooked. Their front hooves stepped on Vittorie's skirts. Vittorie rolled to her side. Her forearms covered her face.

America's hoof pounded next her head. It scraped her ear. The side of her head burned. She looked up underneath the horse. Fear jolted her to action. She tried to crawl, but her knees and toes caught in her skirts. She snatched the material away from her legs and scrambled to one side, away from stamping hooves.

The thieves beat the horses with sticks. Vignoble ignited into a run. Still attached, America's body jerked when the rope went tight. Distraught whinnies pierced the air.

Vittorie choked as someone pulled her up by the collar. Her head throbbed.

"C'est moi!" Gilbert spoke in a whisper. His arm crushed her breast as he turned her backward to his chest. He wrapped an arm around her and lifted his rifle over her shoulder.

One thief ran straight at Vittorie. His face twisted in a demonic howl. He raised his tomahawk over her. Its feather spun on the shaft.

Gilbert fired another shot. The noise rang in Vittorie's right ear. The tomahawk fell at Vittorie's feet. The thief clutched at his side, shot through the stomach. He stumbled and reached out for Vittorie. One finger on his bloody hand was missing. Vittorie escaped his grasp and watched him land hard. She grabbed hold of Gilbert in the dark.

Gilbert wiped his mouth. "*Courons!*" He pushed her from the road into the forest.

Branches struck her face. Flailing her arms ahead of her, she ran and stumbled. Gilbert held onto her. Rocks moved beneath their feet. He tumbled. She slipped. They picked each other up. Her skirt caught on something. She heard it tear but kept running.

Gilbert found her hand in the dark. "*Arrête!*"

She stopped running and folded in half, hands on her knees, mouth open to breathe. "What…about…Smuthers?"

His hand stayed on her back but his knee hit the ground. "Dead."

Heat rose through her chest and up her neck. Tears splashed from her eyes. A high-pitched cry came from her mouth.

"No!" Gilbert said, covering her mouth. "No! Shh…." He pulled her down to kneel beside him. He kissed her forehead, his hand wrapped her head to his chest. "Shh…*je connais*…." His words came with great effort. "Vittorie, *Amour*…I know."

She wiped the wet from her face and nodded. Heat spiked up her throat again.

"They…." He stood and pulled her to her feet. "…will…" He groaned and placed her hand on something she hadn't noticed before in the dark. "…follow…."

The understanding of his words chilled her. She shivered and looked past him for the demons hunting them like prey in the night. Something crawled over her fingers. She recoiled and shook it off.

"Come," he said. "Climb up." She put her hand out and felt rock. Groping around, it leveled out just below her shoulder. Her boot found a toehold. She pushed down with her palms and pressed her torso up above the ledge. Throwing a leg up, she lay flat against the rock, cheek against the cold.

Gilbert lifted himself behind her. "Aaaghh!" He struggled to climb and tumbled beside her. Black dripped from his mouth but he wiped it away. Clenching his teeth, he grabbed her hand and pointed up. "Must...up...."

Like wounded birds they ran, this way and that, around ever-shrinking boulders and fewer trees, at times crawling, always ascending, heavenward.

The ground flattened out at the summit. Tumbling down to the mossy earth, Gilbert covered her with his body, forcing every word from his mouth. "Build...wall...."

Vittorie stared up at him through watery eyes. Understanding how weak he was by how heavy he laid on her, she nodded.

"Stones...," he said and rolled off her.

In the moonlight, for the first time, she noticed black, inky fluid flooding the front of his jacket and reached to touch it. "You're bleeding!"

"Go...." The word gurgled in his mouth.

She found the rip in her skirt and pulled. A long strip came off in her hand. She pressed it to the pulsing hole in his stomach. "Go!"

She replaced her hand with his own over the wound. First, forcing his fist down over the bleeding, and second, obeying orders. Grabbing in every direction, she gathered stones into a heap. Scooping them up, she rushed back to his side and piled the rocks beside him, sobbing.

His military training returned. "Make...a wall." His command came without emotion. He didn't inspect her pitiful work. He couldn't move for the pain overtaking his body.

Her hands shoveled dirt and rocks up to his side, but it was no wall. It might pass for a small mound, perhaps, or a wind break. Nothing greater. From above the tall treetops, a frigid wind swooped down, scraped along the barren ground, and stole over the edge of the mountain into the darkness far below.

Gilbert's left arm reached for her but flopped to the ground, motionless. She knelt and folded her skirt over his twisted legs. Laying down beside him, she pressed her fingers flat to his stomach. He felt warm and wet. New tears stung her eyes. She bit the inside of her cheek to stop the flow of emotion. Her tongue licked over her lips, but fear had dried her saliva to nothing.

Lifting four fingers, she saw the bubble of blood rise through a round space in his wool coat. Raising her forefinger over the bubbling spot, she grit her teeth, and poked her finger back through the hole in his coat.

He flinched and moaned, but his eyes gazed upward. "Do you…see…our star?"

She hung her head, eyes closed. Her tears overflowed.

"Vi…Look…." His soft tone interrupted her crying.

Her right arm stretched to pillow his head. She kissed his eyebrow and looked up. The night's canvas sparkled with brilliance. High above every other hilltop, nothing obstructed their view.

"Arcturus?" She blinked and nodded, seeing the bright red star. "Yes, the Big Dipper's handle curves to it." His warm cheek reassured her. "I see, my love."

His breath caught. "See how…those…stars…point to…that treeline?"

Her whole hand was soaked in his hot blood. She closed her eyes and bit her cheek harder, nodding. The tears poured out, just like the blood, unstoppable.

"…Goo-d…." His eyes closed. "…that is…way back…to Highbaugh's…Mill." His chest heaved. "…They'll help…. must go… at dawn…light…. Promise…." His words came with measured noises.

"I want to go home with you. Together!" She leaned over his neck and wept, and waited for his agreement. None came.

"Run…with…sun…behind right…shoulder…."

Vittorie's body ached. Her head pounded. She needed sleep. "I'm dead if I leave you."

He let out a long breath.

Her head snapped up from his chest. *"Amour!"*

Something changed. His breathing cleared. "...Remember the...first time...we...touched?"

"Bien sûr." She swung her leg to arrange her skirt to cover more of him. "We were children. Playing on the rocks by the river."

"You were...the most...beautiful...light I...had...ever seen." He paused. "Still...are...." He gurgled. She turned his head to the side. Blood dripped out. "I was...ordering...everyone... around...." His eyes fluttered open.

"As usual..." Her intent at humor only interrupted the rush of grief for a second. She let the river flow. "You slipped..." she said between sobs, "...and hit your head...on the rock." Her head was so heavy she leaned it on him. Her whole body shook.

"To my...stupid...shock. But...you...ran...to me...."

"Oui, je me souviens...I remember, Love." She kissed his temple.

"...your...head...my chest...if you could...hear...heart... beat...." His torso convulsed. His shoulders raised off the ground. Unbearable pain etched his face. "Kept...my eyes...closed...extra...long to...feel...you...near." He struggled to keep his eyes open.

She couldn't tell if he could see her. "And you cried." She spoke louder, as if listening might keep him longer. "So I gave you my handkerchief." She kissed him again.

"I...don't...re...member...that."

She nodded. "Yes, you do. I know you do."

His cheek muscle spasmed and he was silent.

"Gilbert?"

"Live...Vi...."

"No!" She dropped her head down on his chest. *"Ne laisse toi."*

The wind howled. It whipped around the hillside and magnified her cries in every direction.

"Pro…mise…me…" he whispered, "…to…live…*Victoire*."

She put her cheek to his and nodded. "Your face is cold." Her hot tears warmed their skin.

44

In the gray morning light, a ten-point buck stepped to the edge of the tree line. Commanding attention, he blew a noisy blast through his nostrils.

The sound startled Vittorie awake. *"Amour?"* she whispered, lifting her head.

Something moved near the trees. She jerked her arm from under his head and sat up, both hands reaching for the rifle.

The buck turned his back to her. Twisting his strong neck, he looked around at her again.

"C'etait un cerf…." she said.

Gilbert didn't answer. He hadn't moved all night.

She touched his hair, which moved, and his cheek, which didn't. His face looked ashen. Every muscle in her body tensed as she sat numb and still.

The forest groaned. Birds called to each other deep in the woods, and a cold wind swirled around the couple.

Gilbert lay lifeless. Smuthers was dead. The horses were gone. She was alone in the wilds of a vast forest somewhere in an uncharted land. No one expected her. No one would come looking for her. *Except perhaps those who followed.* Uneasiness stirred her and she scanned the monotonous horizon. The tree line Gilbert marked last night came into focus. The blowing of the buck called to her again from inside the woods.

She slid Gilbert's knife out of its sheath with trembling hands. Stretching her eyebrows upward, she blinked tears back in order to see. Holding the knife poised above his chest and starting at his neck, she cut the brass buttons off his jacket. Her fingers locked around the button nearest his wounds. She looked away, sawing at the tangled threads until they gave way. The last button came loose.

She gagged at the rawness of the task, but stuffed the buttons down the collar of her coat. They felt like icicles and punctured what warmth she had left in her chest. Her shoulders shook as she forced herself to lift the front of his wool jacket and reach under his lapel. Her fingers felt linen and pulled it out. Her handkerchief, worn but not bloodied, dangled from her hand. She swiveled to her knees but dropped her forehead to his chest one last time.

The sun shifted in its arc and shafts of sunlight penetrated between the dark tree trunks. Sudden brilliance illuminated every dewdrop, and it appeared as though a million candles simultaneously ignited in homage to his sacrifice.

Vittorie opened her eyes. She looked up expectantly to see the eternal part of him spirited away. The limbs of the trees swayed and the sun warmed her back, but she saw none of it. His corpse lay before her, his blood drying on her hands. A fresh wind from the southwest rustled through the pines, extinguishing the flames. The buck blew twice more and disappeared into the forest.

She kissed Gilbert's hair and stroked his face with the back of her fingers. "*Que Dieu vous garde, mon Amour.*" She let out a long sigh, touched the grain of his coat collar and swallowed hard. Shouldering the gun and forcing herself to leave him, she set her eyes on the tree line and walked into the forest.

✳ ✳ ✳

The woods made way for Vittorie as she wove through its trunks and brambles, picking her path and checking her course by the rising sun over her shoulder. Wet leaves muffled her steps. Unable to check her footing on the other side first, she stepped through a thicket, tripped, and fell, unprepared for the landing. She thrust her hands forward and the barrel of the rifle smacked her in the back of the head. A surprised turkey flew up from its well-hidden nest, beating its awkward wings and careening noisily up and away into the otherwise silent surroundings.

"Aahhh!" Vittorie twisted around to see who may have heard. Her heart beat so loud it felt dangerous, but the forest remained as it was. She crawled to the base of the nearest tree, heaving. When her stomach stopped wrenching, she wiped the bile from her lips and leaned her head back against the wide oak. The sun glinted past a sapling beside her and as if searching her out, its light touched her hands. The dried blood looked more red.

The buck blew again from somewhere in front of her. He appeared at the crest of a narrow ridge and lifted his head.

"I can't do this," Vittorie said out loud, pulling her knees to her chest. The wind whistled from the southeast. Sweat chilled her temples and her lower back. Squinting into the sun, she turned until it lit her right shoulder instead and fixed her eyes forward. The animal leapt further into the woods and Vittorie forced herself to rise and follow him. Her feet ran over the uneven terrain and she came bursting through a row of small bushes. The ground unexpectedly sank half a meter on the other side. Losing her balance, she tumbled again to the ground.

She lay in yesterday's narrow trail, cold manure piled on her right amongst deep hoofprints. She reached out to touch the tracks. A sharp pain in her chest made her gasp as tears flooded her eyes. "No!" she insisted, mashing the palms of her hands into her eyes to push them away. She checked the position of the sun and gathered her courage. Darting and faltering, stopping and starting like a wounded bird determined to survive, she ran northwest up the tangled path.

45

Highbaugh's Mill on Bacon Creek

Candle Bailey, thirty and pregnant, hung wet laundry out to dry. "Air's warming up," she said, pinning a shirt to the twine between two cedar posts.

The sun had topped the trees. Three dogs sprawled on the porch, snoozing. A steady southeasterly breeze blew hard enough to be a nuisance. It twirled both arms of the blouse up and over the clothesline. They smacked, cold and abrupt, against Candle's face and shoulder, but she ignored it and pinned an apron next in line.

Her sister-in-law, Emma Highbaugh, younger and unmarried, hoed the garden patch nearby. A boy, ten years old, goofed around with another hoe.

"Mm-hm," Emma said, dragging mud into straight lines. "The creek war't still crisp this morning." She swatted a bug away from her jaw. "T'isn't yet May."

"…but there's promise of a good'n to come." Candle finished both their thoughts out loud and smiled, feeling the sun warm on her skin.

Emma checked the boy's work. His area of the garden lacked any order. Instead, he used his hoe to hack an earthworm into bits. "Get 'em lines straight, Samuel," she instructed, interrupting his attack. Her eyebrow raised at the boy as she continued hoeing.

Samuel wrinkled his nose at her and drew in his breath for an excuse, but Candle caught his eye and shook her head. The boy's shoulders sloped. "Yes'm," he said.

A little girl of six handed Candle the next wet thing. It dripped icy water into her armpits as she held it high. She wriggled away at the surprise and giggled, dropping the garment next to twins sitting in the spring grass nearby.

"Wring it, first, *kleines* Marie," Candle retrieved it from the ground. She spoke the reminder in a soothing tone and stood up, hand on her back.

"*Ja, Mama,*" Marie said, displaying a missing front tooth.

Two of the dogs picked their heads up. Candle sensed something, too. Her palm rubbed over the next babe growing inside her and she turned to look around. A figure burst out of the woods into their field. The dogs jumped up and barked warnings, hair raised, fangs out.

"Mama!" Samuel yelled. He grabbed the rifle laying on the porch and ran with it to Candle. Wrapping an arm around his mother, he hurried them both toward the porch.

Emma threw down her hoe and scooped up the two little ones. She ran toward the cabin, yelling to Marie, "G'on inside! *Lauf!* Run!"

Careening across the wide field, the person ran, rifle raised, barrel to the sun.

"E'rybody inside!" Candle said. "*Oma!*" she yelled toward the cabin.

The door swung open. Oma Highbaugh poked her head out. Her wrinkled face showed immediate understanding as she ushered the children past her. Taking the rifle from the boy, with a thick accent, she said, "Sam, git 'em dogs!"

The women and Sam took defensive positions. Emma took the pistol off its nail over the mantle. Candle put a finger to her lips and gave the children each a corn cob to chew to quiet them. They nodded back with teary wide eyes. Little Marie sat cross-legged in the corner and put a twin in her lap. Sam grabbed the powder horn. Oma stuck the rifle barrel through a hollow knot in the wall and fired skyward. The noise startled them all and started the babies wailing. The dogs crouched under the long table bench.

Candle hugged one infant to her and assured the others. "Jus' to call Pa, Jake, and Joseph in the west field."

One child rocked the other. The toddlers chewed their cobs. Marie whispered prayers.

Ma peeked through a crack between the door and the wall. She watched the person run closer. "S'in a *kleid*."

Emma and Candle exchanged a look. Emma finished checking the pistol and peered out the corner of the window. "T'is the woman from yesterday." She looked as far north and south as her post allowed. "I see nothing chasin' her," she said, moving to the door.

Oma blocked her daughter's path. *"Nein!"*

"She needs help!" Emma said.

"She's a'runnin' fra som'in' we na know," Oma said.

"Nor how close 'tis behind her," Candle said, also looking out the window and watching the runner. "She'll make it."

46

Inside the tiny hovel of that cabin lay Vittorie's salvation. She didn't stop at the edge of the tree line. She didn't look first in case of danger. No. Danger bereaved her in the dark woods. *What could the light do to her?*

Her hips shifted weight. Her legs thrust the rest of her into the heat and blinding light of the open field. Swaying meadow grass, as high as her thighs, covered her feet and ankles. Her rotating footfalls came faster, in spite of the uneven ground. Her heel connected with the dirt and rolled forward to spring off again from her toes. One leg, then the other, first stretching ahead, then jarring the earth in repetition, rifle gripped in hand. Misjudging a stride, her body jerked forward off balance. She bit her tongue as her bottom jaw snapped up. The certain taste of blood caused her to spit, but she kept looking straight ahead, focused.

"Vous plaît!" She intended to yell, but the dryness of her throat held back the words. She wiped sweat off her forehead and smeared it across her tongue. *"Aidez-moi!"* The salt intensified her thirst. "Help me!"

Not waiting for an invitation, she ran up the steps. The door opened and she raced through. It shut with a scrape across the floor and a slide of wood through metal. She stood swaying and panting in the darkened interior. A dim red glow came from the fire burning in the hearth of the crude log home. The sudden end of her sprint caused her head to pound. She reached up to hold it but collapsed to the floor.

The three women worked as though they'd been trained all their lives for this moment. Perhaps they had. Survival runs deep.

47

37.317754, -85.877364 Big Blue Spring

Beside a fallen oak, deep water trickled through the crevice of a rock and formed a tiny pool. Overflowing this natural pocket, the trickle fell downhill for a crooked ways. There, it assembled into a larger pool between a shaded grove of poplars. Two bearded men crouched low behind a limestone boulder within sight of the natural spring. Muscled, silent, rifles in hand, they watched several figures through the trees.

A haggard group of natives assembled around the trunk and the mouth of the spring. Four finished drinking and stood to wipe their mouths dry as their painted ponies continued to drink from the pool. A fifth native helped the sixth to his feet. The sixth native bled from the gut and hung heavy on his compatriot. Three loaded packhorses stood tied to trees. Two of the natives untied them and brought them to the water.

The leaner of the two bearded men shook his head. "Ain't right, Perry," he whispered. "Two Chickasaw. Two Creek." Bushy white eyebrows shaded his pale blue eyes. "Can't make out the last two."

"What does it mean, Middleton, them all mixed in like that?" the younger one asked. He looked fifteen years junior to Middleton, muscled and eager.

"Rogue. Outcasts. All been kicked outta their own tribes… some reason or 'nother." He squinted into the sun watching the thieves. "Now they've banded up. Raidin' on their own."

"So them's one's nobody can stomach."

Middleton shook his head. "Nope. Not even their mamas."

The understanding of who they'd run across settled on Perry. He sat still a long second, thinking how best to go about this thing.

Middleton spoke first. "I'll shoot and reload quick as I can. You hold your first shot in answer to anything they do."

"Right," Perry said.

Providing the necessary diversion, one packhorse whinnied and pawed a hoof at the air. The natives jerked the reins. They beat his rump with a stick. The horse lunged around in a circle. Middleton sighted down the long barrel, aimed, and squeezed the trigger. His gunshot rang out, startling the quiet woods. Smoke rose from the end of the rifle.

The thieves disbanded and scurried into the forest. The wounded native's helper dropped him and he rolled into the water. In a frenzy, four natives grabbed their painted ponies' reins. The packhorses spun in circles, unsure where to run.

Perry fired and shot the fifth native, who reacted to the hit, but was pulled up alongside one of the first four on his horse to escape. In a flurry of heels and elbows, the thieves left at full gallop, dragging the first two packhorses behind them. They disappeared down the trail.

The two trappers crept to the spring. They checked the area, unsure if they were alone. The remaining packhorse stamped its hoof when Perry took the reins.

Middleton dragged the dead native out of the water. "No sense contaminating a good spring." He took the thief's powder horn and knife. "Someone else didn't like this Creek much neither. Look there." Middleton pointed to a gangrenous hole. It gaped in the native's abdomen, a poultice of herbs and cloth shifted by the drag. He also had a large scar on his arm and only four fingers on one hand.

Perry joined him and squatted to investigate. "Day or two old maybe," he said, inspecting the wound. He rolled the body over to view the exit wound.

Middleton looked at the horse and glanced around. "They weren't expectin' nobody."

"Don't suppose they figgered anyone would come up on 'em."

They stopped to listen. The forest was silent.

"Maybe they made sure of it," Middleton said. "Prolly killed off the poor souls. Looks like whoever they were, they were wealthy," he said, touching one of two rifles strapped to the horse.

"Don't suppose dead men have much need o' these things, do ye?" Perry asked.

"If we ever hear of the rightful owners, we'll just give it back." Middleton dusted off his right hand on his trouser leg and spit in it.

Perry spit. "Rightful owners, give it back."

The two men shook hands, the agreement sealed.

"Course, we don't need to go braggin' about our good fortune neither," Perry added.

Both men faced the loot and grinned. Each dug out a piece or two from underneath the strapped linen cloth.

Perry stood over the dead native on the ground. "We found it. Fair."

The two trappers shook hands again.

48

"Git 'er britchins eff!" Oma's order rang out.

"Stay back!" Emma warned the children as their little bodies huddled together. Every eye watched the strange woman. Blood streaked her clothes and skin.

Vittorie went limp. Oma caught her.

"We need to find her wounds," Emma said, unbuttoning her shirt.

Candle spoke to her children, stern and calm. "Face away."

Seeing the back of four little heads, she helped Oma and Emma strip Vittorie's clothes. They supported her, standing her up to get her skirt and undergarments off, for she had no will of her own. Her appendages moved with no resistance. Golden buttons spilled out onto the plank floor.

"War't's 'at?" asked Oma.

Candle and Emma glanced at the curiosity. They shook their heads, no explanation for it. Emma dropped the last bit of dirty clothing into a heap beside the fireplace and retrieved the gold buttons scattered across the floor. She salvaged them in a wooden bowl and put the bowl on top of the mantle.

Pulling the narrow bench from under the table, Oma slumped Vittorie's body along it and stood guard over her. Laid out before her, the stranger's story was spoken without words, written in smooth skin, delicate fingers, dried blood, and the absence of men. Oma smacked the stranger's pale hand to keep her conscious. When Vittorie's eyelids fluttered and closed over bright green eyes, Oma yelled, "She's *tot!*"

Candle scooped the screaming teapot off the tripod and poured its contents into a wide bowl. Emma snatched rags from a low basket. Checking to make sure none of the little heads were peeking, Candle lifted the last layer of clothes covering the stranger's nakedness.

Oma stuck her head close to the body. "Wah't'ehr?" she asked. "Whar't she bled?"

"Don't see yet," said Candle, letting water drip. It moistened whatever mud or blood covered the stranger's arms. She wiped with tenderness.

The three women dipped clean cloths in the water bowl. Each washed an area of skin, searching out wounds.

For Vittorie, the world went red. Fire sparked and hissed. Someone touched her head, her back. Her arms raised without her help. Her shirt nightdress lifted up and over her head, the last trace of dignity cast away from her.

She lay cold and naked. Gilbert's face flashed in front of her... unseeing eyes. Hands waved in front of her face. Women's hands. Someone spoke. She lay alone. Gilbert was gone. "...*accueil...*"

The three women hurried to cleanse their semi-conscious patient, moving like mother birds over their young. Emma worked her rag over the strange woman's neck and arms. Candle checked the woman's head for wounds. If blood had been coming from the head, there would have been a gash under dried blood. Candle found nothing.

"She's going 'gain," Emma said, as Vittorie's eyes rolled back in her head. She prodded the woman's cheek with her knuckle. "Whate'er this poor creature endured, 'tis far too much."

Oma lifted Vittorie's soft fingertips for display. "She war'n't poor."

Emma rinsed her blood-soaked rag in the muddy bowl. "'Tis e'rywhere," she said.

Candle wiped over the woman's chest. Lifting each breast, she checked for a slice through the skin, for some answer to where so much blood had poured from. "*Es tut mir Leid*," she whispered an apology for such familiarity.

"Whar't you 'pologize?" Oma asked. "She *reich* stranger drop a't'yer step." She let Vittorie's arm go so the knuckles knocked the floor. "Wha'r's she bled?"

Candle looked from Emma to the bloody bowl, to the blood-soaked clothing piled by the hearth. So much blood must have a source. She'd nursed many an orphaned calf and goat, and helped nearby mothers through childbirth. Being a midwife and raised as a pioneer, she knew how to aid life along. But each time she'd looked under a blackened piece of clothing to the flesh beneath, there was no answer for the devastation on the stranger's attire.

Oma watched Vittorie's shivering intensify. "Git 'er t' the fahr."

Candle and Emma heaved the bench nearer the flames. Emma added a log. It caught with the blaze.

"Whar's she bled?" Oma asked Candle again.

Candle squatted to sit on a small stool. She wiped her face with the back of her forearm. "The men will…."

"…home…" Vittorie muttered in French.

Candle leaned over her. "What's she sayin'?"

Emma shook her head in reply.

"*Es is nicht Deutsche*," broke in Oma, her German heritage strong. "I *nicht* fin' na woun'."

Emma washed for a second time with smooth strokes over each area. "Mama, please," she said, poised above the stranger's lips. She tucked her own golden-brown hair behind her ear to listen closer.

Candle reasoned aloud. "She's covered in blood, but where's…."

The answer struck them all at the same time. Oma said it aloud. "Naught no'whar," she said, stiffening.

"It's not hers," Candle said.

Emma didn't look up. "It's not her blood."

Oma nodded agreement.

"The woman with the two men yesterday," Candle thought out loud, "kept to the horses. The shorter man said his wife didn't speak English." Her hand went to her mouth. "They must be…."

"Oh, the sweet dear," Emma sighed.

Oma dug through a trunk against the far wall and returned with a nightgown. They slipped the thin fabric over Vittorie's head. Three angels of the forest now watched over the invalid. Moment by moment, they pieced together the crimes against this innocent and her party.

"Surely the others are somewhere safe in hiding," Emma offered.

Candle looked at the bloody linens in a pile at her feet. Emma cried at what she didn't want to know, what none of them did. War still raged on the frontier and the evidence sought refuge among them. Candle wrapped Vittorie in a child's blanket, for she continued to shiver despite the warmth of the fire. Emma rubbed Vittorie's arm and hummed a little.

49

Familiar voices shouted outside and Oma unbolted the door. The men burst in.

Pa Highbaugh, spry at 58, took charge. "Reload the guns. Bolt the door." Wilderness life showed on his face, chiseled by heritage, baked by the sun, lined by each year of survival. He spoke as he moved. "Only inside work today." Seeing the stranger before his fire, he stopped.

His two sons, Jacob and George, came in behind him. Jacob went to Candle and George bolted the door.

"She's t'only whun," Emma said, her eyes directing her father to the bloody clothes piled on the floor.

Pa looked at the small woman in the blanket laid out on his bench and the clothes set to be burned, and understood. "We'll get a search out."

A little voice rose from the blanketed woman. "*Mon mari est... sur la montagne.*"

All motion ceased. Every eye turned to her.

Vittorie repeated her plea. Her eyes glanced at each of them, checking for understanding, her neck craning to see them in the shadowed room. The words became a whisper and disappeared. Only her lips moved.

Disdain clouded Pa's face. "French."

Emma gave Pa a disapproving look and listened closer. "She don't make sense."

Candle spoke. "French or not, we'll help."

As the patriarch, Pa set the rules, but the desperation in Emma's and Candle's faces made him pause. "*Willkommen in den Franzosen.*" He continued firm directions in a softer voice. "Jake, git the Johnson boys. I'll git Bacon Creek." Taking the reloaded rifle from Jake, he added, "George, git the dogs."

Jake pulled various drawers around the small room and stuffed things into pockets. Oldest of the living Highbaugh children, he had his father's features with kinder eyes. The scar across his bottom lip gave him a natural pout that added interest, especially when he smiled.

Following Pa's orders, the younger brother, George Highbaugh, stepped into the second room of the cabin where the three dogs lay. "Good boy, Lazarus." He patted the hound's muzzle and the dog's brown ears flopped side to side. "You, too, Elke." The spotted female licked his large hand. "*Kommen Sie*, Bernard," he said, patting the thigh of his britches while the old dog roused himself. All three dogs sat up. "There's work ahead." He motioned with his finger and the dogs followed him out into the main room.

Candle folded day-old bread and dried meats into a cloth and handed it to her husband, Jake. "She won't be no trouble."

Jake kissed her cheek. "Not for you'n Emma." He glanced at George who was feeding Elke from his hand.

Candle put her head on his shoulder and lowered her voice. "Will you leave Sam?"

Jake nodded.

Emma handed her younger brother, George, the bloody shirt. "How long'll you be gone?"

"Dunno." He held it out for the dogs' noses. They sniffed under and around for the scent.

Vittorie stood up in front of Pa with shaking legs. The long nightshirt swept her thin ankles. She stared at the lean, hardened German. Raising her left hand to the ceiling, she pointed upward and held that pose, one finger in the air. "*Sur la montagne….*" Her eyes moved, searching his face for recognition.

Trying another communication, Vittorie removed her hand from the air and instead stuck it straight out in front of her. Looking at Emma, she held up the hand with five fingers spread. Then she folded down her forefinger and held the pose for a long moment, searching the woman's face for any recognition. Her legs wobbled underneath her, then swayed and collapsed onto the bench, exhausted.

They were deliberate, odd motions. Their importance remained as foreign to the family as the female in the cabin. With the additional bodies inside, the fire, and the afternoon temperature peaking, sweat shone on them all. None spoke French, nor intended to. Pioneer code declared they should shelter the woman. The Bible on Oma's cabinet demanded it. But her silent clues went unheeded and, in the haste needed to mount a search for the men, went overlooked.

With a little food, enough shot, and good tracking dogs, the men were ready.

Pa nodded at Oma before the men left the cabin. "Inside work till we return."

George and the dogs led out, with Pa following. Jake spoke to his children. "Mind your *mutter.*"

Sam jumped from the bunch. "Kin' I come, Papa? Please?"

Jake jerked his head and Sam approached. "No. Don't know what's out there yet. And…" He looked at Candle's large stomach and back to his oldest boy. Lowering his voice to a fatherly tone, he said, "…I need you to look out for your Oma and the *kinder.*"

Disappointment flooded Sam's face. "I'm always left behind. I ain't a *kinder!*"

Jake frowned and looked down at his son. "I need a man to care for things 'til I come back." He handed Samuel a compass.

The boy took the treasure and looked up. His shoulders lifted with surprise, then fell with shame. "I'm sorry, Papa."

"Respect is earned. I expect you to take care of the family." He held the boy's gaze. "If there's any trouble, get 'em to Gardiner. He'll know what to do."

Samuel looked at his Mom and Aunt Emma, at the stranger, and at his younger brothers and sisters in the corner. The compass gleamed in his hand. He nodded. *"Ja, Papa."*

Jake looked around the room at his family. His eyes softened as he caught Candle's glance. His jaw tensed, the scar pinched, and he closed the door behind him.

Emma knelt before the woman laid out on the bench in front of the fire. "They'll track 'em," she said.

With everything to do, plus new attacks on the frontier, the family went back to work. Candle checked the spindle on her wheel and continued spinning flax. Oma returned to kneading bread. Emma held her post next to Vittorie, both arms around the stranger. She felt the woman's shivers abate, her breathing become even, and then watched her fall asleep.

"Good," Emma said. "There will be enough to remember when you wake. Dear Lord, be with all of us…," She unstuck a sweaty lock of matted brown hair from the woman's cheek. "… please."

❖ ❖ ❖

Early the following morning, Vittorie heard unusual noises. Her eyelids felt like America's hoof had stamped down on them. She couldn't keep them open. So, she listened. People spoke from not far away but she couldn't understand what they said. She had to get home.

Lifting her eyelids took monumental effort. Moving her arm seemed like an impossibility. A threadbare blanket covered some exposed straw in a bedframe. Hay poked her in several places. It smelled like sweat and barn, mixed with a strong canine odor. One stool with a caned seat butted up to the head of the bed. Someone had whittled sticks to narrow cylinders with irregular knobs at the end. Three of those wooden pegs jutted from the wall. A soiled apron, the most feminine fixture in the space, hung by its ties from the last peg.

A horse whinnied and stamped nearby. Low tones of male voices wafted through the wall.

"*Vignoble?*" she said, listening to distinct horse sounds. She roused to consciousness and forced her torso to sit up. She leaned her head against the rounded, rough wood and blinked her eyes into focus. From there, she could see a tiny wooden building and a stream. Beyond that, the mounding, tree-covered hills disappeared into one another.

Through the space between logs, she saw men on horses. More horses than she could count through the chink-hole stood outside. Other men milled about, in between reins and pawing hooves. Most had guns. Many had shovels. None dressed like soldiers.

A new set of clothes lay over the end of the bed. She remembered running. She remembered her feet running up two cabin steps and through an open door. A fire blazed. Her clothes in a pile. Naked.

The wind whistled through the cabin wall on the other side of the bed. Solid beams ran across the ceiling. Her fingers touched the brown coverlet over her. Her body felt like it weighed more than the whole world, like a mountain was crushing her down on the bed. She could no longer will herself to move off of it. She fell back into the unsecured sleep of the bereaved.

50

Sam jumped up from his seat by the window. "Pa and the boys are back!" The squirrel-skin frame he'd been curing clattered to the floor. "There's a whole search party!" His boyish interest in men's business piqued, and he pressed his nose to the bumpy glass.

Everyone's attention turned in the direction of the new information. Emma stopped carding wool and set the work in its white oak basket. Marie stopped rocking the toddlers in their cradle. Candle covered the nursing babe at her breast and rubbed her belly.

Oma slurped a bit of stew from the ladle and set it back in the pot. "Run, Sam," she said after swallowing, "and fetch wat'r."

Sam grabbed two pails and flew out the door. He leaped off the porch with a loud, "Whooha!"

The search party consisted of men from about twenty local families—good farmers and hunters. Pa avoided the bouncing boy but tousled the lad's hair on his way up the steps. After a draught of beer, he wiped his stubbled chin and looked at Emma. "We found the two men, both dead."

The collective response from the women was disheartening.

"Since Jack and I'd spoke with them afore, we knew which man declared a wife and so, finding that body…," he took his hat off and scratched the front of his hairline, "…left it alone for the present. We tracked the whereabouts of the horses we'd seen t'other day with the trio. Traced 'em a little ways. Dogs lost the scent and e'ryone's got work to return to."

"What about the other'n?" Candle asked, sliding the babe to her shoulder for a burp.

"Buried the second fellow, the burlier one." He wiped a broad hand over his shirt. "Some felt it important for the wife to be there when her husband was buried. She ready?"

"No, she's been asleep," Candle said, "with all the grief she's endured."

Pa's cheek twitched. "Best get her dressed. E'rybody's got work waitin'. Took off long enough as 'tis."

❈ ❈ ❈

Pa led the family outside, but once there, nodded for Jake to speak to the group.

Jake thumbed a pocket in his pants and stood up straight, flexing his shoulders a bit. "Pa an' George an' I thank you all for coming. A crisis for one means a crisis for all." He waited as a rumble of agreement murmured through the haggard assembly. "A friend—a good neighbor—is not to be taken for granted. Those who come the furthest and need to return to their fields, we thanks you for your time. The rest…," he paused to let the rustle of those turning their horses toward home subside.

Emma came down the porch steps and handed out napkins tied with colored strips of gingham. "*Kuchen* for ya, Mr. Thompson," she said to one old farmer, "jes' to git you home to Fannie."

Jake continued as Emma showed their appreciation. "The rest, we thank you to stay. His wife'll be out directly. There's water at the creek. Emerson, George's got that strap for ya in the barn."

A thin, young man with a reddish beard nodded. George whirled on his heel into the barn with the wiry fellow following.

"As soon as his woman's ready, we'll bury the Frenchman and serve as protection for the burial party. We all know what a raiding party means. Thank you for taking this time away from your own farms and families." Done speaking, Jake put his worn hat back on his head, walked down the porch, and strode to the barn.

Having given out all the food, Emma hiked her skirt enough to run up the steps into the house. Inside, she said, "Marie, come help me," and entered the room of the sleeping stranger.

The little girl nodded but didn't move. "*Ja*, Aunt Emma."

"*Gehen!*" Candle said. "Go!" She shooed the girl in the direction of the store room. It doubled as Emma and Marie's sleeping quarters, where the woman slept.

"Poor soul," cooed Emma, figuring how to rouse the sleeping woman.

Vittorie's forehead, eyelids, and lips were drawn together in an unnatural pinch. She labored to breathe and uttered long moans.

Marie didn't want to come close. "*Sie klingt wie der Wind durch nackte Bäume, bevor die Blätter sprießen.*" Her small hands clutched at the blanket in two fists.

Emma understood the child's fear. "*Ja*, she does sound like the wind through the autumn trees after the leaves have fallen.'" She removed the coverlet and spoke. "*Fraulein*," she said, "I've got to dress you now. Can you open your eyes? Do it yourself?"

The Frenchwoman swallowed. Her eyes rolled but closed again.

Emma placed her hand on the woman's head. No fever.

Marie did, too. "Her hair is soft since you washed it," she said.

Emma shook the sleeping woman's shoulder. She paused, not wanting to say what must be said. "They've found him, *Fraulein*."

Men chatted. Horses pawed the ground beyond the wall.

The woman's eyes opened. She looked downward. Though her eyes remained open, she didn't move. Emma and Marie ruffled a shirt over her head and stood her up. They lifted her feet into a pair of riding britches and put a skirt over top of them. When they sat her back down on the bed, she flopped sideways.

Emma caught her by the arms and held her steady. "Marie, sit there beside her. She's no strength at all."

"*Ja*," the child said, sidling onto the bed. Her bare feet stuck straight out and she wrapped her arms around the stranger, holding on tight.

After wriggling stockings over the woman's pale toes and soft heels, Emma put her boots back on her and laced them with care. She'd never seen a pair of shoes so fine.

Marie noticed. "'Em's fancy."

Emma smiled at the child and wrinkled her nose in play. Her fingers never slowed their task. "*Ja*."

"Bet no mud's in her toes," she said, wiggling her tiniest parts, "like mine."

"*Nein*." Emma grabbed for her brush, but hesitated. "Candle," she called over her shoulder. "Let me hold her," she said to Marie. "Can you fetch my brush from the ledge?"

The door swung open a crack. Candle appeared, belly, then head, baby on her arm.

"What about her hair?" Emma asked.

"Cover it," said Candle.

"I know that, but I don't know how she likes it underneath."

The baby burped. Candle wiped the mewl from its mouth with a rag. The distraction allowed reflection, but the waiting men demanded haste. "Just…," she said, "…fasten it as you do mine."

Marie returned with Emma's brush. Most of the bristles still held a few strands of Emma's hair, the color of the wheat field before harvest.

"*Danke*," she said, taking the brush. Her high cheekbones pinched as she winced at Candle. "But I don't want to hurt her more."

"You're the most gentle woman I know. Confidence, *schwester*."

Emma brushed the brown curls into submission with long, fluid movements. Pleased, she gathered the thick locks in the curve of one forefinger and thumb. With deft twists in a rising motion, she fastened the cascade up into a swirling bun. Securing the knot with three smooth hair rods, she stepped back to assess. One curl needed tucking, but otherwise, good.

"*Gut*," Candle agreed and nodded. "Marie, *nimm das Baby*."

The cherub child slid from the bed, held out her arms, and carried the baby longways out of the room. "*Ja, Mutter*."

With a woman at each arm, they helped the stranger to stand and moved her to the door. Step by step they led her into the main room and out onto the porch.

51

The day itself was sunny with the afternoon heat at its peak. Swarms of gnats and midges swept *en masse* over the swaying grasses, signs of the uncommon warmth that April.

About a third of the original search party milled about, waiting to glimpse the foreign woman for whom all their lives had been disrupted, waiting to march as protection for the burial party. It could have happened to any one of them, to any one of their wives or children. In homage to this pioneer woman and her loss, they forsook their planting day in effort to serve. Sacrifice, the way of life on the frontier, was in equal parts warm, wild, and uncharted.

When the Highbaugh women bolstered Vittorie up on the crude porch, her Frenchness couldn't be seen in any outstanding way. The clothes she wore fit as much as any of the other women's did. They hung a bit loose but were tied up fine. That was enough. Her hair, pulled back and under Emma's lavender calico cap, attracted no attention. Her boots, however, newer in fashion and age than any seen in these parts, with buttons from toe to calf, distanced her from the onlookers. Before her tongue uttered a syllable, they knew. She was not one of them.

Slung between the burgeoning Candle and wiry Emma, Vittorie appeared small and pale. She never looked up; her eyes continued staring downward at her shoes.

Oma, already on the porch with a second basket of warm kuchen, a plate of salt pork, and shelled nuts for the men, yelled out, "*Komm essen!* Come and eat!"

"Where's the *apfel kuchen,* Berta?" red-bearded Emerson joked.

"T'aint 'n'*apfel* left after yer visit yesteryear, Emerson Jaggers!" Oma said, scowling so her pleasure in his comment didn't show. "Ye'll eat last season's raisins or ye'll starve!"

Laughter washed over the group as Berta Highbaugh, stoic and stern, good and trusted, rebuked the ruddy young man. They lined up as they chuckled. None wanted to miss out.

Candle took a thick slice of kuchen from her mother-in-law before the hungry men devoured it all. She put it where Vittorie could see it. Vittorie ignored the gesture. Limp, she stared past it to the ground.

Sweat strung Sam's hair into black strips across his forehead. "Kin I go with the party, *Mutter? Bitte?*" He bounced up and down at the prospect of riding out with all the men.

Candle's eyebrows gathered over her blue eyes. "How would you be of help?"

Jake stepped up behind the lad. "*Nein,* Samuel. You'll stay."

Sam's expression darkened. He looked away from the stranger and his parents and walked around the side of the cabin.

Jake rested a hand on the back of his wife's neck. "He's got to learn, Candle. Respect. Authority. Honor." He looked at the mass of men, ready to move, scarfing down what could be shared among them as a meal, waiting to bury a man they owned in death though never in life. "He will."

"*Ja,*" said Candle, breathing in deep. "How long til you return?"

He kissed her cheek. "As soon as we're done." He nodded at his sister, Emma, and stooped to kiss little Marie.

Marie wiped her mouth. She held the baked treasure in her delicate hand. A generous amount of honey escaped over its edges. Palm to tongue, she licked the gooey sweetness, twice, assured of not wasting any.

Fed and ready to move, men mounted horses. Horses spun and stamped.

George sat astride his horse and walked the large chestnut beside the porch. "Load her on."

Jake replaced Candle as a support for the woman, and he and Emma moved her toward the edge of the ramshackle porch.

"Wait!" Marie shouted. In her hand, she offered her own piece of kuchen to the stranger.

Vittorie's senses awoke to focus on the young girl in front of her. The child's yellow hair hung around her tiny face in natural ringlets. Her rough-sewn shirt and dress swung above her ankles. The apron she wore had one pocket with the seams sewn askew.

It was the girl, not the morsel, that moved Vittorie. The child's face held such a hope with the extended gift. The gesture carried the offer of friendship and wholeness and simplicity as only those tender years can. To refuse such an offer would be shameful, so Vittorie took the roll from the child who stood there, lifting it up. She took it but couldn't bring herself to eat it.

Unfulfilled, her gift not being enjoyed, the child intervened again. She took Vittorie's arm in her two fleshy hands and flexed the appendage with the sweet treat as close to Vittorie's mouth as she could reach.

Vittorie opened her mouth. Moist cake passed through her downturned lips. She bit and chewed, tasting nothing.

☆☆☆

The whole party, made up of eleven men plus Emma and Vittorie, rode alert. The procession moved slow and steady in the direction of the knob. The horses' ears twitched.

Vittorie rode in front of George on the same horse. His arm kept her from falling off. He bent forward in the saddle to duck under an errant sapling branch. Doing so, he squished into her. "Eh…lean t' th' side," he said when the little woman didn't move.

Emma edged her paint horse up next to her brother's. "She doesn't understand you."

"I've got it, Em." George's baritone voice spoke low. "You needn't be a hen." He held Vittorie tighter around the middle as his horse maneuvered jutting rocks in the path.

Emma ignored his word choice. "She could've rode with me."

Done talking, George kicked his horse in the ribs. "She's fine, Em. Leave it be."

They followed the overgrown path between Highbaugh's Mill and the Green River. With the equinox past, spring shoots had erupted from every seed, bulb and branch. Earth reawakened with a green yawn, making the well-traveled trail more difficult to assess. The route dwindled through canebrakes and around bri-ar thickets, then widened again beneath a complete tree canopy content to grow unhindered since the dawn of time. The pioneers journeyed east.

Emma looked past George and cried, nodding. Her bottom lip disappeared under her thin top lip but she rode in silence.

"Cryin' don't help," George said. He dug his kerchief from his shirt pocket and flicked it to his sister.

Emma caught it and blew her nose. The sound made the two nearest riders stare.

George walked his horse beside her, then hung his head and looked at her sideways. "It don't."

She wiped her eyes and dug into her nose with the old rag, soaking up all extra moisture as best as she could. She managed a weak, "She has no one," before fresh tears fell over her delicate cheekbones.

With a shake of his brown hair and determination on his lips, George corrected her. "No, she has you." He waited until Emma caught his eye. "She has *you*."

Emma blew and wiped and nodded. "And you," she said.

George kept his arm around Vittorie's waist to steady her but looked past the animal's ears to the ascent ahead. "Hold with your knees, Em, and tight to the mane. Keep your shoulders to one side and give the horse his head." He watched Emma's grip through the long black and white hair tighten. "He'll find the way, but he may hurdle a few boulders on the way up, so keep your nose off his neck."

Emma's knees squeezed and her shoulder's shifted, but she said, "I know."

$$52$$

Names from pioneer folk were practical, likening the bump in the landscape to a knot on the trunk of a tree or a handle for a door. Neighbors spoke languages from their heritage and common words morphed into new ones. The High German word for hill, *knopf,* lost and gained characteristics. "Knob" became a multipurpose word describing one thing which juts out from another and becomes its own entity. "Hills" were renamed "knobs."

When it came to seeds and solstices, hoeing and shearing, George Highbaugh stood out in no particular way. A simple fellow, farming was what he knew, so farming is what he did. He wore the same britches Monday to Monday, then switched to his spare pair. He had a third pair for important meetings, when he could get away from the fields to go. He wore those to gatherings, funerals, or when the circuit preachers rode through and Candle and Emma shamed him into attendance. The third pair looked just like the first two, but cleaner.

He wore his spare pair on account of the digging ahead.

When he tore one of his weekly britches beyond repair it would get cut up into rags or remade for his nephews or nieces into something for them or the farm. Then, his special occasion pair would become his weekly pair, and it put off going to meeting until the girls could manage to sew him another good pair.

This suited him fine. He'd rather be in the woods or in his fields, spade or gun in his hand, didn't matter. Either one felt right. He could find his way in the wilderness well enough, but preferred the familiar comfort of his own roof, own food, and own porch. He wasn't afraid of much, though he didn't seek out adventure. What he had was good enough and what he didn't have he didn't need. That was the way of it.

It felt odd to have a strange woman this close to him. Her hair smelled like fresh oil and honey, the familiar scent of his sisters' best soap. It caught him off guard. He shook off the encroaching emotion with tabulation. The practical thing to do was to have her saddle with him. Emma was too small to manage her and, if he was honest, Jake was a better shot in the woods. So, Jake needing free hands and Emma being unable and Candle staying back with the children left him the best choice.

The party picked its way up the southeast side of the knob in silence.

It was hard not to think about the body before him. He decided to catalogue the facts as they rode together. Brown hair. Long. He'd seen that when she lay on the bench. Not like dark, rich soil, more like freshly plowed after harvest, when the ground is spent from a season of giving itself to the plants. Her skin was pale and smooth, like the first shoots of onion grass in the spring, their fleshy bulbs hidden just underneath. He couldn't tell the color of her eyes as she was in front of him, but he could see her eyelashes were longer than Emma's. They curled up at the ends. Neither Emma's nor Candle's did that. While Emma was shorter than Candle, and thinner, it was still a wonder to him how small the woman before him really was. The top of her head came to where his lips were. He could see over her clear and free, which was helpful. Everything about her seemed fragile.

For instance, it became necessary early on in their trip to keep a steady hand on her for she was unable—or unwilling, he did not know which—to stay straight in the saddle. It annoyed him that she'd be so careless.

While steadying her, he noticed his hand stretched the whole distance between her hip bone and the bottom of her rib cage, between his small finger and his thumb, without intentionally trying. *Could that be possible?* He applied slightly more pressure, just for a moment, and realized it was true.

Once, she laid her head back on his chest and leaned against him. He moved her forward with his free hand, separating himself from her.

Emma was by his side in an instant. "What's the matter?"

"Nothin'."

Jake slowed pace and walked his black gelding beside George. "Kin you manage her the rest of the way?"

George nodded. He leaned himself and the stranger forward as the chestnut lurched upward.

Cresting the top of the knob, Emma dismounted at George's side. He urged his horse nearer the other riders. Emma walked alongside, her horse trailing by its reins in her hand.

Dismounting a grieving, foreign stranger became the next task. The woman's body, loose the whole ride, felt heavier, clumsier. Emma braced the woman's weight. Jake leaned beside her to catch the falling body. George helped her to descend by portions rather than in a heap. Emma spoke to her as she did to the heifers when they calved—in calm, encouraging tones. While the woman leaned hard on Emma, she stood on her own two feet and walked by herself.

George slid out of his saddle, adjusted its girth, and walked the horse a few paces to a tall birch tree. Wrapping the reins around it, he patted the horse's shoulder.

"Sun's going down," Jake said. He stood behind George, holding a shovel. "I'm ready to get back to Candle and the young'uns."

Behind him, the sound of shovels slicing earth began and he turned to look. Emma knelt with the woman. George didn't even know her, or the man—her husband—who lay dead. The battle occurred without him, its victims strewn inside his territory, one dead in body, one dead in soul, and one sister marked by the reality of it. He wouldn't joke grief away. One thing a farmer knows: Everything has its season, and this was sorrow's. He wouldn't shy away. That was wrong for a man and for the occasion. No. He'd do what the others did, what his sister and the fragile, foreign woman were doing. Be still. Acknowledge. Grieve.

He moved closer to the working shovels and the sound of sobbing and stood still. He saw the dead man was older, but not by much. The cause of death occurred in his chest and stomach as the blood-soaked, white military jacket proved.

He found Jake and stood just behind him. Being taller, he could still see the proceedings.

The purple-gray shade of the deceased man's face verified the hours he'd lain lifeless. Just like an animal killed in the woods, flies swarmed. Maggots twisted in the nostrils and wiggled over his eyelashes. The height of the hillside may have slowed the elements, but nature retrieves her own.

"I'd rather face a rifle," George whispered to his brother, "if it came to that…"

"…than be butchered by a hatchet," Jake said, finishing the thought. "He protected his own." He glanced at the sloping terrain and stretching pine trees. "Led her up here to make their stand…."

With that, the scene came into a different view for George. He'd care for the widow. He'd been angry at the Frenchman for leaving this woman his responsibility. Watching the maggots writhe, he accepted her as a task laid before him. A duty, added to the endless doings of a farmer and a pioneer, to be undertaken with skill and regimen. Unafraid of work, he leaned onto his right boot to shift his weight. He knelt behind Emma and the woman, stretched a hand across both their shoulders as Erving Miller took the preacher's part and began to sing in a low, mellow tone.

53

Once Vittorie saw the shovels and Gilbert's body, she became aware and alert. Kneeling with Emma beside his body, she whispered to him in French, stroking his hair and placing her handkerchief between his chest and hand.

The watching sun continued its westerly orbit over the mountain. Lengthy shadows, in morbid hues of plums and purples, stretched like fingers to touch the crowd.

Jack signaled to Emma and Erving. They'd finished digging the rectangle tomb in the ground. Emma squeezed Vittorie's arm, steeling encouragement for what was to come.

Men's voices, bassy and cavernous, filled the air. The song echoed off the pebbles of the barren hilltop plateau. It vibrated across the space between the knobs, far away and all around, resounding back off-tempo.

Vittorie never stopped her motions nor her muttering. When the singing began, her head turned in the direction of the sound for an instant, then back to the tender caretaking of her love. Her eyes never left him. She tucked his hair and straightened his collar. She touched his stiff cheek, lavender forehead, and eyebrow. She smoothed his sleeve and cupped her hands over his own.

She tried to lay down next to him, but Emma and George stopped her. Strong forearms reached underneath him, twisting his body upward for its final descent. Living souls with solemn voices crowded her. They gripped his corpse. The singing crescendoed in her ears.

One tear dripped down Vittorie's cheek and rolled off her chin. It disappeared into the shredded threads of her husband's jacket. She put her cheek against Gilbert's hair for a last, long minute.

They shifted him away from her. Arms held her back.

Permission given to the grave diggers, they proceeded with their task. Four men lowered his body. Gilbert moved into his everlasting rest deep below the tree line.

The singing stopped except for a single tenor voice. He sang, high and alone.

Vittorie sat motionless. The first bunch of dirt sprayed across his hands, forever clutching her handkerchief.

54

For the Highbaughs, everything went back to how it had been before. After breakfast but still before dawn the following morning, the men went out to the fields. The women finished up with the children, cleared the dishes, and went to their chores.

The sky was robin's egg blue by the time Sam grabbed up the wrapped-wire basket, jumped off the steps, and headed for the henhouse. Marie followed him, the bottoms of her feet scratched and dirty.

"Hold your sister's hand, Samuel," Candle said from the porch. "Don't rile that rooster. And leave the broody hens be!" She plunged her hands deep into the bucket of soapy water but watched her two oldest turn the corner.

Their laughter echoed behind them, the carefree sound of children becoming themselves.

Candle took a step to follow them but didn't. Instead, she gathered another garment from the pile of yesterday's clothes and draped it over the bucket of creek water.

Emma leaned on the slender stick of her broom, distracted by three dark forms circling overhead. "Go away," she said, watching the black buzzards ride the air.

"I've a hope at least half them eggs'll hatch out hens," Candle said, still musing about her chickens. She pressed the edge of her palm across the top of her abdomen, just under her milk-ripe bosoms. Water soaked the front of her apron, tied high to allow for the ever-growing babe inside her.

Emma held the broom with both hands and resumed her work. "I'll do that when I finish here, Candle." She swept the inside dirt out across the threshold. "What can you do sitting down today?"

"I want yesterday washed away," Candle said, grinding George's spare pair over the washboard ribs.

Emma stopped sweeping. "*Ja.*" She laid a hand over the curved top of the broom handle and rested the other on her hip. Her chin lowered and her tone smoothed out like a yard of fresh fabric. "Your ankles look thick to me."

Candle paused midway down the metal board. "*Ja*, I know."

Emma brushed dust in billowing curls out to the grass. "Please…please take care. We can't lose you."

Oma walked out barefoot, her arms full of bawling babies. "I'm goin' pickin!" she said. She passed the toddler and infant to Emma and went back into the smokey cabin.

"Mutter!" Emma said, "Not today, please! Not after…." She jostled the infants in her arms and leaned backward to keep from knocking their heads together. "Stay close to the house."

When Oma walked out again, she held an empty basket and a rifle. Oma took one toddler from Emma and set the child on the porch. When she stood up, escaping smoke circled her knees. "I'll be jes' a *ruthe* inside the wood thar'…na far."

Oma's self-proclaimed arguments went only one way—hers. She talked while she walked, not intending for anyone to stop her. Wild gray hairs blew out from under her cap in the wind. She ambled straight-backed as she could toward the closest patch of pine and cedar trees. "Ef'n we don't fin' more ginger root, all us stomach's'll be achin' wi' *nein* a remedy! Babes *weinen*! Dogs…." German verbage spewed out behind her into the blustery morning.

Her deep blue shirt disappeared into the shadows before either woman on the porch spoke.

Emma bounced the hungry babies. She kissed the precious heads and pressed her cheek against them. "Ohhh, now," she cooed. "Wind's come down the chimney."

"*Konnte sein* I'll stir the fire and then I could spin," Candle said.

"*Gut!* Leave the wash. I can finish."

Candle left the wet trousers. "I'll take *ye*." She pulled the youngest babe from Emma and unpinned her blouse for the child to nurse. "And," she looked through the open door, into the shadowed space, "how long should we let a grieving stranger be? She's not woken once since coming down the knob. Has she?"

"No. Let her sleep today," Emma replied. "Go and sit. I'll check on her when I come in."

Candle honored the wise words, for the babes if not for herself. But before she gave in fully, she turned around on the stoop. "Did Gardiner say anything to you yesterday?"

"He did."

"And?"

Her eyes darted around, uncomfortable repeating his compliment. "He said…he said the woman 'could'n'a come to a more perfect place' to be cared for."

Candle's full lips widened into a grin. "To be cared for by *ye*." Her puffy eyelids squinted. "*Ja,* he's sweet on ye." Heaving a dramatic sigh, she went inside. "You'd do well for him."

Entering the house just enough to fix the broom inside on its peg, Emma gave her sister-in-law a stern look. "*Sitzen!*" she said with both brows arched high. She reemerged with the drooling toddler and a wooden spoon. "There!" she said, setting the child on the porch. Handing the little boy the utensil, she stood up beside the wash basin. "Chew that, little teeth."

The boy's tear-streaked faces looked up at her, spoon in mouth, pudgy fingers. Quiet wouldn't last long. Emma glanced across the field toward the forest and took up the washing. Humming to hide her fears, her hands doused the pant legs again in the bucket of cold water. She scrubbed them hard against the rusting washboard, hard enough to bore a hole. Finally finished, her wrinkled red fingers wrung them out.

The toddler waved his arms. The spoon flew further than he could reach, and he began to blubber. The other twin cried because he heard the first one. Emma dropped the pants on top of more wet clothes in a wide basket. "*Kum*," she said to the tot. Her attention went again to the edge of the field, in the direction of Oma's blue shirt and rifle. "We'll hang the wash and check for bugs in the garden mounds."

55

Emma pounded a heavy oak hammer into a trough of soapy water. The irrythmic banging of wood on wood echoed off May's blossoming hills and hollers. "I've almost finished fulling this last woven piece, Candle. That'll make thirty-seven I'll have for you to sell." She let the hammer splash and wiped the sweat off her face with her sleeve. "Oh, and I checked—you've enough tenter hooks to hang them all but not enough dye."

Candle rocked on the porch, baby asleep in her lap. She quilted a small blanket. "We'll get some next time…." Her sentence stopped short as she touched her belly and let out a long breath.

The wind sucked the side of Emma's faint yellow dress to her thighs and she looked to the horizon. Storm clouds assembled over the treetops at the farthest southern point she could see. She watched them grow and gain speed.

Not letting the weather ruin their snack, both geldings munched sweet spring grasses next to the cabin. The wind humbled the field greens into obeisance and whipped the horses' manes in wild circles as they stretched their necks lower for food.

Marie pounded the handle on the butter churn to make the cream clump. The wooden hull wiggled as the dasher beat the cow's milk inside. Its round base tapped the porch's uneven floorboards. "Papa's back!" she said in her cheery, little-girl tone.

A wagon's wheels turned over the uneven ground. The men had returned. George drove the oxen and Pa jostled next to him on the buckboard. Jake and Sam's legs dangled over the side. Their shoulders slumped. All four bodies swayed with the ruts and rocks in the path.

"Whoooaa," George said, slowing the team.

Pa, Jake and Sam hopped off the level bed. Pa tossed four dead geese toward the porch and adjusted his trousers. Jake unhitched the oxen.

"Saw the rain, did ye?" Emma asked.

"*Ja,*" said Pa. "We got the roof framin' done." His pale blue eyes assessed the storm.

"Wonderful!" Candle said. Eight months of pregnancy plumped her face and neck. Her dimples showed when she smiled. "We kin dress the ducks tomorrow, Pa. Emma made *leberknodel* and we've shelled nuts for supper tonight."

Marie stopped churning and yelled, "I helped with the nuts!"

The Highbaugh men worked like heaven assigned them the tasks; Sam was in training. Jake and Sam each took a handle and pulled the two-man misery whip off the wagon bed. The boy struggled under the awkwardness of the pliable blade. Pa threw rope bundles over his shoulder and gathered the thwart saw and draw knives. George backed the wagon loaded with seed sacks and building tools through the double barn door.

Jake called to Candle on the porch. "Wouldn't help to get the wagon wheels stuck in the mud," he said, "not with the smell of rye bread baking."

Candle's dimples deepened as she stitched.

As Jake and Sam walked together, the long saw caught the wind. Sam tripped, trying to hold his end steady.

"Get up," Jake told his son. "Put your shoulder 'gainst the wind."

Sam picked up his end of the tool as the wind caught the saw again. It pulled him sideways until he did what his father said. Tipping his head of straight hair into the wind like a bull, he leaned his shoulder in the direction of the wind. Jake walked backward into the large barn. Sam, still fighting the other end of the saw, trailed behind.

"Those clouds look like *Zweibruckers* pulling with all their might!" Emma said, eyeing the oncoming clouds.

"What's that?" asked Marie, eager to rest.

"The most beautiful horses I'd ever seen," Emma replied, enjoying the memory. "Marie, *beende das* and *kum* inside. Sam kin bring the churn with him when he comes."

Happy to give her arms a break, Marie spun around. "Kin I run see Papa?"

Emma glanced at Candle, still in the ornate rocker, pulling thread through a small quilt. Candle's eyes crinkled at the girl's sweetness. *"Ja, lauf!"*

Marie stepped down the porch, knees high till the bottom, and ran to find Jake. He emerged from the shadow of the gray building and pulled both sides of the double doors shut. Marie reached him just as he bent over to fix the rod in the ground that kept them closed, hugged his neck, and rose with him as he stood upright.

George had turned out the sandy-colored oxen. Grazing inside the fence just past the barn doors, they plucked light tan reeds with their mouths and chewed, heads down.

Oma scooped up the toddlers from the grass. "War't time t'be inside," she said.

Candle didn't hear. She shook out the quilt over the side of the rocker. The excellence of its repeating dove and tulip motif meant nothing to her at the moment. Her attention was elsewhere.

Vittorie stood in the doorframe of the cabin, more inside than out. One hand rested on the jamb; the other hid behind her back. The effect of sleeping in her clothes, borrowed clothes in particular, gave her an overall rumpled look. Her hair matched; it bunched to the right side with no distinguishable curls. Great waves of her mane coursed in conflicting directions. On the left side, her cheek and forehead were rosy, a distinct line etched from ear to nose. She removed one hand from the doorjamb and used it to shield her eyes as she stood there, roused from interior darkness, watching the family.

"Guten morgen," Candle said, folding the blanket and making the rocker stop.

A sheet of rain advanced on the diagonal from the southwest. The sheer magnitude of liquid descending drenched the trees, evident by the rising cloud of humidity in its wake. The horizon darkened to a dull pewter and the first drops sounded on the roof.

Vittorie walked down off the porch, entranced by the impending deluge. Without warning, she bolted into a run.

It shocked them all. For a moment no one moved nor did anything to stop her. George reacted first. He swung himself bareback onto the chestnut horse.

"Wait!" cried Emma. She was at his side with an outstretched arm. When George rode her way, she jumped, and he pulled her up behind him.

Halfway back from the barn, Jake saw the double riders and looked to Candle for interpretation.

"She's running!" Candle said, pointing a finger in the direction of the creek.

Jake set Marie down and patted her bottom in the direction of the cabin. He sprinted back to the barn and unbolted the rusted rod. "Sam, stay with your *Mutter*!" he yelled to the confused lad.

George and Emma passed the cabin at a canter.

Jake had the black horse trotting in the same direction by the time Pa could reach the barn. He caught the rifle Pa tossed up to him and followed the others at a full gallop.

The wind, aroused to such a fury, drowned out everything but its own sound. Bacon Creek swelled with the hard rain.

Vittorie didn't feel the chilly water as she rushed in up to her knees. She didn't feel the rain splashing on her skin, dousing her clothes and hair. She didn't hear the riders skidding to a stop on the pebbles behind her.

She focused on her hands holding Gilbert's knife. *How deep is a heart?*

Lightning cut a crooked path from heaven to earth. The atmosphere convulsed in a deafening thunderclap.

The double-edged blade looked sharp enough. *How many ribs would feel it slicing through?* She tested it against the bulb of her left thumb. Crimson blood flowed. *Could she push it through her chest without stopping?*

She held the ribbed handle of the dagger. Its blade edged into the valley of her chest.

The gurgling stream bubbled and danced. It licked her dress and pulled her legs downstream, indifferent. Rain washed tears over her jawline and down her neck, wrapping her in its tempest. She opened her lips and yelled, but the wind sucked the sound away, her primal cry voided. Lightning lit the territory in three rapid flashes. Thunder rolled. Her anger uncorked.

The storm's intensity from the southwest had muffled the horse's approach, but it had carried the French woman's shouting to them. George dismounted. The beast turned its rump to the rain.

In the flooding creek, they saw the woman stumble. She splashed but regained her footing and sliced at the air with her knife. Spitting and furious, she shouted into the wind, arms back, shoulders forward, lunging into a fight. She jabbed her knife up, up, wielding the weapon like an assailant intending doom.

Weather and woman collided, an unmatched fury of wrath. Jumping, slashing, she hollered her heartache and screamed out her sorrows. Lightning cracked down to the ground, a jagged testament of force.

Emma slid down beside George, shocked at the display. She grabbed his arm to stop him when he moved to intervene. "Let's let her grieve! Pain's got to get out." With both palms pressed against his chest, her slight frame blocked his path. The sentence choked in her throat. "Mebbe this is the only way she knows how!"

He disagreed. "No need for hollerin' like that."

Jake slowed his horse from a gallop and dismounted to join them.

In the blinding rain and deafening wind, the siblings remained near the horses, several paces from the creek bed. They watched, ready.

Evident rage was carried back to them on ferocious wind gusts. One blew so abruptly George caught Emma from falling over. They moved to the broad side of the horses, using the animals as a windbreak.

George hated inaction. His irritation at being sidelined showed. "Well, if the grief's too much," he said, leaning forward over Emma, "or if she's left her mind, she nor you'll be safe near her knife." His mouth wrinkled down at his little sister.

Another fierce torrent blew the despondent woman in the creek off balance. She fell sideways into the stream, tumbled some before she resurfaced, and crawled back onto shore. There she paused, on hands and knees, some intensity knocked out of her, and pulled her bare ankles out of the swirling currents. Still holding the knife, she sat down facing away from them and rocked back and forth.

Emma tried to go to her but George held her back. "Not you."

The rain beat down on them. Clouds swept northeast. Lightning flickered through their bellows. Instead of a threat, the knife became a conversation piece between woman and storm. Pointing it for emphasis, she jabbed it away from her body and beseeched the imposing sky. The mighty wind blew, forceful and robust. It knocked her backward. Her hands covered her face. Her high-pitched temper dwindled and, instead, her body became racked by long, guttural cries. She shrieked and wailed, and the storm spoke to her in kind.

When the knife fell loose of her grip, she reached to pick up some pebbles around her feet. These she hurled over the water, handful after handful, aimed at the heavens above. She rose but had trouble standing. Her knees buckled and she fell. Scraping a few rocks into a heap, she lay down and stretched one arm over the rigid pile, muttering. A new wave of shaking racked her.

"What's she doing?" George asked, staring at the woman on the ground. The edges of his hat dripped water across his folded arms.

"Whatever it is," Jake said, squinting into the raindrops, "she oughtn't be taking it out on the Almighty." He ducked his head and wiped the wet down his angled nose.

The siblings stayed still. Rain and wind pelted their work clothes. All of them were soaked through.

"Maybe," Emma offered, her intuition acute, "she speaks to Him because no one else understands." She wanted to be near the woman, but turned back to her brothers. "Think of it. Bandits attacked; her man is dead; her friend is dead. She doesn't speak German. What recourse does she have?" Her nostrils flared and reddened with emotion, helpless in the suffering of another. "She's alone. There is no one to avenge her. No target for vengeance. And even if there was," her hazel eyes widened, full of tears, "how does a woman fight such things?"

Her brothers listened and observed the two women—one lost in grief, the other in sympathy—sob out their hearts, words insufficient. Emma's body shook. George's thick fingers touched her arm. She was freezing.

Soaked and spent, the last stones dropped from the grieving woman's grasp. The brothers took that as the signal they'd been waiting for. The storm had calmed, or at least, the eye had arrived.

"I'll go," Jake said. He passed the horse tie and the knife from his own sheath to George and took steps toward the foreigner. "I understand," he said, bending over while he moved closer. He crouched low, hands raised, in order to make himself less intimidating. Rainwater dripped from the point of his elbows. "I understand," he repeated, close enough to make out her features.

Her eyes were closed, her lips a frigid blue color. She shivered worse than Emma. Picking up her knife from the outside of the makeshift rock pile, he secured it in his own sheath. Putting his knee to the ground, he half-crawled to where she would be able to see him. "*Fraulein?*" he said, keeping his voice calm.

She opened her eyes, blinked out the falling rain, and looked from him to the rushing creek. Sitting up, she stared at the hills. Her hands came up to brace her head over her knees, and when they did, a trickle of red coursed down one cheek. Her breathing came in heavy exhales, like a mare in labor. She turned her chin toward him, but her eyes looked down.

He reached toward her, palm up. "Let's get you home."

She leaned her heavy head into his offered hand and wept. Jake wrapped his other arm around her shoulder and let her. Solemn witnesses, Emma and George stood holding the horse ties and each other, soaked to the bone.

They had to get back to the others, to the safety of the cabin. Above the storm, the stars shifted, the day complete. Jake picked Vittorie up under her armpits and raised her to her feet. She whimpered and clung to him as a child would and dropped her head to his chest, as though she had no strength for anything else. Jake walked her back to the others, comforting her like one of his children. Out of instinct, he patted her back.

Emma rushed over. Jake traded places with her, taking the black gelding from George, and the four of them began the soggy walk home.

56

As good mothers did, Candle had an instinctive awareness of where her children were and how they were doing. The new week's laundry washed, she clipped it to the line with straight pegs. The work list never ended on a farm, especially in June for the farmer's wife, but she allowed this time of hanging the laundry to take longer than it should. The newborn slept in the basket by her feet, but she had another reason. She was watching.

Down by the creek bed, Vittorie had been sitting in the same place since morning. She'd taken up a dry spot secluded by towering canes.

In the field behind Candle, little Marie chased a family of turkeys. Their necks bobbed back and forth as they tried to escape her. She enjoyed the game and whooped with laughter as she ran. "Look, *Mutter*, I'm going to catch a turkey and keep it with the hens!"

"Really?" Used to her daughter's ideas, Candle added, "Your father will want to eat it."

Marie stopped, hands on her hips, and stuck out her bottom lip. "*Nein!* He'll be my pet! Catherine has a pet rabbit and her Pa lets her keep it because she named it Hopper. She said you can't eat something that has a name."

"Is that so?"

"*Ja.* I'll name him Ben Franklin."

"Ben Franklin!" Candle said, dimples appearing. "Why Ben Franklin?"

"I heard Papa and Uncle George talking. Every time they said it, their eyebrows got very crooked…" She scrunched her eyebrows together with two of her tiny fingers. "…like this! So, I know it's someone 'portant." She skipped closer to Candle. "Papa can't eat someone 'portant."

Candle hid her enjoyment of her daughter's reasoning skills behind a piece of linen. "You'd better catch him first!"

Realizing she'd forgotten that part, the little girl ran after the last remaining fowl who had not disappeared into the woods. In a laborious display of flight, the heavy bird rose and flew back to the others past the edge of the field. Disappointed, Marie plucked a tall stalk of field grass and ran the feathery head through her fingertips. She tucked herself in between Candle's skirts and gathered strength from being near her mother. She played while Candle continued her work, half-hugging and half-pulling at her mother's legs.

"Did flowers help when our baby went to heaven?" Marie asked. She held on tight to her mother's apron and looked up, blue eyes blinking.

Candle startled and dropped a clothespin. "What, child?" she asked, reaching for another wet diaper to hang up.

"When *das* baby died last year?" Marie asked, retrieving the wooden pin and handing it back.

"*Danke schon.*"

The wind gusted. Its rippled effect blew linens and pants into thin, curvy versions of themselves. This way and that, the unseen force played with the items pinned on the line.

Marie tugged, wanting to know. "Why did we leave the flowers at the creek?"

"No more questions now," Candle said. "Hand me the blouse… there. And a new pin." She held her hand out flat. "Wring the blouse first."

Multiple instructions and drawing the girl back into housework played their part. After several minutes of "helping," little Marie took her curiosity in a new direction. Candle watched as the wind pushed the little girl's blonde hair and tan dress down to the creek. Living by the water, she'd taught the children early its value and danger. She didn't fear for her daughter and the coursing water. But there was something. She watched the golden head travel between swaying grasses, waiting to see where she stopped.

Marie skipped to a low part of the stream. She came to the waters' edge, deciding whether to let the icy water touch her bare feet, when she saw the pretty lady sitting by herself. Picking her way along the tiny, cold rocks, careful not to step on too many of the sharp ones, she tiptoed over to where the lady sat. Marie waited a minute, but she didn't move. One dirt-filled fingernail went to her lips with a new idea. Marie's wispy brows furrowed and she tipped her ear closer to a shoulder. "Did your baby go away, too?" she asked.

Hearing a voice, Vittorie swiveled to see where it came from. She shielded her eyes from the eastern sun. Her cheeks glistened with tears. *"Bonjour?"* she said, seeing the child.

The pair faced each other. Marie stared, questions mounting behind her curled eyelashes. Vittorie gazed back. When the girl stepped closer, Vittorie watched her without moving. Though a child of six, she stood higher than the sitting woman. They were close enough to touch, but they stayed as they were and observed each other instead.

Marie bent down so close to Vittorie's knees that the bottom of her simple dress brushed them in the wind. She leaned forward and, seeing wet on the woman's face, reached out to dry it. She wiped Vittorie's cheeks with the palm of her hand, smearing a bit of dirt in its place. "This is where Mama cried when she lost our baby, too," Marie said. She bent her knees again to check her work. The cheeks were dry, so she found Vittorie's hand and tumbled into a seated spot beside her. Patting twice, she exhaled an extra big breath and settled into finding what the woman thought was so interesting about the faraway knobs.

Seated cross-legged beside the woman, Marie leaned so near that warmth emanated from one to the other. The chill of the wind stopped on that side.

The weight of the child's hand felt soft and genuine, and Vittorie accepted it.

The girl looked out across the water just as the woman did, then moved her other hand in front of Vittorie's face. It held tiny flowers in lavender and yellow, dried leaves, and a bunch of skinny green grass.

For the second time, Vittorie looked into the girl's eyes.

"*Fur dich*," the little girl said, pointing at Vittorie.

Vittorie blinked at the fistful of broken flowers and took the offered gift. Their fingers touched in the exchange.

Marie's eyebrows wrinkled when she saw the fresh tears, and her fingers squeezed tighter as her new friend cried. She rested her head on Vittorie's arm.

From up the hillside behind them, Candle called, "Marie!"

Vittorie's expression changed when she heard the name. The little girl let go of her hand and ran home.

At supper, Marie saw the pretty lady look at her across the table. She didn't look at anybody else. She didn't eat anything either. Not that Marie blamed her. It was asparagus soup and brown bread.

57

Now in the third month of Vittorie's lack of appetite, Emma took action. With the family stretched around the long table, the basket of warm *brotchen* rolls passed around. Everyone reached for their share except Vittorie. She took nothing.

Sitting next to Vittorie, Emma chose a small strip of jerky, three asparagus stalks, a carrot, and one small potato and placed them on Vittorie's plate. She drizzled sorghum on an especially robust *brotchen* and added that, too.

The basket and platters passed person to person around the family table. Pewterware clinked on plates. George took the last *brotchen* and Jake snatched the jerky. Pa folded half the final length of asparagus over with his fork and stuck the juicy vegetable in his mouth.

Sam watched with jealous eyes as his hope of seconds dwindled to precious little. He glared at Vittorie's food and then at her. His nose pinched into wrinkles. "You know she won't eat it!" he shouted at Emma. "Why do you waste it on her?"

"Samuel!" Jake's voice echoed off the wood walls.

The chatter of mealtime ceased. A log moved in the fire. It hissed an orange eruption in the hearth and fell silent.

The boy didn't dare cross his father. He stared at his plate, ears beet red. Everyone looked at Samuel, then to Vittorie, the target of his hot temper. The poor, hungry boy couldn't help it. Tears ran down his face. Tonight's food would once again go to the dogs.

Whether invoked by the hearty smells rising from the comforting food before her, seeing Sam cry, or every person's eyes looking at her, Vittorie did something she had done only twice since coming into the house. She spoke. In a most gentle voice, she said, *"Je vous remercie pour votre hospitalité."* Her green eyes looked up into the dim light. "Thank you, but I'll be going home as soon as I can."

The fire reflected in the pupils surrounding her. The dogs perked their ears.

When she caught eyes with little Marie, the corners of Vittorie's mouth uncurled from the distraught expression she'd worn every day since her wretched arrival and leveled out into a mauve line while she looked at the little girl. *"Je te remercie."*

Any child of France could have understood this simple French phrase, meaning "I thank you." But at this table, which was Vittorie's whole world at the moment, only German or English was spoken. The fact she'd said anything at all shocked them.

The next person Vittorie's eyes connected with was Pa. Not one to be still, he sucked pork salt off his thumb and cut his knife through the fresh creamed butter in the dish. Smearing a healthy dose of the delicious fat on the last bite of his roll, he said, "Well, let's see what we kin fin' ye to do."

58

Day after day, the wheel of life on the Highbaugh farm turned. The whole group, minus Candle and the children who stayed at the cabin, readied themselves to work in the day's planting field.

George lifted his nose and sniffed the air. The front of his tan hair ruffled in the breeze. "Rain's comin' again."

Emma looked at the cows lying down in the pasture. "*Ja*, looks like it." She wrapped the linen strip around Vittorie's left palm for the third time. "*Gut?*"

Vittorie nodded. "*Oui.* Good."

Acting out her question, Emma pinched the fleshy part of her own thumb muscle and shook her head. "*Nein* too tight?" Poking her index finger under the bandage around Vittorie's hand, she seemed pleased to answer her own question. "*Nein.*" The point of her chin intensified as she smiled.

Vittorie communicated with Emma using the few English words she could remember. "Thank you."

Emma tied the two ends into a simple knot above Vittorie's knuckles. With a pat and a nod, she signaled her work complete.

Vittorie smiled to be kind and nodded back. Turning both wrapped palms up, she clenched her fists to untighten the strips a bit. The blisters underneath made her wince so she relaxed her hands.

Emma joined the others in the new field. Pa, Oma, and Jake hoed up the ground in a square as big as two graves. The blades against the rocks in the soil made an irregular chopping sound.

After she heard the digging noises, Vittorie couldn't get any closer. By the time she realized she felt sick, her mouth was full of what her stomach pumped upwards. Vomit spewed over the seed bag. A few chunks of something splashed on her boot. Involuntary gut wrenchings continued, gag after gag. When the heaving subsided, she wiped her mouth on her hands, soiling Emma's fresh wrappings. Embarrassed and weak, she took a few steps nearer the group, unsure what to do next.

Most of the family kept working. Emma said something to the others and walked back to help Vittorie. She motioned for Vittorie to follow her in the direction of the creek.

"Je suis désolé," Vittorie said, full of apology. "I'm wrong." She undid her biled hand wrappings. They slapped against the sides of her dress as she walked so she held her arms out to make them stop.

Emma marched ahead unphased. *"Komme mit mir…*Come!" Pausing to wait until Vittorie caught up, she patted her on the shoulder as they walked together down the last rise to the creek.

The wind cooled the perspiration across Vittorie's forehead like a fresh towel. Her stomach felt more settled and she knelt at the water's edge.

Emma wiped her cheek on her sleeve and pointed up at the lumpy white clouds. *"Schoner tag,"* she said. "Pretty day." The apples of her fine cheeks smoothed out from her smile. "My man died at Yorktown." The words propelled themselves out of her mouth. She looked straight ahead. "Pa said wait to marry till he returned but he didn't…return."

Cold creek water rinsed over Vittorie's hands and she splashed some into her mouth. She spit and filled her mouth to spit again. In between unwrapping her hands and washing, she watched the thin German woman fall silent. Forgetting about her blisters, Vittorie brushed her wet hands against her skirt. Pain stung her palms, so she blew on them and changed to waving her hands dry. "Yorktown?"

"*Ja*," Emma nodded. She folded her arms across her chest and looked deep into the water. "Yes." Their blend of languages seemed to be working.

"*Avec General* George Washington?" Vittorie's eyebrows lifted.

"Yes, General Washington. They want to make him leader of the whole new country." She nosed a rock from the soil with the toe of her worn shoe and tapped it into the water. "Peter—my man—could shoot an acorn off the fencepost better'n either of my brothers…." She smiled but her voice trailed off and her fingers raced to brush something from beneath her eyes. "I'll probably go to Nolin Station after Candle has *das* baby."

The creek ran higher than usual with the recent rains, and they stood there, together, listening to its inevitable flow. An orange and black monarch twirled up from a patch of yellow goldenrod and continued on its quest while the sun baked the rocks at their feet. Emma maneuvered up the bank of the creek urging Vittorie to follow.

The ladies returned to the field with less of a burden between them, more understanding. Neither hurried, wanting to keep the precious bloom of communication open.

"*Mon marier…*my man…*s'appelle…Gilbert,*" Vittorie said. She gasped saying the name, not having spoken it out loud since his death to anyone.

The women's feet trudged down the grasses and their knees punched against the inside of their dresses as they walked, their steps falling together for a few paces as the moment threaded between them. Waving field stems reached for the sun. Each blade whistled upright, eager for its beams to touch them. The day's heat settled in. Cicadas hummed. Woodpeckers pecked holes, and the staccato of beaks punctuated the whirring insect world.

Three neat rows appeared where the rest of the family worked. Pa and George saw the women coming. Pa stopped long enough to gauge their pace, then returned to separating the ground into groupings. George lingered in his looking.

Sam came running as fast as a rabbit through the garden beds and across the new field. He raced up to Jake and doubled over, out of breath. "Ma says there's a party…dozen or so…an' t' come quick!"

Jake lifted his hat to cool the sweat on his dark hair. "Tell her I'm comin'…George too!"

Sam's dark mop of hair had already turned and started the run back. In acknowledgement, one hand raised high in the air. Bare feet flipped up behind him over the red soil.

Pa waved his boys off. "Go on. We'll get the tools and follow. No need Candle gettin' flustered with so big a crowd."

"Thanks, Pa," Jake said. He kept the hoe in one broad hand, gathered his rifle from a seeded bed nearby, and began a steady lope in Sam's direction.

"*Ja,* an' me!" Oma said, a flurry of elbows and knees headed to the cabin.

"I'm comin'," George said. He looked at Emma and Vittorie. "Finish out this row. Kin you carry that seed sack between you?"

"They'll manage," said Pa. "Go on. I'll finish here." Taking the hoe from George, he handed it to Vittorie. "All the way to the end." He pointed to the end of the furrow beside the one they worked on. "Emma, you sow the seed. I don't trust her to know how to space 'em."

Emma gathered her apron into a pouch and Pa poured kernels in until her arm muscles flexed. "Good, Pa, whoa! The furrow's not that long yet."

Pa looked at her, the furrow, and Vittorie. "You've got plenty to do here. 'Specially as I don't know what sort of men are at the Mill. You girls stay here till me or your brothers come back for ya."

Emma nodded when Pa turned his back. She watched his boots leave imprints in the rusted dirt as he went. "How're your hands?" she asked Vittorie.

59

May 21, 1788 - South Carolina's Ratification of the U.S. Constitution. Charleston, South Carolina

The Great Hall at the Exchange and Customs House buzzed with energy. Representatives from every corner of South Carolina had arrived. Salty sea air wafted through the open, second-story windows. The curtains billowed inland, befitting a port city.

Packed in with the rest of the colony's delegates, Charles Cotesworth Pinckney brushed the folded cuffs of his indigo-dyed coat. He gauged his entry. "Exports are a surer mode of determining the productive wealth of a country than any other…"

The crowd parted, hearing a new speaker. Recognizing C.C., they allowed him to pass.

"…particularly when these products are in great demand in foreign countries." He strode to the center of the floor space. "Oxford and Charleston have taught me that." He posed in front of one of the room's two grand fireplace mantels. "While I disagree with some elements proposed today, I do agree with the old adage that…," his dark, lawyer eyes surveyed the room. "…'honesty is the best policy.' In reviewing such of the European states as we are best acquainted with, we may assert with truth that there is but one among the most important which confirms to its citizens their civil liberties, or provides for the securities of private rights, as if it had been fated that we should be the first perfectly free people the world had ever seen."

Agreement rustled through the 222 men. Some sat at tables. Most stood around the rectangular periphery of the room to catch the evening breezes.

C.C. continued. "We have been taught here to believe that full power of right belongs to the people; that it flows immediately from them and is delegated to their officers for the public good; that our rulers are the servants of the people, amenable to their will, and created for their use. How different are the governments of Europe! There the people are the servants and subjects of their rulers; their merit and talents have little or no influence; all the honors and offices of government are swallowed up by birth, by fortune, or by rank."

A murmur rustled through the gathering. Someone shouted, "Ninety-six, what do you say?"

Every neck in the room flounced with a jabot frill craned toward the interruption. Torsoes swiveled to hear the suggested representative from Abbyville.

His response came from the rear of the room. "I've listened with eager attention to all the arguments in favor of the Constitution," said James Lincoln, drawing his hand over the point of his chin, "though the more I hear, the more I'm persuaded of its evil tendency." He stayed in his place as he spoke to the delegates. "What does this proposed Constitution do? It changes, totally changes, the form of your present government. From a well-digested, well-formed democratic, you are at once rushing into an aristocratic government. What have you been contending for these ten years past?"

A strong voice shouted, "Liberty!"

The word repeated around the room. "Liberty! Liberty!"

"Liberty! What is liberty?" asked James Lincoln. The farmer turned judge waited to answer. "The power of governing yourselves." The gravity of the decisions at hand hung heavy on his cheeks. "If you adopt this Constitution have you this power? No. You put it into the hands of a set of men who live one thousand miles from you." His arm swept northward as though flinging something away.

Backcountry Anti-Federalist heads nodded. Heels stomped wooden floorboards.

"It is with pride that I repeat," said C. C., interjecting with a louder voice and drawing attention back to himself, "as old and experienced as they are, they, those faraway kingdoms, are indebted to us for light and refinement." The cupid's bow of his curved lips shone with sweat. "Had the American Revolution not happened, would Ireland enjoy her present rights of commerce and legislation?"

He turned to face John Rutledge, Sr., from Ireland, and held his gaze. The respected attorney mouthed 'no' in response.

"Would the subjects of the Emperor in the Netherlands have presumed to contend for, and ultimately secure, the privileges they demanded? Would the parliaments of France have resisted the edicts of their monarch, and justified in a language that will do honor to the freest people?" He whirled his coattails for emphasis. Catching the intentional gaze of every lowcountry representative, he continued. "Nay, I may add, would a becoming sense of liberty, and of the rights of mankind, have so generally pervaded that kingdom, had not their knowledge of America led them to the investigation?" The soldier turned statesman allowed his tone to cool. His pure white hair curled with the humidity around his stiff collar. "Undoubtedly not. Let it be therefore our boast that we have already taught some of the oldest and wisest nations how to explore their rights as men; and let it be our prayer that the effects of the revolution never cease to operate until they have unshackled all the nations that have firmness to resist the fetters of despotism. Without a precedent, and with the experience of but a few years, were the Convention called upon to form a system for a people differing from all others we are acquainted with. By God, we can accomplish it."

60

Highbaugh's Mill on Bacon Creek

Summer unfurled her glory. The sopping rains of early spring hadn't hindered the season and the wheat fields sprouted their yield.

Vittorie worked behind Emma in the row. She wore a cross-body satchel; its strap rubbed her neck above the collar in the same spot, now raw. Her bandaged hand gripped a fistful of wheat stems. Golden kernels clustered in the heads near her thumb. Bending low, she swung the scythe at the bottom of the stalk. She cut the paltry bunch from the earth and stuffed it in the open bag hanging below her hip.

George sang baritone a few rows ahead with the men. His back bent over the burgeoning harvest as he worked. Jake carried the base notes and kept pace with Pa. Pa's scythe kept rhythm. He never sang.

"If you turn your blade, it will slice them off cleaner," Emma said. She twisted her wrist to show Vittorie the correct angle of the slender half-moon tool. She demonstrated on a new bunch of wheat. Her obvious action needed no interpretation.

"Yes," Vittorie said, blinking the sting of sweat from her eyes. A wasp circled her head and she ducked away from it. The sudden movement jerked her torso in the opposite direction of the daily harvesting and she winced, arching her lower back. The ache intensified and she massaged it with her free hand.

Pa watched her but kept his mouth shut. His scythe never missed a beat.

By the time the sun rose high over the tops of the Eastern treeline, Vittorie's satchel was nowhere close to full, her shortcomings obvious against seasoned farmers in volume of manual labor. Emma emptied hers into the wagon for the third time since breakfast. No one kept count of Pa, George, or Jake.

Harvesting speed varied by tune. The normal harvesting cadence allowed Pa four cutting swings. With a backswing between each slice, that came to eight beats. Slow songs eased the swing speed for the others, but Pa always cut as fast, changing his efforts to double-time when the tune was slow.

Vittorie brushed a fly from her nose and listened, captivated. Her side muscles hurt when she breathed so she just stood there and kept massaging them.

Pa scowled at her non-progress. "Emma!" he said, stopping his work. Both women looked in his direction. The craggy wrinkles in his chin tensed under his straw hat. "Teach her again!"

Emma swung the scythe low. "Like so...." She cut the wheat near the base and held the grains in her other hand for tension.

Vittorie tried. Her grains wouldn't bundle. She couldn't keep them taut. The heavy scythe, awkward in her tiny palm, may as well have been an ax and her task to carve a fine bedpost. She swung against the scraggly handful of stalks. Her blade caught several nearby stalks and mutilated the surrounding wheat.

She turned her back but glanced in Pa's direction, eager to avoid further comment. He'd gone back to keeping rhythm and she exhaled a grateful breath. "No good," she whispered to

Emma, shoulders pinched. "I no can." Her blistered fingers let the rugged tool fall to the ground. "Vittorie house. Want help Candle *avec* baby."

Emma glanced at Pa and rushed nearer to Vittorie. "You can do this." She picked up the cracked handle and held it out.

Wrinkles appeared in Vittorie's forehead. "*Ne jamais...*," she started, frustrated. The correct English didn't come to her. "I no can."

"Did you never farm before, in France?"

"*En France?*"

Emma stopped working. The wind blew the light dress against her thin body. She nodded, her hazel eyes full of encouragement as she waited for an answer.

The question stirred deep in Vittorie. Her knees wobbled. She shrank down to a seated crumple on the ground. "*En France, ma....my...family....*" Her mouth filled with saliva and she looked away, unable to continue for the emotion.

"Well," Emma said, eager to comfort, "you've done enough for today. Come." She ducked her head under the strap of her satchel and removed it from her neck. "Let's go find Candle." Her pink lips widened to a smile and she knelt down beside her friend. "Perhaps you're more suited to inside work."

Vittorie wiped her face on her sleeve. "*Vignoble,*" she said. "Mm...." She pretended to pluck a small thing with two fingers, then made a crushing motion with her fingers against her palm. "Zhh...." This sound accompanied the act of her pouring something out with one hand. She cupped her other hand into the letter 'C' and sipped from the rim of it.

"Oh! You're drinking it!" Emma said. "Your family makes something to drink?"

Vittorie again pretended to pluck a grape. This time she mimed the motion from the head of a wheat stalk.

"They make beer!"

Vittorie's nose wrinkled. *"Non…pas de tout…*no beer." She stood up and remade the plucking motion. *"Vignoble."* But this time she popped one imaginary grape into her mouth and pretended to chew before repeating the grape crushing and pouring it into a glass. She raised her eyebrows, curtsied low, and pretended a second sip from her thumb.

"Oh, wine! They make wine?" Recognition lit Emma's brownish-green eyes. "Like a vineyard! Wine!"

*"Oui! Vignoble…*ah…wy-een." Vittorie emphasized the odd letter sounds to remember her friend's word.

"No wonder…you've never used a scythe in your life! Come on," Emma said, leaving her scythe and satchel in the row and removing Vittorie's for her. "To the house with you!" She linked an arm through Vittorie's.

Being understood brought relief. As the two walked in the direction of the cabin, Vittorie squeezed Emma's arm in a gentle expression of gratitude.

Emma giggled. "I hope you're a terrible cook," she teased. "George is having a hard enough time over you as it is!"

Hearing the familiar name, Vittorie glanced to see the man working the rows behind her. Her eyes caught his. George's song continued even as he looked away from her and went back to his work.

61

The July night air couldn't cool the sun-baked soil fast enough, and George wasn't helping. A makeshift forge, erected at the far corner of the barn, blazed away. He compressed the two handles of the bellows together, and the rush of air fed crimson coals. He watched their intensity grow, satisfied with his solitary task this evening. A bent bridle lay on the anvil, awaiting a beating. The right side of his shirt hung open, ripped under his ribs. He shook his head at the tear. "Emma won't be pleased," he said out loud.

The chestnut horse stretched his neck over the stall wall and pawed his white sock against the dirt floor.

"*Ja.*" George spoke as though the animal understood. "I know."

Vittorie's boots scuffed along the path from the house in the moonlight. She waited under the barn's open doorway before entering. "*George?*" she asked, pronouncing the softer 'g' sounds in his name with her French.

Her presence caught him off guard. He tried not to look too long in her direction. "*Ja?*" Fire reflected in his eyes. He picked up the bridle with elongated tongs and thrust it into the burning heat.

His task at the licking flame drew her nearer to observe more. She moved close enough to touch the bellows at his elbow and stopped. They stood transfixed as the fire roared and retreated.

The wind whistled and the smoke answered by curling toward the exit where it escaped into the star-filled night.

Instead of blundering through a failed communication, Vittorie held out the kitchen tongs Candle sent her with. "Candle send me." One of the sides had melted into an irregular curve and they would no longer clasp.

He allowed himself a moment to notice the curve of her shirt, how she didn't quite fit in his sister's clothes. The borrowed cap on top of her head came up to his chest. He looked from the brilliant green of her eyes to the housewife's tool in her hand. Pulling the bridle from the coals, he laid it on the anvil and smashed at it. Sparks flew as he pounded the metal into its precise shape. The sound of hammer against iron reverberated inside the wooden space, muffled in part by the hay loft and munching livestock.

His arms relaxed and his body weight shifted toward her. "Will you stay?"

Her lips parted without answer. She stepped backward, confused. "*Comment?*" Her forehead wrinkled while she worked to comprehend.

"*Ja*, I want more of you…to know you…." He glanced out the door to where the moon cast a shadow of the forest onto the fields. "…But my life is here. Under the knob. Under his mountain."

The last word overshadowed her interest in his work. She understood. "*La montagne.*"

His blacksmithing gloves and tools anchored his arms in place though his body moved in her direction. "Live here…with me." He bent his head down toward her lips.

"George!" Pa switched the blade of grass from one side of his mouth to the other. His shadow hulked from the doorway to the gravel at Vittorie's feet.

Vittorie dropped the house tongs on the ground and rushed past the old man. George looked at his father and went back to work.

"Awful hot workin' that fire," Pa said.

George wiped sweat from his nose onto his sleeve. He looked at his father but said nothing.

Pa tried another approach. "That's the first shirt you've ruined this season and it's gettin' nigh August. I'd say that's pretty good."

George punished the bridle with a good stoke in the coals and another beating on the anvil. "I gotta fix this 'fore tomorrow, Pa, or we'll not get enough wheat in before the rain."

Pa nodded. Firelight reddened his pale skin. "Ay-yeh." He nodded and returned the grass to his mouth to chew. Turning to leave, he stopped and put his hand on the heavy timber door. "I'll 'ave the girls set ye out another shirt," His boots crunched the parched earth path back to the cabin.

Without looking up, George nodded. His hammering continued.

Satisfied, Pa ambled over to the house, up the two front steps to where the family sat, and with one look back, went inside.

Seeing Pa leave the barn, Candle headed off in that direction. She found her younger brother-in-law as Pa had left him. He continued as if she wasn't there for several minutes, then stopped and tossed his tools back on the bench.

"What?" he said, not wanting to listen.

"Give her time," Candle said in her quiet voice. "It's too soon for her."

He yanked off his gloves and ran a rough hand over his head. "I know."

Two faces, one black and one chestnut, appeared over the side of the stall and Candle stroked their noses. "You're a good man, George."

With a sniff and a stretch, George picked up his gloves and went back to his work, this time more for the bridle's sake than his own.

62

The gibbous moon put on a show that begged for an audience. All the Highbaughs except George congregated on the porch. A whippoorwill sang as the full cloak of sundown enveloped the woods around them.

A light breeze blew in the soft night and each soul rested in the forgiveness a late summer evening brings. Marie and the younger children slept in a row on the plank boards like cooked sausages in a skillet. Candle nursed her recently arrived baby in the rocker while Oma snored in her chair. Pa smoked his pipe. Jake gazed upwards, letting the leather he'd been working on all evening hang loose in his hands. Emma knit while her eyes looked into the night. Vittorie darned socks and pretended not to notice Pa's careful gaze. In truth, everyone awake pretended not to notice Pa's sour stare in the Frenchwoman's direction.

Pa removed the pipe from under his gnarled top lip and knocked it empty against the porch post. "T'morrow, we go to Bacon Creek," he said, turning everyone's attention elsewhere. Stomping up the steps and into the house, he cut the reverie of all, signaling the return to what was.

By the time the sun crested the tree tops the next morning, bare toes dangled off all sides of the wagon between the turning wheels. Vittorie sat next to Emma in a plump tuft of fresh hay with little Marie in her lap. She turned the girl's natural curls into a braid that crowned the child's head. Up front, George hunched over the reins he held, while Pa and Jake kept a lookout, rifles in hand. Oma tatted a delicate edge on a new doily. Sam pet Lazarus, whose panting tongue bobbed lopsided over two sharp bottom teeth.

Pa twisted around from the buckboard to look behind. "I'm going t' buy Albert's mare, Berta."

Oma's fingers moved the thin needles over and under as she glanced up at him. "No more'n twelve linsey-woolsey an' two bags a seed." The stern look she used for bargaining pinched her face together. "Candle n'aye'll 'ave two doz'n aft'r 'at and we'll need 'em to last out t' season," she said, light brown eyes roving over their oldest children and the babies asleep on the straw. Rethinking her trust in Pa to get the order right she said, "*Nein*, George, I'll go."

Used to such marital decision-making, George Sr. rearranged himself forward again and settled in for the rest of the ride.

"I brought my hides to sell, too," Sam said.

"Fine work you've done," Jake replied, his pride in the boy evident.

Sam's chest swelled. He flexed his toes over the edge. "Thanks, Paw."

George turned the team to the right onto a better travelled road. The path widened so the overgrown August grasses didn't brush Sam's feet anymore. The summer's heat had baked the red soil dry, and the wheels jolted over the ruts left by former wagons.

Little Marie popped up from her cozy spot and peered ahead between her Uncle George and Grandpa's shoulders. "I hope I get a sweet," she whispered in George's ear. Her secret told, she leaned back and waited to see the reaction. Childish anticipation rosied her cheeks and the tip of her tongue poked through her lips.

"A sweet?" George said, a chuckle in his cavernous chest. "Y'hear that, Jake? Yer daughter aims to eat a sweet."

Jake smiled at Marie and leaned forward to look around Pa as he responded. "Yep, that's what an uncle's coins are for!"

"Is that right?" George said, his lips spreading into a grin.

Marie kissed the back of George's shirt in anticipation. "*Danke schon, Onkel* George!"

The horse's pulled their load around the last maple grove, and the small settlement along Bacon Creek come into view.

Watchmen hailed the incoming family from a turret above the gate. Jake waved and whistled a signal, and the doors swung wide. Life and activity bustled at the settlement. A man and a horse dragged felled logs by a rope down the center road. Homesteads stood close together, not in a row, with gardens dotted around.

"How come this called?" Vittorie asked.

George turned around at the sound of her voice, but Emma answered. "Bacon Creek."

"Why is 'Bay-kon Crick'?" Vittorie sounded out the new letter blends.

"*How* it came to be called the Bacon Creek Settlement," Emma said, correcting Vittorie's language, "I really don't know." Her hazel eyes scanned the row of public buildings and busy people. "People from different places find themselves living among each other here as neighbors and friends."

Candle unlatched the nursing babe and raised the tiny, wrapped bundle to her shoulder for its burp. "If the Germans had settled it, it would've been named something with a 'burg' at the end of it."

The wagon lurched, and out of instinct, Emma put her hand on Candle to steady her. "Or if the English, then 'town' or 'ton'," she said. "French settlements often end in 'ville'."

Vittorie's face brightened in recognition. "*Oui, en France, c'est...* name... '*ville*'." When she pronounced the word, it had no 'l' sound, just the letter 'v' broke into two syllables.

Emma tried the French pronounciation. "Vee-yuh."

"*Oui!*" Vittorie looked pleased. "Good!"

Pa straightened up. "It's easy to find one's people in the new world if one knows how to understand, how to read, and how to be useful. Be back here in an hour."

The wagon slowed to a stop under a stretching oak limb. Everyone piled off. The men and Sam unloaded sacks, hides, and woven fabric rolls. Emma, Candle, and Oma gathered the children and headed for a building with letters on the window.

Vittorie lagged behind, unsure what was expected of her. It was the first time she'd been anywhere else in America beside the mill without Gilbert. The expanse of dirt, pebbles, and grass widened between her and the family stepping into the shop. Her eyesight blackened a little around the edges, like devilish fingers interrupting her vision. A hollowness in her chest and a dry mouth paralyzed her. Her legs wouldn't move. As Emma's silhouette disappeared behind Candle and Oma through the doorway, Vittorie felt forgotten, her insignificance acute.

A black crow cawed in the branch above her and the wind shook the five-pointed leaves. Three bare-chested men stepped out of the woods. Legs covered with leather and bare feet, they moved toward the wagon and the shop without making a sound. One of them carried a smooth stick.

Memory overtook Vittorie, found its center in the pit of her gut, and before she could get control, she threw up in the shade beyond the back wagon wheel. Hiding there, awaiting the sounds of a fight, she heard nothing unchanged from before. A pair of birds flitted above her, unconcerned about the acts she feared would follow. When no commotion arose, she dared a peek over the wagon bed.

The three bare-chested men stood talking to three men wearing shirts. Their faces were not painted, and their arms hung loose and calm. She realized the men wearing shirts were Jake, George, and a stranger wearing a shopkeeper's apron. The brothers deposited the last of a dozen large sacks of wheat grains and flour on the shop's back porch. The shopkeeper handed them a new bridle and some other items in return. The bare-chested men received something from the white-aproned man also.

Vittorie steadied herself against the wagon. Seeing the simple exchange struck her. She reached into her pouch and pulled out twelve golden buttons. They were the only evidence of her life before this—a lifetime of prayer, a hero husband—a different life in a separate world.

Next, she pulled Gilbert's knife out of her pouch. Its sharp blade lay cool and shiny in her palm. She slid it back into its deceptive hiding place a little too hard. It sliced a long gash in her skirt pouch and she felt it slip down her leg. She pulled up her hem revealing her boots and ankles where the knife stuck gently into the earth. No one noticed.

She looked again at the men. Shirted or not, they all had a knife. Bound around a leg or a waist, the men housed their knives not in a pocket made of cloth, but in a long, triangular leather piece fit to the shape and length of each man's weapon.

That's what she needed. Buttons in one hand and knife in the other, she crept backward, out of view, and ran to the shop.

✳ ✳ ✳

The ride home began with a lurch. Pa drove the team in silence. George and Jake rode beside him, rifles in hand.

"Sam, let your *Onkel* be," Candle reprimanded. "You've chewed his ear since the coins clinked in your pouch. Now, shush." She turned her attention back to nursing the baby and settled the twins with Oma.

"Look!" Emma whispered, folding back paper wrappings to show off her treasure. "I bought a pair of hairpins. See, they've bits of shell in them." Her pretty face glowed with delight, but she bit her bottom lip and held her excitement back.

"I saw you in the shop, Vittorie," Candle said. Her yellow hair caught the early afternoon sun and each cheek boasted a dimple as she smiled. "Did you find something for yourself?" Shortening the sentence to be better understood, she asked, "Something for you?"

Vittorie twisted a bit to show her new leather sheath. It housed Gilbert's knife at her side.

"Oh!" Whatever question circled Candle's mind never found its way out of her mouth. "Why, it fits just right, doesn't it?" she said instead. "And such a fine color, too, like mahogany."

Everyone looked at Vittorie and the practical men's accessory she'd acquired.

"Very fine color," Emma said.

Oma nodded. "Good for killin' varmints come col' wedder in th' autumn."

Vittorie understood less than what her smile affirmed. The family paid her attention and the wagon's wheels rolled homeward over the bumpy highway. Once their interest faded, her left hand slipped into the pocket on her other side and toyed with Gilbert's remaining buttons. Only eight left.

63

Late August heat dried the walls in the cabin and the cracks grew wider as the logs shrank from lack of moisture. Long before the sun was high, sweat dripped down Vittorie's lower back while she dressed. She pressed a hand against her shirt to stop the perspiration's trail and finished tying the apron behind her. Twisting up her hair and securing it with Emma's old hairpins, she wrapped a clean rag over her head and tied it in back under her hairline.

She stopped at the tarnished silver tray serving as a mirror on the wall. Its cracks and age showed a woman, nothing more. She leaned in close to catch a glimpse of green about the eyes. The line of the jaw matched hers from years ago. She turned so her profile reflected and looked as hard left as possible. Impossible as it was to make out many details, she touched the scrolled edge of the mirror and marched into her day.

Catching, killing, and cleaning a chicken called for no frills. Emma and Candle could accomplish it with ease, but the twins were teething and one had colic. The task today fell to her. Tiptoeing past the sleeping babes in the main room, she unlatched the front door and went outside.

Tromping down both steps, her boots made the weathered boards groan. Fog obscured the normal landscape of the awakening day and the barn door stood open. As early as it was, she wasn't the first one at work. Inside, her eyes adjusted. The smell of fresh hay and oats mingled with manure. A rooster crowed. What bit of familiarity it brought calmed her.

In the widest part of the space, George had tethered the chestnut horse. He bent over the animal's leg and scraped the frog of its hoof clean with his pick. "Twent-eh three days in August so far," he said, "and 12 mornings started with fog." He wore the new shirt Emma had sewn for him and his second pair of britches. "D'you know what that means?"

Vittorie listened more because he was talking to her than because she understood. She couldn't pass him to get the blood pot from the barn. "*Nein*," she replied, trying a new German word.

He pointed past her to the fields, rounded and dripping with dew. The hazy lace of low clouds hovered in the stillness. "Every foggy morning in August will equal one snowfall this winter," he said, tapping the pick on the sole of his boot. "Count the foggy mornings and you'll know the winter forecast." He looked at the fields like he and they were engaged in some sort of conversation Vittorie couldn't decipher. "I got a pair of turkeys for you." He set the back hoof down and moved to pick up the animal's front hoof.

"Again, please?" He talked too fast and she missed any word to wrap her limited knowledge of English around.

"Turkeys," he said, nodding his head to the pair of large fowl draped over an overturned bucket just inside the barn doors. "For you."

Four stiff legs bent in unnatural angles protruded from a puff of tawny and white feathers. "*Moi?* Me?"

He scraped dried mud and grass from the v-shape and dropped the second hoof. "For supper."

His intended gift removed her opportunity to try. The dead birds lay waiting with no challenge left, just the work. Her cheeks flushed and she kept her eyes looking at the ground. "T-ank ee-yoo." The words eked between tense lips.

She saw George's face as she marched past him to snatch the birds up and continue her day. His large eyes followed her movements. It made her uncomfortable.

✳ ✳ ✳

"Good thing you cooked two birds, Vittorie!" Emma said. She leaned forward to stroke the chestnut horse's neck. "Did you see Pa take three helpings?" She held up the corresponding number of fingers and laughed, genuine and carefree. Her joy sounded like bubbles bursting.

"*Oui.*" Vittorie urged her horse around three flat rocks at the top of the ridge. She took a deep breath and exhaled, long and slow.

The western sky blushed in fantastic saffron and plum as Vittorie stared into its fading glory. "*Regardez.*" Her tone lost all humor as her eyes searched the peaking knobs before them. "The sky is the only place I find myself."

Emma nudged her horse next to Vittorie's. "What did you say?" Her sweet face held the question as she looked at her friend.

"Look." Vittorie said. She pointed down the ridgeline to the Highbaugh's farm nestled snug in the valley. Smoke rose from the cabin's stone chimney. A dozen horses filled the front yard.

"Another scouting party," Emma said, unimpressed.

The words meant nothing to Emma, but ignited something in Vittorie. Her solace in the evening sunset evaporated. She watched the riders mounting up. Several waved to the Highbaugh men who stood on the porch.

Grief etched Vittorie's face. With a glance to the hills and the darkening sky, she lifted both knees and kicked her heels hard into the black horse's belly. The sudden impact caused the beast to rear up. She leaned forward for balance, sure to keep her face to the side of his mane. As soon as his front hooves touched down again he bolted forward, and she gripped with her legs and fists, crouched low over his body. "Home, boy," she whispered for his ears alone.

He understood. In obedience, his hooves beat the fastest path between the oaks and walnut trees. He jumped a fallen oak and his mane whipped in Vittorie's face. She managed to hold on tight as his body curved through the cedars and down the sloped hillsides. They crossed the west field and slowed up between the maples and oaks at the far end just before the creekbed. White sprays of crystal water shot up from under the gelding's feet. Horse and rider paid no mind. The soaking felt honest and good, welcome after the exertion of the ride. They raced through the wheat fields to the cabin and barn.

Vittorie jumped off her mount before he stopped moving. She threw the reins over the porch rail, bounded up both steps, and ran inside.

"What whar?" Oma gasped. "Whar's th' fhar?"

No one answered. Emma dismounted with less urgency but raced up the steps.

Oma grabbed the girl's elbow. "What's wrong?"

Vittorie appeared back through the front door. She stood in front of Emma and tried to catch her breath. Picking up Emma's hand, she placed it over her own heart, then placed it on Emma's chest. Tears filled Vittorie's bright green eyes, amplifying her clarity and determination. She looked past Emma and the barn to the group of strangers. A peaceful smile broke out on her lips.

Emma saw she had a small bundle in her other hand. "You're leaving." The sentence came out more as a statement than the question. She didn't need an answer. She threw her arms around Vittorie and squeezed.

Pots tied to equine rumps jangled. Men's voices chattered and the group began to move.

Vittorie unfolded herself from Emma. "*Merci*," she said. She looked into the German woman's eyes, deep gratitude reflecting. "Thank you, *mon ami*."

Emma blinked back emotion. Her jaw wrinkled into a smile and she sniffed falling moisture back up her nose. "My friend."

Candle emerged from the house with something in her hands, children flanking her. Vittorie bent down in front of little Marie and pulled a corn husk doll from behind her back. Wrapped in a piece of torn fabric to look like a dress, it fastened with one of Gilbert's gold buttons. The girl let go of her mother's skirt and took the gift. Delight lifted her cherub face before she buried it and the doll back in the gingham folds of Candle's clothes. One by one, Vittorie moved through the family members who had taken her in and made her goodbyes. Each of them had shown kindness to her in their own way.

Candle thrust another small sack in Vittorie's empty hand. "Some brown bread, sorghum, jerky…" She kissed Vittorie on both cheeks. "…dried apples and cheese."

Jake shook her hand and tipped his hat. "Skeggs'll take care of ya." He lifted his chin in the direction of the scouting party.

Pa nodded in his curt way. Unease itched him. His eyes couldn't rest on anything. Finally, he shuffled forward and kissed her on the hand. "*Servus,*" he said, his awkward apology delivered.

She stood up straight but lowered her eyes. Humility is difficult both to give and to receive but she met his gaze. He might have thrown her out; he could have treated her worse. A farmer she wasn't, that was plain. "*Merci beaucoup.*"

The horses' tails swished behind her and she had no more time to explain. God would have to sort it out.

Vittorie kissed Sam on the cheek. The immature lad turned four shades of color and tried to wipe the embarrassment off on his sleeve.

She hugged Oma, who didn't understand what was happening. "Whar't she go'n?"

George took her outstretched hand and pulled her close to him. His other hand touched her side. She expected him to say something, but he didn't. When he stepped back, she felt something leave her.

He held her knife—Gilbert's knife—in his hand. He turned it over in his thick palm and walked away from her, taking it with him to the barn. Dust rose behind him. That knife was the most precious thing she had in her possession. Her chest ached as he walked away with it. She made her feet be still, not run after him and wrench it from his big hand. She couldn't argue it was a paltry offering to this family who'd nursed her and taken her in. If George wanted it, he could take it. They deserved something in exchange, and that's all she had to give.

She turned to the rest of the family to memorize them. A grasshopper jumped and Sam squatted to catch it. One by one she marked them: Candle's blue eyes, the light and goodness that she embodied, and the children surrounding her; Jake's sturdy laugh and steady jaw; Pa's sun-baked skin, wild eyebrows, curled lip, and the hard-set German work ethic that drove him; Little Marie's golden ringlets with their innocence and hope; Sam's youthful energy and boyish outlook; Oma's wrinkled muscles and wiry hair that seemed akin to Pa's brows; and sweet Emma, willowy and good. She marked the ramshackle cabin, hewn and chinked with their own hands. She studied the people, willing Remembrance to record these saviors of hers.

A hot breeze blew from the wheat fields and the mill. She looked over toward the creek and the dark green mounds beyond it. She couldn't live in the shadow of the knob. Wholeness, for her, lay beyond this place.

A chicken squawked and flapped her wings to escape George's treading legs. He approached the side of the porch and when he did, she caught eyes with him and blinked an apology.

The front of his straight hair blew upward in the wind. He squinted into the sun and opened his mouth to speak. No words followed. He just looked at her, breathing. She saw him turn the knife over and over in his hands. This time, though, the blade was sharper on both sides and shinier than she'd ever seen it. He replaced it in her carrying pouch.

"*Merci*," she whispered.

"You can trust Skeggs." he said, nodding toward the retreating group.

Vittorie didn't understand much of what he said, but his heart was evident. That she could see. She smiled, and nodded in gratefulness, for everything.

The first men in the survey party line were already out of sight. It wouldn't be more than a few moments until the last of them would be hidden by the cedar trees and then gone into the woods. A voice in the scouting party bellowed something unintelligible. The sounds of laughter and horse hooves rippled through the air.

Torn at the last minute, Vittorie looked between the unknown wanderers and the family she didn't fit into. She lifted her simple skirt in a sincere curtsy to the Highbaughs. With a last look at Emma and Candle, she ran off the porch and away from their humble sanctuary.

64

The current argument among the party on horseback continued. Sweat rings circled under their jacket arms as they lolled side to side in their saddles.

A dark-haired man in a deep green coat said, "There are, in these founding breaths of America, a…class, well, yes…a class of men who value exploration, bravery…" He chose his words well. "…oneness with the land and those in it. They practice the skill of survival without unnatural domination…" His eyebrows lifted and he looked his fellow travelers over, "…and other ideals which may sound lofty, Russell, but in essence are simply their life choices. As their name suggests, these longhunters, like Skeggs, Dan Boone…" he scratched between his eyes, remembering, "…Logan, Kenton…the McAfees—they would go off and hunt and survive alone for long periods of time."

"But what of it, Abraham?" said the man addressed. "Savages lived in these woods for long periods of time, too, but few have become civilized, if you ask me."

"Don't you find the skills of living off the land to be life in its purest form? Finding food, building shelter out of what could be made with your own hands, with tools you've carried on your person…"

"Ha!" said Russell. "I've slaves for carrying, cooking, and building. We've great estates, both my brother and I." He spoke the sentence as an entitlement. "As educated men, it's our duty to see the right foundation laid in this democracy. To uphold the heritage of our people, increase trade with Europe." He burped. "Excuse me. To build wealth and prove this new nation can provide for itself and others."

Abraham's jaw tensed. "I find the longhunters' way of making peace with others they meet along the way, or living in spite of others who are not for peace, or simply keeping dry on a rainy night, escaping predators, and the like, an artform I admire and aspire to."

"You aspire to be a longhunter, eh, Abe? You'll have to change tailors," he said, chuckling at his own joke.

"Did you know," Abraham said, dismissing Russell's barbed comment, "Skeggs was among the first educated men to venture west over the mountains? Far from your Atlantic shores of Yorktown, or mine at Albany, or Providence, or Charleston, or any of the settlements now flourishing between them."

"Ahhh, the colonies," said Russell, unimpressed. "Our lands are west of Yorktown. I know your kind, Abe. Instead of looking east across the sea, you worship these men who simply turned on their heels and declared just as profound an independence by going beyond the reach of England, or taxes, or really almost all other shackles of our times to this uncharted, undiscovered amalgam of sticks and stones and unfamiliar peoples living here."

"'Worship' takes my admiration too far." Abraham waited to see if Skeggs wanted to interject. Their guide kept silent, so Abraham continued. "But these men were some of the first to reach many of the Native American tribes, the first to see what lay beyond a ridge or on the other side of the valley. Be glad Providence provided a longhunter to become our guide over treacherous terrain to the spot you've been promised, or gifted, or told stories of, you and your brother."

"I am grateful, Abraham, I am. You've won your case. There, are you satisfied? And I, for one, have had almost enough of this treacherous terrain, as you say. Skeggs!" called the heavyset man wearing the fancy blue coat. "You *are* a longhunter, just like Daniel Boone or the McAfees, are you not?" He whipped the stubby horse beneath him with a short crop. "How long d'you say you've been long hunting for?" He asked the question louder than necessary and trotted to the man walking at the head of the group.

"Do you mean since what year have I been longhunting, Russell, or what is the longest time I have been out hunting in the woods?" The longhunter's eyes didn't meet those of his traveling companions. He seemed more focused on the woods, the trail, the task at hand. A woman marched at the tail of his troop, and Henry Skeggs hadn't mentioned her to anyone else yet.

"The longest time." Russell spit every "t" out with effort. "Several months?" he said, taking great care to emphasize his syllables.

"No," said Skeggs. Always in the lead—in pace and in thought— he wore buckskin and leather, and the rocks and wind spoke to him. He listened, then turned through the woods to lead in a new direction, always on foot. "I'd reckon several years, mebbe."

"Really?" The rotund man swatted a bug on his cheek. "That long?" he asked, slapping a second time.

Skeggs withheld his response and busied himself in selecting a camp. The hastening darkness and jovial nature of the noisy group had helped keep their newest member's presence a se- cret, but that would change. He'd taken the several hours she'd marched behind them to put together what he could. After all, a female's presence changes most things. He noticed she didn't look long at any of them, nor did she speak. She kept pace well enough, despite the fact they were on horseback and she wasn't.

When they turned off the trail to make camp for the night, she didn't look winded nor fatigued.

Skeggs selected a wooded glen. He pointed to some oaks. "Jasper, you and your brother will sleep best there."

Flattered, the blue jacket man smacked his horse. "Right. Thank you, Skeggs." Eager to be more comfortable, he urged the short horse to follow directions.

His brother, Russell Hawkes, a great portly beast himself, dismounted with a groan. "Oh! My poor legs! And I believe I've ripped another hole in my knickers. Wretched outdoor life…"

Jasper laughed, still seated in his saddle. He matched Russell in girth but not in stature. "I don't think the country agrees with you, brother."

"I should have bought Lord Cumberly's mare instead of your gelding. She'd not give me half the trouble as this pony." The heel of his shoe snagged during dismount. With his weight unbalanced, he paused, hung with one leg upended, and fell off his horse.

Russell leaned on the trunk of the oak nearest him and howled in laughter. The ruckus rose into the otherwise silent night.

"They're not the best representation of Virginians," said a man with a thick neck and an egg-shaped head. He laid his own armload of kindling beside Skeggs'.

Skeggs scraped grass down to dirt and separated the clods from the blades with a shake. "I know, Abraham," he said, his voice low, "as many entitled landowners before them." He scraped again around in a circle, removing whatever else might burn outside his firepit.

"Whatever land they buy, you'll not have to remind me to purchase a tract far off." He held a branch out.

Skeggs took it. "You'll find there's every sort in these woods."

"Why are they here?" Abraham asked. "They don't fit the type."

"Curiosity. Purpose in their lives." He laid the branch at an angle with two others. "To see the wild West of the Appalachians—not to mention conversation at supper tables for years to come." Skeggs watched the heat lick the dry tinder. "Not so different from most." He blew on the flame to coax it brighter.

"Huh." Abraham unrolled a bed beneath the tallest trees. "I love the sweet smell of the woods."

"Hmm." Skeggs didn't mention the woman with honey-lavender scented hair.

65

The riders finished stretching. Each took a short walk into the woods—for a man's business is his own—and returned again to the communal space.

Tears flowed down her cheeks. She didn't wipe at them. Perhaps no one would notice—certainly not the booted gentry relieving themselves in the trees ahead of her. They were busy chatting amongst themselves as evidenced by various chortles, snorts, and whispers that wafted back to her on the wind. The subject of their secrets she didn't know, nor did she want to. She had her own secrets, and the consciousness of them overwhelmed her.

Vittorie observed the lead man gathering sticks and starting a fire, just like Gilbert and Smuthers would've. His intentional separation of everyone into little groups benefitted her anonymity since the rest of the travelers settled where he suggested. The warm night beckoned the men beyond various trunk clusters, and they slept spread out under the forest canopy.

The sun set below the horizon. It was too late to turn around. *What a stupid idea.* No Gilbert to guide her, to tell her to run or where to find safety. *What was she, a single woman, going to do out in the wild against twelve men with one small knife?* She didn't understand most words spoken to her. She had no money, no assurance.

She stayed quiet, waited in the shadows, and watched him. Not only did he not joke with the others, but his feet made no noise. He navigated around branches and brambles, trunks and rocks like water, taking each object into himself and flowing around it while moving past. He wore a high, fur slipper on each foot.

She stumbled over a root. "Ahh!" Her involuntary cry drew unwanted attention. Several men close by turned in her direction. Her cheeks flushed in the settling twilight. The slippered man tended his fire.

"What was that?" Jasper asked in a hoarse whisper. He curled a blanket under his chin. "Skeggs! Was that another bobcat?"

Skeggs' mound of sticks blazed brighter. "Bobcats do sound just like a woman's scream." His beard and face glowed orange. "I'll keep first watch, gentlemen. Get some sleep."

"Quite!" Jasper said. "Made my neck hair raise."

"We rise early," Skeggs said.

Vittorie blessed his intentional oversight of her. Wedging herself between two exposed roots for the evening, she pulled up her knees and made her shadow fit inside the oak's. The men resettled. The stir of night returned. She put her back up against the generous tree and let herself relax against the broad tree's trunk. Its pointed bark poked through the worn fabric of her borrowed dress. Despite being so uncomfortable, exhaustion weighed her body down. Her nestled spot enveloped her.

The sturdy blaze and general presence of others accomplished much in her weary soul. The burning pop of kindling softened the unease in her chest. A whippoorwill sang its distinctive three-syllable song. Low whinnies from the horses tied to nearby branches added to the lullaby. Sleep almost settled over her.

A shrill call went through the air overhead. Another followed, closer to her. Three shadowy figures appeared out of the woods. On the other side of the fire from her spot in the oak roots, faces glared at her through heightened flames. Without hesitation, and with her hand on her knife, she darted into the woods behind her. The small fire wasn't enough. It couldn't light her way very far. She blinked against the darkness. Her feet didn't stop. Her hands punched out in front of her, ready to knock limbs—sapling or *sapien*—away. Fear returned full force. She could break her neck running but she didn't care. She would not die by their hands.

Tightening her grip on the knife, she shrieked and she ran, taking her vengeance on the blackness that had snuffed out the light of her life. There was no moon. No time to find the stars through the canopy of the trees. She tripped over something. The ground punched her chin and stole her breath. Splayed out like a chicken to be stuffed, she panted and stayed still, careful to keep a hold on the knife.

Light from somewhere glinted on the blade. From her fallen spot on the ground, she clenched her teeth to quiet her breathing, but it didn't help. Over her own panting, gasping breath, she heard the sound that unstrung her, the sound she'd listened for on the hilltop her last night with Gilbert. It hadn't come then. It came now: someone searching for her.

He pursued with intent, not with the haphazard steps she'd taken. Every moment brought him toward her hiding place among the underbrush.

Swaying grasses moved in the wind and wiped the damp night on her skin. She lay stiff but flinched away from the wet ferns in her face. She lay unmoving, unable to move. *Could he see her?* She strained her eyes side to side, unwilling to move her head. Fear choked her. *What would happen if he found her?*

The wind whirled. It lifted the branches full of leaves above her. Tree frogs shrieked a deafening chorus. The noise muffled his approach. She sprang up from her hiding spot toward a clearing in the darkness ahead. Shafts of moonlight reached her through the twisting leaves overhead.

A voice yelled from behind. "Ssttyawp!"

The word swirled in her brain without any meaning attached to it. Instinct pivoted her a few degrees and she kept running in the precise, opposite direction from his sounds. Memory sparked a fire in her legs and propelled her on. The night Smuthers died. Gilbert bleeding on the mountaintop. Images presented by her fears matched the sounds trailing her. No question lingered. She wanted to live. She had to.

"Stop!" the voice called again, close by.

She raced with her arms out in front of her. Tree limbs, saplings, branches—all collided first with her forearms. She swung down and away to protect her face. Death at the hand of this assassin, or worse, became real. Something shifted in her. With a clarity she hadn't had before, she decided she could and would—if she must—kill the man pursuing her. On impulse to declare his impending death, she shouted, *"Laisse-moi!"*

More light penetrated her surroundings. She burst into a clearing.

"Arrête!" the voice called out.

Hearing her native tongue startled her. She obeyed, stopped in her tracks, and spun around, knife in hand, ready to strike. Her eardrums pounded the echo of her racing heartbeat and she gulped air into her dry mouth.

No footsteps. No wind.

A hard blow from the right sent her falling to the ground. He was on top of her. Her fist clenched and stabbed into his back, but only her fist pounded fabric. No knife! Her palm was empty!

"Laisse moi!!" She twisted underneath him and clawed at the ground. *Perhaps the knife hadn't fallen too far...*

He grabbed her around the belly. His weight pushed her down. He had her wrist, both her wrists.

She screamed. *"Aide-moi!"*

"Madame, s'il vous plaît! Arrête! Pour votre santé!" He yanked her to her feet, but kept hold of her hands. "Please, stop!"

Leather-like arms wrapped around her torso. She bit into his sleeve.

"Aarrghh!" Stung by the bite, he swung her around, unharmed. When he relaxed his grip, she dropped down to the ground. The clouds moved and a moon appeared. The half-light gave form to her shadowy attacker. She hurled herself at him, fingers toward his eyes. He knocked her arms away and grabbed one wrist. In a single movement, he wrenched both arms behind her back and twisted her with his body down to their knees.

The celestial shift of the clouds revealed what she hadn't seen before. Centimeters in front of her, not one full step more, the ground disappeared. If she'd continued her course she would have fallen into a hole as wide as three wagons. Her hair stood on end as she panted, hung over its side. "Aahhhh!"

He wrapped one arm around her waist keeping her safe. *"Madame!"*

A branch and some rocks slipped over the edge. He held her, breathing loudly himself, and they waited. No sound followed. No bottom found by the falling debris in the cavernous hole.

"S'il vous plaît!" He scooted backward and dragged her body with him. "Wait, please!" His heart beat slow and strong against her back. His grasp relaxed. They lay there a moment, the woman and the woodsman, one holding the other, and the other clinging to the first. Placing himself between her and the pit, with a calm and steady voice, he said in French, *"Madame,* please…I am a friend."

She looked over his shoulder again at the cavernous hole, then into the silhouetted shadows of her attacker-turned-savior's face. *"Je comprends,"* she said, lightheaded. "You speak French?"

"Yes."

"You don't want to hurt me?" she asked.

"No."

The thrill of hearing her own language spoken burst out of Vittorie's mouth so sudden it startled the man. Girlish laughter echoed in the night. He looked around. For the first time in a long time he found himself unsure how to respond. Her laughter intensified. Tears ran from the outside edges of her eyes.

"Can you stand?" he asked, reaching a hand out.

She doubled over and brought the back of her hand up to cover her mouth, hysterical and open. *"Arrête!"* she said, mimicking his voice, reenacting his attempt to stop her. The little button of her nose bent sideways and a fresh peel of high-pitched squeaks erupted.

Not amused, he folded his arms over his chest. He cleared his throat and stamped a moccasin. Attempting to regain proper etiquette, she breathed in deeply through her nose. Sobriety returned, but giggles followed. A long exhale ensued. She sat up straight, intending to quit, but it was hopeless.

"Who are your people?" he asked. Her mannerisms, like when she covered her mouth, were refined. She was alone, yet her personality was soft, like someone used to being protected.

Pointing at herself in mock seriousness, she repeated, "Do you want to hurt me?" Unable to stop laughing, she lay down on the ground, face in the moss.

He saw nothing funny. "My name is Henry Skeggs."

Her shoulders shook. The high squeak returned, followed by shortness of breath.

"I intend to return to camp for some smoking of a certain dried leaf." Realizing she wasn't ready yet, he paced a minute, and sat down a safe distance away from her. "My native comrades had promised such, and brought it to our campfire tonight."

" Look at that!" She pointed to the hole. "I could have dropped in and…" Amazement soured as she heard what he said. "Native comrades…tonight….” She pointed back into the forest. “Those men killed my husband!” she said, wiping her face.

“Not those men,” he said.

“They were men just like that! How do you know?” The absence of his reply unnerved her and she cursed the loss of her knife.

“Those men are my friends.”

“Are you a murderer, too, then? And a thief?”

“Are you a woman used to yelling at men?” In response, he rose up from his seat on the ground, retrieved his gun from the backside of a nearby maple and started to leave. “There’s more than one reason I choose to live alone, not the least of which are the freedoms from a woman’s tongue.” He wiped a hand down his beard but stopped before leaving her. He shouldered his rifle. “I’m a scout. A guide. It’s my business to know these woods, and the people in them, as well as I know my own soul.” He watched her as she listened. “You’d be safer at my campfire with *those* men tonight than out here alone in these woods.” With that, he walked under the broad arm of the silvered maple.

The coolness of night had settled and she shivered, reviving her fears. Standing up, she checked around for her knife. Not seeing it, and not knowing her way in the dark, she jogged to the first tree and put her hand on its cracked shell. She couldn’t hear him moving through the woods. “*Attendez, s’il vous plaît!*” she called after him. “Wait, please!”

He appeared beside her, making no sound.

“My name is Victoire Mon… LeClerc.”

The name rang in his remembrance and he looked at her as if for the first time. “Skeggs,” he said, sticking out his hand for her to take it. Her delicate hand slipped inside his. She curtsied once, out of habit. Introductions complete, he led her back into the spotted moonlight of the twittering leaves, back in the direction they’d come from.

By the time they reached camp her muscles ached and her soul was tired. Her chilled body in wet clothes drew near the fire, despite the presence of the three bare-chested men. She sat down closest to Skeggs, as far from the others as she could while still feeling the heat of the fire. Her stomach rumbled, but exhaustion overtook her. Food she would find tomorrow. She fell asleep with the image of the slippered man and his presumed murderous companions sharing smoke from a long stick burning amber hues into her dreams.

66

Skeggs awoke after a few good hours of sleep. The worst part about leading survey parties wasn't the terrain, nor the hazards that came along with it. No. It was the survey party. It didn't take much for Skeggs to know a man—the girth of his belly, the threads of his clothing, the look in his eye, the tell of his handshake. Women were much the same. He comprehended them after a very short time in their presence, even a shorter time than it took him to figure out a man. Women were simpler to him. Generally, he had less to do with them anyway.

Fools and preachers believe all men are good. That hadn't been Skeggs' experience. All men were liars; only their actions meant much of anything. If you watched a man long enough to see what he did, you could discount everything he said and make a fairly good guess as to what he'd do next. That sort of observation gave Skeggs what he needed to know about what a particular man would do before he did it.

He still had a good four hours before any of the party would be up. The night waned past the time for owls, but wasn't early enough for doves. He used the time to observe. His senses took in everything: the movement of the wind through the top leaves in the maples, a mouse racing around one of the Hawke boys' satchels. It stopped once to sit up and listen before scurrying on. The

French woman slumped over, asleep on the hard ground. Unlike most women, she puzzled him.

Russell Hawkes snored an obnoxious amount. Skeggs glanced around, his gaze checking between the tree trunks, grateful for no movement. Knowing these woods and being welcome by French, Dutch, Native, or any man alike meant only half-peace. He always made room for caution. A snorer could become a call for a rogue man or beast to investigate. Skeggs pinched Russell's nostrils closed till he sputtered awake, snorting and disgruntled.

"What the devil?" said the pompous landowner, then he saw Skeggs' face. He knew by the look on it what the conversation would be about. "Damp Virginia air…." Russell apologized and turned over on his side.

Skeggs had a way of making his point without being heavy-handed. He circled the small party, navigating their perimeter in his moccasins.

Russell watched him till Skeggs' shadow mingled with the night. Unsettled by the sudden sensation of being alone in the woods, even with other sleeping gentlemen, the portly man raised up on his forearms. "Skeggs!" His whisper scraped harshly against the slumbering night.

Skeggs' form materialized between two oaks a little further north. "What, Russell?"

Embarrassed by his childish display of fear, and hoping, of course, to be denied, he asked, "Want me to come along?"

"Twelve miles comin' today. Better rested if you sleep a few more hours. I'll not be far."

"Right. Good thought at that. Twelve miles. Ohhh…"

Skeggs didn't stay to hear him go quiet. He needed to find some breakfast.

67

When Vittorie awoke the next morning, three pieces of smoked meat stuck out of her sack. They did not taste like the ones from the mill. Beside them sat a few, overlapping maple leaves topped with a small mound of fresh blueberries. She mashed the tart, sweet fruit between her tongue and teeth, holding the juice in her mouth a moment before swallowing. She bit hard on the jerky to break some off. Its toughness contrasted nicely with the juice of the wild harvest.

The morning's attitude and atmosphere were gray. But as moods and weather can, the indeterminate sky gave way to soft white clouds with a palette of aquas and roses. No ceiling nor portrait at the king's palace in Versailles rivaled it. Something like peace hovered on her shoulders while she chewed. She breathed in deep, very glad to be alive. All was not well, but fear and grief had been put a little further away for the moment, and that felt good. Somewhere nearby, she had a friend.

In good enough spirits, Vittorie stayed at Skeggs' side all morning, clucking away in French. "Am I talking too much? *Alors!* What a magnificent view! See how the fog clings to the valley? *Monsieur Skeggs*, do you see? Have you seen anything like it before?"

Skeggs flickered a glance in the mentioned direction for manners' sake and walked past. "Yes." The Hawkes men hadn't risen yet and he'd had enough of their laziness. "Load up without them," he said to Abraham and the others.

The party mounted up sans the Hawkes. As the others' horses trotted past, the two pork sausages in their bedrolls woke with a start. Fury lit indignant at being left behind. As just punishment for their behavior, Skeggs led their horses away with him, forcing the men to walk and carry their own loads. There were more than a few chuckles at their expense by the departing associates. They wheezed and crouched to pick up their lodgings. They bustled and bumped into each others' rear ends and turned, cursing and sputtering.

At the top of the next high hill, Skeggs tied their horses to a tree.

"I don't know…what you think…you're about…Henry Skeggs," Jasper wheezed, doubled over to catch his breath, "but…I have something…something…to say…." His shouts echoed up around the hillsides from the bottom of the valley. "…about…your ungentlemanly behavior!"

When the brothers did arrive at their horses, the audible cursing of Skeggs had stopped. They needed their breath to fill great lungs and force their hefty selves forward so as not to be lost in the wilderness. Humility is a mighty force, and forgiveness is its kin. The brothers were accepted back and all in the party realized Skeggs was in charge.

When the sun shone from the front and to the right of them, Skeggs stopped the troop at a stream. Trees overhung the riverbank on one side. "We'll rest here for a bit."

Soaked with sweat, Vittorie wasted no time finding a bare patch of ground to sit. Smelly as the rest, she watched them think nothing of stripping down to their britches and shirts and flinging themselves pell-mell into the refreshing pool. Two of them waded in, glancing behind to Skeggs for reassurance of safety. The younger men splashed and played—some overpowering others, some standing out of the roughhousing, but laughing and gloating in turn.

"How like boys they still are," Vittorie said out loud. No one heard her, but the French felt delightful in her mouth.

Skeggs lounged on the breezy hillside beneath the bowing branches. He lay on his side, one knee and one elbow bent in relaxation.

"You don't smell like the others."

Amusement curled the corners of his lips. "Thank you," he said, tugging a long grass from its anchor in the earth. He put it in his mouth.

"How can you keep so clean when the others are so...not?"

He looked at the swimmers. "I know where the watering holes are." He walked to where she sat and took off his hat, careful to stand so the sun wasn't in her eyes.

She lifted her hand to shield them anyway. The tree leaves glinted sunny pinpricks behind him.

"About knocking you down..." He began with the deep calmness. "It was for your own sake."

She waited, but he didn't go further. "I know," she said. There was another long pause between them as each wondered if the other would speak. "*Merci*," she added at last.

He nodded several times but said nothing. Instead, he reached into his boot, pulled out a knife, and handed it to her. Only it wasn't a knife; it was *her* knife. Surprise washed over her face. She looked up to question him, but he'd already turned and was rising. She held the gift and returned it to its home on her hip. When she looked up again, he'd stopped walking away and was facing her.

"I'm taking them over the next hill," he added.

Not understanding why he said that—nor why she was being left out—showed on her face, clear as the water.

His eyes checked the sky, then the horizon. "The river's yours."

The men were gathered and gone in minutes. He was the last one she saw disappear over the far side of the small hill opposite the stream.

She hurried to unlace shoes and remove socks, and her bare feet brushed the soft grass at the edge of the creek. The chilly water sent a brisk rush through her. It began at her toes first, then her ankles, and by the time it reached her knees she didn't care if her skirt got wet around the edges.

The stream sang around her, a melancholy tune without words. Sadness cloaked her. She spread her fingers and let clear rivulets thread between them, lingering. With the men out of sight, and the hills engulfing her tiny figure there in the water, she gathered her skirts up higher with one hand and listened, proving she was alone.

Splashing water over her face and neck rejuvenated her. It washed away more than red earth and sweat. Bending her face down to the surface, she sucked water into her mouth, held it on her tongue, and swallowed. Holding her breath, she stuck her face below the surface and opened her eyes. The sun's rays wiggled in patterns over the rocky bottom like the lace on her bedskirts back home.

That memory was too much. Jerking her head up to erase it, she lost her balance and fell backward. The shoulder of her blouse and her left ear got soaked before she righted herself. She reprimanded the ill-mannered stream with a smack of her open hand.

"Stupid!" she chided. Her hair wet, her dress wet, she waded toward the far shore. Before she reached the bank, she dropped her skirt and let it drag in the water. Swinging her arms front to back, she took three leaping steps and flung her full body under the water. She rolled onto her back and let the flow of the more powerful body carry her.

Blinking water from her eyelashes, she gazed up into blue sky. Rounded clouds hovered in small patches high overhead. As she floated, water edged the space around her face, from her chin to her chest, and filled her ears. Her hair wriggled outside its usual crown, loose and untamed. Liquid lifted her breasts. It filled the place between her skin and clothes, and she basked in the solitude of being carried by tears deeper than her own.

68

"She'll be counted as my ward till we reach Nolin." Skeggs took occasion to look each bearded traveler in the eye. "Having a woman among us changes nothing. You'll each see your lands in the same timing as promised." He waited for the murmur to quit. "There's no change in plan so your fees remain unchanged. That answers the brothers. Pickering, what's bothering you?"

The man he addressed had hair stuck half-dried across his forehead. Sensing the eyes of the group on him, he wiped it to one side. "Well, Mr. Henry, sir…." He couldn't hold Skeggs' gaze and took his hat off to inspect the broad brim. "Mr. Henry, I just think…it's not proper."

Several others dropped their eyes to the ground. The Hawkes brothers smirked.

"What are you talking about?" Skeggs asked.

"Well…her," Pickering said. "…not proper for you to have… her."

Agreement muttered through the clustered group. Several heads nodded. The Hawkes sniggered.

"Let me tell you where I stand. I'm here to do a job," said Skeggs. "Before she arrived, I had the dozen of you to transport from Lexington to parts unknown and back again. That remains. The difference is now I have thirteen." He checked the position of the sun and wanted to move on, but hadn't set a time for her to rejoin them. His return to search for her would stir more unrest among the other men. "Her arrival surprised me as much as you."

"Who is she?" Abraham asked.

Skeggs lifted his shoulders. "You've seen how little I've spoken to her." He shook his head. "She speaks mostly French." He removed his hat. "I believe she came from France with her husband after the war. If I'm right, he fought with Washington under Rochambeau and they were looking to settle here."

Respect rippled like a wave across the men's faces.

"So, she has told him who she is," Jasper said. He looked two or three of the others hard in the eyes.

"No, Jasper. She hasn't." Skeggs let their conversations fall silent before he continued. "I took her husband and another soldier to search out land on the Green River. My understanding was they had put money down before they scouted it with me, and afterward planned to complete the purchase. She wasn't in the party, but the Frenchman talked about a wife back in Lexington, waiting on him. My guess is," he looked over his shoulder and yanked his neck in the direction of the hill and stream beyond, "that's her."

"But where's the Frenchman?" Russell asked.

Jasper added, "And how did she get here from Lexington without him?"

"Does anyone else speak French?" asked Abraham.

All except for the last question went unanswered. A complete round of "nos" ensued.

"Skeggs, you'll need to question the woman," Russell said, forgetting his humility.

Before Skeggs replied, Abraham held up both hands. "Gentlemen! Let's remember we are gentlemen. How many of you are married men?" He kept one hand in the air as others raised theirs. Jasper and Russell were the last to acknowledge.

"I feel something has happened unexpectedly to her," Abraham said. "I've noticed her crying. If Skeggs is correct, there must be more to her story." He walked in front of the others as he talked. "She arrived after we stopped at that mill. They must know more." He snapped his head up with resolve. "Let's return her there."

"She doesn't appear to want to go back," Skeggs said. "She hasn't asked me to return her."

Most of the men didn't need to look any harder into it. They took it as it was, as Skeggs had put it to them.

"Are you singling her out for yourself?" Russell asked.

Ignoring Russell's question, Skeggs said, "Going back adds time—and further payment—onto the trip. I'll ask her more about her intentions when it's suitable. Her business is her own, just like any man here. However," he lowered his voice and stared at the Hawkes, "I want your word she'll be treated as an equal. She's no one's servant, slave, or handmaid."

"Yes, yes, you have our word," Russell said, his full lips wrinkling into a smirk. "But there is the question of payment." He looked at his brother.

Jasper smoothed the lapel of his embroidered jacket. "Yes, has she paid her way, like the rest of us…equals?"

69

"How is it you speak French?" Vittorie asked, hopping over a root. "You're the first person I've met, really, who can."

His backwoodsman's attire looked like any other English speaker. When he spoke English, no French accent prevailed. His facial features, hidden by graying hair and baked by decades of sun circles, revealed no certain parentage. Sharp aqua eyes pierced.

"My mother taught me," he explained. "And I studied some."

"From France?" Delight filled her eyes.

He shook his head. "She was a great learner, and teacher." He pulled up a root through the center of the path and tossed it, twig and tendrils, into the underbrush. "Plus, I soldiered some."

"Would you write a letter and send it back to France for me?"

"I could see what might be done. It would be rather hard for them to respond without you being planted anywhere as yet, though. You don't write?"

She looked elsewhere to avoid his gaze but shook her head. A little bird with shocking azure feathers swooped up to a limb. Something very interesting happened under its wing and it stuck its beak in to investigate.

Vittorie watched the finch. "No," she said, pretending to be distracted. "Gilbert and I intended for him to write once we settled. Now, I can't imagine telling them."

The bird ruffled its wings. It cocked its head and peered down at the passing people.

"Where did you soldier?"

"Couple different places."

"At Yorktown? My husband fought at Yorktown."

A woodpecker nearby pecked for bugs in a pine trunk. The hollow echo moved through the branches overhead. Skeggs didn't answer.

Vittorie looked up for the source of the sound. "I understand the fighting at Yorktown won the war for America," she said. "That's what Gilbert told me." She moved a leafy fern to the side and stepped onto a narrow patch of moss. "But acts in war can be exaggerated at times. Not to say he meant to. Just…have you heard that? About Yorktown?"

Skeggs moved with the agility of a deer, never tired, never winded. "He told you right. The French influence and aid at Yorktown helped the Continental Army suppress the British stronghold there. I witnessed General Washington sign the terms of surrender at Redoubt 10."

"What is…ten?"

"Redoubt 10. A strategic stronghold we took. Once that was secure, it allowed the Allies to retake Yorktown. Lafayette and Hamilton led. Do you know where your husband was?"

Her curls swayed back and forth. "He didn't speak much about it."

Skeggs chose a narrow path between dense trees. They walked at the head of the party, him first and her following. The horses trailed single file. The sounds of varied gaits and sure footfalls interrupted other conversations behind them.

He plucked a broad leaf, bigger than his hand, careful to save the moisture collected in it. Rounding the sides, he opened his mouth, and let the water drop off onto his tongue.

Vittorie moved closer to the tree and found a limb her height. Mimicking him, she plucked and rounded and drank. The water tasted cold and fresh, and she smiled, grateful for the simple necessity. *"Merci."*

He didn't smile back, but he didn't not smile either. His blue eyes squinted at her and looked down a moment, before he strode past her. "It's not exactly a watering hole," he said to the rest of the men, "but anyone who's out of water can quench a might of thirst. We'll pause a minute to get refreshed."

The horses filed forward and riders dismounted around the maple grove. Some, who had full waterskins, turned the skins up still sitting in their saddles. Others watched Vittorie continue to drink from the leaves and tried it themselves.

"Gentlemen," Skeggs said. "May I present Madame Vittorie LeClerc. Her husband fought for our cause under Rochambeau at Yorktown."

Hearing the introduction and the news, Abraham dismounted and took off his hat. Rummaging around inside his saddle bag, he found what he searched for and walked toward Vittorie. He bent one arm at the elbow before his waist and folded into a bow. "Madame," he said. "It's a pleasure to make your acquaintance."

Embarrassed by the unwanted attention, Vittorie clutched the seam of her skirt, pulled what extra there was out to the left a little, and curtsied.

He handed her a dry waterskin. "I noticed something has happened to your waterskin and you are without. May I offer you an additional one I happen to have on hand?"

She blushed, not understanding.

Skeggs interpreted in French. "He has an extra waterskin if you'd like to use it."

"Good God," Russell said. "What a display. I disapprove of airs wasted on the lower classes. She's only a peasant. Let her drink from the trees, Abraham." He snatched at the empty waterskin. "That skin's worth a small bag of Spanish milled coins."

Abraham anticipated him and jerked it away. "My waterskins, my purse, and my manners are no concern of yours."

Skeggs held a hand out before Vittorie toward the offered skin. "If you'd like it, it's yours."

Vittorie curtsied to Abraham and again to Skeggs. "Thank you." She curtsied once more to Abraham before taking the offered gift. Abraham walked back to his palomino, and Skeggs looked hard at Russell until he, too, went back about his business.

Vittorie studied the water pouch. The supple hide curved into a rounded shape with immaculate stitching, turned inside. It felt soft as she ran her fingers over it. They left three lines through the grain of fine hair. The rim of the piece was crafted from a fine metal, without a flaw in its curvature. Rawhide string, wound tight several times just below the mouth, connected the bag to the tarnished silver circle. A craftsman's detail crested the stopper with a shape, two lines that met at one point.

"What is this?" she asked Skeggs in French, pointing to the engraving.

He scraped his knife blade down a wiry strip of sapling and looked over. "The letter 'L.'"

"Ahh, yes," she said. "Why?"

"'L' is the first letter of his surname. Lindo. Abraham Lindo."

Abraham scraped sweat off his saffron-colored horse. He wasn't close enough to hear his name spoken and proceeded to pull burrs out of the animal's white mane.

Skeggs threw the sapling to the side and cut another. "His family is from South Carolina. In Indigo."

"Is that a place?"

"No, it's a plant used to make deep blue dye. They came from London a generation back and have done well for themselves cultivating the plant."

"Ahh, indigo! Yes, for fabrics," she said. "We arrived in South Carolina. At Charleston." Her normal chatter waned. She went silent, staring at the waterskin in her hands. "They came upon us so sudden in the twilight...taking everything. Gilbert...." She stopped speaking, skipping over raw memories. Grief shadowed an important key deep in the recesses of her mind. Had she not been alone, had there been others to speak for her, those lost words may have unlocked a pathway for her—very near to this present place. But she was alone. And she couldn't remember.

"Are you alright?"

Her delayed answer told him the truth. "...*Oui*...Yes...thank you." She touched the sewn edge. "This is very well made. I know a little about sewing." She brushed at a dirt spot on the bodice of her dress. "I didn't make this," she said, attempting to make light of how much she disliked the fabric. "I ruined mine. The family at the mill were very kind. Their daughter and I were about the same size. About."

Skeggs looked her in the face, not over her body. "That was lucky."

"I don't believe in luck."

"I see."

"I used to have more faith."

Skeggs' aqua eyes looked up from his work. He knotted the strips in his hand together and pulled tight. "Me too." He held out what he'd been working on.

"What is that?"

His face relaxed and the edges of his mouth lifted a bit. "This'll keep your water on your waist."

The cloth Candle had packed food in for her now wrapped as a belt during the daily walks. It wrinkled around her middle.

Underneath it, her knife pouch slung down from a barn rope she'd tied over her dress.

Her hands reached out to take the twisted sinews. "Thank you," she said, before she'd deciphered how it worked.

"So, you're a seamstress?" He demonstrated as he held the looped sapling. "Run your belt through here and then tie this part closed again." Relinquishing it, he changed topics. "Sewn for many wealthy families?"

"Yes," she said, looping and retying it as he'd said. "My own." The words were honest.

"That's what I thought." He left her and walked over to the men. Slinging his long-barreled rifle over a shoulder, he shouted, "Let's head on."

Metal clinked as horses chewed bits between their teeth. Foreign voices spoke syllables which made no sense to her. She ducked behind a maple, leaned her rifle against its backside, and hiked up her skirts. Squatting down, she spread her feet wide and listened. Urine splattered hard against green sprouts. A red bug with black dots walked up a slender shoot of something growing in front of her. Finished, she squeezed her muscles to dry off. Standing up, she smoothed the front of the coarse brown linen and settled the hanging waterskin and knife pouch over separate hips. She patted the front of her dress again, checking for specific bumps. Yes. Seven buttons still snug inside.

Rejoining the mounted group, a small man approached her. His brown eyes set wide apart in his square head. "*Madame*, would you prefer to ride? I could walk instead."

She searched for Skeggs, but he was too far away and busy with a spotted horse. A flush of heat spiked up her neck to her cheeks. Her sense of fellowship wilted. Ignorance washed her brow. "*Eu...*," she said, stammering.

The horse pulled at the reins he held out. His teeth looked worse than the nags.

She glanced past them for any help. Skeggs put the appaloosa's foreleg down, but didn't turn around.

"*Je suis désolé!*" she said, before she curtsied and ran to find the one person who she understood.

70

Skeggs couldn't escape the feminine form shadowing him. He listened and asked questions in French as they picked their way up and over the knobs to Nolin Station. "What was done to recover the stolen items?"

She changed the gun to the opposite shoulder. "A search party of area farmers went out."

"How extensive was the search?"

"It was a difficult time. I don't remember." She showed more fear in relating the details of her tragedy than sleeping outdoors or traveling with a band of strange men.

"Do you have a written list of items lost?"

"In my mind." Cool air rosied her cheeks despite the somber conversation. Silver clouds escaped her mouth as she spoke. "An abundance of seeds for late vegetables and, of course, the remaining apple, peach and grape seeds not planted in December. Necessities, such as gunpowder, pepper, salt, wine…." She scrunched her eyebrows, remembering. "An herbal tonic Mrs. Brown insisted we take. 'Use it religiously,' she said. She told us she had used it many times to ward off common ailments here."

"Mmm-hmm." Skeggs tromped up a hillside. His moccasins crunched crimson and yellow leaves underfoot. "Anything else?" He turned to check on the seated gentry who moseyed behind.

Her strides were two-and-a-half to one of his. "Blankets, outer garments, some books and maps."

"Books?"

"Gilbert could read and write." She selected a particular leaf from the ground and fiddled the perfect orange specimen in her fingertips. "It was coming in to fashion—salons where ladies would learn as men do. But, my parents are…aristocratic." She stuck the leaf in her belt. "I had my sewing and my family. I think if we'd stayed, Gilbert would have wanted me to learn. Oh! Gilbert had some other legal papers from the land office after we made the downpayment."

"That's something could be tracked."

"*Monsieur Vaughn* was an…awkward…man. He ignored us mostly. And there were bottles when he opened cabinet doors in his office. Perhaps he could be asked for help?"

Her willingness to trust him—a man she met three days ago—and march into what life a single, illiterate woman alone might find in the wild surprised him. "No. Mr. Vaughn is no longer living. I took a survey party through Lexington last month and learned he'd…died.

"That night…Gilbert said we were so close." She untied Candle's cloth from her waist and used the fabric as a shawl. "We climbed to the top of a hill, and the stars are the same here as France. Gilbert showed me how to return to the mill using the stars."

"Then he died? On the top of the knob."

Noises in the air stopped her. "Yes."

High overhead, a flock of honking geese rearranged themselves in formation. The massive arrowhead shape splintered; the fowl in front moved aside. A bird at the end broke into the wind and propelled itself to the empty space. When the new goose led, two straight lines emanated at right angles off each of its wings. The original pattern repeated with fresh strength at its helm.

"*Que magnifique*," she said.

"Yes, they are magnificent. Those are the Canada geese." He paused the party's northeastern trek and everyone watched the flock flying south. "They winter in the South," Skeggs said, "and will fly back home for the summer."

"Marvelous how they do. Where would you go if you could fly?"

He enjoyed her appreciation in watching the aerial precision. "I'm fine on my feet."

Vittorie craned her neck back. She blocked the sun, putting her right hand beside her face. "Home."

He watched her wipe tears away. Her eyes shone a spectacular green, like the liquid brilliance of the gorgeous dogbane beetle. "Is that where would you fly to, *Chrysochus auratus*?" he asked, nicknaming her after the leaf bug.

"So many, together," she said, enthralled by the community above. Another tear dripped over her jaw as she shrugged. "I don't know. I have no place *to* go, no money, but I couldn't stay there…"

He shouldered his rifle and marched on. "What else was taken that you remember?"

Both hands wiped wet off her face. She blew air from between her lips and raised her eyebrows. "*Eu…*matches, a scope, seasonings given me by our cook…my wedding trousseau! I sewed all of it myself while he here, in America.…my mother's pearl earrings and necklace. My father's vest…"

Vittorie darted off the trail. Surrounded by denser woods, she collapsed. Autumn's pageantry fluttered down around her.

"Whoa! Hold up!" Skeggs stopped the first horse, Abraham's palomino, with his hand. "Hold the others here, Abe. Got a slight delay."

Hidden from the group's eyes, she cried, her shoulders shaking. "My father said…" she began as Skeggs approached. Tears raced down her cheeks. She wiped them on her collar and wrists, but they kept coming.

Skeggs crouched in front of her and rested his elbows over his knees, balanced. He had an incredible ability to be still.

"My father said…give the vest to his eldest grandson…" Grief consumed her. She fell over. "My family cross for their eldest granddaughter…" Her sentences were cut short with sobs and saliva dripped from her mouth as it hung open in agony.

Skeggs reached forward but stopped. Her acute pain affected him. Knowing how it feels to be separated, he laid his hand on her back.

71

Nolin Station. Western Virginia Settlement

Larger than any outpost Vittorie had seen since Lexington, Nolin Station showed signs of abandonment. Absence of upkeep had weathered all structures into pale shades of gray. Front doors hung askew. Composed of wood or stone, crude buildings still crowded the center core, built with materials the original craftsmen had on hand.

Abraham and the other men of the scouting party dismounted. They attended their horses but remained just inside the entrance. Few people milled about. A woman helped a small girl avoid fresh manure in the street. A horse and rider turned a thin corridor between buildings as he snapped the reins.

Two men waited outside a newer log structure. Skeggs greeted them with a nod. "I see the LaRues are still in health."

One leaned against the doorframe. The other sat astride a barrel. Both held flint-lock rifles.

"Phillips gone to the Cumberland?" Skeggs asked.

"No, ye've caught him. He's inside," said the barrel-sitter with a backward jerk of his head. "Ah see you got your hands full, Mr. Henry." He smiled in Vittorie's direction.

"Nothing that can't be worked out." Skeggs stepped between them to let himself through the door.

Vittorie breathed the crisp autumn air. Tree limbs above rooftops waved crimson, amber, and rust. The sun shone. When the wind blew, it sent a half-rainbow of leaves showering down the narrow streets below. Four men worked along the perimeter, uprooting pointed stakes and hauling them off on a flat sled hooked to two donkeys.

Skeggs reemerged. "Greet your fathers for me, would you, boys?" The door banged shut. "Come with me," Skeggs said in French to Vittorie, walking off the plank-board porch.

She followed. After several paces, she noticed she was the only one running after him. "Where are we going?"

"Hodgen's Mill."

"Why?"

"Because you need a family."

"What?"

"It's about a two-mile jaunt. Can you make two more miles today?"

"What's a mile?"

"Kilometers." He rested his arm through his rifle strap and looked at her. "A little over three kilometers." When she thought about it too long, he shifted his weight, turned, and took off at a slow jog. "Keep up."

She stuffed the little bag of belongings in her shirt against her belly and retied her belt underneath it. Beginning to jog behind him, she grabbed the butt of her rifle. Its strap wrapped over her shoulder but holding it this way stopped its errant swinging and forced its movements to coincide with the thrust of her arms, the cadence of her feet. Her other arm moved in syncopation.

They loped down the steep hillside, feet pounding faster near the bottom. Vittorie's knees jarred as the ground leveled out flat again.

"What about the others?" she shouted. "Aren't they coming, too?"

"Nope. You need a house. They're searching for land." His legs swished through the high grasses. "I know the family, and Phillips agreed."

"Who?" She kept her blouse tucked in to run and didn't interrupt him.

"Phillip Phillips, at Nolin Station there. He's been here since the beginning, really. They call that Phillips Fort now, but I know it as Nolin Station. He's become a judge. Learned his boyhood from the natives. Been a surveyor over much of this area. Station's mostly disbanded, as you see. Building farms further outside the settlements is safer these last few years."

"How…can you say that…."

He didn't answer. Instead, his feet turned onto a road cut with a plow. She broke through the last grasses herself and the road was a welcome change. The lack of opposition around her feet and ankles made it easier to stretch them and keep up.

His moccasins made rhythmic noises. "I'm sorry," he said. "I realize that isn't your experience. The tribes ranged this land for centuries prior to Europeans. There's been much misunderstanding where property boundaries and treaties are concerned." His whole body moved as one, limbs propelled by muscles at solid joints around his core. "Except for the attack on your party, there hasn't been hostility in this area since…well, two or three years. It doesn't make sense," he said, running and talking with ease. "For many moons, there had been peace."

Vittorie ran in silence. Both thighs felt tight. Her feet hurt. Yet she pounded them down, one after the other, to stay with the one man who seemed to know these woods and everyone in them. The dry dirt path meandered through the field, then a hedgerow of maples. After it they came upon descending hills stuck with huge gray rocks bigger than she was, laced with white marbling.

This part of the country was full of angles—hillsides up and great slopes down. Massive trees stood alone and the road snaked past, only to happen upon a whole grove of another sort and then a bunch of mixed trees. The terrain allowed a person to run it. No bluffs or cliffs appeared, just mounds of golden earth high as mountains without snow. Autumn yellows and oranges and reds popped out of summer's green tapestry spread out all around them.

At the top of one particularly high hill, she slowed. The view took her breath away. *"Mon Dieu!* I have never seen so beautiful a fabric swath as this!"

Seeing her ecstasy in the landscape, he stopped running and walked in a half-circle back to where she first stopped.

She faced the setting sun and shielded her eyes with a hand. "How far we can see?"

The wind blew to cool their sweat and the smoldering sun radiated the last heat of the day.

"Some peoples say, 'Sky threw its cape over Earth here, and their embrace birthed the country you see.'"

"I like that."

He pointed to his left. "Over that ridge, that's the north fork of the Nolin River. The Widow Sellers has a farm there."

"Is that where we're going?"

"That's where you're going."

72

Skeggs opened the metal gate of a house with a blue door and deep blue shutters. Matching glass windows flanked both sides. Entering the property of a house with some wealth made Vittorie insecure. "I can't go in there," she said, halting outside the wooden fence. "I'm not dressed."

"That's the first thing you've said that makes you sound like a female. You've been dressed the entire time I've known you, let the record show. And besides," he said, walking back to hold the gate open for her a second time, "you're coming here to work, not sit."

"Work?" she asked, embracing the idea. "What kind of work?"

"A farm always has work." He motioned with his hand for her to walk through. "What you ought to be asking is 'what are the terms?'"

She crossed the small pebbles that created the property border. The gate creaked closed and Skeggs resumed the lead to the brick house. Three steps were hewn from stone, dark gray in color, and wide enough for two people to walk up together. Skeggs pulled the brass knocker up and rapped it down twice to announce their presence.

In France, she would have been able to approach with confidence, to speak with wit and intelligence. Her too-small clothes, ripped at the shoulder and torn at the knee, embarrassed her. It lacked multiple layers. It had no petticoat. No skirting flounced beneath. The sleeves had the meanest gathers at the seams – not pleats. Stitching existed to hold pieces together, nothing more. The weave was even, but offered no details. No knots of pink thread created flowers; no reds nor yellows added highlights and shadow. Nature herself colored the flax that spun into skeins on the Highbaugh women's wheel. It fell over her hips, straight down from the old rope belt. It covered her.

She breathed out a little too loud.

"You'll get along fine, here," Skeggs assured her.

Vittorie looked down at her dress. In the summer it had been itchy. At night, it kept her warm. Wrinkled and ripped at the moment, however, it was in abysmal need of washing.

A lovely, dark-haired woman opened the door. "Mr. Henry! How ya be?" Her smile spread between two sculpted cheeks. Her dyed-blue dress fit her well, her shoes were polished, and a pressed linen apron wrapped clean around her middle.

"Fine as a frog hair, Miss Grace. Mrs. S in?"

"Come in, come in," the woman said. She stepped back and waved her arm to speed their decision. Eyelashes curled above her dark brown eyes. Her burnt-butter skin hadn't a wrinkle. She smelled of wood smoke and wax.

She caught eyes with Vittorie. Without even a glance at the offending outfit, the dimples pulled her cheeks into another genuine grin. "Welcome to you, Miss."

Skeggs and Miss Grace exchanged more words Vittorie didn't understand.

"Wait here." Skeggs motioned to a bench above an oilskin rug in the hall.

She sat. Skeggs followed Miss Grace through a red door on the right, and when it closed behind them, all familiarity disappeared. She was left alone. The hall was quaint, informal. The only furniture besides a boot scrape and a gilded mirror was a carved table near the bench she sat on. Spying the mirror, she jumped off the seat and looked at her reflected self.

"Oh!" she cried. Disgusting smudges of mud streaked her jaw. Wild hair puffed out around her head in every direction. *"I look like the fountains of Versailles—with no wig!"* Raking her fingertips through the mess of hair, she attempted to coax it into a manageable shape. Her curls refused the coercion, so she licked her fingertips and smoothed. Unsuccessful in the day's heat, she threw her wrists up. "Now I look like the baby chicks, just out of the shell at the mill—some feathers wet and stuck down tight, others poofed up and fuzzy." Her fingertips tried again but her hair only volumed higher. Unable to manage any better, she mumbled to herself, "If the estate owners have any curls among them, they'll understand."

She stuck her chin out at the mirror for a look at the smudge, then glanced around for a wash basin. Finding none, she licked her fingers and wiped at the dried mud. Instead of cleanliness, three additional marks appeared where she'd wiped.

"Ugh!" She wiped her dirty hands on her skirt. Unsure what other help could be extracted from the simple hall, she picked up her linsey-woolsey hem and bent her face down to it, rubbed her chin and cheek with the underside of it and checked in the mirror again. The dirt came off but her cheek glowed bright red. Checking each cheek back and forth in the mirror, she rubbed the other side till it also glowed. Once the reds matched, she returned to the bench. Hearing voices behind the red door, she untied the cloth from her waist. Having another quick thought about her hair, she wrapped her head in the fabric and sat down again, folding her hands.

The door at the far end creaked open. Skeggs' clear voice and a different female voice finished speaking. The woman's voice sounded like a large bell, deep and sturdy. Vittorie stood up and smoothed her skirt, awaiting further introductions, but the door closed again. Skeggs and the bell voice spoke in hushed tones. Tempted to put her ear to the door, she leaned in its direction, but remembered her upbringing and straightened up. Their conversation continued in English, so she waited. Standing there felt awkward, so she sat. The door flung open once more and Vittorie rose to meet them.

A tall woman with speckled gray and white hair led Skeggs through the doorway. "Well, she looks healthy!" The woman's deep voice bellowed out against the wooden walls. "Look at those cheeks! Bright as a red-feathered cardinal bird!" She stuck her face down lower to get a clear look at Vittorie. "Henry said you've met misfortune on the Wilderness Trail but you're handy around the house." Her gown flounced as she moved, petticoats assured. The solid gray coat she wore fit her well and puffed full at the sleeves. Her dress was of gray and white-striped cotton, pinched and tucked with European elegance. Silk ribbons edged the bodice.

"Mrs. Sellers, may I introduce, Mrs. Gilbert LeClerc," Skeggs said.

Vittorie curtsied but her face burned redder. "Hullo," she said, remembering her upbringing and practicing her English.

"Very well, dear," Mrs. Sellers said. "Ask her what she thinks, Henry."

Skeggs stood between both women. He addressed Vittorie in French. "They need help in the kitchen three days a week. Some of the other families around…"

"Tell her she'll have every other Sunday off," Mrs. Sellers interrupted.

According to the lines on the woman's outfit, Vittorie guessed the undergarment used stays for shape. For a woman of her height and age, the bosoms that bobbed at the top of the shirting must have had support. While tasteful, vertical ribbing inside the dress was almost certain.

Skeggs nodded and continued. "Other families might have things that need doing the other three days, so you might gain additional income to buy your indenture back faster. And, every other Sabbath you'll have off. There's a closet back of the kitchen that could be cleaned out for your quarters. She'll pay you one day for every two weeks you work, the rest to be your room and board. The other families can trade or pay you outright. What say you to terms?"

His question at the end came without warning. She looked past him to the tall woman peering over his shoulder and nodded. Skeggs retrieved his hat from a hook on the white-washed wall and stretched his hand for the door.

"Are you leaving me?" The words were said before Vittorie had time to check them.

Depressing the latch, he exited but stuck his head back in. "I'll check on you," he said. With a smile she hadn't seen before, he looked from Mrs. Sellers back to her and shut the door behind him.

Vittorie watched him through the mottled glass window until Mrs. Sellers said, "You can call me Samantha. We believe in first names here. Let me show you around."

She left the hallway, leading Vittorie from the window and into the next phase of her life.

73

"Mr. Sellers' people were originally from England. Norman origin, so there may be French in the ancestry somewhere, like yourself. I was raised in Virginia—Williamsburg—and when I married Mr. Sellers, he gained land, slaves, and not an unsubstantial sum through my dowry." She laid her long fingers on the straight back of a dining room chair. It stood at the head of a fine, rectangular table with smooth benches down either side. No matching chair paralleled it at the far end. "The silver in the cupboards, candlesticks, servers, all came through me. Though Mr. Sellers did give me the soup tureen as a wedding present."

Not understanding the whole story, Vittorie watched the woman's mouth. She pieced together what words she could: French, Sellers, land. When Mrs. Sellers paused, Vittorie followed her gaze to the delicate soup tureen of blue, yellow, and pink flowers painted on a cream background. The oval soup server's matching lid had a raised leaf painted emerald green on top.

"I bore him three sons and a daughter," she continued. "Edward, Elias, Ebenezer, and Charlotte. All the children are married now with lands of their own around Nolin." She stiffened as she spoke. "Mr. Sellers died April 1785, and as I disagree with the bondage of another human, I declared our slaves free. Charles would turn over in his grave, if he could. I'm leaving this farm to the current members of the family who work it, regardless of heritage." Her defiant brown eyes stared at Vittorie.

This being the woman's house and Vittorie not understanding it all except for the passion, she kept silent. They moved into another room with two windows. Each one had print fabric in yellows and blues draped over a rod. The curtains cascaded in symmetrical folds down each side of the casement with a delicate, scalloped effect.

"I am the mistress of the manor." The sentence sobered Mrs. Sellers as she said it. "As a widow, I'm no longer considered '*feme covert*'. Legally, I'm '*feme sole*'. According to Mr. Sellers's will and colonial law I'm allowed to preside over the estate. I live here now alone with Grace, Clem, Faith, and Rightly. We work the land and make it home."

Two upholstered chairs in a seaside-blue fabric sat on opposite sides of an impeccably carved white-oak chest. The three front panels had raised floral patterns, bordered on all sides by thinner strips of wood. Each of these strips had been carved into round and swirling motifs, the workman's premiere talent.

The artistry of the chest appearing here in the woods surprised Vittorie. She walked around a painted oilskin rug in the center of the room and reached her fingers out to touch the intricate details on the ornate furniture piece.

"No! Please don't touch!" Mrs. Sellers said.

Vittorie's hand snapped back to her side. With no way to explain her appreciation of the furniture's design, she moved away from it and returned to Mrs. Sellers's side of the room.

Waving a lengthy arm, Mrs. Sellers said, "There was nothing here before us." Obvious pride filled her eyes. "Everything you see, we've established."

She led them out a back door and down a rough stone pathway past the plucked remains of what looked to have been a lovely garden.

"There's the chicken yard, smoke house, upper fields." She pointed high to the north. "The lower fields are beyond."

She talked too fast for Vittorie to pick out many words, but she followed behind the willowy older woman anyway.

The wind brought a familiar scent to Vittorie's nostrils. She sniffed the air, insistent for another whiff. Distracted from her tour, she saw a particular green shoot in the garden by her knees. Picking one bright stalk, she inhaled and plucked another from a second bush and then a strip from a third, smelling each in turn.

Mrs. Sellers kept talking, unaware she'd lost her audience in the herb garden. "'Round there's the stable and woodpile. North fork of Nolin River's right through those cherry trees."

Their path came to an end at a smallish building separate from the others. The wood slat structure was square with a tall roof and a foundation made of rounded stones.

"You'll begin your days here," Mrs. Sellers said, "cooking." She opened the door and let Vittorie step inside.

Along the biggest part of the far wall yawned a vast, stone hearth. Crackling heat from burning logs on the firedogs warmed the cozy room. Overhead, heavy crossbeams dried bundles of hanging herbs and strands of garlic bulbs. Wooden boxes on shelves under the window held potatoes. On a round worktable in the center of the room, a bushel of apples overflowed. One caned stool tucked under the table; another doubled as the current resting spot for an apron and shears. Pots and fire pokers hung from wrought iron hooks under the mantel. A stack of kindling filled a woven basket. The space was tidy and neat, with necessary utensils placed orderly on shelves.

"Many hands make light work, especially now the children are grown. There's always something to be done, seems like."

Vittorie's fingers wandered around the room touching the pots, spoons, skillets, and food. She lifted an apple to her nose. It smelled of heat and juice. She paused at the north-facing window with a view of the back fields.

"Do you understand anything I'm saying?" Mrs. Sellers asked.

Vittorie lifted a ladle from its hook. Her eyebrows relaxed. "'*Femme couvert*', *non*. *Femme sole*, yes.You are own. I live here," she replied in halting English. "I work…to you."

Satisfied, Mrs. Sellers clapped her hands together. She laughed a great laugh, straight from her belly. "Yes!" she said, gazing out the open door. Her expression clouded. "Let's see about your room." With that, she turned away and headed back to the main house. Vittorie assumed she was to follow, which she did, and closed the kitchen door behind her.

74

Uncle Clem and Rightly worked in the upper fields. Sunlight washed their rows in blinding effects as they cut the last of the hay.

"We goin' be don' t'day, Uncle Clem?" Rightly asked. Just eight years old, he swung his small scythe with ease.

"Keep workin' until they ain't no mo' to do," Clem said. "Soon's we tie the last bundle an' set it in the loft, I'll let you know we's done."

"Sho' seems a heap mo' 'an las' year." Rightly's 'r' sounds faded off, indistinct.

"Livestock'll need it all t' make it through t' spring. Hits gone be a col' wintuh." Clem's deep voice exaggerated the last two words, emphasizing the drop in temperature he expected.

Rightly chuckled at the older man's humor. Clem laughed along with the boy. Down by the house, Vittorie carried two old cots into the yard. The sight of a new person caught their attention, but didn't slow their work.

"Look d'ar," said Rightly. His arms kept moving, but his eyes watched the strange woman.

"Mm, hmmm." Clem acknowledged the information as he wrapped another bundle.

"She's wo'kin'," Rightly said.

"Sho 'nuff." Clem cut and bundled along the row, distracted by the activity down by the house.

One by one the butter churn, a small stack of wood, and a spinning wheel made their appearance on the back lawn.

Rightly stretched up on his heels and waved one pink hand to a woman milking a fawn-colored cow in the lower field. His mother, Faith, acknowledged him with a nod. Rightly pointed to the mystery woman up at the house. He scrunched up his shoulders and bent his elbows with palms up in a silent question. "Who she?" he mouthed down the hillside to her.

She nodded again, hands above the pail. When he didn't quit, she stopped her work and shooed his attention back to his. Wrapping a crocheted shawl over her shoulders, she sat on the three-legged stool. "Ah seen huh." Her fingers encircled the Jersey's pale udders. "Ah s'pose we'll learn mow at suppah..." She gave a strong nudge as a nursing calf would. The repetitious squirt of fresh, creamy milk hit the side of her pail again. "...what 'nother woman's doin' onnuh fahm." But she, too, watched the new business with interest.

75

Vittorie emptied the large closet in back of the house that Samantha had shown her. Swept and scrubbed, she replaced what was necessary to create a bedroom out of the space. An open bedroll filled two-thirds of the area, leaving a third on one side for walking and hanging things.

Having no extra wardrobe and few items of her own made it simple enough to keep house for herself. She laid the rifle at the head of her bed and pulled the stuffed sack out of her shirt. The sheath and knife she retied and stuck back inside the pouch in her skirt. A rusted nail became the hook for the piece of cloth Candle gave her.

Gilbert's buttons spilled out. She stared at the seven brass orbs tipped on their edges and strewn in a misshapen line. Kneeling down, she lay beside them and rested her head on her hand. Touching one, she let the outer rim circle around on the rough wood floor, examining it. Double circles coursed around the outside edge, except where two of the ends met in budding petals. Centered above those was a single raised bump, but in the center of the button itself were two shapes next to each other. The first, like a teardrop, disconnected at one of the top points and drooped inward toward the middle. The second, like a horse's back legs, had one straight line and one bent in a hard angle in the middle.

Her thumb brushed over the symbols, whatever they were. The buttons sealed him up, kept him warm, decorated him with honor. They meant Gilbert to her. She looked at the knife sheath and rifle. Those came from him too and were memories to her, not weapons. She sighed and got up. Time to work. She passed a small boy heading into the hallway. Rightly carried new bundles of flax indoors.

"Ah need maybe fow-uh mo', Rightly," Grace called down the stairs after the boy.

"Yes, Miss Grace," he said on his way past Vittorie.

Vittorie touched the sanded railing of the staircase and walked up. In the first room to the right she found Grace restuffing Mrs. Sellers' bed.

"Fresh stuffin' gon' make this wintuh pass a 'hole lot bettuh," Grace said to Vittorie standing in the doorway. "Clem done said it and he's nevuh been wrong yet. That man knows!" Her eyes bulged for emphasis and she shook her head, pushing hay into the linen sack sewn to fit the frame. "Grab that side and shove it in deep."

Vittorie guessed more than understood what Grace's motions meant and she walked across wide oak planks to the bedframe to do as she was bid. Grace's manner put her at ease and the task took the worries from her mind as she worked them out through her hands.

"Ah thinks he's got a weathuhvane for a backbone and barometers bobbin' in his blood. Some people jes' know." She tossed a pillow to Vittorie and a folded square of cotton. "And Clem's one who knows. If he say it's gon' be cole, you may's jes' git your wool stockins ready by the side o' your bed, Miss Vi, an' you sho' gon' be glad you did."

Rightly returned, arms loaded, hesitant to speak to her. She smiled as he passed and he smiled back but quickened his step past her. He set the bundles at Miss Grace's feet and left.

"He's quiet as a mouse, sometimes," Grace said, "but, Lawd, don't that boy know how to holluh at the river!"

Vittorie smiled. "I no speak English good. I learn."

Grace smoothed a cotton sheet over the plump linen mattress and set two pillows at the head. "You'll do jes' fine, Miss Vi." She looked Vittorie over, then patted her arm. "Come on, it's time t' git suppah on. You ken he'p me today. Tomarruh, Mrs. S gon' tell me what's your'n to do."

76

Vittorie was carrying extra firewood to the kitchen when she saw a woman approach with two milk buckets balanced over her shoulders. Careful to keep her back straight while her foot snagged a rope latch, the woman lifted a door in the ground with her foot and lowered the two buckets down. Finishing her job first, she wiped her hands on her apron and stood up to face the newcomer.

"I's Faith," she said, golden eyes sparkling. Rightly came from the smokehouse and walked past them. "Tha's'un my boy, Rightly."

"Vittorie," Vittorie said, pointing to herself.

"Tha's fine," Faith said, slow and easy. Her collarbone showed at the top of her round neckline. She pressed sweat off her forehead with the back of her hand.

Both women drew in a breath to speak at the same time but stopped. Faith smiled and waited.

"*Qu'est-ce que c'est ca?*" Vittorie tapped her toe on the door in the ground. "What is?"

"Rutt sella?" Faith's hair parted in the middle and curled to frame her face. "Kep 'em cole." She opened the door with her hand this time and it stayed open at an angle.

Vittorie followed her down inside, touching the cold stone walls. Wooden crates stored potatoes, turnips, parsnips, and onions. Baskets overflowed with carrots and apples. On a narrow

361

stone ledge above a dozen metal milk jugs, individual eggs lay cushioned between fabrics.

Vittorie stood beside the large orange vegetables she'd seen in Charleston. "I no know this."

"Punkin," Faith said, showing a little gap between her two top front teeth.

Vittorie touched its skin and repeated the new word. "Punkin." Her eyes darted around the secret room full of edible treasures. "Rutt sella." Her stomach growled. Overcome with gratitude, she grabbed the dark-skinned milkmaid's hand and gave it a quick squeeze.

Startled by such ease, Faith returned a little squeeze before letting go. She smiled at the new woman who didn't know what a root cellar was. "Where do you come from?" Faith asked, then restated with more hesitation between words, "What…is…your…country?"

"France. *Et vous?*" Vittorie asked.

"Mali." The word leapt from her heart and spilled across her lips. "In Africa." Sadness wreathed her face. She forced a smile, but grief remained in her eyes.

"Africa," Vittorie lowered her voice, "is *belle*…beautiful…people. You want…go home?"

Faith lowered her eyes at the compliment. "Beauty is not always a gift." She saw the questioning look on Vittorie's face but changed the subject. "This land is wide and Mali is far. No one waits for me there. I got no money to cross the sea, an' I have Rightly." She glanced up the steps to the clouds. "Do you miss France?"

Vittorie understood all but the last sentence. A dull ache weighed on her chest. "*Mademoiselle France?*"

Faith said it differently. "Here, it is wild. Tall trees. Few people. No boats." She picked up an onion from a basket and smelled it.

Wrinkling her nose for effect, she passed the root vegetable under Vittorie's nose for her to smell.

Vittorie took it from Faith's outstretched hand, happy to find something familiar. *"L'oignion!"* She wrapped both hands around it and inhaled again. The willingness of this other woman to communicate touched something deep inside her.

Faith laughed at Vittorie and pointed to the onion. "In Mali, we eat this," she said. Pinching the tips of all her fingers on one hand together and bringing it to her mouth, she pretended to bite. After a moment of chewing, she smiled and rubbed her belly.

"En France, aussi. What eat Mali?"

"Mali kisses the ocean." The pink of her palm cupped, then lifted up and down like the waves of the sea. Then, she pressed the palms of her hands together and wriggled them back and forth, like a fish swimming through water.

"Ah, *poisson!"* Vittorie said. She made the same motion with her hands and repeated, *"un poisson."*

"Fish." Faith rubbed her belly, smiling.

"Feesh." Vittorie made the fish with her hands again. She made the fish swim up to her mouth and pretended to take a bite, chewing vigorously. Enamored with her newfound friend's ability to communicate, she finished the charade with a dramatic swallow.

The ladies laughed together. Empathy lit their hearts and reminded them who they were, where they came from. When the humor faded, they stood silent, each traveling in memory to kingdoms far away. The women recollected themselves long ago, savoring the precious individuality of once-daily life, life before standing in the musty cellar. Here, the familiarities of home were removed except in dreams or conversations like this. For a moment, they were rich again.

77

Mornings came early the world over, but none so early as on a farm. Vittorie barely slept, intending to make a good impression her first day of work. As soon as she could see the form of her hand in the dark, she was up and out the back door to her kitchen.

By the time Clem and Rightly shuffled past to finish the upper fields, they saw the glow of fire and smelled cooked herbs in the air. Rightly looked in the kitchen window. His breath fogged the very image he wished to spy on. "I can't see."

Clem laughed as he wiped it free with his sleeve and licked his lips for the promise of breakfast. "We shall see what we shall see, Mistuh Rightly. Both Miss Grace an' your mama's good inuh kitchen. But I sho' know I plannuh be hungreh thus mo'ning, and with the harves' on us, and Miss Grace and Miss Faith so busy, I's tired of stale cakes an on'y buttuh." He tugged the boy's ear in play and walked down the path to the fields. "Ano'w pairuh han's gon' be welcome on thus fahm, fo' sho'."

"Fo' sho'." Rightly repeated Clem's happy tone.

When the meal bell rang later, they'd had already put up eighteen sheaves. The calm surface broke in the wash basin as they plunged their hands in to wash up.

"Go back'n'use the lye," Faith called to Rightly. His hands were still dirty as she turned him away from the door which led to breakfast. He trudged back to the soap and the bucket.

Grace helped Vittorie carry two large covered skillets from the outdoor kitchen's fireplace to the dining room table. Steam wafted around the room. Everyone breathed in the good smells. Vittorie looked pleased when she removed the first cover and displayed the fruits of her labor.

The dining room was on the north side of the house, so the brass oil lamps were lit. More than light glowed on the faces gathered around the table. Vittorie took the long kitchen knife and sliced into the savory galette. Plates were passed.

As each person was served, they held something up, saying its name aloud. Grace started first. Passing the round disk in front of her to Vittorie to be served, she said, "Plate." Vittorie pushed the triangular piece off her server with a knife, not understanding. Grace tapped on the pewter and repeated, "plate."

Vittorie's eyes widened, accompanied in motion by her eyebrows. "Play-t," she said, with much emphasis on the "T."

Rightly jumped in next. "'Poon," he said, eager to not be the only one with lessons anymore.

"Spoon." Grace corrected him.

Vittorie repeated, "Spoon."

Serving another plate, Faith added, "Ah-pple." She held a red one up.

"Ah-pple." Vittorie smiled.

Uncle Clem took a bite of the steaming food on his plate. After a long chew and swallow, he announced, "Tha's jes' fine!"

78

Harvest continued well into the warm September. No matter what fruit or vegetable was gathered or washed, new energy filled the group. The congenial air of friendship continued and Vittorie learned new words. She helped anywhere she could. In turn, she had many teachers and learned quickly. In the chicken house gathering eggs with Rightly and Grace, all three could be heard counting aloud, "...twent-eh-seven, twent-eh-eight..." Clem taught her "rain" and "coat." She learned simple verbs like "pick," "hold," and "give." The new environment, new focus, and friends were good medicine.

With the decreasing daylight winter brings, the hens laid less. Vittorie brought two or three chickens into the kitchen with her for the day. The light of the fire warmed and confused them as to how long the sun really shone, so they laid more for her. The Sellers family did as much as they could to store food for the winter ahead. The root cellar held tomatoes, summer squash, potatoes, garlic, gourds from the fall garden, carrots, leeks, radishes, apples, pumpkins, mushrooms, a few days' milk, and all the smoked meats. Simple as it was, it lent the Sellers farm comfort and security, the essence of home.

The first Tuesday in October was dry and crisp with smoke churning out of the kitchen chimney all day. Rightly peeked in the open door. He watched as Vittorie stirred the largest black pot.

"What'cha cookin', Miz Vi?"

Vittorie shrugged and pulled the paddle through a savory liquid. A carrot surfaced.

"I foun' three broody hens backside o' the smoke'ouse." The boy set down the bucket of ashes and stared at her, the dark skin of his sweet face beaded with sweat. "Ma tol' me not to gathuh those eggs. If'n I don't, they'll hatch under their ma's wahum wings."

Intending to send him on his way happy, she handed him a fresh yeast roll. Instead, he padded barefoot across the stone floor and tucked both legs under him on the stool. Dried garlic hung just over his head.

"Ducks an' geese 'r' hard to manage," he said. "They lay their eggs out on the groun'. Not in a nest." He bit the roll with his side teeth and kept talking. "Las' win'er we found eggs frozen on the groun'. Mama cried. I was hungry." He swallowed and bit again. "Now I's searchin' all'a time fo' them's ducks. We gonna pen 'em this win'er. Clem an' I."

He pointed at a little spade she'd forgotten in the potato basket. She nodded out of politeness. He burst into a grin and jumped down. Gaps for new teeth showed in his eight-year-old mouth. Pulling a string from his pocket, he tied the garden tool to his belt and spun his hips back and forth. He stopped, then started again, enraptured. Finally, he gave it a tug to make sure it stuck fast.

"Tha's fine!"

His joy caused Vittorie to smile for real. She needed the spade to dig weeds, but that could wait. It did her good to see Rightly happy. He deserved it. He wrapped his thin arms around her filthy skirt. His hug was so tight, it almost knocked her over.

"*De rien!*" she said, brushing off the importance she felt for the boy. "Tha's alright."

Faith stepped up to the doorway, a milk bucket in each hand. "You behavin'?"

"Hm-hmmm!" Rightly's mouth was full again. "Look! She said I's could use it!" He brandished the shovel. Scooting past the buckets and his mother, he paused for a second in the long shadow of the house. Waving back at Vittorie, the boy disappeared around the blue aster bushes.

"Ah'd like halfuh that boy's happiness." Faith let the pails clunk on the kitchen floor. Not a drop spilled. She lifted her arms and pressed her shoulder blades together to flex the opposite muscles.

"Ah know." Vittorie drained the cheese molds, catching the liquid in a bowl. Afterward, her fingers separated the cheese from the wooden mold. "Lookuh tha' cream!" White foam frothed at the top of the steel buckets.

"Three heif'uh's wiv' calves produce milk so plen'iful that ah take a pail each innuh mornin' and evenin', and there's still 'nuff fo' every calf." Faith rubbed her neck muscles in deep circular motions. "How you doin' t'dee, Vi?" Her deep-set eyes looked at her friend with concern.

Vittorie salted the cheeses. "*Fromages.*"

Faith picked up another wet mold and held it in her hand. "Cheeee-z."

Vittorie turned her back to Faith and took a metal rod off its hook. "Chee-eeze," she said, as she poked the fire.

Uncle Clem knocked on the open kitchen door. He kept his boots outside but poked his broad shoulders in. "You goin' have time t' learn in the smokehouse t'dee, Miz Vi?"

"Yes." Vittorie wiped extra salt off her hands. "T-ank ee-you for ash."

"Well, I 'preciate you makin' soap fo' us all." Clem had a way of turning small works into great appreciation.

"Yer venison yes't'dee was de best you evah done smoke!" Faith said to Clem. She stopped rubbing her neck and folded her slender fingers together in front of her worn linen dress.

Education in many forms served as a worthy distraction from endless grieving. Vittorie learned a lot watching the methodical way Clem worked in the smokehouse. She was never present for the butchering, but the details of curing meats helped focus her mind. New words filled the forefront of her brain, pushing older memories back in the process.

Clem smiled without showing his teeth. His cheeks puffed out about as wide as they could as he enjoyed the compliment. "Ah suppose ah done alright with that'un. Ah'll sen' Rightly fo' you 'rectly after, so you don't need to be there at the first."

79

Carrying her garden spade and a small egg basket, Vittorie walked to the hen house. Her breath puffed before her in the cool, morning air. It felt good to be awake with purpose.

She paused halfway between the house and the chicken coop for a second, just to be still. A candle lit in the upstairs window. Grace was awake. As she continued on, the leather of her boots stretched more with each stride. The sky was pale blue on the eastern horizon. A rooster crowed. Calves old enough to be separated lowed for their mothers in another field. A bell rang from a sheep's neck in the east pasture as the flock grazed. Inky black crows flew overhead.

"Away," Vittorie said aloud. "Fly away."

"Wha's that Miz Vi?"

Clem's voice in the darkness made her jump. "Good mo'nin', Clem."

He wore his wool coat, three buttons undone. "You doin' alright this mo'nin'?" His breath misted between them against the lavender sky.

She nodded, unable to break the stillness with the truth. Her vocabulary failed.

"D'you know this in' ma fav'rite time a day?"

She shook her head. "Is it? It is beauty."

"Ah feel like, mo'nin's like this'n, God's done up t' something and if ah'm quiet, He'll let me in on what He's about."

Wrapping her shawl tighter, Vittorie said, "Ah like that."

"Yes'm, mo'nin' prayuhs is my fav'rite." He bent his head in a gentleman's nod. "You take care, Miz Vi. Novembuh beauty gon' get col' soon 'nuff t'dee. If'n you needs a coat, you see Miz Grace. We boun' t' have anothuh 'roun' someplace fo' yuh."

"Thank yuh, Clem."

"T'aint nothin', Miz Vi." He nodded to her once more. "You'ah mo' impo'tant thanuh coat."

She watched the great form of him move down the path to the barn, so big and so kind. Through the upstairs window, she saw the light of the candle from Mrs. Sellers' room behind lace curtains.

Three steps over slate stones and she opened the kitchen door. Shivering off the night's chill as she entered, she squatted before the fireplace to light the logs placed the night before. "Grow," she said, coaxing the flames in her native tongue, "you've much to accomplish today."

$$80$$

Christmas Eve. 1788

Vittorie spread out everything she'd made. Five handmade offerings for the family lay in one pile on her open bedroll, a variety of her very best handiwork. For Clem, she'd sewn a new shirt, deep burgundy with embroidered edges in a robust brown. His buttons were fabric-wrapped with embroidered wheat details on them. For Rightly, she'd sewn a wool coat and waistcoat in a plum-color with the same brown embroidery as Clem, but with less detailing. Maturity mattered. The coat Rightly had been wearing was threadbare and so small he had to keep his elbows straight gathering eggs.

Vittorie refolded the pieced and quilted lap blanket for Faith, who needed the extra warmth on frigid frontier evenings as she worked late into the nights. For Grace, she'd trimmed a lovely new apron and tatted delicate curls around the edge. For Samantha, the matron of the estate, she crocheted a delicate collar in soft ivory thread. It fastened in back with a thick, mother-of-pearl button.

Vittorie stepped back and checked her work. Her bottom bumped against the wall, close as it was in her makeshift room.

There was a light knock. "We r'all in the parlor, Vi," said Faith's voice from the other side of the door.

"Thank ye," said Vittorie, smiling at her familiar name. "One mo' minute, please."

She gathered the gifts in the little blanket Grace had lent her and headed downstairs to join the festivities.

The parlor glimmered, dressed for the occasion. Everything glowed in saffron hues, warm and inviting. Samantha had set out extra candles and decorated with evergreen boughs across the mantel. The window sills and above each doorway were dressed the same. They looked like the matching sabot sleeves on her old green taffeta dress. Happiness edged some of the grief over in her heart. She bit the inside of her cheek and rushed to lay her gifts next to the fireplace. Its flames were brighter than usual. She stared into them, transfixed, blessed for an occasion to distance her sadness.

Clem brought in extra wood and piled it in the wood bin. "Merr-eh Christmas, Miss Vi." He held out his hand, and when she took his, he clasped a rough right hand on top. "We'uh glad you come to us." He kept his voice low, the words for her alone.

She couldn't help the tear that raced down the curve of her left cheek. They never touched during work or life, but tonight, on the celebration of heaven reaching down to earth, the firm grasp of his hands was healing. "Thank ye," she said.

"I's a wond-eh how y'all have dec'rated," he said. "Right purty." He dropped her hands and thumbed his suspenders.

"*Joyo No-el!*" Rightly bounced in singing, lifting the mood with his childish delight. He wiggled and giggled, giddy with youthful anticipation, and repeated the French Christmas greeting she'd taught him. "*Joy-o, No-el! Joy-o, No-el!*"

"*Tres bien!*" Vittorie said. "*Joyeux Noel!*" The double patches on his knees made her sorry she hadn't made breeches for him yet.

"Time for gifts!" Samantha said, tapping her spoon on the silver for attention. "Rightly! Come first!" She pointed to a worn blanket covering something tucked behind her chair.

Being the only child gave Rightly certain privileges unusual the rest of the year. He ripped the cover off. "A toy wagon!"

"And the wheels really spin!" said Samantha, not letting him lose a minute.

"Can I hitch Anderson to it? He's big 'nuff to pull me, ain't 'e?" asked Rightly.

Clem and Faith exchanged looks. "Spring is still a way off," Faith said, unsure how to respond to Rightly's request to harness the goat.

"Oh, I think he's old enough," said Samantha, settling deeper into her chair. "He's got to learn how to handle a team sometime." She passed around the plate of Vittorie's home baked sweet rolls from the side table, reserving an extra one for herself.

Rightly paused, caught between them. Faith put on a smile for her son but her eyebrow raised like the hair on the dogs' necks when they scrapped. Rightly gave Samantha a hug, received two sticks of candy, and sat himself quietly next to his mother.

"I guess I'll go first," Samantha said. She passed around a piece of stick candy to each, some store-bought mints, and a gift befitting their work. Clem received a new ax head and Grace a thick wool shawl. "I paid Vittorie to crochet it!"

"Oh, it's fine!" said Grace, feeling the softness of the indigo-dyed wool.

Doubly pleased to see Grace's pleasure in it, Vittorie smiled. "We hoped you'd like it."

Faith received Grace's old boots to wear plus a new purple handkerchief.

"To wrap your hair in," Grace said.

Faith folded the small piece of cotton again and laid it atop the boots. "Thank ye."

Vittorie unwrapped her brown paper gift to find four matching bottles. She opened the first and sniffed at its contents. "*Poivre?*" The translation wasn't coming to her.

"Sea salt, cinnamon, fresh pepper, and allspice," Samantha said, helping. Her whole face creased as she smiled.

"*Sel et* Pep…," said Vittorie.

Grace corrected her. "Salt."

"Salt," said Vittorie, "pepper, cinnamon, and…." She passed it for the others to smell. "*Merci beaucoup.* Thank ye much." The delightful gifts made her warm inside. There'd be new opportunities open to her in her cooking because of them. The present really was for the household, but the expense for spices was high. Her gift had cost the most.

"Ah'll pass 'round next," Clem said, surprising them all. He'd whittled wooden animals in perfect likeness—a fine horse which resembled Samantha's own for her, a cow for Faith, a fox for Rightly, a whippoorwill for Grace, and a crowing rooster for Vittorie. Everyone thanked Clem, and Rightly and Faith hugged him in appreciation.

Rightly and Faith followed in passing around gifts, with Faith officiating and Rightly passing. Rightly took his job quite serious. Faith had stuffed small burlap pieces with dried herbs left over from the garden into small sachets. Each was tied with jute and decorated with a piece of torn linen.

Vittorie recognized it. "Faith! Is your…you break good dress to give us ribbon!"

"Jes' from th'inside hem," Faith said. Her eyelashes fluttered at being found out.

Vittorie also noticed the jute from what Clem and Rightly used to bundle hay with. "*Merci,*" she said, as Rightly delivered hers. Rising, she crossed the room to give Faith a hug. "Thank ye."

Grace had dipped candles for each of them. She passed the slender tapers out from a little white oak basket she'd made. The basket she handed to Samantha.

"Lovely! Your handwork improves every year," Samantha said. "Thank you, dear Grace."

Vittorie went last. As each person opened their gift, she saw true joy spread over their face. It washed over her, each wave compounding the one before. Through this cavalcade of tiny appreciations, she was overcome with emotions and darted out to the kitchen. When she returned with more rolls, everyone overlooked her red face and believed the serving of sweets to be the reason for her quick escape. All was not perfect, but it was well.

After the singing and the stories, Rightly fell asleep in front of the fireplace, one arm draped through his wagon's wheel. Faith stroked his forehead. Clem snuggled in the Philadelphia Chippendale chair Samantha was so proud of. He snored with his mouth closed and his chin tucked in his collar. Samantha gazed into the fire while Grace hummed and rocked in the rocking chair.

In the matching Philadelphia Chippendale chair, Vittorie sat, welcome in the room. She licked some honey from her lip and chewed her sweet roll. It tasted nothing like Cook's back home, but it wasn't awful. The others enjoyed them.

"Thank you for the happiness," Faith said to the others as she scooped up her son. Rightly's weight looked easy as she lifted him in her arms. "Ah'll leave the wagon for tonight."

"G'night, Faith," said Samantha.

"Thank ye for the friendship," said Vittorie. "*Bonne nuit.* G'night."

Mother and son left with Christmas blessings. Grace roused Clem and they headed upstairs.

"G'night, Vittorie LeClerc," said Samantha. Her long fingers rested on Vittorie's shoulder as she passed by. "I'm glad you've come to us, dear." She gathered the empty plate with only honey dripped where the sweet rolls used to be and carried it into the dining room. "Merry Christmas to you and may God bless you. You've certainly been a gift to us." She took a lamp and went to bed.

Still in her chair, Vittorie let the sounds of the fireplace lull her in the empty room. "*Oh, Gilbert,*" she thought, sitting beside the flickering fire, "*how I miss you! How you would have enjoyed a night like tonight.*" But, of course, if Gilbert had been there, she wouldn't have been there either. She would have been with him. The ache in her heart, her one constant companion, grew somehow a bit more distant. Though she knew a hard cry would follow later, she was happy in this room with the light and the love, and that was miracle enough for now.

81

Christmas sparked an idea in Vittorie's mind. During the new year's cold winter months, she embroidered a bolt of blue ticking to sell back at a higher cost to the trading post. She chose three bold colors of thread—a lemon yellow, a dark aubergine, and a spiced orange. Stitched into curling fronds and strong stems, wending their way up the ticking staffs, they made her yearn to keep the fabric herself with how they complemented each other.

"How'd you learn t' stitch like that?" Grace asked, resting the needle and linsey-woolsey piece in her lap.

"In France," Vittorie said, "all little girls learn." Her 'r's' sounded throaty from her native pronunciation, but her vocabulary had improved.

Samantha looked up from the book. "There's enough finished fabric there to cut several men's coats and waistcoats, depending on the buyers. You've truly improved its quality, Vittorie. It's very finely done."

Clem kept whittling. "The twenty-sixth o' March ah'm goin' t' see Isaiah about seed. You kin ride 'long."

"An' Clem'll watch out for ye. Make sho' Mistuh Isaiah Gardner is fair in his purchase o' your work," Grace added. She'd set her jaw just so. That was her way of declaring a thing, and when she declared a thing, it *was* so.

"Yes," said Samantha. "That will be good." Everything settled, she looked down again at the book in her hands. "'Cast your bread upon the waters, and in due time, it will return to you,'" she said, reading the night's passage. "Ecclesiastes eleven, the first verse. What do you think that means, Vittorie?" Her light brown eyes waited, expecting an answer.

"*Pardonnez mo*i?"

"…English…."

"Again, please?"

Samantha lingered in her gaze but then reread the passage. "'Cast your bread upon the waters, and in due time, it will return to you.' What do you think it means?" She took a mothering role, especially with Vittorie, though education ran deep in her veins.

Caught off guard, Vittorie found a ready excuse. "*Eu*…just sewing."

The wind howled outside and drove the rain hard against the glass window behind her. Vittorie flinched. The pain of a year ago overwhelmed her, brought on by the March showers. It was all she could do to squash the grief down and sew. To be lectured in English—belittled before everyone—was more than she could bear. The correct response evaded her.

Rightly sat at Faith's feet, his tired eyes now wide awake. Grace looked up from polishing the candlesticks.

Vittorie felt hot. The room spun. She focused on the sewing sitting in her lap and picked it up again.

"That's right," said Samantha. "We sow our seed, but God is in charge of the return of our harvest." Mistaking 'sew' for 'sow', she approved of the simple answer. "Do you have a favorite verse from the Bible you'd like to read us, Vittorie?" She held out the large book.

"I do no read," Vittorie said, quieter than usual.

Samantha's eyebrows sprung up. "Well," she said, surprised. "It's late enough. Good night, everyone."

Sitting on the far side of the room blacking his Sunday boots with coal from the fire, Uncle Clem tossed it back into the flames and rose first. "G'night."

Everyone but Samantha and Vittorie packed up, said their good nights, and walked out the door to their quarters. Vittorie watched them go. Rain splattered the southwest wall, and she shuddered.

"It does seem colder tonight," Samantha said. "Take this with you." She handed Vittorie the worn blanket, then put seven English coins into her other hand, payment for the month.

"Thank you," said Vittorie, throwing the blanket around her shoulders. She glanced out the window again. The rain had no intention of letting up.

Inside her sleeping closet, she unrolled her bed and laid the coins out in a row on top of it. She pulled at a brick in the wall near her bed. It wiggled loose easy enough and she set it aside. Reaching into the secret spot, she pulled out a folded burlap napkin. Inside lay Gilbert's last seven buttons and two gold coins. She added the seven new coins and started to fold it again when she stopped. Plucking one coin from the bunch, she moved it over by itself and hid the rest behind the brick, replacing it with care. The cracked mortar blended in with the rest of the wall. No one would have guessed the hairline crack went all the way through, and that with one solid tug, the whole thing gave way, revealing treasure indeed. The single coin she slipped into her skirt pouch, gave it a little pat, then slipped herself between the two blankets of her little hay bed and fell asleep with another new idea. Like the embroidered fabric, this one excited her. A ray of hope brightened another little spot in the shadow over her heart.

82

March 26, 1789

"Hol' on jus' one moment there, Miz Vi. I know you'll be tryin' to jump off yo'sef but jus' hol' on an I kin' he'p you down from the carriage ladylike." Clem slowed the team and hitched them to the post, walking over to her side and extending his hand.

"You don't need t' fuss to me, Clem. I kin get down same you."

"Miz Vittorie, I would be he'ping any lady down like my mama raised me. You don't have t' feel special if'n you don't want but I'm gonna stan' here jus' the same with my hand ready."

"Tank ye, Clem. I know. Jus' feels proud."

"S'only pride if we can' t'accept he'p e'ry now 'n'agin, Miz Vi."

"You're right."

"It won't al'ays be hard, Miz Vi. It'll come 'roun'. You'll see."

"If you say so, Clem. Hard me for to think on."

"Uh-hm. I unnastand. But you'll see. It'll come 'roun'."

He handed her Grace's handmade white oak basket from the back of the wagon and took the steps up to the trading post door. Its large brass handle dwarfed in his hand as he pulled it open for them.

"Merci, Clem."

Vittorie's arm looped through the handle as she clutched it to her nervous stomach. Buying things in a store was not the same as selling things to a store. Reaching her hand in her pocket she felt the one gold coin. One coin wasn't enough for what she needed. She had to convince the shopkeeper to buy her work, French and female notwithstanding. With no confidence to speak English with strangers yet, her work would have to speak for itself.

The trading post smelled of tannins. Leathers and pelts from different animals lay on shelving around the edges of the simple room. Around the three columns which supported the center of the building were barrels and more shelves. A long counter ran the length of the space on the left side. All the wood inside was unpainted, except for a sign behind the counter. Vittorie saw the letters: T, R, A, D, I, N…The last letter of the first word escaped her memory. Before she had time to decipher the rest she was interrupted by the store owner.

"Mornin', Clem. May I help ye?" The man behind the counter had a high forehead and very white hair which stuck out of a small cap. His vest was dark gray over a shirt that bloused out down his arms with a tight cuff at his wrists. He continued to measure beans into a scale even after he asked the question.

Clem crossed to the counter. "We've got some fabric for ye, Isai-yuh. Miz Vit'rie done 'broidered it in her way so's to look mighty fahn now. Jus' ye look'n see. Will ye?"

Isaiah glanced at Clem, then Vittorie. "Jes' a minute, Clem. I'll be right with ye." He dumped beans from the scale's mouth down into a sack, twirled the back and tied it with some baling twine. "Fabric, ye say. We've got plenty o' that right heeyah." He thwapped several bolts behind him with his knuckles. "Jes' come down from Lexington las' week. S'pose I kin al'ays look, though, right?" His smile showed a side tooth missing top and bottom. "I've got your order already roun' back, Clem, once you-ah through heeyah. Jes' show Jackson the slip and he'll he'p you load it."

There wasn't much open space left on the counter so Vittorie dug into it and pulled out the blue ticking she'd finished. She'd barely set it down when Isaiah picked it up and rubbed it between his thumb and forefinger. Remembering the beans, he set it down again and brushed his hands on the apron across his waist. "Al'ays dust in packaging things. We don't want that on the fabric, do we?" He smiled politely at Vittorie, but being unfamiliar with his speech, her mind worked on translating his words. She smiled back on instinct to hide her hesitation.

"She done all the work he'self, Isaiah. All this wintuh. She very talented."

Isaiah peered over his glasses at the fabric. His chin tightened as he inspected the work. "I see that. Young lady, how'd ye like t' be paid—goods in-kin' or dollahs and cent?"

Vittorie looked at Clem. "What are terms?"

83

Spring came again with a bucket. More like a thousand buckets with a hundred holes in each rounded bottom. It poured every day from March thirtieth to April twenty first. Mud found its way onto Vittorie's utensils and into the food. Somewhere around April eighth she gave up tiptoeing between the kitchen and house. She raced the raindrops and did her best not to drop any food from the platters nor drench herself in the process.

The perpetual chill in the air meant the fires burned longer into the season than normal. Vittorie stoked the kitchen fire from before the sun rose till after it set, as well as the one in the dining room. Samantha oversaw the parlor fireplace. Faith fed the small ones in the family's quarters. Dampness clung to everything.

Vittorie could be kept warm enough in her bedroom if she pulled the edges of her blanket up and tucked them underneath her. That's the one way she could keep from freezing. She moved her cot against the bricks which doubled as the back side of the living room chimney. They stayed warm a couple hours after the fire died.

Her cheeses needing a mold casing flourished. Those that didn't need such dampness were brought up to the kitchen. The coolness usually provided by the root cellar pervaded in her kitchen, except when the fire drove it away.

She baked two days a week, early in the morning. On the other mornings, she set new seeds in the ground with Faith, plucked chickens for the pot, or harvested.

On April twenty-first, the buckets finally found their bottom and emptied out. Vittorie kneaded raisin cakes. The drumming on the kitchen's roof eased up so gradually the silence caught her off guard. She walked outside and turned a floured palm upward. Two small drips fell into her hand as the wind played with her apron strings. She squinted up to the bluing sky.

Grace strode outside, both hands on her hips. "It's about time! Thank ye, Jesus." She burst out laughing and returned to the house.

By the end of May, wild blackberries budded out in plenty. All the winter had come and gone. Golden fields bowed when the wind rolled. Lambs leaped in play. Everything was putting down roots and pushing up shoots—squash, beans, and corn. The first strawberries of the season were thinking about turning red. Redbud trees bloomed along the fence rows and just beyond some of the fields. It was the time of year with a rhythm to it, which Vittorie needed. Better weather refreshed her, plus the familiarity of place and her improved skills provided some peace and a little pride.

That made it all the more disconcerting when, carrying a load of clean laundry back from the river, Vittorie froze, awash in memory. A certain smell in the air carried her back home across the Atlantic. She closed her eyes and the soft anise scent from Cook's warm-baked cookies transported her. In her mind, she saw her childhood chef hunched over pots, face ringed in a halo of sweaty curls. Heard the sound of her mother's petticoat brushing down the steps into the garden, her sister laughing.

Alone on the path between the river and the kitchen, shielded by the summer show of hemlocks and walnut branches, she set her basket down, fell to her knees beside it, and wept. Fading black-eyed susans populated her path as the sun warmed her hair and the wind kissed her temples. A window opened in her soul, fresh and painful. She cried so hard drool ran down her chin. It mixed with the salty tears that washed her face. Strong enough to grieve openly, she let the cry pour out. Things she couldn't regain flooded past. Questions she couldn't get answered raced away. Guilt over the happiness she didn't feel right having inundated the moment.

A cowbell tinkled. It reminded her of life, of responsibility. The mournful lowing sounds of the heifers parading home to be milked meant supper would be expected soon.

She ran to the river to wash her face and returned for her basket. It didn't feel as heavy as before. She strung the laundry on the line behind the kitchen, pinning skirts, pants, and linens up to dry in what was left of the warm day. In France, she had servants to do this very job for her. She burst out laughing, shocked at the sounds of hysterical joy erupting instead of grief. The laughter kept coming, gushing out irreversibly, cleansing her from the inside out.

Hearing something unusual, Faith put down her milk buckets at the kitchen door and ran around back. "What's wrong?" she asked Vittorie.

Instead of answering, Vittorie leaned into the building to steady herself. With one hand covering her mouth, she giggled uncontrollably. "I do no think…" Tears poured out of her eyes. She made gasping noises to catch her breath. "…cry any more tears! No more cry!" The effort it took to finish that sentence struck her as funny. She doubled over in a laugh so deep there was no more sound, just motions.

Concerned, Faith grabbed her around the waist and hauled her to the house. "'Mantha!" she shouted. "Sa-mantha!" She coaxed Vittorie by speaking like she would to a birthing heifer. "Come on, now. Can't be fussin' like this, hear?"

Powerless, Vittorie fell to the ground. When her bottom touched down with a thump, she let out a whoop and laughed louder. Tears kept falling.

"'Mantha!" Faith yelled, fanning Vittorie with her apron.

Grace appeared from around the corner, broomstick in hand. "Lord A'mighty! What happened?"

"I jes' foun' her this way!" Faith said, still fanning.

Samantha held the broom in defense and looked around for a varmint. "Is she hurt?"

"No! She's laughin' cryin'!"

"I ain't neveh heard o' such a thing!"

Faith grimaced consent. "Me either, but I been fannin' a while now and that's what this is."

"Ah knewd a body kin only shed so many tears fo' grief." She fanned with the broom. "Mebbe she done cried all those and now the Lord given her happy tears at the bottom o' her bucket."

"Fo' sho'," Faith said, not sure at all.

"What's the mattuh?" Clem lumbered around the corner, out of breath, with Rightly beside him. "We heard the shoutin'." They fanned, too, without knowing why.

Vittorie sighed, interrupted by some hiccups, and wiped her face. "*Suis désolé*," she said. "I sorry. No worry."

"Oh, we worried alright," Grace said, her voice definite. "Honey, if I wasn't worried about you befo', I am now." She tossed the broom to Clem, and knelt her solid body down. On the ground next to Vittorie, she grabbed the little Frenchwoman into a big mama hug. "You goin' be aw-right. Yep. You is." She kissed the top of Vittorie's head and patted her hair down in long, calming motions, rocking the foreign woman back and forth as a child. "Lord, but you is."

84

A plentiful harvest brought in another glorious fall which gave way to winter. Practicing her handiwork on snowy evenings before the fire provided her an opportunity to sell in the spring. Working each week on the Sellers farm and others around added to the bulging burlap behind the brick. Her English kept improving, her fear of speaking lessened, and her second March on the Sellers farm arrived with wind, not rain.

"You're becoming quite known, Vi," said Samantha, poking her head into the kitchen on a Tuesday afternoon. "I was stopped by no less than three people today in town."

Pink flushed over Vittorie's pale cheeks. She tasted the soup and swallowed. "Yes?" Returning to the worktable, she diced green onion shoots.

"Your work's being sought out for its particular intricacies and whirling curls of decorative thread." Enjoying the notoriety, Samantha's shoulders bounced with glee as she recounted the messages. "Your'n is unlike anything being made or brought from the coastal colonies even!" She glanced around the room as if checking for listeners. "The supply of your fabric for men's shirts at the post is low. And," she stepped inside completely and lowered her voice, "the ladies will buy more if you visit them with your basket at home."

Vittorie moved a chopped, green pile to one side of the block. "What do you say?" Selecting another several stalks, she continued to slice.

"Go today! Go!" Samantha clapped her hands for emphasis.

The smack made Vittorie jump. "I have work…." She motioned to the simmering pot over the flames.

"I've spoken to the rest. Grace agrees with me. She'll finish out here today and you go visiting. With your basket."

A half hour later, wrapped in a thick, crocheted shawl, Vittorie carried her large white oak basket up the front steps of Mrs. Randolph's house, their nearest neighbor. Woven by Grace with willowy canes tucked and looped in precise proportions, the basket had a round mouth and sides, but a sturdy square base.

Up to its usual tricks, the wind whipped against Vittorie's cheek and froze her nose. "*Arrête,*" Vittorie said, speaking to the unseen gusts. She covered her nose a moment with gloved fingers.

Mrs. Randolph's maid let Vittorie in and seated her in a small parlor to the left of the entry door. It didn't take long for Mrs. Randolph to settle herself and the tea to be poured. Sipping from English cups, Mrs. Randolph surveyed the newest dainties. "You've come to me first, haven't you?" She peered at Vittorie through her eyeglass rimmed in mother-of-pearl.

"Yes." Vittorie lifted the saucer and raised the cup to her lips. The temperature of the liquid in her mouth warmed her. It tasted of mint. "What flavor tea?"

"Apple mint. I'll send you with a sprig from the garden." Holding a piece of plum linen with chartreuse and ruby threaded embroidery, she sighed. "Well, if I don't grab you first, Mrs. L— and you know who I mean, though I shan't gossip about her, no— always seems to buy up what she knows I would like then flaunts it from her carriage as she passes!"

Wagon wheels in the street rolled past. Mrs. Randolph strained to see.

"No, not her," Mrs. Randolph said, settling herself again in the tufted chair. "I wouldn't be surprised if she does drive past my gate specifically! I would never be so bold, I can tell you that."

Vittorie took another delightful sip of tea, the aroma and liquid warming her. Every town or city with people in it has its gossips. Vittorie played the part of the foreigner well, remaining outside the circles just enough to be accepted into each—though wholly a part of none.

"Let's see what you've made this month, shall we?" Mrs. Randolph began rifling through the remainder of Vittorie's fine handwork.

House after house, teacup after teacup, settee after armchair after bench, each woman in Nolin Station supported Vittorie's work. The coin in her pocket had grown into more because of her diligence, and Vittorie supported herself, plus helped a few others. Hadn't Faith been able to buy Rightly a new pair of shoes? And a stick pin with a jeweled head for herself for Sunday? Clem found himself a knife just for filleting his fish, and Samantha bought herself a bell that tinkled lightly when she tapped its porcelain sides. Grace wore a new hairpin. With each gift a bit of her savings toward returning home were whittled away. No one asked how the others came by these things. Some things don't need to be spoken of. While France seemed further away than ever, belonging somewhere she was happy wasn't.

85

After a good year of selling her wares at the post or home to home, the families of Nolin Station knew Vittorie was a widow. Many were in the same position. They'd lost their beloveds to war, sickness, or age. Though none were as young as she—and they believed that to be a singular difference—the community undertook the matter as though they'd birthed her themselves.

After church the third Sunday in May, the illustrious Mrs. Randolph informed Vittorie of the situation. "A suitable husband should be found for you, dear." Her voice raised to an officiant tone, loud enough to reach the tip of the new chapel's pointed spire. "It's not too late for you yet!" she said in front of everyone milling around the wide plank steps.

Agreement from the parishioners spread like honey over hot bread. The men, especially, listened.

That shouldn't have surprised her, but it did. Heat flushed up Vittorie's neck and burst red on her cheeks. "Ah'm content."

"Of course you are, dear," said Mrs. Randolph. The pearls in her ears dangled as her big head nodded. "It's better that young people have each other before they get old." She shared her opinions as facts. Their understatement confirmed their truth. "You would do well to remarry." Her eyes narrowed. "You're young and pretty and resourceful. Why should you live alone?"

"But Ah don't live alone," Vittorie said, her comments falling on deaf ears. "Ah love the family Ah live with."

Mrs. Randolph's decisions came with finality. "As well you would. You're kind-hearted and so are they." She patted Vittorie's shoulder and leaned closer. "Choose well, for you'll have your pick, I dare say." She waved her finger in the direction of the men, winked one eye and left.

With the air still cool the next day and little chance of rain, Vittorie walked to the trading post to sell her new handkerchiefs to Isaiah. No need to bother Clem about the wagon. "God bless you, Henry Skeggs," she whispered as a yellow finch flew to a redbud branch beside her. Gratitude for the man, for the part he'd played in creating these new opportunities in her life encouraged her. She walked at a steady pace down the road, happy to have choices.

Once the trading post came into sight, she saw no less than seven men standing on the steps outside the store. They shushed and stiffened as she approached, and smiled directly at her—each sporting one of her blue-ticking shirts! The oddity of being the object of their attention as she climbed each step was unnerving. The whole situation embarrassed her.

Once inside, she sighed in relief and scurried up to the counter, ready to talk about the business at hand. "Good mo'ning, Mr. Gahdner," she said, doing her best to remain unruffled. She rested her basket on the counter between them and uncovered her newest work.

A businessman with a soft heart, Isaiah Gardner counted her handkerchiefs. "...Four, six, eight...." He motioned with his head toward the crowd outside. "Busy today," he said just as the front door opened.

"Yes." The approaching men distressed her.

In groups of twos and threes, the men got closer. Suddenly very interested in pick-axes, the price of millet listed on Isaiah's board, and new leather straps, they loafed nearer to the counter. All wanting to be available when she turned around, they crowded Vittorie till she squashed up tight to the wooden sales desk.

"Be with you in just a moment, gentlemen." Isaiah lowered his voice for her alone to hear and spoke with intent. "You don't have any more shirts for me today, do you? I've had a run on 'em, you see." His salesman's eyebrow curved.

"No," Vittorie said, "but Ah've got mo' fabric bolt. You like me make more?" She relaxed, happy for the distraction from the impending swarm of suitors.

"It'd be good for both our businesses if you could."

She nodded, aware of the shortened distance between herself and Isaiah. She kept her eyes on his tablature.

"That's five men's handkerchiefs, one lady's embroidered kerchief, two linen tablecloths, and three table crochets from you today. And, this is yours," he concluded, counting money into her palm.

She smiled genuinely. The coins and paper in her hand felt fantastic. She stuffed the payment deep into the pouch between her skirt folds and rearranged the pleating to hide its presence. "I price some to next week."

As Isaiah helped the next customer, she scurried to the far right side of the counter to examine the fabric. The tight weave of the gray linen inspired her. Another had wool dyed to a deep rust color. A third bolt on the shelf sported a pale shade of yellow cotton. Inspiration gathered in moments like these set her for weeks, and she lingered over the possibilities.

When she'd stayed long enough that most of the men had left the shop, she waved goodbye to Isaiah and exited herself. But walking outside, the awkwardness returned. The men were still there, and now each also wiped his forehead with one of her handkerchiefs. The youngest one, she noticed, even used her ladies' embroidered handkerchief! One last farmer named Hank stood on the bottom step sulking, fists deep in the pockets of his britches, without any handkerchief at all. As Vittorie rushed down the steps trying to avoid the men, she bumped into Hank and lost her balance. His hands flew out from his pockets and he caught her by the elbows.

"See there," he said, with a silly grin. "I got the girl!"

Vittorie chuckled, embarrassed. "Thank you, Hank," she said, recovering. "Ah'm standing by self now." She'd settled more into the fabric of their world every day. To think of them as suitors made her shy. She preferred things as they had been, lonely and uncomplicated

He released her, but his knees stayed bent, his broad palms ready should she need his assistance again. "Yer welcum."

She distanced herself from them and forced a smile. "Good day, Sam, Noah, Reuben…" She looked at each man as she addressed him. "…Benjamin, Gobel, Thomas, Mordecai." She curtsied and hurried into the streaming rays of sunlight across the path toward home. The lane curved as it always did, and the gate that had welcomed her, nay, taken her in, over two years ago came into view. Her heart leaped at its familiar groan as she stepped through. Home was an adjustable word.

86

June mornings brought blackberry picking and cooking syrups and tarts, so by three o'clock the desire to wash intensified. A cloud passed overhead. Vittorie stuck her head full out the kitchen door to check if her plans needed changing, but the cloud held no gray. She smiled and grabbed a small white oak basket she'd made herself. Perhaps she'd find more berries. A basket was always useful. Sweat ran down the small of her back. There wasn't time for a full swim, but there was the promise of refreshing herself.

There were never enough days of good weather for swimming, especially with so near and so lovely a spot on the Nolin River as by the Sellers farm. Vittorie tried to get someone to slip away to the river with her at least once a week. But today, Samantha had Grace and Faith working with her, so they were unavailable. Rightly would have lived in the water if Faith let him, but this afternoon Vittorie knew he was busy with Clem shearing sheep. The water would be hers alone.

The intoxicating pull of the river gurgled up in her soul, rushed her through her daily chores, and danced her feet over cascading beds of moss and limestone to its elusive banks. Her favorite part of the path was the last rise of earth before the first sight of the river, guarded closely by cherry tree sentinels, leafy and green. Her heart skipped a beat as she crested the hill. She could hear the river running but couldn't see it yet. And then, with neck stretched full out, another step, and oh! There it was—altogether new and so comfortingly the same.

She stopped for a minute, saying hello in her heart to her friend—for so she thought of the river. It was here she had space and time to think over her life, her artistry, her recipes. In the water or out, this place refreshed her, body and soul.

She waded in, holding her skirts up to her thighs. The water ran colder today. A fish swam below the surface on her left. Three hummingbirds busily gathered nectar from a vine with orange, trumpet-shaped flowers. She heard their miniature wings pound the air in low tones as they darted, ruby-throated, in and out of the petals. She'd ask Clem what kind of flower attracted hummingbirds later. Perhaps they could plant some near the house.

Upstream, the sweetest blackberries grew on canes overhanging the river's edge. She made her way to them, tightening the muscles of her legs against the strong current. Cold water swirled between her knees as it surged downstream. She carefully placed each foot on tiptoe before applying her full weight to the stones along the rocky bottom. One particular branch with large, dark berries swaggered in the breeze. In length, the fruit measured half her pointer finger. Picking the nearest cluster, she popped one in her mouth. Hot juice burst out. She plucked more into her cupped hand.

Her basket sat forgotten on shore. Wading back to retrieve it, she pulled the bottom of her skirts up higher, holding them in place by tucking the hem into her tight waistline. Stepping gingerly over the mossy rocks and out of the water, her fingers clasped the woven handle of the basket firmly before she splashed back into the stream.

Fish darted back and forth under the clear water. She watched them, confident and peaceful. Lowering her basket, careful not to distract the swimmers below, she jerked it up fast, hoping for a catch. Water drained out through the bottom. No fish. Repeating the trap—this time pushing it lower beneath the surface before pulling it up—proved successful. A good-sized crappie flopped inside.

A male voice laughed. "Natives fish like that."

Vittorie whirled around.

A man in rolled trousers lounged on the bank, one leg dangling over the edge, ankle in the water. He held a cane pole and fished from a protruding rock.

In her haste, Vittorie misstepped. She plunged entirely underwater losing berries, basket, and fish.

The man rose to his feet and jumped in. His pole bounced off the boulder, pulled by the current to parts unknown.

Her feet found the bottom. When her head cleared the surface, he was reaching for her, holding her elbow. On instinct, she yanked it away. He found it again and lifted her up.

"Catch your breath?" Blue eyes looked into hers.

She wiped wet hair off her face and blinked up at him. Not understanding his last word, she asked, "Catch my fish?"

Accepting it as a challenge, the man dove back under the water. He surfaced further away and with strong swimmer's strokes closed the distance between himself and the basket. The tide kept her floating basket just out of his reach, carrying it away.

Before she could see if he'd succeeded, both man and basket careened around a bend and disappeared.

"Oh!" Vittorie cried, more for the loss of the man than the basket. Lunging through the chest-deep water, she tried to catch up. The current pulled her with ease. She saw him stand up near the far shore. He raised both hands in the air to her. No basket.

"Come back!" she cried, not loud enough for him to hear.

His arms pulled him back through the water.

Walking against the current was hard enough. His struggle swimming upstream made her heart weaken for him. She sloshed out of the water, lowered her skirts and smoothed her hair.

And there he was, dripping wet and grinning like her impish nephews used to do. Disarmingly so.

"I owe you supper," he said, genuinely apologetic.

"No need."

He wasn't finished apologizing. "I'm sorry. About startling you, I mean." He stood, wringing out his pant legs, never taking his eyes from her. "I came here to fish."

Something about his halting speech made her not run away as she originally intended to. The lavender linen of her dress clung to her body, accentuating every curve.

He brought his arms up to wring out his sleeves, splashing green river muck on her face. His smile melted. "Oh, I'm so sorry!" He stepped closer and wiped her eyebrow and cheek with his thumb. Algae removed, he stopped short. "That wasn't appropriate either."

Stepping back, she stumbled again over the uneven rocks. He reached out to grab her and held on until her feet settled between the shifting pebbles on shore. Then he released her and waited.

"*Merci.*" She smoothed her bedraggled hair away from her face. "Thank you." Her cap hung askew by a few stalwart pins. Her curls, dark and long under the water's weight, covered her shoulders.

"Forgive me," he started again, "for the whole mud incident and…touching you." His hand waved around near her face mimicking his prior actions. He fixed his arms stiff to his side for fear of repeating his casual faux pas.

She pulled her dress away from her shivering form. "I do." A puddle enlarged around her feet as the tempo of dripping water slowed. "Any good fishing?"

His mouth wrinkled, unsure of how to recover. He looked down the river. Shaking water from his hair, he shrugged. "Well, let's see…" As soon as he looked back at her, a smile washed across his face. "I've not only *not* caught a fish myself today, but I've managed to help you lose yours! So, I'd say right now…" his laugh diminished into a carefree sigh, "…I'm minus two." He wiped off his beard and chuckled.

Taken by his genuine ease, she laughed too. "Maybe tomorrow," she said, with a slight tip of her head, "you try again."

"*À demain,*" he added.

Her eyes sparkled at his French. He bowed low, sopping wet, to hide his enjoyment of the moment. She gathered shoes and stockings and, with a glance back to the stranger, ran barefoot toward the farm.

87

"Soundin' like someone's happy." Faith smirked. "I heard you sin-gin'." The pale pink dress suited her mahogany skin and comple-mented her rosy cheeks and thick, curved lips.

Vittorie shrugged. "A little." She wore a light green linsey-woolsey dress over a capped-sleeve shirt.

"Well, if you is, I's jes' sayin', tha's jes' fine," Faith teased.

Vittorie's shoulders relaxed. She appreciated the kindness of her friend.

"I heard Miz Sellers sayin' we might all head to the crick this aftahnoon. You comin'?"

Vittorie stirred the kettle with a long wooden spoon, her gaze transfixed out the window. "I am."

Faith took a deep breath in through her nose. "Tha's good. You makin' yo' sassafras tea?"

"I is," Vittorie responded with mock demureness.

"Listen to her speak that good English! Mm, mmm. And she can cook! You goin' get snatched up yet, Ms. Vi. Mmm, hmmm. Some handsome soldier, wounded in battle, but still doin' fine, he's gonna hear about yo' cookin' and yo' good heart. Then he's gonna get a look on ya...it won't take five minutes to fall in love."

"Faith!" Vittorie said, "Stop." She ladled hot tea into pitchers to cool.

"Five minutes!" Faith's collarbone showed above the top gathers of her shirt. "You mark me." She corrected herself for emphasis. "Less even—if he's the kine' o' man I pray for you."

Vittorie's ladle stopped mid-scoop. "Why do you pray for me?"

Faith looked straight at Vi. "You 'memba Miz Sellers readin' the story of Adam to us? How he was God's man and named all the animals?" She dipped a finger in the milk pail and flicked it at Vittorie. "How they all marched in front of him so he could do his job but all the while he's a thinkin' 'they ain't none like me?' Well, you's like Adam here." She picked up a chicken egg from the bowl. "I love ya, don't mistake me, an' you brought somethin' with you that we didn' have afore you come." She held the egg and pointed a finger at her friend.

Vittorie's eyes said enough.

"But I think there's more for you in this worl'. And God's th' only one I know big enough to bring ya to it. Or bring it to you. I know you and He's got business to straighten out." She set the egg on the table. "That'll come. Meantime, I been askin' 'im for ya." She wiped her palms on the brown, twirling embroidery of her apron. Reshouldering the buckets, she deposited them in the cellar and collected the ones Vittorie had emptied out already.

Vittorie poured the rest of the kettle into a single cup. The spout hung upside-down as the last drops fell.

"You go'n be fine," Faith said, stepping back through the door. "'Finuh than a frog hair' as Mr. Skeggs likes to say." Then she laughed at the woodsman's silly saying.

"You all gave me everythin', Faith." Vittorie put the kettle down. "What did I bring?"

"You'll figure it out." Faith walked away with her empty buckets through the grass. "Right now, I's thinkin' it's yo' blackberry tarts, but that might be my stomach talkin'." She chuckled at her own joke.

"I had nothin' when I come." Vittorie finished the thought alone. She hooked the kettle on its nail by the fire and readied a basket for the family picnic by the stream.

* * *

An evening at the river brought a welcome rest for everyone. The sun glinted over the water as the leaves twisted above, shielding sore muscles from the harvest heat.

Everyone cooled off by playing in the water and soaking in a few precious moments of reprieve before tomorrow's labor. Uncle Clem found himself a stick, affixed his hook and a string, and nodded on and off with his line tugging against the moving water. Faith and Rightly lay on the warm rocks to dry off. Vittorie rested with her head on her arm in the sweet grass, idly twisting Gilbert's wedding ring on and off her finger. Samantha combed a bag of flax. Grace hummed on and off. She put words for them all to the song in her heart.

"When my heart is heavy,
and I'm feelin' low,
I take my burdens to the river's flow.
When I am tired, Lord,
when I am weak,
with my heavy burdens,
Jesus I seek."

The heart of the new song resonated deep inside Vittorie. Maybe it was Grace's beautiful tone or the plaintive way it chorused once Uncle Clem and Faith joined in. Her heart melted while her eyes kept watch over the water for another chance meeting with the fisherman.

"So come, Lord,
and carry me home.
Take now these troubles

I carry alone.
For I am weary,
and you are good.
You lighten'd my load,
I knew you would."

They sang it over and over, adding a part or changing volume in turns. By the end, Vittorie could hum along.

When their song had run its course, they all dropped out except for Grace, who sang the last line again, alone.

"I knew you would."

Vittorie had never heard anything so captivating. It stuck with her for days.

$$88$$

Vittorie's ingenuity wove itself into the fabric of Nolin Station. Owning "the French woman's work" became a status symbol in the very best homes; knowing Vittorie herself was an attractive prize indeed.

Samantha invited her closest friends, Rose and Evelyn, to a gossip session masquerading as a midday meal. Vittorie prepped all morning for the occasion. Samantha picked fresh flowers for the table from the garden. Everything looked beautiful. Vittorie wove in and out of the party of three seated around the table, serving each from a silver tray.

"What sweet surprise do you have for us today, Vi?" Samantha asked, proud as a peacock that Vittorie lived in her house.

"I thought dinner would never come. I've been so looking forward to it," Evelyn said.

Vittorie situated a personal skillet in front of her. Steam rose from the black pan, the savory smell intoxicating.

"Who'll thank the Lord?" Samantha asked.

Grace appeared in the doorframe, her eyebrow raised in playful critique. "You ladies bettuh thank Him. I already tasted what Vi's done cooked up fo' you."

"Oh Grace! Don't' spoil the surprise!" Samantha said. "Will you say grace for us?"

"Grace by Grace!" Rose said, giggling at her own joke. "Please, Grace." She bowed her head over folded hands.

When the other ladies closed their eyes, and Vittorie had finished serving, Grace began. "Precious Lord, we thank ye. We thank ye for savin' us all, in every way. Thank ye for helpin' us fin' our way and for bringin' us all together. Our hearts are Your'n. Amen."

Vittorie opened her eyes and tucked an errant curl back under her cap. "Thank you, Grace."

Grace gave Vittorie a squeeze around the shoulder. "Clem, Faith, Rightly, an' I's headin' to the rivuh." She raised her eyebrow at each of the ladies around the table. "You all behave." As the door swung shut behind her, she added, "Save's repentin' latuh."

The blessing said, forks were grabbed and knives sliced into action.

Evelyn got a bite between her wide lips first. "Mmm!" She closed her eyes to chew.

Rose blew over the morsel on her fork. Waiting for it to cool, she said, "Samantha hasn't stopped singing your praises, my dear, since your first summer here and those blackberry tarts." Her eyes glinted at Vittorie. The wrinkles under them crinkled into deeper lines. "My, you look lovely today." She turned to Evelyn, her younger, more practical sister, and raised her voice. "Doesn't she Evie?"

Not willing to be rushed through her lunch, Evelyn chewed and swallowed. "Yes. You don't have to shout." Addressing Vittorie, she said, "You know my son." She readied another bite and held the steaming chunk just above the skillet. "Thomas, Jr." She watched Vittorie's reaction to his name. "Well, he keeps his eye on that store for whenever a certain young lady brings any new thing in." Having promoted her offspring, fork went to mouth and she chewed again, eyes wide.

"IF she remarries…" Samantha wiped her chin with one of Vittorie's embroidered handkerchiefs. "She's sworn she'll have none but a soldier." She joined Evelyn in eyeing Vittorie's response.

"If, if, if," sing-songed Rose. She tapped her sister's skillet with the fork in her hand. "It's a big world out there."

Vittorie poured apple mint tea from Samantha's silver pitcher, ignoring their stares.

Rose changed tactics. "There's actually quite a few men come lately on account of stories from the trading post steps." No longer childish in her tone, but matter-of-fact, she leaned forward over her plate for emphasis. "Quite a few."

"I'll leave you to eat," Vittorie said. "My English is still learning, but I understand good enough." She teased them, purposely regressing in her English fluency.

Samantha returned to her mothering role. "And coming along just fine. Go, dear. We're fine here. It's delicious!"

With two hands on her tray and a bump of her hip, Vittorie hustled through the door and out of earshot. The three eaters watched her through the window, munching away.

Once she passed through the door of the separate kitchen, Rose put a hand on Samantha's arm. She leaned in, whispering, "I invited one of them today!" The faintest bit of food stuck on her bottom lip as she laughed into her napkin.

Not understanding, Samantha furrowed her brows. She crouched forward and shook her head. "One of what?"

"A man!" Rose spat out with glee. "I invited one to dinner today!"

"Rose!" Samantha sputtered. "It's not even your house!"

"You don't mind." Rose waved away her friend's astonishment with a handkerchief and continued. "One of the Overmountain Men. Fought at King's Mountain in the Revolution. Turned the tide of the war!"

"Single-handedly, no doubt," Evelyn chided, grabbing her glass. "Shhh! Here she comes!"

Vittorie returned, a tray of dessert and fresh pitcher of tea in hand. She set them on the side table.

Enraptured with her food, Evelyn asked Vittorie, "What do you call this magnificent creation?" She chewed and swallowed and added more to her mouth.

All three ladies looked at Vittorie, wrinkled faces trimmed in lace. She looked from one to the other at a loss. Evelyn tapped her skillet, eyes wide with expectation.

After several stalling noises, Vittorie offered, "Um…American Wild? It's all the land—pepper red, beans *françoise,* squash…" She took a moment to select the right words. "…eggs, turkey…pig, rosemary, garlic, *fromage*…cheese."

A few short knocks on the front door interrupted them. Samantha left the table to see who it was, casting a look of rebuke at Rose. The diners hushed in effort to hear any conversation from the front hall. They heard the door creak as it opened on its hinges. Conversation ensued. There was a pause, then more than one set of footsteps returned to the dining room. Samantha entered, followed by a man. Not just any man. Behind her, in military garb, strode the man from the river.

"Captain Frazier," she said, beginning introductions, "you know your Aunt Rose, of course, and…well, how would you be related then to Evelyn?"

Rose glanced between the two young people, her triumph complete. "She's my sister, so his aunt through marriage."

"Quite," Samantha continued in confidence. Her voice softened as she turned to Vittorie. "May I present Mrs. Vittorie LeClerc."

"Ladies," he said with a stiff bow. Turning toward Vittorie, he made another small bow for her alone.

Samantha didn't know what to do about her friend's game of hearts, but one look from the man to her ward put her more at ease. "Vittorie was just telling us the name of this scrumptious plate she concocted. 'The American' it is!" she said, sitting down again. "You had it in my house first, Evelyn." She poked her fork for emphasis in the direction of her friend. "Remember that!"

Rose wiped her mouth under her napkin. "Come in, John."

The three women made room at the table. He pulled up a chair and joined them. His eyes followed Vittorie until he made himself be entertained with the others at the table.

"Thank you for your hospitality, Mrs. Sellers. And the invitation, Aunt Rose." The women nodded in turn. "How's Thomas, Jr., Aunt Evelyn?"

Not waiting for the answer, Vittorie retreated to the kitchen. She paced the floor a minute. Wiping her face first, she grabbed the water bucket and poured it over the dirty utensils in the dry sink. Plunging her hands in, she talked to herself with rapid rebukes. "*Il est ici!*" she said, wiping cooked egg off a spoon. "American Wild. *Voici! L'Americain.*" Frustrated at her emotions, her argument began in high-pitched French and lapsed into unintelligible noises. Head shakes, tsks, and puffs of air followed.

89

In the dining room, dessert's conversation came to a close. Napkins wiped mouths and were laid beside bowls scraped clean.

Rose took Evelyn by the arm. Sauntering sister and self past Samantha out the front door, she giggled. "Thank you, Samantha dear. See you Thursday!" With a childish grin, she waved a hanky at her handsome younger relative. "Bye, John!"

"Wait a minute, can you?" Evelyn said, annoyed at being tugged. "Tell Vittorie dinner was delicious. And tell her Thomas Jr. will call later!"

Samantha waved and nodded. "So lovely you both came today. Thursday, and yes." Closing the front door behind them, she took hold of the captain's arm and walked him toward the back door. "Being from the Watauga Settlements, Captain, I have some questions for you about cultivation and order. Statehood being upon us any day now…What do you say about it?" she asked, keeping her arm linked through his and pulling him through the dining room.

"It depends on what you mean," Captain Frazier said, recognizing the opportunity to linger. He glanced out the back window. "Establishing self-governance is difficult. Too firm a hand and we're back to kingdoms and peasants. Too lax…" He exhaled and shook his head. "Chaos."

His answer was grounded and correct. Most important of all, it impressed Samantha.

"Sounds exactly like gardening." She opened the back door and held out her other arm for him to lead outside.

On the distant hillside, sheep lazed in the shadow of the maple trees studding the fence lines. No smoke rose from the slaughter house this hour of the day, and a gray donkey lifted his head among the field cows.

Captain John Frazier stepped over the exterior threshold of the house onto a wide, stone step. Before him stretched the path leading to the garden.

Vittorie knelt by an herb bed. She yanked a weed, saw him, and held it limp in the air.

"Hello," he whispered.

The door shut. Samantha hadn't accompanied him. Vittorie returned to her gardening without comment. Plucking another weed, she added both to a basket beside her.

"You are the French woman living with Mrs. Sellers?"

"The French widow, yes." She watched him with curiosity, though kept her hands in the dirt. "And you are Rose's niece?"

He scratched his face and nodded. "Nephew."

Embarrassed at her mistake, she returned to pulling overgrown green shoots.

He moved to where she worked and squatted down. Thinking better of it, he sat, cross-legged, close to her. Pinching a plant on his right, he brought the thin stalk under his nose. "Rosemary! I thought I smelled it in your meal." He looked over the organized pattern of buds and flowering stems. "Your garden is robust."

She couldn't help but notice his intelligence. "It grows well here."

"My name is John. Everyone calls me Frazier."

Content with her work, she gave herself permission to look fully at him. His eyes beamed happiness, like the color of an afternoon sky. "Victoire. Victoire Monet LeClerc. Everyone calls me Vittorie."

A smile sprouted on him with an honesty she'd seen at the river. Fiddling with the twig in his fingers, he asked, "I don't suppose you'd like to give me a chance to explain myself, say, tomorrow afternoon?"

"Why do you need explain an'thing to me?"

He rose to his knees and pressed up, using the fence to help him stand, and brushed dirt off his pants. His jacket and knickers fit him well, worn, but not worn through. His boots were well-used yet clean. For a soldier, he carried himself with a relaxed demeanor. It suited him. His wide mustache hung down on both sides of his mouth, neatly trimmed. His eyes were beautiful.

Just then, Samantha opened the back door, startling them both. "Take the day off tomorrow, Vittorie. I'm going to Rose's. Grace can cook for the rest."

Excuses ripped away, Vittorie looked back at him, still searching for a reason to say 'no.' Instead, she could only see how blue his eyes were and realized how peaceful it felt to look at him.

"Please," he added.

"*Oui.*"

90

Seated on two fine horses, Vittorie and Frazier descended to the river's edge, then maneuvered the animals over gnarled roots toward a wild meadow.

He wore a shirt of her blue ticking. "I love the landscape here. It reminds me of growing up in Carolina."

"North or South?"

"North. My family farmed near the Yadkin River."

"Ah miss the salt air of sea. En France, my family grow vineyards near ocean." The wind played with her hair, braided loosely down her back.

The color in her cheeks and the light in her eyes captivated him. "Do you intend to live again on the coast?"

Her eyebrows wrinkled. "Coast?"

"By the ocean. Now that you live over the mountains, do you still want to go back to the ocean, or are you happy here?" He slowed his horse so she could walk her horse alongside.

"Ah miss water." Her smile tightened. "Ah miss many things." She looked away. "Why you are alone, Captain?"

"A country boy is never truly alone if he knows the trees and can find water."

The muscles in her cheeks drooped. "Have married?"

Reaching in his saddle bag, he pulled out a waterskin. "Five years." He passed her the skin. "Drink, to keep hydrated. We're leaving the shade."

She drank and passed it back.

"Emily. She liked to make things for me." He capped the skin and stuck it under the leather cover of the saddle bag. "When I left to aid the cause, my friends laughed at my handmade... everything."

Vittorie's hands relaxed their hold on the reins. She repeated the part she didn't understand. "'...Ate the coz?'"

"No, aid. 'Aid the cause'...the Revolution." He picked a burr from her horse's black mane. "When news came the British had left the northern colonies and moved the war to the southern colonies, I joined. Patriot, of course! I was at Cowpens and King's Mountain. I would have served till the end, but took a shot through the thigh." He patted his leg over the spot.

"Again, please." Her shoulders hunched forward as she leaned toward him, listening. "What happened your leg?"

He made the sound of a rifle shot whizzing through the air and used his hand to illustrate the bullet landing just below the crease of his hip.

"*Jamais, Mon Dieu!*"

"Yes, though I didn't even realize it at the time—everything happens fast in war. Spent a month recovering. It missed the bone, tore some muscle. I do pretty well to hide the inconsistency in my walk."

"I see."

"Figured you did. Let's race the field. Want to?" he asked, turning his horse by the reins.

"Where Emily?" Vittorie held her horse back for his reply.

Drying heat baked the open field. He turned his horse toward a small grove of poplars. The coolness of the woods welcomed confessions.

"She died. Yellow fever. And our son. They'd been buried a week when I got home."

"Bandits shoot Gilbert, and friend, Smuthers, settle with us. Gilbert die, next *matin*…morning, in my arms. Germans bury him." Once she began, the rest poured out. "Ah miss him." She checked his interest to see if she'd said too much.

"Go on, please."

"Other times," she said, wiping her neck, "other times I think I am child then. Big hope. Don't know this America, don't know fear. I no hope like child any more."

"It isn't childish to want happiness. Do you know the document, the writing, by which we declared our independence from tyranny holds that very tenet as a truth? 'That all men are created equal…." He swung an arm out wide. "…That they are endowed by their Creator with certain unalienable rights, that among these,' and here they list three items that belong to a man as a right, under God…'That among these…." He held up his hand in front of her, counting out each word. "…are life, liberty, and the pursuit of happiness.' You see, in these United States, each individual is responsible—more than responsible, held accountable—for finding what their Creator has endowed them with and add to the greater good by supplying it out of their own pursuit of…." He stopped short for her to fill in the empty space.

She watched him but said nothing, so he said it. "Happiness."

"…'appiness?"

He thrust out his arms with emphasis. "Pursuit of Happiness! Yes." Perspiration beaded his forehead. "Joie de vivre!"

"Kentucky law say be happy?"

"No. America's law says go find your happiness. And yes, if Kentucky succeeds in becoming our own state. We fought for every colonist's right to pursue…."

She tipped her head to the side, not understanding.

"To chase after, to explore—what it is they desire. What was woven by the Almighty, before time began, into the very fabric of your soul." He wiped moisture down his mustache. "*Vous comprenez*, soul?"

"Non. I don't understand."

The strong smell of horse sweat in the summer heat mixed with the breezy scents of cedar and honeysuckle.

Vittorie pressed a handkerchief over her forehead in a series of small compressions. "My father work...works...in court of King Louis XVI." Her skin glistened. "He's quiet man."

Frazier's face elongated. "The king?"

"*Non, mon père*. My father." She liked not being the only one who misunderstands. "He prefer long walk to long conversation, unless you'ah talking about *le government*."

Recognizing the French word, he pronounced its English equivalent, emphasizing the 'o', 'r', and 't'. "Go-vern-ment."

"*Oui*, yes, govern-ment. Or his vineyards. *Ma mère...*"

"Your mother."

A nod. "...spoke for him in all else."

"Sounds like a capable woman."

The large body of a blue king skimmer dragonfly lifted off the fanfared petals of a wilting white morning glory. It zoomed past the fuzzy heads of several wild garlic stalks and eventually set down beside the yellow bloom of a soft velvet leaf.

"She is. Very." Vittorie conceded another nod. "I have her eyes."

"They are beautiful."

Her lips curled up at the edges. "I think like my father, but I am not a mother. *Peut-etre* I be more like my mother if I have...if I...am mother, too."

"Perhaps. Do you want children?"

She turned away. "I think I...."

"Who does your creativity come from?"

She shrugged. "I don't know."

"I like to sing. My brothers in the Watauga Settlements, the place I left before coming to visit Aunt Rose and meet you, called me the Singing Statesman."

Her head bent to the side. "Again, please?"

"They called me the Singing Statesman."

"Before?"

"Rose is my aunt?" He shifted in his saddle.

"*Non*, after that." Her eyebrows lifted in a question.

"Before I came…to meet you." Caught in the confession, the tips of his ears burned red. "Henry Skeggs is a friend of mine from before the war. He knew Dan Boone and me as kids on the Yadkin."

Her expression softened at the name of the slippered man. "You know Henry Skeggs? Oh. And who?"

"Dan Boone. Daniel Boone. He's fairly well-known. Explorer. Pioneer. He and I grew up together in the mountains of North Carolina. Skeggs used to visit my parents on his scouting trips through the Blue Ridge, or *Quirank*, as Powhatan called them."

"Powhat-an?"

"Great chief—like a king, a leader—of the Cherokee native people. Before so many colonists came. Every new group wants to name a thing in their tongue."

"Gilbert told me…I think no kings in Oo-nited States America. But you say he is king. Did you know king? Powhat-an?"

"No. He lived long before now, but his people are strong. Many of his children's children's children still live here. They're some of the native tribes in these parts."

"Why you want meet me?"

He studied the curve of her hairline and the point of her chin, unable to look away. "I was willing to give my life for my colony. I'd never thought about living wounded." He stripped a handful of maple leaves from a low-hanging branch. "America won her freedom." He rubbed the neck muscles of his bay horse. "After I lost my family, and almost my life, it crushed me. I slipped into a…a darkness? A part of myself I didn't know was there. Maybe it wasn't even me." Ripping the leaves into pieces, he continued. "I tried to drown it." He acted out taking a drink from a jug. "I didn't mean to tell you all this. I mean, I did, just not today. I never thought it could be any different for me."

Sincerity washed over his expression. "It was all I knew. Anger. The fight against tyranny. Skeggs told me once the fight against tyranny will always exist. It was him who suggested I learn law and government. So, I did. I like being left alone, keeping my peace. I'm level-headed. Pretty good at legislating, actually, if it doesn't sound too conceited to say so." He hung his head and threw up his hands. When he did, his reins slapped his horse's hide. It made the animal flinch, sending the beast sideways, closer to Vittorie and her horse. His knee banged hers. "And then last year, I heard stories."

He paused and looked at her, gathering strength. "I heard about a lot of things. One of which happened to be a beautiful young widow. She was brave, kind…good. I didn't believe in her at first. No one like that could exist, not out here anyway. How could someone come so close to death, be so mistreated, and not be bitter like I was?"

"You don't…."

"Please, let me tell you. I want you to know." He swallowed. "I thought about how strong you must be, how you came to have such character. I wondered if you really were as beautiful as he'd said and if you'd already been snatched up by some…," he sat up straighter in mock bravado, "…lesser man out here." He still had her attention. "I found myself wondering. I found myself thinking. I found myself telling Aunt Rose I'd come visit."

His horse pawed the ground. The sound of urine streaming against unsuspecting leaves below grounded the conversation.

"So much for my deep confessions," he said, embarrassed. "I realized how selfish I was acting. I remembered how much passion and devotion I had for people before Emily died, for their rights. And I thought, 'Here's a woman'..." He didn't look at her long as he raced through to the end of his argument. "Here's a woman deserving of love." Ending his speech, he fidgeted with the reins, which made his horse whinny.

Vittorie sat quietly. Concern showed on her face.

A breeze tempered the mid-June heat. The river gurgled on the other side of the black raspberry bushes. "I had to come and see if...see if a man could pursue happiness after great loss," he said.

"After fighting you go into government? What you want now?"

"My own land. To farm. I'd like a family."

"I used to want those things." She plucked a few ripe berries. "But my life go a different way."

"This river doesn't run as straight as a bird flies, but they both can reach their destination."

She held her palm out flat with several berries for him. "I'd rather am the bird."

✳ ✳ ✳

As the horses arrived at the front gate, fireside orange and musty plum edged the skyline.

"T-ank you for the ride," Vittorie said, her tone cordial. "I did much enjoy your company. Good evenin'."

"I still owe you a supper, if you'll allow me." Reluctance edged the easy manner he'd carried himself with all day.

She smiled with an openness that drew him to her and she whispered, "I release you from your debt."

Dismounting, he put his arms around her waist and helped her down. "Thank you for today," he said. She smelled like heaven. "I hope to call on you again."

She curtsied, bending her knees deep but straightening up fast. Back within the familiarity of the farm, she snipped the cord of the connection. "I cook here for this family. I create in the evenings t' have somethin' t' give. I don't know when t' be free next."

A whippoorwill called, announcing the day's end. She'd missed supper.

"Would you be happy if I called on you again?"

"Mr. Frazier, it's been a long day."

"Just Frazier, please. Or John."

Walking through the gate, it closed behind her with a clink of the latch.

"I'm sorry if I scared you."

Her dress rustled around as she turned to face him. "Scare me?"

"I led with my emotions instead of common sense. Perhaps I should have waited to speak of all that."

The wind stirred, blowing ribbons and curls across her face.

"I respect you honesty." She removed tendrils of her hair from her mouth. "Will you let me think it about?" She encouraged him with a smile. A very little smile.

91

"That John Frazier's becomin' a regulah sight aroun' here, Miz Vi!" Faith pinned a large pair of Clem's wet britches on the line. "This'n the third day this week he's helped Clem'n Rightly harvest." She peered through hung laundry for her friend's reaction.

"He works for free." Vittorie pinned Grace's apron strings up. "An' we can use the help."

Faith brushed the dangling impediment aside. "He works b'cause he's in love."

Vittorie looked at her friend as though she'd just heard concerning news.

Stepping between the woman and the line, Faith slid the basket of washed laundry away from Vittorie with her leg. "You like him. I see it. What's the matter?"

"I don't know."

"I do. You's afeared."

"No, I'm not."

Faith folded her arms like when she corrected Rightly. "His presence on the farm soothes ye and stirs ye at the same time."

"I like this little space on earth. For a while now, I have. With him here there is something…."

"You'ah not meant to stay as you are. You'ah meant t' grow."

"Ah is!"

427

"Ah am," Faith said, correcting her language. "An' no you ain't. You'ah pushin' the good out of yo' life 'cause you's holdin' on t' the old man. Well, the old man is gone, Love. It's no hurt to let him go. He's already gone. What's the word in your language for a gift, an extra special, jes' comin' once, you bettuh grab him, gift?"

Vittorie held the taut line for support and hung her head. "*L'agniappe.*"

"La'nap."

Faith's intentional failure at saying it right made Vittorie laugh. "*L'agniappe.*" She rolled the 'n' extra long.

"Mm-hm and you best l'an-yap him up!" Faith turned Vi to face her. "Grievin's got its place. I know. But it ain't livin'. Love is knockin' on yo' door an' 'less you wannuh sleep innuh closet forevuh…."

"*Oui, oui*…yes. *D'accord.* I'll try harder."

"Tha's part o' yo' problem, Vi. It's not something to make hard. Let go." Her words hit their mark. "Look at 'im." She looked in Frazier's direction.

Grace carried a basket of fresh-picked sweet corn around the backside of the kitchen building. "What'uh you girls doin'?" She saw the direction Faith and Vi were looking, so she looked, too.

Vittorie sighed. When she followed Faith's gaze, she saw Frazier bind a bundle and toss it to Clem. Shirt sleeves rolled, his sun-kissed muscles gleamed.

He raised a hand in salute to her. Uncle Clem shook his head and leaned back, enjoying himself in a laugh.

Grace chuckled, "That man's in love if ever one was."

Vittorie gave a little wave in return, hiding her happiness behind the billowing linens.

92

Vittorie brushed off her hands. With her work finished, her heart wondered where *he* was. Stepping outside the kitchen door, she stopped. Something lay in her path.

A large stick lay sideways across the threshold. Stuck in the crook of its two largest branches bloomed an arranged bouquet of wildflowers. Clutching up the surprise, she breathed in a multi-colored aroma. She held the bouquet for a long moment, as much to temper her wild rapture as to savor the gift.

Her fingers found a thin, lavender thread tied to the bouquet. It led off down the path where it connected to another little flower and another, as far as she could see from her little stoop. Elation filled her soul and adrenaline powered her legs. She leaped and hid a squeal of delight behind the scrumptious nosegay. *Could being so happy all at once be acceptable?*

As her feet followed the intended course, she wound the skein back up. She skipped to the next stem and untied the new flower, adding it to the growing bouquet. A vibrant cluster of orange butterfly milkweed flowers plumped up beside its cousin, the blushing red milkweed. The tower-shaped cascading bell petals of false dragonhead in faintest violet and white highlighted the circular gyrations and radial symmetry of a brilliant citrus-colored common sunflower. She extricated the striped and hazy hues of multiple purple meadow phlox from its entanglements, and added the lovely specimen to the bunch in her hand.

The thread led down her favorite path to the orchard, where it ended. She twirled around a cherry tree, already in love with the afternoon full of promise, the fragrant pause heightening the anticipation of her destination. When she arrived at the crest of the hill, she saw what she'd hoped for. Down by the water, Frazier crouched over a fire, cooking. Two plates sat on a blanket just out of reach of the water's edge where a hollowed log boat rocked lazily back and forth.

She called to him. "Are you expectin' someone?"

Her presence startled him, but then his unraveling smile appeared. He'd shaved. His mustache was thinner and his beard gone. It showed off a dimple in each scruffy cheek. "Please," he said, ushering her to a seat on the blanket.

She knelt down on the soft wool and made herself as comfortable as she dared. Being the center of so much attention overwhelmed her, and he hadn't even served the food yet. Frazier hummed and flipped something in the pan. When he looked over in her direction, his eyes fell on something to her right. Beside her sat a new basket with a hinged top. Baling twine tied into a makeshift ribbon and bow indicated it was a present, for her. She looked back at him for permission.

"A replacement," he said with a nod.

She pulled one end of the bow. The ribbon came undone. Lifting the lid off her new basket, she reached inside and pulled out a delicate bird's nest. Its hollow overflowed with maple tree seedpods.

A strong gust of wind blew, disturbing the contents of the nest in her hand. It sent the tiny, pale shapes twirling up and away. Losing their updraft, the winged pods cascaded down around her in a fanciful whirligig shower.

"*Oh, merci!*" she gasped.

The rapture of her expression and unconscious slip into French proved thanks enough for him. He stirred the contents of the skillet, enjoying the moment with her. "I think there's something else." He peered into the basket with a quizzical expression and handed it back to her.

"*Encore?*" There, in the bottom, lay one white feather. She lifted it out, touching the quill point and pinching the spine lightly between her fingertips, smoothing the vane. "What is this?"

"'You'd rather be….'"

"…the bird…."

"…than the river." Her smile increased at his perception.

Frazier took the fish off the fire and put one on her plate. "Perfection," he declared over his own cooking, awaiting judgment.

She took a bite, chewed, and made a sour expression.

Horror streaked across his face. "It's not good?"

She almost choked, laughing at her own joke and swallowing at the same time. "Ahaha! No, it's delicious."

He fell down beside her in relief, very close. "Say that in French."

She didn't move away. "Say what?"

"Delicious," he said, eyes intent on her lips.

"*Dé-lic-i-eux.*" It was nearly impossible not to pucker her lips pronouncing it, but she tried. Her head bobbled side to side. "*Come* ça. Sounds almost the same." Her body ached to be held by him.

"Almost? It is the same." When he laughed, his bottom lip appeared out from under his mustache. "Like *we* are the same."

There was no denying the truth those words held. So opposite, yet so aligned. He noticed her hesitate. Her eyelids came crashing down. Thick eyelashes flashed. But today was the day he had to know. It couldn't be put off any longer.

The fire crackled as the logs burned, and the night air settled into a cool September temperature as they ate.

He stabbed at his plate. "What do you love about it here?"

"I don't know."

"No? Then why do you stay?"

"I have a good life with Samantha and Grace and the family." With a forced laugh, she added, "I don't have much choice."

"Of course you do." His tone changed. "Everyone has. I took this wound in my leg to make sure of it. In America, we are free, Vittorie. Not bound by class or title, only by our laws and our convictions." He took her hand. Their fingers wound together and he kissed hers.

Surprised at how comfortable, how good, that felt, she looked into his eyes. "You have big hope," she said. "And goodness." With her free hand, she put the last morsel of food in her mouth. After chewing a moment, she asked, "Rosemary?"

"Very good."

"Why do you stay?"

"I'm not. I'm leaving."

Vittorie felt sick to her stomach hearing the news. "When?" she asked, lifting the pitch of her voice to mask her emotions.

"They've asked me to help start a settlement North of the Cumberland River, about 100 miles south of here." He kept hold of her hand.

"That's far."

For lack of another response, he shrugged.

"And you're going?"

"They have a need for more men with my skills. They've asked me to help write the plan for self-governance."

A fish jumped, breaking the surface tension on the water. The river moved on, erasing its place.

He stroked her cheek with the fingers of his other hand. "Vittorie Monet LeClerc, be my wife. Come with me."

She pulled her fingers away. "It's hard to start all over."

"Harder when your heart is someplace else."

Her brain clouded over the correct English words. "Dinner was beauty." She couldn't get out what she really wanted to say. The moment ruined, embarrassed, she stood up. She brushed the crumbs off her skirt and took in a deep breath, but no more words came out. She shook her head and turned, half-running, half-scrambling up the path back to the house.

Frazier leaped up. "Vittorie!" He watched her go. The lavender cord between them reached its breaking point. He felt it tearing out his heart. He'd leave the river and the station alone. Ready to be done with all evidence of romance, he wadded up the blanket, dishes and all, and chucked it into the boat. His mind whirled. His chest had a pain left of center.

He grabbed the frying pan, kicked sand on the fire, and ran a hand through his hair to ease the ache coming on. Only one thing could fix it, and she was running farther away. His temples throbbed, and he took a deep breath to calm down.

The sound of the water annoyed him. He watched it racing away from him, too. He loved her and he knew it. She loved him. He knew that. *Why didn't she know it?*

With the answer in mind, he spun around to chase after her, almost losing his balance in the suddenness of his decision.

But she was close. Running back to him. Stopping in front of him.

She sucked her breath in hard. "Everywhere I look, I see only you."

That was all the permission he needed. Her love confessed, he wrapped her in a kiss, passionate and tender, like she'd always been his, like she would always be his. Under the waxing grin of the crescent moon, he committed all his soul to her, all his love to her, body to follow.

93

Vittorie tossed her bouquet of yellow American lotus bundled with fragrant white water lilies high over her head. Her lemon-colored dress billowed over Frazier's colonialist uniform in the last windy days of September. Cream piping complimented the floral details she'd stitched into the sheer cotton overlay. He kept his hand behind the small of her back as she turned around.

Vittorie laughed with glee at her friend's turn of fortune. "Haha! Faith caught the bouquet!"

Faith looked radiant.

"Good!" Frazier said. "I wish her well. Skeggs!" He clapped the woodsman by the forearm. "Thank you, you old black bear. You were right."

"Humility suits you, John." Skeggs kept hold of Frazier's arm. "Congratulations. Did you hear? Rhode Island ratified in May. That makes all thirteen colonies."

"I bet the vote was close," Frazier stepped back beside Vittorie. "Last I heard, they were split nigh even."

"Aye, t'was. 34-32. Concern over continued slavery one of their chief oppositions, which I agree. Though I'd rather have them in the Union. Greater good on the side to fight it."

"I suppose commercial trade twisted a hand in their votes."

"Correct. Federal government threatened they'd be cut off."

"Cut off? Where would they go? Pirate trade over the Atlantic? It's not like they could journey west over the mountains." He stomped a daddy long leg off his boot.

"I'm honored you came, Henry. We're forever grateful to you."

"Where do you plan to settle?" Without waiting for the answer, Skeggs turned to the bride. "If he gives you any trouble, he'll have to answer to me, *Ursus Americanus*. That's the word of Henry Skeggs, the old Black Bear."

Vittorie reached for Skeggs and took both his hands in hers. "*Merci, mon ami, pour tous….*" Gratitude for his kindness overflowed her heart. She kissed his haggard, brown knuckles.

"English please!" joked Frazier. "My French is limited, and I'd like to know why my wife is distributing kisses!"

Baked with age, Skeggs' face creased into lines as unique as the horizon. He held Vittorie's gaze, and the intensity of his aqua blue eyes focused on her alone as he listened, taking time to receive what she'd said. "Bless you, sweet girl." The corners of his mouth turned up, but as fast as a squirrel shakes its tail the satisfaction dissipated. He patted her hand and let it go.

Frazier scooped her hand to his arm. "Did you know, Vi," he said, "before you stands the best distance runner I've ever met?"

"I believe it."

"It's true. And I've never seen him on a horse. Ever."

Samantha's approach turned the conversation in a new direction. "Here's your walnuts, Vi. Rightly's been guarding this basket from the other children till now! They're wrapped so pretty!" She played with the lid and handle strap. "I like that color ribbon. You are so creative, Mrs. Vittorie Frazier!" She dabbed an eye with her hankie. "And when you've finished passing those out, come and eat you two. Hello, Henry! I hoped you might be in our woods today!" She swayed toward him, feet planted. "You're welcome to stay." Equal in age, her tone piqued higher as she spoke to Skeggs.

"Thank you, ma'am. 'at's very kind." The outdoorsman in him resurfaced. "Unfortunately, I must leave directly."

"Can't you stay to eat? We've Clem's stew, good ale, Vittorie's own soft cheeses, butter enough for all the bread, plus beans and roasted corn. And…," she paused to lengthen the temptation, "… Faith made fresh cream from the Jersey girls this mornin'. She plans to serve it over the last o' the strawberries with mint."

"You were the right place for her, Katey. Thank you." He spoke the truth like it hung from trees where anyone could have gathered it. "Got a long road ahead, but thank you much. Better to run on a might empty stomach than full as a tick."

"Katey! I haven't heard anyone call me that since…well, I don't know when." Her hat flounced in the breeze and she reached to repin it.

Vittorie took the basket from Samantha. "Why does he call you 'Katey'?"

"Samantha Katherine." She brushed a ladybug off her glove. "Samantha seemed too formal when I was a child. Ere'body called me Katey, except my Papaw. He named me 'Diddlebug.' Oh my!"

Skeggs settled his faded, unlooped hat over straw-gray hair and pulled it down to his brows. "Mr. Frazier. Mrs. Frazier. Mrs. Sellers."

Rightly ran over, pulling Faith along by the arm. "Kin Ah pass the gifts out, pleeeeease? Ah promise to give ere'body some!"

"Ah said he had t' ask you," Faith said, smiling. "An' Ah was ready to fetch them berries, Miz Vi…Mrs. Vi. Ooo! That sounds good. Ms. Rose and Ms. Evelyn have finished their stew and done been askin'."

"Yes, thank you, Faith. Rightly, give your Mama the first sack o' walnuts and then you kin give them all away!"

Vittorie turned to say something to Skeggs, but he was gone. Only the berry bushes remained, dripping with vines of yellow honeysuckle, and a hummingbird, drinking deeply. Someone struck up a fiddle, and Frazier led Vittorie to dance with their guests.

438

94

"I thought you said you didn't have much." Frazier gawked, hands on hips, at the growing pile to be loaded on the wagon.

"I don't. But a home's gotta have a spinnin' wheel an' Samantha said is extra, so I might's'a well take it. An' Clem tol' me take his extra box for salting, sayin' we get a farm." She pointed to a bucket next to more items in a row. "We need a milk pail. And Isaiah gave us the butter churn for a wedding gift."

He pointed to a carved-out wooden piece shaped like a miniature canoe, filled with fabric-covered things. "What are all these?"

"Grace gave her dough bowl to me an' those plates are from your family."

His look questioned that. He hoisted the churn into the back of the wagon with a grimace.

"Rose brought them over last week," Vittorie said. "Said she was glad to have them passed down to family."

Rightly unlatched the gate from the inside. He walked it as wide as it would open, until he fell into the stalks and dying leaves of the bushes. "Go 'head, Mama," his voice chirped out.

Faith leaned back as she carried a stool in front of her, feet first. "Thank ye, Rightly. Hold it wide for Uncle Clem."

Clem toted a matching carved bench in one hand while he gestured with the other. "Bring the rug, Rightly."

Once the man and long bench passed the gateway, the boy ran back toward the house.

Grace met him on her way out. "Ah got it. Go help Samantha!" She marched straight out to where Frazier stood in the back of the flat wagon. "Here, John," she said, waiting for him to take it. "This can't set on the groun'."

"What is it?" John asked.

"Rag rug!" Grace answered with enthusiasm.

"Woven from e'ery scrap o' fabric to pass through the house in th' las' year!" Vittorie beamed. "Isn't it marvelous? Grace and Faith made it for us."

"An' these are from me," said Clem, tapping a knobby, dark fingertip on his bench and stool.

Frazier hopped down to inspect the bench. The seats were sanded smoother than a calf's nose as he ran his hands over it. The tri-colored wood traded between sand, rose, and sorrel brown. Every joint held fast. "Hickory?"

When Clem nodded, his whole chest moved. "Worked on it in the evenin's evuh since you been courtin' Miz Vi."

"Clem, this is fine work. I'm honored. Thank you." He reached for Clem's hand.

Clem pulled him into a hug. "God go wit' ye." He stretched out his other arm and pulled Vittorie in. "You take care o' each other, now. We won't be 'round t' look out for ye."

"We will," Vittorie said, but her voice trembled.

The front door creaked on its hinges. Samantha emerged from the house carrying a basket. Rightly darted ahead of her with a wide, flat box.

"Here y'aruh! Miz Samant'a said this'n is'n fo' you!"

"It *isn't* for me?" Frazier teased. He took the box and patted the boy on the back of his shoulder. "I think you've grown since yesterday, Rightly!"

Rightly's smile spread ear to ear. His adult front teeth shone white and bright in the center of his mouth, one overlapping the other a little. "Hear, Mama! I tol' you!" The pink of his tongue showed through the gaps where his canines would be growing through the winter.

"It's for you," Samantha said, huffing and shuffling to catch up. "It *is* for them, Rightly, hon. Clem, would you lift those three things inside the house door and bring them out for John?"

"How big are they?" John asked.

"There's the quilt and some table doilies, besides this oak basket with cold meats, cheese, and bread. Have you a little bit of money, John?"

The idea of her asking him that struck Frazier wrong, but he bit his tongue. "Yes, ma'am. I promise I can take care of her."

"It's not a question of might, John. As her representative parent, it seemed right to ask before I send her off into the wide world again."

"We're going to be fine. She's going to be well taken care of, you have my word." He waited for her to stop arranging things in the wagon and look at him. "You have my word."

Samantha touched his elbow. "I know. You'll write." To hide the emotion welling up in her eyes, she turned away from him. "Goodness, look at the sky. It'll be noon before you're saddled. Rightly, Faith, everyone say your sayin's." Leading by example, she put an arm around John's shoulder. "G'bye, son. Be good to each other."

"With my life. For my whole life. You have my word."

Samantha waved a hanky. "Clem!" she hollered. "They're underway. Did you say farewell?"

Clem jogged his solid frame out to the gate. Faith and Grace and Rightly clung to Vittorie and he finished out the group embrace. Giggles erupted from inside the family circle.

"Oh," Vittorie cried, "I have t' go now or I never will! Thank you, thank you…*merci, mon Coeur.*"

Faith's high cheekbones glistened with the tears falling over them. "An Ah'm go'n keep up yo' cheese-makin'," she promised as she struggled to keep her composure. "It'll be like you's right…," she lifted up her elbow and made a fierce point down to the ground beside her, "…he-uh." After her bold declaration in front of everyone, her delicate hand landed on her chest where it bounced twice. "Right he-uh."

From her seat beside John on the stiff buckboard, Vittorie placed her hand over her heart and made a fist. "Right he-uh." She kissed her fingertips and waved to the Sellerses. Loaded down with the love of so many, it was hard not to cry.

As their wagon lurched into the unknown, Frazier read her heart. He put her head down on his shoulder and kissed the top of it. With a slap of the reins, he drove the team of horses forward.

95

1802 - Cader Edwards' Home. Goosehorn, Kentucky

A lovely cottage rested amidst snow drifts, hung from the heavens by the single strand of smoke rising from its chimney. Men's voices laughed from inside warm windows.

The merry party of three burst into a new round of cheer. Skeggs sat closest to the fireplace, long rifle taken apart over his legs. He oiled the barrel with a limp rag, shoulders rounding as he chuckled. "I remember!"

Perry, the man to Skeggs' immediate right, laughed longest. His loose bottom lip flopped free, due in large part to the lack of many remaining teeth. His jaw worked like a steer, chewing away when he closed his mouth. "That spring o' eighty-eight were a wet'un," he said. "Middleton an I, we was trackin' fer a land party. Twenty Virginians, which we handed off to you, Skeggs." Dirty fingers wiped saliva off the bottom of his face. He spread it across the chest of his shirt. Feeling his pipe, he pulled it from the pocket.

Skeggs huffed, trying to keep from laughing again. "T'was a party of eight, Perry! Not twenty," He rested the rag on his leg; his fingers trembled on their own.

"Well, they seemed like to twenty, fussy as they were," said Perry, chuckling.

"Extraordinary!" Cader Edwards, the evening's host, sat across from Skeggs enjoying his company. The young surveyor took his feet off the patterned footstool and leaned forward. "That was twelve, fourteen years ago, Skeggs! Is there a man in this country you haven't met? Or that you don't remember?"

Skeggs worked his rag over the gunstock maple. "Oh, some, I s'pose." Aqua eyes peered through wrinkled lids, piercing as ever.

"Not if they've been anywhere in 'ese woods." Perry snorted, holding the pipe in his hand.

Cader opened a box above the mantel and refilled his pipe. "Apparently, they *are* his woods. He knows them like I know my own home. Extraordinary!" He puffed till it smoked and sat back in his curved easy chair. "Go on. What happened next?" His loose hand draped over the rounded armrest.

Skeggs reconnected the spiral bore. "The party of Pennsylvanians you and Middleton took south of the barrens April 1788 was eight men. McGary traded me for the Virginia party partway. That's what I remember."

Wide-eyed, Cader poked his pipe at Perry. "Memory for figures he's got, eh?" Smoke puffed from his mouth. "Go on, Henry."

"That's right," Perry interrupted. "We jes' brought 'em from Lexington. McGary switched parties wi' ye there in the barrens."

"They were searching the boundaries of a hundred thousand acres north of the Cumberland," Skeggs continued. "South of the Kentucky line...well, Virginia in those days."

Perry gazed into the roaring fire, jaw gumming. "Ye know, we had an adventure there." Deeply settled in his chair, he stared at the flames as if in a trance. "I've rarely spoke of it," he said, furrowing his brows. "It happened right here." He bent a finger toward the snow swirling outside. "At the spring. After we left ye,

Middleton an' I come across some no-account thieves. Surprised, they were, on seein' us." He chuckled in his throat.

"White or red?" Skeggs asked. "The thieves."

"Red," Perry said. Thought and fire overtook his tongue and he paused, staring.

Cader looked between his two house guests—one bent on confession, the other tracking details—a smile growing. There's clout in being the first one to know a thing: It gains one much in the eyes of the listeners when one passes it on again.

"Red," Perry repeated, "happened to be. Was a might find we had there, at the spring with 'em indians."

"Which spring?" asked Skeggs.

"Big Blue Spring." Perry jerked the pipe and thumb over his left shoulder. "Jes' outside yer door there. Middleton and I happened upon six indians makin' off with a killin' if ever I saw 'un."

"April of eighty-eight?" Skeggs loaded the fire to keep the memory burning. "You're sure?"

Cader handed Perry the tobacco box.

"Thank ye," Perry said, taking the snuff. "Sure 'nough. We happened upon 'em sudden like." Not typically the center of such attention and feeling an unaccustomed freedom, he grew more animated. His shoulders sloped; the volume of his voice dropped. As the others listened, he stared at a knot in Cader's floor. The pipe in his right hand wound about in the air. At particular junctures, he clenched it between his canines. It wiggled while the words spilled out from his lips. He was no longer in the room with them. He was at the Big Blue Spring, finding treasure.

Tracking each word, Skeggs leaned on Cader's mantel. His long rifle rested against the hearth. "So, you never found the owners?"

"Naw," said Perry.

"Still have anything?" Skeggs asked.

"Naw. I've no use for fancy things like that. Jes' gimme a bit more than my own skin to wear, enough to eat for the day, and a fire to set by." He took a long pull on his pipe. "The wife still has a gift I gave her, though. She'll ne'er part with it."

96

Long rifle in hand and bundled in fur-lined skins, Skeggs tromped through thawing snow to pay a visit. Perry's fence, broken in three places, reflected the man. The tin roof was worn thin. The front door had come off one hinge. It cocked so as to never keep winter fully out nor the fire's heat fully in. Perry seemed a man pleased enough to have a cabin and a roof and a wife; how he kept them was his business.

"Hullllooooo, Perry!" Skeggs called from the gate.

A woman's harsh voice answered. "Hullo?" The crooked door wiggled as she squinted through the gap. "Who is't?"

"Henry Skeggs, ma'am. Perry at home?"

"Oh-ho!" Perry shouted. "Bring him in!"

After much marital shouting and the door jarring, it opened. Skeggs ducked under the low frame. Perry sat him at the kitchen table and the longhunter set his satchel to one side. An iron pot bubbled over the roaring fire, but Mrs. Perry paid it no mind. While Skeggs talked, her full attention stayed focused on him. She scrunched her mouth and furrowed her brows as the men explained the reason for Skeggs' visit.

"An' what do the likes of 'im want wiv it?" came her direct reply.

Mr. Perry's shoulders drooped. "I was jes' tellin' him at Cader's last evenin' about the find at Big Blue Spring…."

"Ooohhh, another story, was ye? An' there's time for that?" She'd a heart as big as her middle, which was to say, her heart was prodigious indeed. Years of hoping for things and being disappointed jaded her. She'd grown weary of always being kind and good-natured. "We got's a river run down th'inside wall, only enough vittles for two days, an' ye've got time for stories? About mine undergarments, no less?" Mrs. Perry crossed her plump arms, gripping the spoon like a saber.

Skeggs cleared his throat. "If you please, Mrs. Perry…."

She turned to him. "If yer so interested, why'n't you fin' yer own woman, Mr…?" She left off, realizing she'd forgotten his name.

"Skeggs. And I'll fix you some pitch."

Lifting the pot, she moved it to a stone on the floor to cool. "Ey?"

"For the roof." Skeggs gestured in the direction of the leak.

"See? There." She lay the spoon beside Perry and retrieved another one from a bowl on the cupboard. This one she set before Skeggs. "A *hard-workin'* man." Her fists went to her wide hips and she stared at her husband, judging the effect of her words.

Mr. Perry wasn't as rough as he appeared, at least not where the missus was concerned. "Got some pigeons 'fore the storm…." A sudden air came about him. He seemed smaller than last evening. Nothing of the bravado and honor from the storyteller of the night before could be seen in him at the present moment. Now, he was seeing himself through her eyes. Worse, she was telling him how he was seen in her eyes. It had an ill-effect on him, as it might on any man in his position.

Turning her attention back to Skeggs, she asked, "What in'erest have ye in me vest?" She set bowls of stew by each spoon.

This was the question Skeggs'd come for. He'd not expected it so soon, nor so easily asked. "I know a woman like yourself would want to do the right thing if she learned the rightful owner…," he paused for the last few words to hit, "…who valued the item highly and became a widow in its loss…had been found."

This noble thought was new to Mrs. Perry. She sucked broth off her thumb.

Skeggs saw her generous bottom lip quiver as he continued. "And would pay to replace such a valuable thing, to be sure." Skeggs let the weight of his words hang in the room.

Mr. Perry slurped. Mrs. Perry slapped a mighty forearm down on the table to quiet him. It worked.

She stared back at Skeggs, as she might size up which chicken to pluck from the yard for supper. Standing up and turning around, she grunted. Her wide girth bumped the table and chair on the way to the makeshift cupboard behind her. From inside a clay canister she plucked something soft and silvery, which she laid on the cleaner part of the table in front of Skeggs. "The problem is, Mr. Skeggs, I could never fine anyt'ing to wear wiv it."

Judging from appearances, it might have fit around her forearm. In actuality, its creator intended it as a vest for an entire woman. Skeggs decided it best to let that pass unspoken.

"An' here," she continued, pulling a paper from the inside vest pocket. "I've 'anded it to many an learned soul and naught nary a one could a read it t' me. Do ye read, Mr. Skeggs?"

Her honest question, so full of genuine curiosity, buoyed Skeggs' hope of acquisition. He took the small scrap from her outstretched arm and positioned it before his eyes.

She leaned down with her face next to his. Her backside bobbed behind her as her knees wiggled in expectation. Of all that was unhad or unattainable for her in life, this one gift, with this one paper, had been the true mystery to come to her. "Ye think, on this frigid win'er mornin', wit nothin' but stew and spring drippin' in, ye might'n read it me?"

Ignoring the bosoms at his elbow, Skeggs focused on his task. "It's written in French, Mrs. Perry. A note on moral and religious duties addressed to a young bride-to-be." He handed the paper back to her. "From a…," he narrowed his gaze and moved the paper further from his eyes, "…clergyman, looks like."

Mrs. Perry's hand flew to her mouth. "Oh, the sweet dear," she said, blinking back tears. "Oh, Mr. Perry!" She draped her arms around Mr. Perry, whose shock at the sudden turn of emotional events caused him to be more pleased with Skeggs by the minute. "Had I known, I should've given it up long ago." Pricked by the thought of withholding a piece of this young widow's trousseau, words spilled out of her soft heart. "I'm so sorry," she cried out. "Oh, Mr. Perry!" She repeated. "I didn't know…the sweet dear…."

"Perhaps," Skeggs said, "you have been its safe-keeping these fifteen years."

This happy thought made tears well up in Mrs. P's eyes. A smile spread between her pink, chicken-thigh cheeks. "Do ye' t'ink, Mr. Perry?" Her voice softened, and as she stood with her arms still flung around his neck, she seemed more suited to his size.

"Perhaps," Skeggs interrupted, "when you're paid for its safe-keeping, there might be enough for an outfit more to your liking."

Extricating herself from her husband, Mrs. Perry lifted the delicate vest in her hands and held it out for Skeggs. Evidence of Vittorie's skill in curling emellishments covered the garment.

"Do you really t'ink so, Mr. Skeggs?" she asked, child-like hope in her eyes.

Skeggs tucked it inside the worn leather satchel that never left his person. He put a tiny sack of coins on the table. "I'll see what might be done."

Mrs. Perry wiggled in excitement. "See, Mr. Perry? Mr. Skeggs knows what to do wiv' it." In her newfound exuberance, she offered him a skillet. "Cornbread?"

97

Summer, 1802 - Davidson County, Tennessee

If twelve years is a long time for a Tennessee cabin to bear the brunt of summer heat and winter bite, the Frazier home weathered well. Their house stood complete on a stone foundation in rectangular shape. One door opened in the center front, with one equal and opposite out the back. Every window had shutters and a sillbox planted in herbs or flowers. The weather-beaten threshold showed wear. Opposite the kitchen garden, a smallish orchard grew on the property's north side—apples of various sorts, damson plums, and pears. Taller trees bordered the edges like a hemmed doily. Wildflower hills spread around the wider landscape toward the Cumberland River.

A carved headboard framed Vittorie. "Bedtime!" she called.

French touches accented rough-hewn wood around the room. It set a wonderful atmosphere. Oil lamps cast soft light over prints she'd painted on the walls. Seven children sprawled around her. The tousled heads ranged from ten years old down to two. Four of the seven were boys.

John Frazier climbed the broad, smooth stairs he'd cut and placed years earlier to the children's attic bedroom. Enjoying

453

the scene set before him, he leaned a shoulder outside the door frame and observed.

Vittorie patted little bodies above and below the covers. "Shhh, now. Quiet up." She patted her own large belly, pregnant once more.

"Momma?" Anna, her eldest, had inherited her mother's and grandmother's green eyes. "Tell us about when you were my age."

"No," said her second son, Lee. "Tell us the story of when you crossed the ocean to meet Father." His thick hair needed trimming.

The older children had all heard the story before. Some held a sibling on their lap, or nearby enough to poke as needed. They giggled with excitement, the whole group a happy sort of tangle.

"Hmmm…let's see," Vittorie said. Silver streaked the brown curls lolling over her shoulders. "I was born in a whole 'nother country called *France*."

Auguste, the eldest son, interrupted. "Where everyone speaks French because the King says so!" Pulling a blanket off the bed, he wrapped it around his shoulders and balanced a tiny pillow on his head like a crown. Everyone laughed and he sat down, triumphant.

Vittorie continued. "Your *grand-mère* et *grand-père* had a vine-yard. We grew grapes on a hillside by the sea. After my chores were done, I would run up the hill and sit, looking out across the village, dreaming of life in America."

No more than four, Little Henry piped up. "Did you dream of me?"

Vittorie tickled his belly. "*Bien sûr*! I dreamed of all of you."

Too excited to be patient, John, Jr., called out, "Then you got on a big ship!" He stood on his tiptoes and reached high into the air.

"Yes," Vittorie said, acknowledging his addition to the story with a smile, "but it felt very small in the great big ocean."

A moment passed between husband and wife when Frazier entered the room,. "Your father was here already." Her tone softened.

"Very lonely," he added, eyes on her alone.

"And very brave," Vittorie said.

Showing his humorous side, Frazier said, "And then she fell in love with me!"

"Father!" said Anna.

Frazier took over the storytelling, wide-eyed and dramatic. "And then, one by one, you all popped out of the garden and she kept bringing you in! 'Keep them out!' I would say, but do you think she would listen?"

Vittorie kissed the top of Marie's little head and rolled herself out of the children's sleeping spot. "No! I wanted them all!"

Interrupting the bedtime mayhem, from the front pasture came a loud, "Hulllloooo, Fraziers!"

Anna, Auguste, and Henry rushed to the window first, each calling out in turn. "Hullo-o!" "Why, it's Mr. Skeggs!" "Henry!"

"So much for bedtime!" Vittorie lowered the fabric curtain between the boys' side and the girls' side of the sleeping loft. "A quick hello and then to bed!"

Frazier helped her descend the stairs.

Skeggs held three pheasants by the legs. "I come bearing gifts!"

"None needed!" shouted Vittorie, her delight in his arrival apparent.

"Like the in-laws I never got to know," Frazier joked. "Come into civilization, man!" He took the pheasants.

"*Bienvenue!*" Vittorie kissed Skeggs hello on both cheeks. "Do you never age? Your hair is barely grayer than the last time we saw you."

Skeggs looked pleased and changed the subject. "Civilization, huh? How are the civilized faring these days?"

"Wrote the charter years ago," Frazier said, "but it's a challenge, same as ever."

Vittorie returned with a basin and linen towel. She set them in front of Skeggs. "Thank you for the poultry." She poured water from a pitcher. "Still wandering your knobs?" Her tone implied it was spoken as a compliment. She brought what was left from dinner to the table, *pot-au-feu* and rolls with butter, jerky, and blueberries.

Skeggs washed his face, neck, and arms and seated himself at the table.

"He's amazingly fit for any man, let alone one of his age," Frazier said. "Look at him! What brings you our way?"

The smell of Vittorie's cooking put a smile on Skeggs' face. "*Merci*," he said to Vittorie. Sopping bread through his bowl, he answered Frazier's question. "A story I heard over winter."

"Your stories are always excellent." Vittorie filled his glass with a pale ale. "But it's an awfully long way just for that."

Skeggs glanced at Vittorie, hunting a bean in his bowl. "It's about you."

Several little heads peered over the balcony. His attention to their mother's cooking brought whispers and giggles from the audience above.

"*Moi?*" She smoothed her dress over her belly. "Can't be very interesting."

In true storyteller fashion, Skeggs prolonged their anticipation. He finished his bowl and bread, then tipped back in his chair and rubbed his eyes a minute before continuing. "For forty years now I've made my home, when I chose to, with a family by the name of Edwards, Cader Edwards, near Big Blue Spring. Not far from where we first met, Vi. It's all Kentucky now." He upended his glass, finishing the drink. "Cader's nigh his fortieth year. Surveyor. Wife, some young'uns, intelligent…. Good folk."

Vittorie poured him more ale.

"Last winter, I'd taken in with the Edwards', and one snowy night Cader and I were by the fire telling stories and such. A good time. Man named Perry, neighbor by half a mile or so, joined us. Perry's a rougher character in appearances, though not a bad sort by any means. Well, I've been over these woods several lifetimes worth, and turned out Perry'd done some work with land parties over the years. He's by no means a man of letters, but can do the job tracking and such. Solid folk."

"I'm glad to hear you're not living out of doors all the time, Henry," said Vittorie. "Last winter was very cold." She wrapped a berry-colored shawl around her shoulders.

"Turned out I'd taken over a survey party once from Perry. He was with a colleague of mine from the war named Middleton, not long after first meeting you at Highbaugh's Mill." His aqua eyes looked over at Vittorie.

The passage of time, and a good life with Frazier, had done much to heal the wounds left by that first American spring in 1788. Vittorie's eyes dropped for a second. Frazier wrapped her hand around his arm and pulled her closer.

Skeggs nodded before continuing. "Perry told a story which connected with a part of yours."

Vittorie sat up straighter, thinking there must be good reason for him exhuming this part of her past.

98

Vittorie held her vest in her hands, its fine silk thinned over time. Decorated with threads her fingers created decades ago, a world away, her fingertips followed the floral curves of the bodice. She touched its silver button clasps.

Incredulous, Frazier said nothing. He tapped a finger on the table in thought. Even the children, still awake in the loft, refrained from ruining the delicate moment with words.

Vittorie herself broke the silence. "How did you know it was mine?" she barely whispered.

Skeggs answered in his quiet way, "Put dates and places together."

"They met the thieves within two days, and saw the horses and all our things," she said. "So near…."

"Not three miles away," Skeggs confirmed.

Vittorie spun away from them at the table. "If they'd told anyone about it sooner…." The house felt cramped. Her hands shook.

From above, young Anna saw her mother burst into tears. "Momma!" she cried.

The family stayed silent while Vittorie grieved all over again. She leaned her head on Frazier who comforted her in whispers. He smoothed her hair and she wet his pocket handkerchief thoroughly.

When she could keep the intermittent tears off her cheeks with a mere flick of her forefinger, she simply said, "You certainly do know your woods, Mr. Skeggs." With a pat for her protruding belly, she asked, "How can I ever repay you?"

He picked up his spoon and empty bowl. "This'll be fine."

She burst into a laugh and reached to take his bowl. "As much as you like and more!"

But Frazier caught her arm and seated her again. Taking the bowl himself, he heaped it to overflowing and set the bowl before their hero.

Vittorie stretched her hand across the table to touch Frazier's arm. "*Amour*, please send money for a wardrobe for Mrs. Perry. What was lost has now been found."

Frazier kissed his wife's forehead. "At least a good day dress, my love, as Henry promised."

Vittorie took her vest off the table and laid it out over a wooden chest in the corner of the room.

Anna's sleepy voice popped over the balcony. "S'beautiful, Mother. You made it, didn't you?"

Vittorie nodded at her girl's understanding. "In France." With a blown kiss, she instructed, "To sleep now."

As if waiting to be released from her watchman's post, the young girl's head touched the pillow and she breathed evenly like her siblings, fast asleep.

99

Perry's house in the spring looked worse without snow to hide the details. It now had a patch of dark pitch over a large portion of roof and tall weeds sprung up in the yard. Perry held a group of men spellbound. They stood where the garden intended to grow. His rake lay beside him on the ground, and his hands jabbed and punched as he spoke.

Mrs. Perry preened herself in a new eggplant-colored outfit. She fluttered like a peacock, humming and hoeing, and beamed as he spoke.

Skeggs walked past the Perrys, returning from a hunt. He carried his long rifle. A dead partridge swayed from his satchel.

"There we were, s'rrounded by twelve thieves," Perry continued. "I shot one, dead 'tween the eyes."

Skeggs acknowledged the Perrys with a nod without slowing his stride.

"Th'others run off," Perry said. "But the one I kilt had only four fingers, with a nub where the fith yous'ta'be."

Skeggs froze in his tracks. "You didn't say it that way before," he said with a scowl.

"What?" Perry asked, aware that his tale had grown. Not intending to get caught, he began snorting through his nose.

"Four fingers. You didn't mention one only had four fingers." The other men backed away, suddenly finding importance in being elsewhere.

"Ohhh, that," Perry said, rubbing a hand over his double chin. "A nub where the fifth yous'ta'be." His head jiggled up and down.

Skeggs thrust the partridge into Perry's chest and let it go. Headed in the opposite direction of the Edwards home, where he was originally heading, he launched into a slow lope for a long run.

Perry fumbled with the bird. "Change your mind, then?"

100

Skeggs held his firearm and a wrapped satchel above his head to ford the Green River at Big Buffalo Crossing. The strong current fought him as he swam, but he touched bottom close to the far shore and hauled himself up by a beech root. Unfolding his satchel from the coat, his pipe dropped out unnoticed. He continued on, water spraying from him with every stride.

A barren landscape yawned before Skeggs as he ran, his pace easy, his breathing deep. The forest behind him, he tracked along the descending ridge of the hunting fields burnt off by the natives. The hills peaked lower. The ground stretched longer, sparsely brushed with waving grasses and single, scattered trees. Three pillars of smoke rose to the southeast of him, past a wild apple grove. His stomach growled. His legs churned on.

He rested only when necessary, and for twelve days ran, foraged, slept, and ran some more. A thirteenth moon found its place, rising southeast of him. He slept against a cedar, but after a few hours began again, feet pounding their tempered beat. Morning dew cooled him.

He kept a panting doe in his sights and tracked her over the western Appalachian terrain. Carrying nothing but necessities, water pouch, knife, and satchel, his feet sailed over the ground, barely moving the dirt.

The doe's lythe movements turned erratic. She panted heavily, finding no rest from his pursuit. Her hoof struck a boulder, leaving a scar.

He followed the same path, silently gaining ground. Sweat dripped off his darkened skin. Wrinkles from age and sun were out of place on the lean musculature of the older man's bones.

In fear, her fragile legs stretched past the width she could maintain. Every stride, each inhale, strained her heart.

His sweat and breath ran in a cycle, one conditioned the other. His pursuit intensified. His skill outweighed her own, and in the wild, that was law.

She couldn't shake him. The full sun moved overhead, but he remained close. She couldn't keep ahead of death. Her heart spasmed. Her little legs faltered. She wobbled and fell down. Exhaustion overtook her and she collapsed, dead. Running to her expired form, he knelt and felt for a pulse. He whispered over her, honoring her life, acknowledging her sacrifice.

With the doe around his shoulders, Skeggs picked his way up a narrow mountain pass. The steep incline hid its treachery in dense green foliage, covering the deathly descent like a shroud. The valley floor yawned hundreds of feet below. The distant sound of the Tanasi River wafted up. Skeggs stopped in his tracks and looked up. Overhead, a red-tailed hawk screeched.

"Hello, Louie," Skeggs said aloud.

A pointed arrow stung the red-oak tree in front of his nose.

101

Upper Sequatchie Valley, Tennessee

Three warriors escorted Skeggs. The hawk rode the arm of the one minus an eye. Down a winding trail they trekked to a make-shift outpost of varied luxury. In the clearing, four dilapidated cabins clustered around a storehouse. Children chased skinny dogs off its porch. Bone wind chimes moaned hollow calls. Brightly colored fabrics knotted on breezy clotheslines. A good piece of river rolled further down the incline to the east. Canoes rested, beached high on the hillside, awaiting escape.

Skeggs carried his gift around his shoulders. The dirt path widened. His captors led him to a man in a Louis XIV-style chair, its rounded wood frame draped with satin and furs. On the throne sat a man with dark freckles and skin leathered by life. His ninety years had worn on him so the dermis stretched over his bones looked painful. Thin and frail in body, French Louie remained quick in mind. He lounged, awaiting the longhunter who'd trespassed into his forbidden kingdom.

All merriment halted when Skeggs approached. Whistles and tambourines ceased. Even the wind chimes paused. Skeggs removed the doe from his shoulders and laid it at the older man's feet. Stepping back from the gift, he stood quietly.

Louie rose with the aid of a woman who looked no more than fifty. Her full lips curved down like the tips of a sourwood leaf. Her dark eyes were cold.

Louie held out his arms. The sleeves of his robe dangled low. "You've come for my birthday, I see. And with a gift," Louie said, moving around the carcass within arm's reach of Skeggs.

"How old are you this time?" Skeggs asked.

Louie put two hands on Skeggs' shoulders, and kissed him on both cheeks.

"Ninety-three," Louie whispered, turning their direction toward the store. "But I tell the ladies sixty-six."

Skeggs dipped his head to honor his host. "Rotten liar."

Louie scowled at him. "You know I didn't make my living on my looks. Come in." He motioned his guards away and beckoned Skeggs to follow him.

The old storefront served as Louie's current living quarters, a more private setting. Skeggs ducked hanging hooves, drying bundles of herbs, colored glass, and silver trinkets stuck into the ceiling. Another person skulked around the dim room; its dark form passed behind Louie. As Skeggs' eyes adjusted to the lamps, he could see it moved like a female. The quiet woman's black hair flowed free to her waist, but her movements jerked like they pained her.

"You are my honored guest always, as I have told all my family here. I can never repay the debt I owe you," Louie said, being helped into a chair by the sourwood woman. "And I'll never want to either!" A laugh wheezed through his airpipes and ended as a cough. "I'm sure it'd be well over what I can afford. Though I can afford much."

The quiet women swept a severed chicken foot and three candles off the tablecloth in front of Louie. She set down a bottle and a metal goblet. Louie motioned for Skeggs to help himself to a chair. Skeggs accepted, and she set a similar goblet in front of him.

"Forty years since I've seen you. I'm not the man I used to be," Louie sighed. "How'd you find us?"

"Heard you'd closed down the Obey's River outpost. Knew you'd moved north from Lookout Mountain."

French Louie smiled, raisin lips stretching over scattered pebbles in his mouth. A goat ran through the room.

"I've always prided myself in knowing you as I do." Louie drank to his own joke and inspected his glass. "Spanish treasure ship," he said. "Best thing that happened to me in '79." He fidgeted in his seat. "Most men in my position, well, haven't lived as long as I have. Thanks to you. Ha! Thanks to you!" His cough returned.

Skeggs turned the goblet in his hand. Rubies encrusted the widest part of the bowl and a darker set of stones edged the rim. "You're doing well for yourself."

Louie poured them each another drink and took a swallow of his. The pink of his tongue poked through tooth-free holes when he winced. "Walk with me."

Weak-kneed, Louie grabbed Skeggs' arm for support. The quiet woman moved a curtain. A door opened and they stepped into a jungle paradise wreathed with cages. A pair of peach macaws screeched. A mountain lion paced, and several monkeys swung overhead.

"I don't get out as much as I'd like to," Louie said. "They tell me the settlements are thick as thieves, pardon the expression. But I'm out. Done. For the most part. Traffic has stopped as far as I'm concerned." He feigned disinterest.

One cage stood empty. Skeggs backed away from it as a large, yellow snake lowered itself from the poplar tree behind him.

Louie knocked it down with his walking stick. "Indisa!" he called. "Put Sequatchie back in her cage!" He turned to Skeggs. "An addition from East India traders."

The sourwood woman retrieved the escapee.

Louie nodded in her direction. "What do you think of my newest addition?" Skeggs's non-answer reprimanded him. Louie changed tactics. "War is a terrible thing. I know you disapprove of my menagerie."

Continuing along, they arrived at the dock, which had been ornamented for a makeshift party. Torches jutted out of the embankment. Bottles and wax-filled shells lined long tables that overflowed with food. Ornate china bowls spilled over with spiced seafood and venison.

Louie's arrival stirred a commotion, and before he sat at the head of the table, he raised his arms. "We feast like kings tonight for my friend is here again! This is the one I've told you about! He who saved my life. I owe him a debt I owe to no other. He saved me when others would not have." He lowered his arms and lifted a glass. "To the Longhunter!"

There was a beating of drums and music as the women served from the heaping bowls of food.

"How is your family?" Skeggs asked. He poked his knife into a piece of meat and ate.

The lace cuff around Louie's hand fluttered. "If I let them, the women complain, the men rebel. I have thirty-two great-grandchildren and eight great-great grandchildren." He poked Skeggs in the ribs with a chicken bone. "No heirs for you, Longhunter?"

"You are alert as always." Skeggs peeled the translucent shell off a crayfish and dragged the tender crustacean through a silver dipping bowl of sauce. "How do you keep yourself so well?"

"Tea," Louie answered. "Three times a day. Walk as much as I can by myself. I perform all the necessities," he said, distracted by a raven-haired beauty carrying a pitcher. "And you?"

"Necessities, yes." He looked away from a younger, dark-eyed beauty eyeing him across the table.

"You are a simpler man than French Louie," Louie said as though he were someone else. "Ha! And a good thing, too. You know, I think if you were a man like me, I'd be dead!" He let the woman clean his fingers on a cloth before picking up his spoon. "I would have let me die that day on the Cumberland. You could've taken my business for yourself." He narrowed his eyes at Skeggs as he gnawed sinew from bone, sucked off his fingers, and wiped them on a silk scarf under his plate. "No. You are not a man like me. But, look! In my age I am become a man like you! Hunh!" He slapped Skeggs on the arm, laughing.

Skeggs dropped the crawdad in front of him, but smiled at his host. "Are you?"

"I'm simple now. I like a fire and my women to warm me at night. My family around me, the children to play, the dogs to bark...no, not the dogs to bark...but...." His expression changed again to distrust. "Tell me, my friend, why are you here?"

Nothing can be trusted in the devil's den. Glad of the noise around them, Skeggs swallowed what was in his mouth. "I come to ask you about a four-fingered man."

Louie's eyes left his friend to scan the table and the exact location of his sons. None of them were paying attention. He hunched over his plate without looking up. "Speak to me about it again." He picked something from his mouth and put it in the silk. "Later."

The sourwood woman signaled to some of the young women who started to dance in a circle. Tambourines clattered. Except for Skeggs's, no glass remained empty long. He was exempt, by Louie's orders.

102

Most of Louie's men passed out. Some went off with a wife or available girl. A few sober men stood guard, far away, as the bonfire burnt down to embers. Louie lay on a bed of furs strewn over the ground near the dying fire. Indisa lay with him. Skeggs stretched out opposite them in the dirt.

"I want to tell you a story," Skeggs said, catching Louie's attention.

"You mean a lie?"

Skeggs shook his head.

Louie propped himself up a bit higher. "Will I like this story?"

Skeggs looked at Indisa and back to Louie.

"Go on," Louie encouraged. "She no longer has a tongue."

Skeggs paused a minute before continuing. "You used to trade with a man who had four fingers?"

"Old Cinquo, but you already know that. In fact, Cinquo once said it was you who had some part to play in the loss of it," Louie said, wriggling his fingers. "Anyway, Cinquo is dead. Why?"

Skeggs told Louie the promised story of lovers, of the attack, of Vittorie being a French woman—a fact to win her favor in this king's court—and of her uncommon qualities.

Louie stopped him. "She's a woman." He belched. "What's so uncommon?"

"I'm sorry you can't meet her."

Too many years a thief, vaguery displeased Louie. He searched for explanation. "She is beautiful?"

"Yes."

"Hair?"

"Chestnut curls. Teeth, matched and clean, plus eyes a man isn't likely to forget." Skeggs enjoyed painting a picture for the withering man. "But there is more to her," he tapped his chest, "inside."

"A woman who thinks she can think is never good for a man," Louie sniffed.

"She has courage."

"What has she done that she's so brave?"

Skeggs laid his trap. "She never asked for the life of another in payment for the murder of her husband."

"Perhaps he was weak and not worth avenging. Or she isn't beautiful, as you say, and couldn't find anyone to avenge him with payment of a woman's kind." He looked at Indisa. "Or she is weak?" He spit each possibility at Skeggs, daring him to confirm the truth. Skeggs's silence unnerved him the most. "So, what does she want instead?"

"Nothing."

"What!" Louie's temper flared. Indisa flinched. "Why are you here, then?"

"You owe me your life, Louie. A life! Something Cinquo took from her that no one can restore except you, if you can and if you will."

"What do you mean?"

"Do you ever think about your own death, Louie? Who awaits you?"

Louie grimaced in pain. His lips smacked. "Every night. What of it?"

"Do you remember when Cinquo died?"

"Who can remember everyone who dies?"

Skeggs pulled his knife from its sheath.

Louie remembered. "Yes, yes!" He waved the knife away. "I learned of it not long after. His men sold me two horses and goods."

"Anything else?" Skeggs asked, gripping the handle.

"I sent the horses down river right away, naturally. Hid the rest till months later." Honesty hurt. "Their raid was quite valuable."

"Anything of value in particular?"

"Gold. Silver. Bullets. Silk dress. Sold that to a Nickajack chief for his white bride, which I also sold him." The lace cuff whirled. "I sold it all." He whispered to Indisa, who wrapped herself in a fur and walked to the back of the storehouse. Louie watched her go. Alone, Louie whispered, "I did save one thing. On account of the spirits."

103

Louie used women and men as a blacksmith might work his tools. If one rubbed him the wrong way, he plunged them into a fire until they could be molded for his further use. Whoever wouldn't conform was cut off. Indisa's loss of speech indicated her clipping.

The quiet woman appeared. She helped Louie rise from his cushions, and Skeggs followed. She walked with Louie to the store and into a dark corner of one of the very back rooms filled with trunks of all sizes and colors, mostly crafted of leather and wood. There she gave Skeggs one silver candlestick and lit another, which she set on a shelf. Louie crowded over her, whispering, "Around 1790! Hurry!" His hands circled each other. His mouth twitched.

"1788." Skeggs took the liberty to correct him in the important detail.

Louie didn't like it. "1788!" he said, bending over the quiet woman. "I know I kept it." His fear grew. "And it best be here!"

The quiet woman rummaged through the room. She toppled one trunk off another and turned them one side to the next looking for markings which corresponded with the year Louie demanded. She returned with a medium-sized trunk, set it between the two men, and beat on the lock with the hilt of a dagger. Her blade flashed through the air, and both men jumped back.

Louie stopped her with another wave of his hand. He pulled a chain from around his neck with several keys on it. Inserting an unusual skeleton key into the lock, the latch turned. He raised the lid with tenderness and lifted out several wrapped packages. These he set to the side. "Fetch it out," he said, motioning for the woman to do it.

Reaching all the way to the bottom, she pulled out a small scrap of burlap and unfolded it. In her palm lay an ancient gold cross. She held it out for Louie but he shuddered, moving away from it.

"I don't want to touch it," he said, waving it over to Skeggs.

Observing the fear it held for the man, Skeggs held out his hand, and she placed the piece in his open palm.

An artisan's skill was evident from every angle, even in the dim light. Etched in its corners, decorated with the smoothing of its own metal in several curves, long lines flowered into vines. It had a clasp on its back for use as a pin, and a loop in its top, allowing it to be hung from a chain as a necklace. Five unique, precious stones gleamed around its axis.

Securing it safely beneath the folds that had hidden it so long, Skeggs refolded the burlap over the treasure and tucked it deep into the satchel at his hip.

"You said that she is French?" Louie asked. Skeggs nodded. The woman held something else out. "A friend of my friend?"

"A good French friend."

"A life for a life, a friend of my friend. It must go back. Then the spirits will be at peace." He handed Skeggs some papers. "And these." He shrugged. "Paper is easiest tracked."

Skeggs examined the papers. "This is a good thing, Louie."

"This redeems me?"

A smile hinted across the trapper's lips at the black-hearted acquaintance of his asking such a question. "I'll see what might be done."

104

Frazier Farm. Davidson County, Tennessee

Vittorie's cross lay in her lap, the burlap flapped open across her knees. She clutched it to her heart and stood up.

When Skeggs finished reading aloud, he held the documents out for her to take.

The intensity of everything hit her. She slumped down in a heap on the top porch step, wrapped both hands around the papers, and put them close to her lips. She sat with her eyes closed to the setting sun, but fire-red reflected in the tear coursing over her cheek.

"Thank you," she said. "Thank you, Henry Skeggs." She leaned against the post and wilted lower. "And what about him? The wretched soul. Does this redeem him?'" Tears wet the cross in her hand. "Can it redeem someone who stole so much to return so little so long after?" She wiped her cheek and opened her eyes. "Henry." She knelt before him and took his hands in hers. "Whatever made you do this? I'm no one to you. And I'm not brave like you told him."

The longhunter pulled her to her feet in his quiet way. Other than that, he didn't respond.

She returned to the table. Her fingers trembled, so she passed the treasured pages with the black markings over to her husband. "Again, please," she asked.

Frazier handed one to Skeggs. "This one is in French."

Skeggs didn't need to look. "It's the marriage certificate. Soldier in the King's forces named Gilbert LeClerc to Vittorie Monet. Signed in the town of Nantes, France."

Vittorie pressed her fingers against her lips for a second. "Village, Mr. Skeggs. *Une ville en France.* 'Town' is English."

Frazier read the papers in his hands. "This is a land title for…" He held the paper closer and squinted. "…200 acres Northwest of Green River by Big Buffalo Crossing." He flipped the corner over to read the ones behind it in the stack. "And these are bonds for the same. This one," he said, shuffling papers, "this one is land for a William Sm…Smuthers. And this," he said, handling another, "is his honorable discharge from the Maryland Line."

Overwhelmed, Vittorie took Skeggs hands and kissed them. "*Merci beaucoup, Monsieur Henri.*" She disappeared into the house, but returned after just a moment. "Does the land have any value?"

"I crossed Green River this summer, and last, on my way to see you," Skeggs said, "right at the Big Buffalo Crossing." He moved a chair closer to the table and sat with them. "Timber is plentiful. Oaks, maple, nut trees, cedar. River runs strong. I've fished it. And there are a few settlers with cabins I saw."

"What if I wanted to claim the land?" Vittorie asked.

Frazier interjected. "Sorry, Vi, but the first problem is women can't hold property rights under current American law."

Skeggs rubbed the stubble of his chin. "But she's French."

Vittorie's interest piqued. "*Oui?*"

"According to the legal rights of foreign citizens after the Revolution," Skeggs said, "signed in the Treaty of Versailles…."

"Oh! Versailles! Do you know my father told me about meeting Monsieur Franklin and Presidents Adams and Jefferson when they worked on those documents with our King. Of course, they weren't Presidents yet when they met my father."

Skeggs continued. "Under the Treaty, Vi, you maintain French citizenship here in America, including all rights afforded French citizens. And a French woman can own property herself." Skeggs tapped the paperwork.

"So, if I wanted to claim the land I could, even now?"

"Against any other purchaser." Skeggs looked at Vittorie. "Someone was looking out for you."

"*Mon père....*"

"*C'est vrais.*"

Frazier sighed. "English, please."

"Her father." Skeggs interpreted. "But you'd have to pay the notes with interest, since the dates due, and all permanent improvement value. Which, unfortunately, is more than the land is currently worth."

The papers had value as signed documents verifying key moments of her existence. That ended it.

"Though they're of high value just as they are in this home. Thank you, Henry," said Frazier. "As for anyone else, save Smuthers' relations, which I've no idea how to begin to locate, there seems little value in them now."

Vittorie's fingers returned to the cross in her hand, a balm of health to her heart. "Our home is here. God has restored a piece of my heritage that has great meaning to me. I'm grateful to Him, and you, *Henri*. Let the Green River flow as it may. I'm not connected there anymore."

Frazier kissed the top of her head and Skeggs nodded in acknowledgement. That chapter was closed.

105

1815 - Big Buffalo Crossing area of Green River in Kentucky

Three hundred and sixty miles of water zigzagged westward through a definite gorge, central in the state of Kentucky. The Green River and its healthy tributaries flowed thirteen years more, hydrating the lush landscape. Amos' flatbottom ferries brought lumber and supplies to settlers along its banks. Buffalo decreased. A development began in their place.

Richard J. Munford slouched in his favorite chair, his countenance darkened. He watched the logs spark in the fireplace.

Above the angry wind and September rain, the distinct sound of a knock came at the Munford's front door.

"I've sworn off knocks and visitors! Since the sentiment in town has turned ugly. Demand I repay them *their* money! As if they don't harvest and farm it and eat its produce."

Mrs. Elizabeth Munford stuck the lit end of her tinder stick against the candlewick. Seeing it light, she replaced the glass. "Now, dear, I thought you said Robert was working on that with you and you'd had…."

The knock sounded louder this time.

"Don't answer it!" Munford said. "Calling me 'cheat' and 'crook'…to my face!"

Seeing he didn't intend to move, Mrs. Munford went to the door herself. From his seat by the fire, Munford cringed, awaiting the harsh tones he feared. None came. He couldn't make out what was said, only that it was a low voice, a man's voice, and then his wife's, which sounded cheery enough still. The door closed. A draft blew around him and he pulled his blanket tighter. Hearing two sets of footsteps, he twisted to see who had passed the guard at the gate and was being ushered in to see him.

"Come in, Mr. Meredith," Mrs. Munford began. "Richard has been healing and will appreciate a friend about now." She hooked Mr. Meredith's soaked coat on the rack. "Caught cold returning from representing the Commonwealth last week." Turning to her husband she added, "Mr. Meredith's been caught in this weather for two days, can you imagine? Thomas sent him up as the Inn's full. I told him he could spend the night in the spare room." Having stated things directly, she resumed a humble posture. "More tea, dear?"

"Meredith! Ho, man! Come in. Tea, what?" With a new war with Britain begun and problems with settlers burdening him, having to concentrate on tea confused him.

Mrs. Munford had already removed his empty cup to refill it. "Tea, Mr. Meredith?"

"Anything stronger?"

"Coffee?"

Not what Meredith had in mind, but the presence of a lady such as Mrs. Munford—who was currently even more entitled to her present authority with Munford ailing—caused his request to go no further. "Thank you."

She left for the kitchen. The two men were alone.

"Hullo, Meredith. Been a while," was all Munford could muster.

Meredith could see the state of his friend and, being no stranger to monologue, began a conversation he intended to keep up, one-sided or not. He scooted his chair right up next to the fire, knees to the heat. "Haven't seen you, what, since the year the spring winds blew down Dutton's Feed Store." An average man with long fingers and narrowish eyes, he had a pleasant enough disposition.

"How's Dismal Creek treating you?" Munford asked. "Why anyone would name a place that I'll not know. I'm dismal enough without living in a place actually called Dismal."

"Runnin' high right about now," Meredith replied, concentrating more on the fire than his friend. "'Preciate the hospitality, Richard. A man could swim standing up out there and I've two days 'fore home."

Munford nodded. "Stable Old Toby already?"

"Lost Toby last year." Meredith shook his head. "Colic. Got a five-year old quarter named King. 15 hands. Good for wading creeks," Meredith said, chuckling at his own joke.

"Would you like some...no, she's gone to get it. Oh, you don't know the trouble I have, Meredith. I wouldn't wish it on ye for a king's ransom." Munford rubbed his forehead and down his face. "Fort McHenry withstood a 25-hour day of British Naval bombardment in Maryland little over a year ago, but in the morning the flag still flew!" He grunted. "I feel as besieged here on my own land!"

Mrs. Munford returned and set a mug in front of each man. She also set down plates for each with sliced meat, warm bread, pats of pressed butter, and cups of steamy soup.

"Thank you, truly." Meredith bowed his head.

"Thank you, dear. Meredith, did you stable your horse?" Munford said, forgetting he had already asked. Realizing his friend was praying, he bowed his head and waited until Meredith raised his again. "What did you say its name was?"

Meredith slurped his soup from the cup. He swallowed fast. "King. Yes. I took the liberty what with the weather and all."

"I told him that was fine, dear," said Mrs. Munford. "What color is your new horse?"

Caught with food in his mouth a second time, Meredith swallowed and put the cup down in his lap. "Dun."

"Oh, fine. If you two need anything I'll not be far. I've some work to do in the parlor." She patted Mr. Munford's arm and left them alone.

"I'm sorry to hear things aren't going well for you." Meredith selected a thick piece of mutton.

Munford perused the options. "Just all this paperwork and legal matters, they're like to be the death of me." He picked out some mutton and bread.

"What? With the town?" He folded the mutton into his mouth and chewed. "I thought you were selling things off fine, growing like a poke stalk."

"Selling, yes." Munford scooped a bit of soup into his spoon and blew it cooler. "Collecting, no. Too many rumors about murders and French women. No paperwork to prove it!"

Meredith choked. He wiped his mouth on the back of his hand, then noticed the napkin beside his plate and used that, too. "Did you say 'French women'?" There ought to be something interesting in a conversation started like that.

"Yes. French women. Or woman. One woman. You see, I've gotten mixed up in a title search for my own lands." He leaned closer to Meredith. "I bought my lands outright from a Robert Vaughn, who'd had a survey made of the 2500 acres right where we sit. Paid coin, no notes. Done."

"When was this?" Meredith asked, buttering bread.

"'03. No, '02. Also the year I tried my hand at asparagus plants." He shook his head. "Lost the whole crop of them."

"Frost?"

"Rabbits," Munford said, chewing a bite of his sandwich. "Anyway, Vaughn's a decent fellow. All's on the up-and-up so far as I know, and what do you think? Vaughn's dead. Estate insolvent." He threw up his hands and fell back against the chair. Soup splashed on the floorboards. "Insolvent!"

"I'm sorry to hear that, but how are you affected?"

"Rumors! Lies! Half-truths? Full truths? I don't know, but every hill in these hollows hides a different story of a Frenchman, an Englishman, and the Frenchman's wife who bought this land years ago from Vaughn." Glancing in the direction of the kitchen, he wiped the floor with his napkin. "Both men were murdered as they come over the hill called Frenchman's Knob." He motioned with his thumb over his shoulder as if the place loomed just outside his window.

Meredith stood up with his plate. "Curious that the Frenchman should be murdered in Kentucky on a hill named Frenchman's Knob." He moved about the room as if gathering clues.

"No, his murder was the reason for the naming of the hill," Munford said, clarifying the error of his friend. "He's why it's called 'Frenchman's Knob'."

"Oh," said Meredith. He continued about the room and spying his coffee, seated himself in his chair for a hot drink. "I know the story exactly. Met the woman myself once in the Nolin Settlements but that was, oh, twenty-five years ago."

"Really?" Munford's reaction dribbled soup into his lap. "Go on!"

Meredith swallowed a large gulp of coffee. "Last I heard she remarried a soldier who fought at King's Mountain. They moved south, I think. West? More'n that I don't know."

"You see, that's as far as I can ever get!" Munford chose another slice of mutton. "Someone's heard something, known someone, but not for years, or they aren't exactly sure of what they were sure of to begin with…." He slumped, exasperated. "How am I supposed to find one Frenchwoman in the whole of America?" The meat flopped around as his hand flailed in a circle. "A woman!" He stuffed the piece in his mouth, and as he swallowed, his depression returned. "There's no way to track her! She can't own land, buy, trade, or sell. If it were a man, I could follow him legally. How do they expect me to produce one woman? But I definitely need to take care of collecting on all this land. I've lent out notes, in good faith, to good pioneers, that is my trouble."

"Well, I know one thing," Meredith said.

Munford's attention had gone back to his fire. "Hmmm?"

"I just heard a strange story about your French woman not a fortnight ago from a man recently seen her."

Munford dropped his teacup outright. "What! How?"

"Man named Henry Skeggs."

"How can I meet him?"

"He's a Kentucky man. Explorer, hunter, guide. Land locator. This country wouldn't *be* without him, or men like him. Ever heard of Daniel Boone? Kenton? Logan? The McAfees?"

"Who hasn't," Munford said, retrieving his cup.

"All part of a group known as The Longhunters. Could track a man or beast for days by runnin' 'em down on foot. No bullets. Just strength for strength outdistance 'em." Meredith enjoyed the added mystery.

"Run 'em down? What? Are you getting to the bit about the French woman?"

Meredith leaped forward and acted out his speech, ignoring his host's question. "They'd head off into the wilderness by themselves when there was naught here but the natives and God Himself." Adding emphasis to the next point, he crouched low, back hunched over, shoulders scrunched up around his ears. He stretched out his fingers like rounded, bared teeth. "No one would see 'em for months when they'd go on these...hunts. They'd take a gun, sure, but they'd just outrun a deer till it fell down dead. Natives taught 'em how. Battle between man and beast."

The fire cast a shadow on the wall behind Meredith. Munford squinted as he listened, entranced by the story and the oddness of the teller.

"They'd explore and come back with tales of adventures that kept civilized men awake and cowering in their beds at night." Ending with a fierce stance over Munford's chair, he sat back down and resumed interest in his coffee. "So, when civilized men wanted to know what was west of the sea, men like Skeggs became their guides."

Munford's fingertips released the edge of his armrest. He relaxed back into his chair as Meredith drained his cup. "Were you ever an actor?" he asked.

Meredith recoiled.

"You never know what people were before they came to Kentucky," Munford said, flipping his toes under a blanket. "A peasant may have been a king. A poor man may work here and end a king. Anything is possible. Everyone can be reborn here."

"What?" Meredith looked confused.

"I'm sorry. Go on."

Instead, Meredith yawned a ferocious yawn and rose to go upstairs. "Yes, Skeggs told me a curious story about your Frenchwoman not a fortnight ago."

"You've said that, Meredith. Go forward."

Meredith put a foot on the bottom stair. "Anyway," he said, yawning, "Skeggs is your man. Sure 'nough. No need to thank me. No trouble at all." He'd reached the top step.

"But Mr. Meredith!" Munford shouted.

"Hmm?"

"How do I find him?"

"I don't know. I found him at Cader Edwards' place, over by Blue Springs, a fortnight ago. G'nite, Richard. Thanks for the bed."

106

"It's no less than a miracle how you've recovered from all that was ailing you, dear," Mrs. Munford said, sweeping the front stoop. "Meredith's visit did you good."

Puddles shrank to manageable size and the sun shone. Munford walked his horse out from the stable.

"I barely slept the night Meredith stayed." Munford mounted his horse on his second attempt. "Jesse knows to keep working the south pasture," he said, reminding her of the order of things while he would be away. "And when they break that colt, make sure they only do it in the early morning or late afternoon so he doesn't overheat. You'll have to oversee the harvesting plus your normal inside work with Susannah. Just give the extra squash away. It's a sin to let it spoil. I'll be back as soon as I, whoa!" His horse wouldn't cooperate until he took charge.

"I know, Richard. I've told you I mean to put up enough squash and bring the rest to Mrs. Bolton."

"Don't bother hosting any neighbors," Munford continued, not paying her attention. "And don't go visiting any of the farmers. And don't go into town!" He scanned up and down the lane before he walked the horse out. "Best just to stay home. Why don't you just put that squash up? We'll eat it over winter."

Mrs. Munford handed him his hat. "Good-bye, dear." She turned and walked toward the house.

"Don't worry about me. Everything's in order. I'll return as soon as I can. Elizabeth!" he shouted.

"Yes, dear," she said, returning from the inside of their garden gate.

"You look lovely in that shawl."

She blushed. "Hello to Mr. Skeggs for me, dear."

"Will do. Right, then. Off to see the legend. Gee'ap!" With a kick of his heels, he and his horse were off in the direction of Blue Springs.

107

Cader Edwards' Farm. Goosehorn, Kentucky

In the secluded clearing above Cader Edwards' actual homestead, Skeggs worked some squirrel over a fire in front of his small cabin. The spot had a view, good kindling, and protection from the western wind. It was as good a place as any for an old man on his own.

The wind gusted an unexpected noise. Skeggs heard the single horse and rider before he saw them. A man in a fancy coat rode up to Cader's door, tethered his horse, and was invited inside. Possibilities being endless and visitors being few, Skeggs finished his supper, kicked dirt on the flames, and after a time, made his way down the hillside.

Cader's home sweltered with the fire burning in the hearth. His eyes twinkled, though the areas around them had gathered a few more storylines. He puffed on his pipe while Mrs. Edwards instructed their daughter in her knitting. Their boy carved an owl out of cedar while three younger children played.

Skeggs carried in a fresh stack of wood and shut the door behind him.

"Here's the man you want," Cader said.

Munford jumped up like a schoolboy, unable to contain himself.

Enjoying the position he found himself in, Cader said, "Henry, this is Richard Jones Munford. Trying to organize a town at Big Buffalo Crossing and having some trouble. Hopes you might know what's to be done."

Skeggs put the wood down and reloaded the fire.

"How do you do, Mr. Skeggs." Munford didn't figure the answer to his quest would be as backwoods as the man before him. "I've been trying for months to discover the missing link in this endless legal mess. I bought land on Green River, organized it into plots. I leased my land to good folk to till and keep as they will. But, the story of the Frenchman and a murder circles round and chokes my livelihood. No tenant will pay me anymore since I can't prove I'm the rightful owner. How should I have known the land was sold once before I bought it to become a town? I tried to find Vaughn. I've done my due diligence. How am I to find one lonely woman, the Frenchman's widow, who's mixed up in the middle of all of this? I can't. Which brings me to you!" He snorted and sobered himself with a false cough. "So, the mysterious French widow. My friend, Mr. Meredith, said you knew her?"

"You haven't heard the whole of it, Munford!" Cader interjected, turning to his disheveled old friend. "Tell him about the summer after you met with Mrs. Frazier the first time, and Perry told the story the second time."

The boy spoke up. "Tell about when you ran to see Old Louie!" He spun around with excitement. "I love that part."

"Ran to Old Louie?" Munford asked. "Where's that?"

"It's not a where it's a who," the boy said.

"Whom, Bobby." Mrs. Edwards corrected her son. "Mind your manners."

Skeggs took his familiar place on the wooden stool and picked up where he left off working a hide. "Why a town?" Skeggs asked, looking the newcomer over.

"Men want the freedom to govern themselves, but we all have this dang internal need for each other, you see, which makes Munfordstown the perfect place."

"Munfordstown?"

Munford laughed. "My botany skills being what they are, I had no hope of naming anything else in this beautiful countryside after me. Eh, do you know what that is, botany?"

Cader smiled at the comment. "Do you know what botany is, Skeggs?"

"*Je peut parler avec la femme Française, si vous voulez,*" came Skeggs' unoffended reply. "Would you like to converse in French? *Et, oui. Je connais la botanique.* I know a little about botany."

Munford's jaw dropped. "He speaks French?" It made waves in his double chin. "I just didn't think…."

Cader poked him with the butt of his pipe. "You can learn a lot in these woods," he said.

Overcome, Munford knelt before Skeggs to deliver his plea, formed over many months, to this haggard old man. "I need you to speak for me," Munford begged. "You are the only one who can do it. You know the trails. You speak French!" His eyes widened, astounded.

Embarrassed, Skeggs backed away.

Mrs. Edwards shot a queer look to her husband, but Cader waved her off so as not to interrupt the show.

Munford continued. "Will you go and see if the Frenchwoman will give me a quitclaim deed for the lands? I bought them in good faith from the proprietor, Mr. Vaughn. He's now deceased, his estate insolvent." Munford clutched his palms together. "And could you return with documentation which proves I have the right to continue with my town, and appease my conscience and my tenants and erase the rumors blackening my good name?"

"How do you mean to negotiate?" Skeggs asked.

Used to such questions, Munford said, "Spanish milled coins are most reliable for weight. I can send you payment in that form. Or gold, if she prefers."

"Wouldn't you want to go yourself?"

Munford stood up slowly, sat back in his chair and rubbed his knees. "I don't see how I could be useful in any way that you yourself wouldn't be more so."

"You could meet Mrs. Frazier."

Munford shook his head. "You already have an open line of communication, as I understand it, which I would only hinder. I wouldn't mind going at all if you thought I really could be of some usefulness." He ended with a fit of coughing.

Cader removed the pipe from his bottom lip. "How do you mean to go, Henry? It's over 100 miles, and even if you could, you shouldn't be running around the countryside by yourself anymore. Mrs. Edwards would be up every night worrying about you." He came to his real point at last. "At least let me go with you."

"Should either of you be running around in the woods at your ages?" Her husband's use of reasoning to invite himself along on the escapade was not lost on her.

Cader offered an immediate consolation. "Would you consider going on horseback, Henry?"

Skeggs looked past the hide in his hands to the moccasined boots wrapping his feet. "I'll see what might be done."

"Excellent!" gasped Munford. He wiped sweat off his forehead and stuck an old hanky back in his pocket. "Lots of paperwork ahead of me. Wish I could be joining you in the country." With a sturdy handshake for Skeggs, he added, "You've saved me."

108

Frazier Farm. Davidson County, Tennessee

Two ladders leaned against mature apple trees. Vittorie's grown children picked plump red fruit and passed it down to younger siblings, who collected it in several baskets. The late afternoon sun beamed sideways, illuminating the scene.

Vittorie pushed leaves off the path up to the front of her house with a long-handled broom. Her back muscles ached when she twisted. She had stopped to brush gray curls out of her eyes when two unfamiliar figures on horseback rode up the lane.

It took a minute for Vittorie to recognize the riders, but this time she did before the children. "Why, it's *Henri*! On horseback! Clara, get your father from the shop and tell him Henry's come."

With the horses watered and grazing, the men found a warm welcome inside the Frazier house. Twenty years of Vittorie's French decorating filled the American log home. Dried lavender lay on window sills. Embroidered fabrics appointed handcrafted wood furniture. Evidence of a homespun life surrounded them. She set a fresh baguette, blackberries, and square cheese before them on the table, then peeked under the lid of the cooking pot and removed supper from the heat. Autumnal scents from the simmering chicken and apples in cream of the *poulet au cidre* circled the room.

The purpose of their visit leaked out before Frazier had time to return from town. When he did arrive, Vittorie filled him in, starting with the least important news first. "Sweetheart, they want to organize a town."

"Who does?" He looked from one man to the other. "Henry! Welcome! And welcome, friend." He shook Cader's hand. "John Frazier."

"Cader Edwards. You've a fine home, here, Mr. Frazier, and lovely family."

"A Mr. Richard Jones Munford," Vittorie answered, as the men greeted one another.

"Hello, Frazier," said Skeggs, clasping forearms in their familiar way. Nodding to Cader, he added, "He looks after me a bit, so when he asked if he could join the trip, I accepted."

"On condition that we ride some of the way." Cader laughed.

"I noticed!" said Frazier.

Vittorie put her hand in her husband's. "They want to pay us for the Green River land and to start Munfordstown."

"Pardon me?" Frazier looked shocked. "To pay...us?"

Skeggs answered in his calm way. "One hundred and fifty dollars. Plus, interest from the time of the original down payment."

Vittorie could hardly say the words. "One hundred fifty dollars!"

"Plus interest," Cader added.

Frazier laughed out loud. "Skeggs, you are the most...wild man I've ever known!" He smacked the table. "But I won't do it. I won't take the money."

"Why?" Vittorie asked, surprised at his abrupt close of the opportunity.

"I've nothing to do with that land, Vi. I never have," He took her chin in his hand. "It's yours. They may pay *you*, if you like. It'll be whatever *you* decide."

Vittorie bit her bottom lip, beaming. Getting up as quickly as she could, she retrieved the land titles from a small box in her cupboard. "Gentlemen, you'll witness me sell my land today! Clara, go fetch your brothers and sisters in to see!"

A girl of thirteen rose from her needlework at the table and ran out the door. As Vittorie watched her go, she was reminded of another young woman, in another place and another time, who loved to feel the wind in her hair and the ground under her feet. Within moments, the children bumped through the door.

"Come in and be quiet," Frazier told his children. He brought the inkwell, blotter, and quill pen from his desk. "Your mother, a citizen of France and an American, is giving permission to these men to found a town because she owns the land. Herself."

Skeggs took a paper from the satchel on his hip. The straps and sack were new, though the stitching echoed his old one. "Cader will witness Mrs. Frazier—Mrs. LeClerc—signing her name…here." He indicated a place at the bottom of the page.

Vittorie signed in the presence of all the witnesses in swirling indigo ink. The wetness of it gleamed, iridescent in the lamplight.

"Oh, Mama, look!" Clara sighed. "Your letters look beautiful." She squeezed Vittorie's shoulders.

Skeggs hefted two burlap bags from his satchel. Munford's Spanish milled dollars and gold clinked as he passed them over to Vittorie.

She looked around the room at her children and squeezed Frazier's hand. "I do have one request of *Monsieur* Munford, *Henri*." Her green eyes glistened. "Please ask if he might consider changing the name to 'Munford-ville'." She straightened the crocheted table runner under the bowl of acorns. "'Town' is so… English."

A certain smile worked its way around the corners of his lips. "I'll see what might be done."

EPILOGUE

1842 - Frazier Farm

Vittorie kissed her fingertips and touched them to a new marker set just outside the apple orchard. "*Merci, mon amour,*" she whispered. The stone bore the name of the last man she loved, John Frazier. Savoring the early morning moments in her orchard, she took her son-in-law's outstretched arm. "Thank you, Everett."

Two saddled horses grazed beside him. Everett laced the fingers of his hands together for Vittorie to step into. She bent her knee and he helped her up onto a demure dappled gray horse.

"Are you settled alright?" he asked.

She nodded. "I'm good, dear."

The windows on the log house were closed up. No light flickered inside.

Everett mounted the bay horse and signaled the driver of the wagon ahead. Two large Belgians pulled and the loaded wagon lurched forward. Strapped under tarps lay everything—outside of her family—Vittorie held precious in the world.

"He'll take the main route and meet us in Monroe. Are you ready, Mum?" Everett asked. His forehead had broadened from where a hairline used to be. Still, the white in his full mustache and beard distinguished him as a middle-aged man.

"I've been ready. Waitin' on ye'," she said.

He smirked at her confidence. "I wish you would ride the carriage, Mum. The way north to Kentucky's long, especially not on the new roads."

"I'll arrive in my own way, if you please." A rifle lashed alongside her leg, she nudged the horse forward. "I thought about writing President Tyler to let him know my cabin was available if he needed it."

"Did you?" Everett laughed at her joke. "Well, Clara and James'll be here by next month and have the house full of life again, don't you worry. You're going to like Monroe County, Mum. It has hills and hollers the way you like. Anna's been so beside herself with excitement over you comin' to live with us I don't think she's slept in months. The girls neither."

The path from the house blossomed with redbuds. Leafy green shoots emerged inside last year's black raspberry bushes signalling another summer of fruit. They rode single file through the once-wild woods in peace. Past the last fence, the path became a lane, which by full light widened to a road. They followed it eastward through the afternoon along the Cumberland River. Pausing to rest during the hottest part of the day, they continued forward long after the lightning bugs flashed in the night.

In a particular place near the bottom of a bellowing waterfall, she halted in the moonlight. "Stop, Everett."

"You alright, Mum?" He dismounted in a rush. "I should never have agreed to riding into the night."

"I insisted. Help me down?" He did and she threw her coat over his outstretched arm. "You might want to turn around."

"What are you doing?"

"Undressing. Turn 'round, please." Her dress and next her petticoat pooled on the ground around her ankles.

He heard ripples and a quick glance confirmed his fears. She moved in slow strokes through the water. "Do you think that's wise, Mum?" His tone suggested otherwise.

"Shhh, boy. We're in Kentucky now. Stop worryin' and live." She swam, slow and lazy, in the broad pool. Above the mist of the cascading falls, a rainbow crystallized in full spectrum. "Look!" she gasped. "It's true. John told me about the moonbow, though I scarcely believed him." Stretching her arm forward, she came back to shore, humming a tune from long ago.

After she dressed, they found a shallow spot and crossed to the other shore and slept. The rest of the trip continued fully clothed until they arrived at Anna and Everett's house in Monroe County a day later.

Teenage granddaughters greeted her at the gate. "Grand-mère! Grand-mère!"

"Oh, Sage! Christina! How tall you've both grown! And Christina, look at your apron!" She took Everett's arm to dismount and the girls squeezed her tight. "Oh! What good hugs. Your mother told me you kept practicing. You've gotten very good with your needles!"

Inside, Vittorie removed her gloves and set them on a low table in the front hall. She checked her face in the small mirror above it, once for dirt and once for memory. She smiled, despite the pain in her abdomen, and wiped sweat off her forehead.

Anna set the rifle against the doorframe. "The girls are unloading your things, Mum. You're going to love Kentucky here with us."

But Everett caught Vittorie just as she crumpled to the floor.

"Momma!" Anna screamed.

Vittorie looked at Everett. Her lips had no color. "A priest, please," she whispered.

✳ ✳ ✳

When Father DeLuynes arrived from Bardstown, Vittorie was in the backyard on a bed of pillows. Resting under a Catawba tree high on a hill, she kept her eyes closed with a pained look. Sage read to her. Christina stroked her hand.

Gathering his robe, Father DeLuynes ran up the hillside. Sage put down the book as he laid his hands on the old woman's head and whispered a prayer.

The girls left their grandmother with him.

"*Victoire*, hear me you can?" he asked. His 'r's softened in his throat like the non-native English speaker he was.

Vittorie shaded her eyes with her hand. "From where do you come?"

"The Trappists, near Bardstown."

"No, before then. Before America."

"The Brittany region of France," he replied taking her hand.

Color returned to her cheeks. "Do you know the family of Monet?"

"My father was friends with a Luc Monet who lived in the village south of me."

"Luc…Was his grandfather of the same name?"

"*Oui*, I think. Yes."

Vittorie smiled. "That is my nephew!" Her eyes, grayed green, sparkled inside sparse gray lashes. "Can you believe it? Oh, will you tell me of my family! What can you say of the house of Monet there, and of France?"

The shadows lengthened and fell over her as if she'd closed her eyes in one tiny blink and forgotten to reopen them. The wind blew across her cheek. Vittorie died that afternoon as the priest spoke his benediction, the time of day when the sunlight streams in from the side of the world and colors ignite in one last brilliance. Her spirit caught away, there would be no more gathering it back.

NOTES AND
ACKNOWLEDGEMENTS

I began researching the story of Frenchman's Knob shortly after my own move to Hart County, Kentucky in December 2007. Having studied French since third grade and lived in Paris for several months during college, finding the highest peak in my new locale named "Frenchman's Knob" captured my attention. Fresh off the road from touring with my sisters in our band and finding for the first time in my life that I was terrible at everything I tried to do (putting up goat fencing in January, I'm thinking of you), I felt lost, ill-equipped, and alone.

Writing about people and their stories made sense to me. I had been writing three-and-a-half-minute musical stories for Nashville or New York to broadcast for the last ten years. But now the band had broken up, my dyed-red hair seemed misplaced among my sweet Amish neighbors, and I was practically the only woman within a 50-mile radius who wasn't already married with children nor a fabulous cook.

So, when Nadine Hawkins delivered Florence Edwards Gardiner's little green book of her father's (Cyrus Edwards) stories about the landscape and its people and casually said, "I've always thought someone should write a movie about the second story, the one about Frenchman's Knob…" I was hooked. I knew storytelling. I could research. And I did.

✻ ✻ ✻

Not surprisingly, people—both past and present—have been my greatest resources. Some references on this list are personal interviews, others are trips my family or I took to the actual, historic sites. My favorite interview memory begins along a walkway of rose bushes that led to a comfortable home, fascinating conversation over homemade chicken salad and pie, and a personal driving tour past an old barn still sporting a certain yellow necktie. Thank you, All, again.

It may seem odd to acknowledge the land itself, but remember: roads and borders are relatively new, man-made concepts. In researching American Wild, set centuries earlier than this author's birth, I spent much effort and time locating the regions, areas, forests, rivers, springs, and trees (yes, even trees) named in documents as markers and pathways for natives, longhunters, explorers, and settlers. This work led me to a humbled empathy for the lives of these ancestors. It brought their everyday adventures into calloused and living color for me, and caused deeper understanding of their struggle, reasoning, tragedies, and victories.

First, let me apologize to anyone or any place I've left out of this short list to follow. God knows. Now, let me start by thanking the country that enamored me from the beginning.

<u>FRANCE</u>

My first step onto the tarmac at Charles de Gaulle airport was unlike any other footfall of mine before or since. Your language, history, architecture, art, and people beckoned me early in life, and still does today.

The University of Paris: my professors, friends, and those I met along the way.

Paris, France, its living and historical treasures and surrounding countrysides, including The Palace of Versailles, The Louvre, and Monet's House & Gardens in Giverny.

Chez de la Motte Rouge: To the fine family who housed me during my three-month tenure. You treated me like your own and watched over me. You are kind, generous, and good. Thank you.

Aaron Chabot, who hosted Thanksgiving dinner at his apartment on 28 Novembre 1997, and all my international friends and expats who shared a veritable feast abroad. I still have our menu and guest list. Salut!

CALIFORNIA

Barbara Nicolosi Harrington, Origin Entertainment, Founder & Chair Emeritus, Act One, Inc.: I will always remember "…the writer's ultimate gift is to sit and stare open-mouthed…" Thank you.

Candy at Alan Wertheimer's office: My notes reference you often as a help and encouragement.

CONNECTICUT

Westport and the Compo Beach cannons: You fueled my love of the Revolutionary War era.

Mystic Seaport: Thank you, Mindy and Carol, for answering my questions about ships arriving after the Revolution carrying passengers, not cargo. My visits to you are very present in mind.

Jim and Janet Bair: Two of my very favorite people ever. Thank you for your love of literature and for reading early drafts. Your honest edits were necessary yet kind. You've been my teachers and now my friends. Thank you.

GEORGIA

Cecil Murphey, New York Times bestselling author, speaker, teacher: The seeds of your mentorship took years to germinate and blossom. Thank you for your faith and patience. Robert says "hello!" Twila Belk, thank you so much.

Stan and Carol Cottrell: Your hospitality, friendship, and good taste are remembered fondly. Thank you, and thank you for introducing me to Cec.

VIRGINIA

Yorktown, Jamestown, and Williamsburg, Virginia: Your ability to transport visitors today to life centuries ago is a distinguished art. Keep preserving it.

Mobjack Bay Coffee Roasters & Petite Café, caretakers of the Cole Digges House circa 1720, Yorktown, Virginia.

JJ and Penny: You housed, fed, kayaked, and toured us through your lifelong love of Virginia. I delightfully await future fireside chats.

WASHINGTON, DC

Library of Congress: The architecture and austerity in this stately facility are inspiring. An under-marketed treasure.

SOUTH CAROLINA

Historic Willington, South Carolina, and the Willington Bookshop & History Center: Thank you for staying open when I couldn't decide how many books Robert would let me pack the car with.

South Carolina State Parks: Your living history, woods, wetlands, trails, fields, bookstores, markers, coastlines, camping, and fishing keep me happy and grounded.

Kings Mountain State Park: The battles commemorated here gave hope to farmers and settlers that they could join together and that their backwoods skills were to be prized highly. In learning why and how you were significant, I realized what kind of a character Frazier must have been, just as he became a second chance at love and hope for Vittorie.

Hickory Knob State Park.

Musgrove Mill State Park: Thank you, Dawn Weaver, Park Manager, for your love of the park and sharing the stories.

Charles Towne Landing State Park: Your walking trails, zoo with only native animals, and The Adventure ship brought things to life for me.

Ninety-Six National Historic Site.

Cowpens National Battlefield.

South Carolina State Museum: Days of education and fun.

Old Santee Canal Park: Thank you for preserving the architecture, animals and plant life of the lowcountry so simply.

Cypress Gardens: Thank you for your "Free for County Residents" days. Because of your generosity, I took my young daughter and sat among your wildlife without financial worry. We soaked in your atmosphere, boated through the swamp, and learned more details of South Carolina's plant and animal life.

Summerville, SC: For being lovers of history yet not afraid to grow. Thank you.

Main Street Reads Bookstore in historic downtown Summerville, and The Monday Night Writer's Group: Shari, Regina, Emily, Adam, Hannah, Sharon, Doug, Karen, Rebecca – and all the others who sat and mused. You were my oasis. And to Kat Varn, author of Gardenia Duty, who's author signing drew me like a moth to the flame.

Magnolia Plantation: Not only for your breathtaking wildlife and manicured grounds, but for the sign you've posted where British General Cornwallis came ashore on his march to Charleston and on to Yorktown.

The Huguenot Society of South Carolina.

The Old Exchange and Provost Dungeon: All ships and their cargo passed through this portal when entering Charleston's harbor. The US Constitution was ratified on the second floor of this building. Hannah – you were a wonderful assistance.

Kahal Kodeth Beth Elohim.

St. Michael's Church, Corner of Meeting and Broad Streets.

St. Philip's Church.

The Old Slave Mart Museum.

Mepkin Abbey: Beautiful grounds by the Cooper River are a sanctuary of peace and prayer. This abbey originated from the Louisville diocese, the Bardstown Gethsemani Abbey, where Father DeLuynes left to give Vittorie her last rites.

Fr. Joe Tedesco, at Mepkin Abbey: You gave your precious time to help research and connect the dots to Father Charles DeLuynes for me, and graciously taught me about the priesthood. I am so thankful. I appreciate your thoughts on the soul: going from entitlement to love and service to fellow man, to becoming one with God's plan for your life and partaking with Christ in service to man by obedience to God. That is an adventurous life.

Chris Weatherhead: Thank you for sitting with me while my leg healed and brainstorming rewrites and publishing options.

Clarence Felder: Your encouragement as an artist and writer is heartfelt. Thank you so much.

Rich Carnahan and everyone at Publish Pros. This book launched because of your visionary acceptance of this work, the efforts of your creative team, the editing and friendship of both you and Mary Hall (noted in the Kentucky section for her own merits) and lots of patient teamwork. Thank you so much for the laughs.

NORTH CAROLINA

Cherokee, North Carolina and The Museum of the Cherokee: Thank you for your storytelling and cultural preservation of such precious people.

TENNESSEE

Lookout Mountain, the Tennessee River, Obey's River, and Sequatchie Valley.

Goodlettsville, Tennessee.

Nashville, Tennessee.

Greg Seneff, Esq., and family: Thank you for your ability to befriend artists and help them walk straight. Thank you for mailing query letters, for being there, and for being a buffer.

KENTUCKY

The Abbey of Gethsemani, Trappist, Kentucky: This Abbey is a community of Roman Catholic monks belonging to the worldwide Order of Cistercians of Strict Observance, commonly known as Trappist. God bless you for your delicious fudge, your living testimony of service and faith, and your open doors.

Western Kentucky University: Thank you to Professor Lynwood Montel, Professor Ron DeMarse, retired Professor Cory Lash, and your friend, Bently, who read my original American Wild film script.

Louisville International Film Festival and Kentucky Center for the Arts, where I met that year's winners, Bob and Nancy Gregg: Bob, you told me American Wild was "…fascinating. Too beautifully written to be a screenplay. Make it into a novel. It is a great story, well told with superb characters." I said I'd call when I was done. I apologize, I've misplaced your number.

Kentucky Arts Council and Kentucky Living Magazine: You have inspired and educated me.

Hart County: Thank you for your green historical markers, your commitment to preserving arts and culture, and going above and beyond to make sure visitors and locals still build positive community. Thank you for embracing me. I have so many sweet memories.

Hart County Library: To Vicki Logsdon and Debi, who answered hundreds of questions, looked into copyrights, and helped me out of dead ends in research countless times. God bless you.

Heartfelt thanks to the Hart County Homemakers Association, and all my "aunties" who exercised me through my pregnancy and blessed our home with gifts and prayers, the late Patricia and Howard Margolis (your lilies photograph hangs in my kitchen), and the late Rose Bostic. (He doesn't need much watching over, but I'll keep an eye on him just the same.)

Barren County, the town of Hiseville, and the City of Glasgow, Kentucky: An historic treasure trove still rolling with gorgeous farmland.

South Central KY Cultural Center & Museum: Thank you, Mary, for researching "poles" and what it means in length these days. June Jackson, your enthusiasm spurred me onward. Thank you,

Deana Snow, (who's Duval ancestors attended St. Joseph's School in Bardstown) for sharing your birthday treats with me on May 17, 2011.

Warren County and Warren County Public Library: Thank you for the green historical marker on Highway 31 E about the Long-hunters. The first words on it are "Henry Skeggs," which showed me this story was bigger than Munfordville's Green River or Hart County alone. To SKyPac: I have officially broken my leg—though not with you—and it's not all it's cracked up to be. You, however, are still awash with stage lights in my memory. Thank you. To all my fellow stagehands who encouraged me on our loading dock breaks to drink milk while pregnant for "calcium, calcium, calcium." The baby is fine (and so are my teeth) ten years later. I will always love the theater.

Monroe County, Kentucky.

Elizabethtown, Kentucky.

Cave City, Kentucky.

Bernheim Forest.

The Kentucky State Park System, specifically the John James Audubon State Park and the Cumberland State Park and surrounding areas. It is here that I have Vittorie night-swim on her final journey back to Kentucky.

Mammoth Cave National Park. The Big Woods.

The Cities of Hodgenville and Bardstown, Kentucky: For your current charms and being where the Stations originally were.

The Cities of Lexington and Louisville, Kentucky.

Horse Cave, Kentucky.

President's Office and Campbellsville University.

St. Catherine College, Springfield, Kentucky.

Munfordville, Kentucky and the Green River Basin: Thank you for preserving your character and history, but mostly, thank you for welcoming strangers. I was one of them.

Old Mt. Olivet Church in Munfordville, Kentucky.

Everyone at the Hart County Welcome Center, and Carolyn Short at the Hart County Historical Society, and others who guided me through Roy Cann's works, Nolin and Philipp's Station, the Rolling Fork River, trees marked and referred to in histories and specifically in Cyrus Edwards' book. My hours spent there were not enough, specifically in the Skeggs/Thompson research. Carolyn, your oral histories defined how I saw things—through your eyes as a child— and helpd me envision a wider river basin at Big Buffalo Crossing than is there now. Also, Ms. June Burke, Doris Cloar, and many others, for the years you safeguarded letters, stories, artifacts, and carried all the knowledge forward. You strengthen our tomorrows by your values and efforts.

Nadine Hawkins: your gift of a little green book forever changed my life. You "ignited the pilot light" in me to dig deeper, to search out the story. Thank you for loving your land, your history, and accepting strangers as family before anyone got married. You are my example of a fine Kentucky woman.

Virginia Davis, author of "The Iris's Secret" and other wonderful

Hart County stories, and an advocate for Hart County in every good way. Judy Sizemore and Lucille Harp, thank you, dear ladies.

The Berry Center and Wendell Berry.

Michael Srygler Jr. and Rene Srygler: You've helped more than we speak of. Thank you.

Dian Knight, Kentucky Film Commission Office: A visionary.

Sheryl Bailey and family: Your recipes, hospitality, and holiday picnics by the Green River are far from forgotten. Thank you.

Don Waddell and your lovely wife: You told me stories only locals know. You sacrificed several good-weather days to drive me around Hart and Barren Counties so I could see for myself Henry Skeggs' gravesite, Blue Spring Creek, and the Three Springs Area where you grew up. Your willingness to share the sadness, secrets, and griefs of families living and dead humbled and educated me about the strength of those who live in Kentucky's countryside.

Athyleon and Lee Tindall: Thank you for letting us come pick apples, sending us home with your fresh-grown produce, teaching me to piece a quilt and quilting it yourself, for giving my wee babe and I a safe space to run away to when life seemed so sparse. You made us abundant.

Bonnieville, Kentucky, the Bacon Creek Historical Society, Kimmy Cook, Linda Watts, and Daryl: Thank you to all of you who love your roots and who traipsed me around Frenchman's Knob so I could see the Blue Hole and the hilltop for myself.

To my Honey Run Homemaker friend Bessie Johnson's son, Don, and to Daryl Thompson: I needed your understanding of how the topography of the land has changed over the last 200 years. Thank you so much for taking me to Shirt Tail Spring to locate the murder sites.

Mary Hall at Publish Pros: Your careful editing and home base in Kentucky cinched my trust in you for this task. I so appreciate your awareness, effort, time, skill, and the care with which you helped birth this story into the light. Thank you so much.

Mary Margaret Villines: You are such an encourager.

Dr. Ann Marie Hemmer: Thank you for answering my medical and emotional questions.

To all the people I've ever questioned about rifles, military strategy, horse tack or blacksmithing, gardening, seeds, farming, sewing, quilting, cooking, money, and life. To everyone who passed on a skill, art, or handcraft's specific process to someone who would never master it like you have, but you spent the time anyway—thank you. You may think it a small thing, but I don't.

All the Kentucky farmers and gardeners: Without your patience, my ignorance of the land and how things grow would still be embarrassing.

Brother Phillip and Linda Trent: you've been so wonderful. Thank you.

To my friends and family at IMC: You represented so many generations of what I was reading and writing about. Hold onto each other. Tightly.

Sammy & Marilyn Thompson: Your humor and cookies still intertwine our Sunday afternoons.

Sherry "Honey" Lowell: Your abilities with animals, carpentry, befriending strangers, and raising grandsons has widened my scope of women at every age. Thank you for shampooing the nursery carpet in the trailer, and for shipping homemade goodies across the mountains in December.

To all my Amish friends and neighbors in Kentucky who shared their recipes, histories, sewing techniques, equine and bovine knowledge, handcraft and woodcraft skills, funerals, weddings, and ways: Thank you for building a life with my family, especially when you came over to reignite our pilot light after storms because you knew we didn't know how.

To those of you who have been so kind, prayed for me, worked with me, and who hold the line where you live so artists and authors like me can learn from you and grow into better people: May God bless you. Truly.

To my aunts, uncles, cousins and beyond: Keep connected. I miss you.

To my sisters and their families: I will always love you—no distance considered. Thank you for your forgiveness, oppositeness, and for making music with me during those seasons. So good. Allicia, your comfy abode, equine knowledge, and calm spirit will always be a landing pad for me. Ariana, your talent with green things and how to turn them into amazing foods will always impress me. Brittany, you see more than you credit yourself for and that is the first step.

To my parents, whom I love: Thank you for the support, encouragement, and examples of discipline. I would need those lessons to run the race of this book's journey. Thank you for being available, even now. I value your wisdom. You are amazing. Dad, your wit in spite of it all. Umma, your clarity in seeing others. Mom, your love of ancestry, and your move to Kentucky, where I learned about this story. I love each of you.

To my in-laws, Everett and Lou Ann: You are The. Very. Best. God knew. And you do, too, but I'll tell you again how precious you are to me. Thank you for letting me write above the shop, for scrambled eggs, for summer swimming sessions, vacations, forgiveness, and most of all, for your son.

To Robert: You're still my favorite. And look! It's really a book now.

And to my children and grandchildren: I applaud you becoming yourselves, especially when it's hardest. Bravo. I love you so much.

BIBLIOGRAPHY

"All Tennessee, U.S., Wills and Probate Records, 1779-2008, Results for Frazier." Ancestry. November 20, 2023. www.ancestry.com/search/collections/9176/?name=_frazier.

"The American Revolution: A Timeline of George Washington's Military and Political Career During the American Revolution, 1774-1783." Library of Congress. November 20, 2023. www.loc.gov/collections/george-washington-papers/articles-and-essays/timeline/the-american-revolution/.

"Antoine Groignard" Wikipedia. January 13, 2021. en.wikipedia.org/wiki/Antoine_Groignard.

"Baroque Dance." Wikipedia. July 16, 2022. en.wikipedia.org/wiki/Baroque_dance.

Behre, Robert. "Annual Repairs on the Wooden Ship Adventure turn into an unexpected adventure." *Post and Courier.* April 10, 2019. www.postandcourier.com/news/annual-repairs-on-the-wooden-ship-adventure-turn-into-an/article_4cb95fb6-4ccf-11e9-9767-9b5301cdeaaf.html.

Blanc, Georges, and Coco Jobard. *Simple French Cooking: Recipes from Our Mothers' Kitchens.* London: Cassell & Co., 2001.

Burdick, Kim. "Fever." Journal of the American Revolution. November 12, 2015. www.allthingsliberty.com/2015/11/fever.

Callahan, James Morton. *History of West Virginia, Old and New, Volume 1.* American Historical Society, 1923. books.google.com/books?id=czQT AAAAYAAJ&printsec=frontcover.

Baird Chambliss, Landon. *Baird-Davidson-Rogers-Woods & Allied Histories,* page 6. Hart County Historical Society.

Clark, Robert J., et al. "Speculative Hunting by an Arachneophagic Saltacid Spider." *Behaviour.* 137, no. 12 (December 2000): 1601-1612.

Cline Crabb, Opal. *Henry Skeggs, Longhunter, and the Captain Cader Edwards Family,* 1765-1820. Calhoun, KY: O.C. Crab, 1978.

"The Colonial Period: A Timeline from George Washington's Birth Through His Marriage and Early Career, 1731/32-1773." Library of Congress. November 20, 2023. www.loc.gov/collections/george-washington-papers/articles-and-essays/timeline/the-colonial-period/.

"Colonial Travel." Constitutionfacts.com. October 27, 2019. www.constitutionfacts.com/founders-library/colonial-travel/.

"ColonialWilliamsburg." October 13, 2019. www.colonialwilliamsburg.org.

"Courante." Wikipedia. March 11, 2023. en.wikipedia.org/wiki/Courante.

Craddock Lafferty, Susan. "Before It Was Hart County." *Hart County Historical Society Quarterly.*

"Creek Burial Customs." Access Genealogy. September 22, 2019. www.accessgenealogy.com/alabama/creek-burial-customs.htm.

Davidson County Tennessee Wills and Inventories, Vol. I. Davidson County, TN.

Delany, Joseph F. "Rev. Charles Hyppolite DeLuynes." In *Historical Records and Studies, Volume 10,* edited by Charles G. Hesbermann, 130-151. New York: US Catholic Society, January 1917.

"Difference between Sorrel, Chestnut, and Red Roan Horses." Knowledge Nuts. December 18, 2013. knowledgenuts.com/ difference-between-sorrel-chestnut-and-red-roan-horses/.

Draper, Lyman C. *King's Mountain and Its Heroes: History of the Battle of King's Mountain.* Cincinnati, OH: Peter G. Thompson, 1881.

The Early Republic: A Timeline of Washington's Presiding over the Continental Congress, His Presidency, and Death, 1786-1799." Library of Congress. November 20, 2023. www.loc.gov/collections/george-washington-papers/articles-and-essays/timeline/ the-early-republic/.

"The Edict of Toleration." Musee Protestant. October 5, 2019. www.museeprotestant.org/en/notice/ the-edict-of-toleration-november-29th-1787/.

Edwards Gardiner, Florence. *Cyrus Edwards' Stories of Early Days and Others in What Is Now Barren, Hart, and Metcalfe Counties.* Louisville, KY: The Standard Printing Company, Incorporated, 1940.

"The First Marylanders." Maryland Office of Tourism. October 9, 2019. www.visitmaryland.org/article/first-marylanders.

"Forest Types." National Park Service: Blue Ridge Parkway VA. November 3, 2019. www.nps.gov/blri/learn/nature/forests.htm.

Fransisco, Darlene. "Munfordville, Kentucky Proudly Preserves its Wartime Heritage – including, some say, a wartime ghost." HistoryNet. September 23, 1996. www.historynet.com/munfordville-kentuckys-civil-war-heritage-nov-96-americas-civil-war-feature/.

"French Wedding Traditions." French Bedroom. September 25, 2019. www.frenchbedroomcompany.co.uk/ blog/10-french-wedding-traditions.

"Frenchman's Knob." Kentucky Land Heritage Fund. Bacon Creek Historical Society. 2010.

Fukai, Akiko. *Fashion: The Collection of the Kyoto Costume Institute, A History from the 18th to the 20th Century*. New York, NY: Taschen, 2006.

"Georgian Architecture." Wikipedia. September 30, 2019. en.wikipedia.org/wiki/Georgian_architecture/.

Gibb, Carson. "Introduction to New Early Settlers of Maryland." Maryland State Archives. October 9, 2019. msa.maryland.gov/msa/speccol/ sc4300/sc4341/html/intro.html.

Gragg, Rod. *Forged in Faith: How Faith Shaped the Birth of the Nation 1607-1776*. New York, NY: Howard Books, a division of Simon & Schuster, Inc., 2010.

Greene, Jerome A. *The Guns of Independence: The Siege of Yorktown, 1781*. New York, NY: Savas Beatie, 2005.

Harp, Lucille. "Becoming Woodsonville." *Hart County Historical Society's Quarterly*. Summer (2008).

Hartley, R.R., et al. "Notes on the Breeding Biology, Hunting Behavior, and Ecology of the Taita Falcon in Zimbabwe." *Journal of Raptor Research*. 27, no. 3 (1993): 133-142.

Hill, Bob. "Parklands." Kentucky Living. July 1, 2011. www.kentuckyliving. com/archives/no-title-2646.

"Historic Charleston." Explore Charleston. October 5, 2019. www.charlestoncvb.com/media/media-kit/historic-overview/.

"An Historical Map of West Virginia with Pictorial Landmarks Along James River and Kanawha." OldImprints. October 23, 2019. www.old-imprints.com/pages/books/40378/west-virginia/an-historical-map-of-west-virginia-with-pictorial-landmarks-along-james-river-and-kanawha. (Site discontinued).

"History of St. Augustine, Florida." Wikipedia. October 22, 2023. en.wikipedia.org/wiki/History-of-St._Augustine,_Florida.

"History of the Origin of Vittles for Food." Culinary Lore. April 25, 2016. www.culinarylore.com/food-history:vittles-origin/.

Hood, Marjorie, and Ruth Blake Burns Fischer. *Tennessee Tidbits 1778-1914 Vol. II*. Vista, CA: Ram Press, 1988.

"James River and Kanawha Canal." Wikipedia. August 14, 2023. en.wikipedia.org/wiki/James_River_and_Kanawha_Canal.

Jelatis, Virginia. "Indigo: 1747-1802." South Carolina Encyclopedia. August 5, 2022. www.scencyclopedia.org/sce/entries/indigo/.

Kennett, Lee. *The French Forces in America, 1780-1783*. Mt. Pleasant, MI: Bloomsbury Academic, 1977.

"The Kentucky Heritage Land Conservation Fund protects Hart County's Frenchman's Knob." *Hart County News Herald*. September 6, 2012. 1981. www.newstogo.us/editionviewer/default.aspx?Edition=c96db7ba-b8ca-47d6-9f4c-184f86c2c855&Page=8290bd43-9b9b-4af1-8c53-bfef7fd14b04.

Kumar, Mohi. "From Gunpowder to Teeth Whitener, the Science Behind Historic Uses of Urine." *Smithsonian Magazine*. August 20, 2013. www.smithsonianmag.com/science-nature/from-gunpowder-to-teeth-whitener-the-science-behind-historic-uses-of-urine-442390/.

"Lafayette." Wikipedia. October 14, 2023. en.wikipedia.org/wiki/Gilbert_du_Motier,_Marquis_de_Lafayette.

"List of French Army Regiments." Wikipedia. June 4, 2023. en.wikipedia.org/wiki/List_of_French_Army_regiments.

"List of French Units in the American Revolutionary War." Wikipedia. April 3, 2023. en.wikipedia.org/wiki/List_of_French_units_in_the_American_Revolutionary_War.

"List of Ships in the Line of France." Wikipedia. July 21, 2022.
    en.wikipedia.org/wiki/List_of_ships_of_the_line_of_France

Mance, Kim. "A Mushroom Cave in France That'll Make
    You Feel Like You're Shrooming." Conde Nast Traveler.
    March 3, 2013. www.cntraveler.com/stories/2013-03-03/
    gourmet-mushroom-cave-loire-valley-france-vacation.

"Martha Washington." History of American Women. January 12, 2009.
    www.womenhistoryblog.com/2009/01/martha-dandridge-custis-wash-
    ington.html.

"Martha's Biography." Martha Washington: A Life. www.marthawashing-
    ton.us/exhibits/show/martha-washington–a-life/.

"Maryland Emigration and Immigration." Family Search.
    October 23, 2023. www.familysearch.org/en/wiki/
    Maryland_Emigration_and_Immigration.

McCandless, Peter. "Revolutionary Fever: Disease and War in the Lower
    South, 1776-1783." Transactions of the American Clinical and
    Climitalogical Association. 118 (2007): 225-249. www.ncbi.nlm.nih.
    gov/pmc/articles/PMC1863584/.

McCutcheon, Marc. *The Writer's Guide to Everyday Life in the 1800s.*
    Cincinnati, OH: F&W Publications, Inc., 1993.

McDougall, Christopher. *Born to Run.* New York, NY: Vintage Books,
    2011.

McNamara, Rieman. "Thomas Heyward, Jr." 2007.
    www.dsdi1776.com/signers-by-state/thomas-heyward-jr/.

"Memories of Life on a Farm." *Hart County Quarterly.* 27 (1979).

Middelton, Carol. "About the Creeks." Roots Web. September 22, 2019.
    homepages.rootsweb.com/~cmamcrk4/crk4.html.

"Museum of the Cherokee People." September 22, 2109. www.cherokeemuseum.org/learn/faq (Site discontinued).

"Muskingum River." Wikipedia. July 3, 2021. en.wikipedia.org/wiki/Muskingum_River.

"Muskogee Creek Language Words." Native Languages of the Americas. September 22, 2019. www.native-languages.org/muskogee_words.htm.

"Native American Baby Names for Boys." SheKnows. September 22, 2019. www.sheknows.com/baby-names/baby-boy-names.

"Native American Indian Facts." Native American Indian Facts. www.native-american-indian-facts.com.

O'Donnell, Patrick K. *Washington's Immortals: The Untold Story of an Elite Regiment Who Changed the Course of the Revolution.* New York, NY: Atlantic Monthly Press, 2016.

Olver, Lynne. "Colonial Food." January 3, 2015. www.foodtimeline.org/foodcolonial.html.

Olver, Lynne. "South Carolina Foods." Food Timeline. January 30, 2015. www.foodtimeline.org/statefoods.html#southcarolina.

"Palace of Versailles." Wikipedia. October 5, 2019. en.wikipedia.org/wiki/Palace_of_Versailles.

Pinckney, Charles. "Speech in the Ratification Convention, 14 May 1788." *The Debates in the Several State Conventions, on the Adoption of the Federal Constitution, Volume 4,* edited by Jonathan Elliot, 318-332. Philadelphia PA: J.B. Lippincott and Company, 1827.

Rastatter, Paul J. "Prisoners of War during the American Revolution." Varsity Tutors. October 9, 2019. www.varsitytutors.com/earlyamerica/early-america-review/volume-6/pows-during-the-american-revolution.

"The Robert Munford File." Hart County Historical Society.

"Rochambeau." American Battlefields Trust. October 15, 2019.
    www.battlefields.org/learn/biographies/rochambeau.

"Rochambeau." Wikipedia. September 28, 2023. en.wikipedia.org/wiki/
    Jean-Baptiste_Donatien_de_Vimeur,_comte_de_Rochambeau.

Rodriguez, Emily. "Feme sole." Encyclopædia Britannica. June 7, 2017.
    www.britannica.com/topic/feme-sole.

"Route 176." US Ends. May 28, 2023. www.usends.com/176.html.

"Royal Deux Ponts Regiment." Wikipedia. October 29, 2023.
    en.wikipedia.org/wiki/Royal_Deux-Ponts_Regiment.

Rubin, Julian. "Oxygen." February 2018. www.juliantrubin.com/bigten/
    oxygenexperiments.html.

"Sash Window." Wikipedia. August 28, 2019. en.wikipedia.org/wiki/
    Sash_window.

"The Settlement of Maryland." History. March 23, 2021.
    www.history.com/this-day-in-history/the-settlement-of-maryland.

Taylor, Dale. *The Writer's Guide to Everyday Life in Colonial America from
    1607-1783*. Cincinnati, OH: F&W Publications, Inc., 1997.

"Thomas Jefferson Biography." Th. Jefferson Monticello.
    October 10, 2019. www.monticello.org/thomas-jefferson/
    brief-biography-of-jefferson/.

Tower, Stefen. "Treaty of Hopewell." Wikipedia. October 8, 2023.
    en.wikipedia.org/wiki/Treaty_of_Hopewell.

Varn, Kat. *Gardenia Duty*. Tampa, FL: Gatekeeper Press, 2019.

Wallenfeldt, Jeff. "Northwest Ordinances." Britannica. April 16, 2023.
    www.britannica.com/event/Northwest-Ordinances.

ABOUT THE AUTHOR

Enamored of the natural world and the human experience in it, Marissa Hale has traveled to eleven countries on three continents and visited thirty-eight of the fifty United States. She learned French at a young age, studied in Paris, France at the American University there, and graduated from Wheaton College with a degree in Communications. In many ways, her life paralleled Vittorie's journey to Kentucky and beyond: Everything she knew was suddenly stripped away, she didn't know where to go nor how to move forward from there, and she was lost in the same region.

However, the kindness of Kentucky strangers helped Marissa along and, in the end, she lives a success story with her husband, relationships, and discovering her own path.

Before *American Wild*, Marissa wrote songs and screenplays, performed for crowds of thousands, and taught elementary school art. In addition to writing, she now owns a general contracting company and makes her home in South Carolina with her husband, children, and grandchildren.

Learn more at MarissaHale.com.